SPARROW IN THE SUN

DANIELLE BULLEN

SPARROW IN THE SUN

SPARROW IN THE SUN

SPARROW IN THE SUN

Gloir do Dhia. For all that is written and failed.

Gloir do Dhia.

Copyright © 2024 by Danielle Bullen All rights reserved.

No part of this publication may be reproduced, distributed, or transmitted in any form or by any means, including photocopying, recording, or other electronic or mechanical methods, without the prior written permission of the publisher, except as permitted by U.S. copyright law. For permission requests, contact Danielle Bullen.

This book is a work of fiction. Names, characters, businesses, organizations, places, events and incidents are products of the author's imagination. Any resemblance to actual persons, living or dead, events, or locales is entirely coincidental. All remedies in this book are fictional and not intended to be used for medicinal purposes. Please seek medical council from a doctor before attempting to use any remedies, herbal blends or any other medical advice from this book.

Book Cover by Danielle Bullen @danielle.bullen.author
Title Illustration by Kate Lab @kategoescreating
First edition, 2024. Printed in the United States of America.
Editors: Copy and Line: Katelyn Walker, Worldbuilding and Dev Madeleine Bullen, Proof: Esther McIntyre and Manuscript Citique: Jasmine Fischer.

All rights reserved. No part of this may be used in any form of A.I.

To Cathryn

Thank you for loving nine wild, motherless children when the world went dark. "There is a friend who is closer than a brother." Proverbs 18:24. Thank you for sharing what you love with us fearlessly and joyfully; through classes and cake and white chicken chili made well.
We love you, Aunt Cat.

Table of Contents:

Glossary
The Old Poem
Prologue

1: Lív
2: Salves & Stones
3: The Dark Watches
4: Fear
5: New Orders
6: Sradfaang
7: Departure
8: The Mountainers
9: Flames and Fire
10: Flagroot
11: Fort Barchot
12: Wolves
13: Falling Rain
14: Sikkerhet
15: Eerol
16: Hallsong
17: Kúráh Talk
18: The Harper
19: Desperate Light
20: Blood Sparrow
21: Pounding Feet
22: Harbinger
23: Bloodsong
24: Darkfall
25: The Night Watches
26: Wounds Tended
27: Gold Trim Soldiers
28: Of Table Talk
29: Ágë
30: Eusebus
31: New Stones
32: Out of the Mouths of Infants
33: Only Hearsay
34: Claw
35: Bones
36: Ragnar H'olbrenkir
37: Máthanmôrs
38: The Healing Ward
39: Arrivals
40: Tejan
41: Emissaries from the West
42: The Lady
43: Dark Hall
44: Gulliame
45: Lord Baldwin
46: Before Dawn
47: Light of the Road
48: Campfire Talk
49: The Horse Plains
50: Vidar
51: Night Songs
52: Eye Diggers
53: The Sword Tree
54: The Fields of Andelor

Epilogue
Acknowledgements
About the Author

Glossary:

Seasons:

Lív: New life, Spring—Mark, a flower on a tree
Strále: Summer. Sun beam months. Warmth—Mark: Grass knee high
Innhöstig: Harvest. The Harvest of fields and orchards—Mark: Ripe fruit
Samling: Gathering. The season between the Harvest of fields and the first snow fall. Mark: End of Harvest.
Gråsving: Gray turning. Winter. Gray fall. Mark: 1st snow or frost in the Southern Countries. Beginning of the darkmoons.

Common words:

Fortnight: 14 days. 2 Weeks
Watch: About 3 hours. There are 8 watches in a day.
Turning: Roughly 1 year. It is a full turning of the seasons, even if the months have not all gone or have more than gone by.
Darkfall: Night.
Landlot: People. Persons of any race, frequently shortened to lot.
Lot: Slang for 'landlot'.
Kúráh: Woman. Formal or respectful. Can be used in place of lady. Denotes some form of respect.
Civ: Girl or woman. Casual. Can be heavily derogatory or just casually used.
Sonyá: Literally 'sir' or man. A term of respect or honor. Can be used in place of lord, on a minor lord.
Lede: Less commonly used word for 'sir.' Most often used to denote respect or honor to those in rank above you, or to the elderly.
Gót: No. Negative.
Aye: Yes. Affirmative.
Goodling: pet word of affection, used commonly on hounds, but also sometimes on children by nursemaids and mothers.

Ürâ: Mountain slang for man. Uncommon.

Millitary:

Knoc'gnori Warriors: Highest ranking officers in a sub-unit of the military, answering only directly to the monarch of the land they operate in. Traditionally only goblin soldiers complete the rites to become a full Knoc'gnori. There are only three ranks within them.

Military rankings:
Recruit: trainee.
Soldier: Any soldier out of training. Unranked men.
Private
Lieutenant
Leiutenant Commander
Captain
Major
Lieutenant Colonel
Colonel
Rear upper general
General
General of War

Pronunciation guide:

Auvridal: AHV-ri-DAHL
Menantian: Men-AY-shun
Eness: EN-ess
Blåthjortt: BLATT-yorT
Gråsving: Gr-AHS-vigh
Lív: Li-f
Fár: Fa-er
Einion: E-ni-UN or ae-NI-aaN, pronounced differently by different local dialects.
Sradfaang: SR-AD-fa(h)-ang. (The second 'a' is nearly silent.)
Elnial: EL-nih-EL
Fian: FI-ahn
Sonyá: sohn-y-eh
Civ: K-if
Lede: LEE-dey.
Krevák poison: CREE-vack
Maa'eulé: Mah-EU-lay
Knoc'gnori: NAUK-nor-EE
Cavene: KAH-veen
Kûráh: KOO-rAH
Ürâ: OO-rAH
Gót: Goh-tt
Aílé: EY-lee
Georwyn: GE-ohr-whyn
Sikkerhet: SI-ker-HETT
Fitzclaste: FITZ-clay-st
Tejan: TEY-ann. (Teja: TEY-yah.)
Ciaran: SEER-ahn.

The Old poem

Auvridal, of the high plains and low valleys. Auvridal, lost to shadows.
 A child will come, a man in his time.
And hope will dawn, with songs of life to a people long in darkness.
Songs of healing through the Sparrow, the Blood Sparrow.
Shadows will cry out and new voices will join,
Voices from a people not your own,
Swords from a land over far mountains,
 Hands from a land of brothers.
The time is drawing near, or did you not wonder when the Swan would come?
 The Eastern Swan. The warmth that sought him seeks him now,
But its hands shall reach into darkness and come out empty.
Cruelty shall lead to freedom, gold shall be wrought,
The Corvus shall guide, and these darkest parts will at last see light.
When the North Spring freezes and shadows draw long,
The High Lands shall come down and bring arms.
Hope from the hills. Strength to a dying land.
Auvridal, of the war-torn people. Auvridal of the sold.
 Days will come when you seek life,
And Life has sought you first.
Let the air crack and the ground shake.
The Guard will not give up his task until the dead rise again,
Let the red rim flow my brothers!
There is light where the Dark once dwelt.
Let the red rim flow my brothers,
At the Hands of Joy is sorrow's song gone.

Prologue

Lights dance in the castle, overshadowing the shouts, the screams. "To the king! To the king!" There is a wail, high and clear, the king's mother, her aged voice cracking, and the clanking of soldiers' feet.

Death, within the castle walls. Death, within the royal bedchamber.

The queen's eyes are livid, her women weeping, all of them weeping and there are figures, slipping out windows into the darkness beyond. One of them is caught, cornered, guards shouting, weapons drawn. The figure draws his own, staring. "Maá'eulé come." He brings his knife up, blade moving toward his throat, and a guard's hand wraps around his wrist, drawing back the blade. The figure's eyes shift, swirling a thousand colors, all centered around the deep yellow of fear.

The guard grimaces, pulling him. "You will answer for the crimes against our king, Hylethlan. May his soul move on in peace to the Bright Halls where yours will never go."

The figure spits, and the guard jerks him forward, shoving him toward the stairs. He is taken, his hands bound, the deed already done.

The king is dead.

Long live the queen.

I

Lív

They did not work.

My eyes stare back at me in the distorted reflection of the bronze disc in my hand. The middle is bright, polished to a shine, and within it my eyes reflect gold and red, both pale—fear and anger. *The herbs did nothing to slow it. I am nearly out of ashwag. There will not be any for more than half a turning. It is still the only one that has made any difference, slowed the change at all. But it is not enough.*

I flick my gaze to the words across the page before me, the writing cramped along the page, each word underlined, the red of the pokeberry ink already fading. The sheet beneath it crinkles as I lift it, paper frayed near the edges. *Nothing has worked, not in five full turnings of seasons. Nothing has dampened it, or even slowed it enough to help.*

Curse it.

Fár was wrong. Or I am not the one to find it. There are few herbs left to try in these hills, few names not underlined on the page, and the ink is fading out. Our people are dying, hunted by this sign of their blood, and I am failing them.

•▶|◀▶|◀▶|◀▶|◀▶|◀▶|◀•

I lift the crock from the cloth, set it on the shelf. The glaze gleams purple in the early light, a pot for bone-setting salves when the days grow shorter again. The others beside it fill the shelves, crocks still waiting for harvesting seasons to come in full, for poultices, salves, teas, and tinctures. Something cold and damp bumps my arm, a puff of breath sliding across my skin.

I glance down. Blåthjortt's hound eyes meet mine, his tongue lolling, tail bumping the table behind him. He lowers his head, brushing my elbow with his muzzle. I half smile. "Do you wish to go out to roam now, goodling?"

His tongue lolls out again, eyes lighting up. His tail wags faster, blue-gray fur swishing too close to the new salve on the table. I lift my hand under his chin, step backward, and he moves with me. "It is time to hunt for herbs." His tail wags faster, his head turning toward the door. I smile and glance toward the fireplace. Steam drifts off the pot, the surface of the liquid motionless, quiet in the shadows of the hearth. I run my hands down my skirts, knocking the dust back to the dirt-packed floor. It is cool beneath my bare feet. I step forward, lift the basket from the shelf. The knife hilt thuds softly inside, blade bright in the morning light.

I turn toward the door, step through, Blått just beside me. I run my hand along his back, higher than the basket on my hip. He barks and bolts, vanishing through the low boughs of soft green leaves, the early leaves of Lív, the season of growth.

I step through the branches, duck under the soft pink oak leaves. Trillium dots the hillside, three white petals on each tiny plant. Bloodroot lies scattered beside them; their blooms smaller, far more delicate than the thick flowers of the trillium. The flowers on this hill are only white, only ever white when leaves come out again, and the trees begin to shade over. Sunlight cuts through the trees, leaving trails in the last of the morning fog, slices of gold in the pale greens of the world. I smile.

A bird calls, three notes, sharp and fast. It echoes off in the woods. A bark sounds. I step under a branch, leaves brushing against my hair, pulling pale strands free. I glance over my shoulder. There is a small puff of gray against the dawn sky, through a break in the trees. *Fire in the village, a half-watch's walk from here.* I follow the smoke with my eyes. *Good fires, or ones that bring news and trouble?*

The smoke is pale gray, a small puff of it. *It will be cooking fires, and nothing more. Common fire.* Another bird calls, the sound soft, even, the call of a mourning dove, and there is silence in the forest, wind brushing through the trees. I turn away, strands of hair brushing across my face, light as the morning dawn and a mourning dove calls.

II

Salves & Stones

Blått barks.

I glance up, and he vanishes through the open door, a rabbit tail gone into the brush, or down its hole. Blått's barks grow louder, his great paws scraping at the side of the bush where small leaves dance where the rabbit once vanished. I click my tongue twice—a command. He barks louder, not glancing toward me. *He cannot hear me.* My hands set the crock back on the shelf, and it thuds heavily, solid and full. I turn toward the fireplace, sprinkle a dusting of leaves into the pot hanging over the flames. Steam catches on my fingers, thick and heavy, tallow bubbling below, already green with herbs.

I turn back toward the door, press my hand against my skirt. Blått is gone, his place beside the brush vacant now, a bark fading into the distance. *Perhaps the rabbit took its chance in the open spaces.* I grimace and step up to the doorway. There is no trace of blue fur out in the hundred trees and the pale green underbrush now. I purse my lips, glance down at the table. Plants are set in piles around it to be crushed, boiled down and blended, or hung up to dry. *Work for the days to come.* I shove the sleeves of my dress up and step forward, grip the pestle. It is cool, smooth stone, heavy in my palm. I grip the tip of the chamomile stalk, pull the flowers from their places. The buds fall softly, landing gently on the stone of the mortar. *Chamomile for simple salves, for tending small wounds and common ones. The crop looks to be large this turning. Treul will be grateful for that.*

I grind the pestle down and twist. Yellow dots coat the end of it, cover it like bits of down feathers. I press harder, turn the pestle. *Lív is come. Hunting season will have come again with it. Soldiers will be heading out to do the Queen's bidding and hunt down those who bear the blood of my people, slaughter them in the streets of their villages. There will be no snowfall to keep them safe anymore, to slow travel and block the mountain passes that keep the soldiers at bay. And there will be nothing more to try, no more herb combinations that I have not tried, until Strále is half over, the season nearly gone, and hundreds more are likely dead.* The pestle grinds into the chamomile blossoms, crushed gold clinging to its end.

I lift it, scrape off the fragments into the crock, waiting. *How many more moons need to be thrown aside preparing for this next Gråsving, waiting for plants to grow, seeds to come in, flowers to bloom and fade again?* I purse my lips, press the pestle down once more. *Ailé was right to doubt that anything could be done for them, for us, though she did not know that I was trying. Did not know that I was one.* I lift the mortar, scrape the bowl into the crock, fragments of the flowers falling into rest, bright specks in the dark of the greens below.

Would it be worth the danger and time to travel and read from a healing script, in a town? I shake my head, place more herbs into the vessel. *The cities are too far, and the risks too high. If I leave, there is no guarantee I will not be caught and hung before I even arrive.* I shake my head. "You have been down that trail before. The strife is too high everywhere now." I press my hand against the table. *Fár, you said this could be done, but what if it cannot?*

I clench my jaw. *There ought to be something else left to be done other than waiting and trying out here, in these forests, in this hut. More herbs to try somewhere else safe.* I lift my head. *Creator—.*

My hands still.

There is a man in the doorway. His hat is in his hands, eyes earnest, uncertain and wide, his clothing ragged. My heart slows in my throat. I look down sharply, press my leaf-gritted fingers against my apron. I clear my throat. "Pardon." My eyes burn—I bite it back, force back, the changing of the colors.

I lift my eyes again. *He may not be able to see the color from there, coming from the light of the world beyond into the darkness of the cottage. But it is not worth the risk.* I snap my gaze over him, keep my eyes low, hooded. *He is worn, but not haggard, not as ragged as he seemed a moment ago. No beggar man. But I can tell nothing of his intentions. His expression is wary, as it should be. These are not times when strangers should show up at homes unannounced.* He shifts his hat in his hands once more, angling his stance. "Pardon, kúráh. I am sorry to trouble you, but I've mislaid the pathway. Could I trouble you to point me back t' it? I ask you nothing but that, and I am sorry to be intruding on your home." His accent is faint, hard where the words roll.

I incline my head, press my hands against my apron. "Aye." I step away from the table, back toward my cloak, keep my eyes down. "I will show you the way but cannot take you to it. The road is a long ways from here. You have strayed far from it, ürâ."

He inclines his head, straight forward and a tilt to the left at the last moment. *Honor and appreciation.* I incline mine back and gesture toward the open spaces beyond the door. He steps away, his eyes cast toward the ground. *Nervous. Troubled. But he is not watching me. He does not know. Is he nervous for his sake, or hiding something?* I step up the hillside. "Where were you coming from, ürâ?"

His eyes move toward me, back straightening, hand twisting his hat. "I came from Béhla and was to be heading toward Glynfolath, near Fort Berring. I left the road to watch a stag, a foolish thing. But do you know the place?" His hands slow their twisting on his cap, eyes raise to mine.

I nod. *There is no movement in the hills, no sign of Blåthjortt. He left when he would have been most appreciated here. I am alone.* I lift my hand, point to the path down toward the village. "I do not know where the Fort is, but Glynfolath is along the highway. If you follow this path, it will take you back to the village, Amyé, the only one within more than half two days of here. From there, ask directions and they will be given to you, to the highway. It will be at least half a watch of walking before you reach Amyé. I would stay there tonight, or you will be alone on the roadways after dark falls. They are quiet people and as trustworthy as you can expect to find."

He inclines his head, his hands pressed sharply together, the hat blurring the gesture. "Thank you, kúráh. Thank you very much. I am sorry t' have troubled you alone, while your man is gone. I know it is not welcome, to have strangers in your home right now, and it was a kindness for you to show me the way."

I incline my head. "It is little trouble. May you be well on your roads."

He bows again, turning toward the path, shoving his cap onto his head. There is a pack on the ground beside the oak tree, near the herb patch in the sunlight. He heaves it onto his shoulders and nods again, the same bow as before. I force the smile to my lips, and he turns away, moving up the slope between the dancing red of the maples branches, his steps quick and ambled, a tilt to his back. There is a bark in the distance, up on the hilltop, far from the path and the traveling man. *He did not seem suspicious of me, or alarmed, more than anyone would be in these days. He cannot have seen my eyes change, or he would have run or taken me in. Unless he would get help for that.* I shake my head, my eyes on the trees. *Blått is late. He would have been little help, had he been here, but he would have discouraged a man looking for trouble, had he been in doors or near, at the very least.*

My eyes move back to the slope. *Travelers do not come through here, not often.* I wrap my arms around my waist. *No one comes through here, not unless they are looking for poultices, after harvest is gone. It will pay to be on watch for the next few days for others. If he sends soldiers for me and I am not prepared, the end will not be kind. I have been hiding from that for too long to fail now, to be found now.*

•▶|◀▶|◀▶|◀▶|◀▶|◀▶|◀•

I slip the knife under the leaves of the calvesfoot stalk, my feet sinking deeper into the mud of the mossy waters along the creek side. I glance down, step forward. The hem of my skirts is slipping down, brushing the surface of the murky, brown stream. I grip the side of my skirts, pull them higher, tuck them into my belt. Wet fabric slaps against my calves, water trickling down them into the stream once more. I shake a strand of hair out of my eyes, stoop, slide my blade through another stalk. The stem falls sideways, catching on the one beside it, and the second bends beneath its weight, sinking into the slow waters. I lift them both, slide the knife through the second, and tuck them into the basket under my arm. The basket is nearly full, stalks and leaves hanging over the rim of it, flower blooms mixed with the leaves. I flick my eyes over the patch, stalks thick and full, reaching up toward the sky in the tree dappled light. *The late frost does not seem to have affected the calvesfoot this turning. There is no lack of it here, the patch wider than it was last Lív.* I straighten, press a hand against my back. It aches, dully.

Moss squishes beneath my feet and I step forward, mud slipping up between each toe. There is movement on the edge of my vision— Blåthjortt. He stands, raising himself from the leaves of the nettles he settled himself in, stretching above the half-crushed stalks. I glance over the stems beneath him, grimace. His tongue lolling out, eyes alight, the whole bed of nettles crushed in his wake. I tuck the basket against my hip, shake my head, a grin tugging at my lips. *I will have to find another patch of nettles this Stråle. This one will only half recover from him before harvest, if he does not sleep in it again when we come back for them.* Blått moves toward me, his eyes alert, tail wagging. I click my tongue, nod up the slope. He barks, jumping into a lope, and is gone behind the trees in a breath.

I start after him, glance up toward the sky. The air is heavy, space between the trees dark gray, the clouds thick with rain that will be here in a quarter watch or less. The leaves on the trees are pale, color muted with the deep gray of the sky. The forest is silent, nearly choked with it, no sign of wind, no breath of movement, but for the hound's darting lope between the brush. I turn up the hill. He is near its crest, head and tail barely visible over the bushes along the slope and the hundreds of ground apple plants along it, their leaves bright green, still young. He drops back onto his haunches, his tail gone, and I grasp a branch, pulling myself up the small drop-off. I step around the tiny plants, clustered among the fallen leaves and Blåthjortt is off again, darting through the trees, his fur caught in a stream of sunlight for barely a breath before it is gone again. Dark clouds churn, the forest still so quiet, so still. *Stifled.*

I lift my head, glance along the trees. *Something is off.* I tuck my skirts more securely into my belt. There is a heavy stillness in the forest, more than that of the storm rolling overhead, more than the silence of the winds. *Or perhaps I am mistaken. It has been half a moon since we had a storm.* The air smells damp, feels heavy on my skin, heavy in my lungs. Sweat clings to my hair.

I take a step down the hill, the crest gone, slope before me, thorns pressing against the soles of my feet. Something pulls at my skirts, tugging. I weave them around my fingers, pull them free from the branch gripping them. I glance up from the leaves. The cottage is just down the hill, smoke curling between the branches in a small stream, white among the dark overhead. I press my free hand against a tree, step down again. Blått barks, somewhere down the hill. *In the cottage.* His bark is muffled, sharp. I slow my steps. My eyes burn. *Perhaps a coon got in. It will be going for the honeycomb...* I step faster, lift my skirts, and the stalks of the calves-foot slap against my back. Blått's bark sounds again and there is a swear. A man's voice.

My heart stills, my hand half on a tree. *That is not the voice of the traveler, come back again.* My eyes burn. I shove back the change, pull in a breath. *It will be a man from Amyé, come with a request from Treul.* I flick my eyes around the clearing. There is no sign of anyone else, no movement in the stillness of the forest. *Not soldiers come.* My heart lightens. I drop the handful of my skirts, step down, planting my foot against a stone. *Answer his question, send him on his way. He will have only come to fetch something, something Treul has not enough of or to ask a question. He will be on his way again swiftly, as they always are.*

"Oiy, Tram—" my head shoots up. A voice, but it is strange, different. "—keep that hound back. It's big and I do not like its face. Looks to mean trouble. Or hair-brainedness." My heart sinks. *There is more than one of them. It does not sound like any man I have heard before in Amyé.* I drop half down behind a bush, my knee sinking into the earth. *Why would they have gone in on their own, if I was not here? There is no Tram in our village, has not been before. But there may have been new settlers since I was last there, moons ago.* My hand tightens on the basket, the branches brushing my back. *I do not wish to enter with an uncertain quantity of unknown men in my home. There is no wisdom in testing what they have come for on my own.*

A figure steps around the side of the cottage, a horse saddled behind him. *They have horses.* My heart sinks. There is no sign of the gold trim of soldiers on his shoulders, no glint of the Mark. *Wealthy men, then, off the roadway. Is it not strange, that a man and a party both have strayed from the road in these last few days? That has not happened in many seasons.*

The man is well kept, his clothing dark, groomed. *Not a guide, nor do the men inside sound to be. They ought to have hired one, to come through these mountains, not have tried it on their own if that is how they strayed from the road. You do not come through the mountains without a guide to lead your way. But why then, did they enter my home while I was gone?* A voice cuts out, from the cottage again. "Dall, get that thing out of here and find the owner. They will not be far off and we do not need any more trouble today. We've had blazin' enough already."

The man beside the cottage flicks his gaze up. *He'll see me, before I have risen, see me hiding here, and I will have lost any control over all that is going on.* I stand, straighten my spine. I take a step down the slope, lift my eyes, as though I have been moving down the path this whole time, not crouching behind the brush. He is watching me, his garb all strangely black and undusted, like a memory. I lift my chin. "May I help you?" My voice is soft, but he lifts a brow, his shoulders straightening, back ramrod-straight like that of a soldier. My heart twists in my chest. I shove back the changing of my eyes—gold will be easily visible, even beneath the shadows of the darkening sky. I even my breath. *Soldiers do not wander on their own. They go with orders. These men seem ill-prepared, unsuited for the woodlands. They seem lost.*

He nods his head, just barely, hand leaving the reins of the horses. He turns, stepping forward, once, precisely. "Are you the owner of this cottage?"

I incline my head—respect without recognition—move down the hill. He is only a few steps away now, his cloak covering all of his garments, leaving only his black boots visible, dull beneath the trees. His face is not bearded, a few stray hairs straggled on it, like the ghost of a beard, a man who cannot grow one or is too young to have tried. I half flick my eyes back to his boots—they are scuffed, well worn. *Perhaps not a wealthy man. Perhaps an assistant to one, and more prepared for the roads than I thought from the hill.*

He clears his throat. "We have taken possession of this hut. A member of our party has fallen ill and we will retain it until he is well enough to take to the roads again. We ask that you not interfere with our business and keep out from underfoot until we are on our way, within two days. Any resistance would be unwise and fruitless. Please remove anything you need from the hut."

My eyes burn, beginning to shift and I shove it back, hard, keep it down. *Curse it.* My heart thuds in my chest. *Take control. Do not let them take this. They cannot take possession of someone's home like that, not as travelers. I can ask for help from the village if they do, if they try again. The village would help me, for this. Illness I can help with.* "How ill is he, your companion?"

He glances at me and back at the doorway. "That is not your concern. Your concern is to keep out of our way, during the duration. Please remove anything you need swiftly." His gaze lands back on me. "But first, you seem to have a hound. Is he aggressive? Will he do harm?" He lifts a brow, his expression watchful.

I purse my lips. "Only on command." His hand shifts beneath his cloak, back tensing. I step forward, ignoring his movements. A shiver crawls up my spine. *Take control. You can handle illness. Get them on their way within a watch or send them down to Treul in the village below, where they should be, to a healer who is one in practice.* "I know something of the healing arts. If you will allow me to look at him, I may be of some aid to you while you are here, so that you can be on your way again sooner. The road is a long ways from here."

He glances at me, pausing only breaths from the door. "You know something of healing, or you are skilled in it?"

I brush my sleeves down my arm, adjust the basket against my hip, face him. "I am a healing herbalist. It is my trade. If you will let me look at him, I may be able to help you on your way."

He turns full toward me, eyes scanning over my frame, over my clothing. Mistrust creeps in them, sharp at the edges, mirrored in the set of his clean shaved jaw. I wait, and he speaks, stepping aside from the doorway. "Come in then, healer." The last word is sharp, distrust in his words, in his stance. I step through the doorway and wind brushes through the trees, a sudden breath in the stillness, throwing leaves across the floor. There are three men inside, one standing beside my hound, his hand on Blått's head, another sifting through a bag on the table. There is a man beside him, in a chair, slumped against the table and his face ashen, veins protruding across his forehead, purpled even in the shadows.

I step forward and the man behind Blått jerks a sword out of the folds of his cloak. "Not one step closer, kûráh, if you value your life. You will not go close to him." I swallow hard, look down quickly. My eyes swirl. *Curse it.* I bite it back. *Take control.*

I swallow hard. "I cannot help if I cannot see him. I am a healer."

He lifts the sword, the point raising at the edge of my vision, toward my throat. "I will not have any low-birthed herb monger touching him. Step back. Leave. Now." There is iron in his voice. I step backward, Blått's eyes lifting to mine.

"Let her through, Dall. She is going to check on him. All the ones around these parts are like to be low-birthed. She at least looks to be an herbalist." *The man behind me.*

The sword lowers, the man swearing, and I step forward, over to the man slumped against my table. *Praise Elnial my notes are not still out.* The veins across his face are dark, gnarled, thick with stagnated blood. *His skin is paler than I thought beneath them.* I swallow, look back at the man in the doorway. "What has happened?"

He lifts a brow, face impassive. "It is not for you to question. You said you could tend him. Do so or get out of the way and we will find someone better."

I straighten. "If I do not know what happened, I may treat him for the wrong disease." I press my hands against the side of his neck, against a purpled vein. Heat sears my hand, sweat clinging to my fingers. I jerk my hand back, snap my eyes down. "What happened to this man?" My eyes fly back to the one in the doorway. His back is still straight, arms folded more precisely than I have ever seen, everything about his stance sharp-edged.

He exchanges a look with someone behind me and half grimaces, looking up toward the ceiling. "He was cut by a blade, on his arm. We suspect there was poison on it."

I glance down once more at the ill man, my hand pressed against the table. His face is gray, almost green, veins protruding out of his forehead in a sick, darkening color. *What causes that? That combined with the fever?* I clench my jaw, glance down at his arm. It is soaked, soaked with dark fluid. I grip the sleeve, rip it open and his cloak dips back, the faintest light falling across the wound. It is a small line across his skin, marred with dark fluids and I can hardly make it out in the darkening room. *The storm must be close now. We need light.* I turn, point toward one of the corners where the lantern sits, unused since the dark moons. "Light that, please, one of you. I cannot see him." The air is so still, charged with the energy of the world before a storm strikes. I suck in a breath, look down at the wound again, stoop closer. It's dark, blood crusted to it and there is no sign of bandaging, no sign of an attempt to staunch it or care for it. The crust around it looks wrong, the same dark veins, nearly purple, threading through his arm. *Krevák poison.* My eyes shift, burning. *This man is dying. I will do what little can be done, but this man is dying.*

Tell them frankly. I force my eyes to still, to be gray in the shadows. "How far did you travel to come here? If it is not far, his family should be gone for. This is no simple poison. It is krevák, and few men have ever survived it. He may not have his mind, when he wakes again, if he wakes again. His family should be gone for."

One of the men straightens, his already impossibly precise posture sharper, the lantern in his hand casting shadows across his face in the pre-storm air. His face is like a stone, expressionless. "If you value your life, you will ensure he is one of the few that do." I shake my head, knock the cloak away from the unconscious man's shoulder. Something glints on it. *Gold.* My heart stops in my chest.

I push the cloak further from his shoulder, and there is further gold, the gold that I've only seen from a distance, seasons ago—gold trim of a soldier, a queen's man. *The Queen's men.* My eyes burn. I shove back the change, force it down, and my heart thunders in my chest. *An officer.* I swallow hard, busy my fingers testing the edges of the crusted wound. *He can make threats, can take my home. There is no one to challenge it for me, not in this village or any other. If this man dies, will they carry out the execution on my floor, or will I be taken to a city as a captive for failure to save him? No one will look for me until the winds of harvest have come, and they look for salves and find my corpse. All my work will have been in vain, wasted on this ground.*

I purse my lips, glance over at the man by the door. He is still holding the lantern, watching me, shadows dancing along his features. I reach my hand out, for the light. My eyes flick back to the man on the table. *He would be better tended by Treul, in the village. He has tended far more illnesses than I have, is far more skilled.*

I lift my eyes to his face, the pallor of it ashen, like a death mask. *And if I take him to Treul and he dies, it will be Treul's head on a pike and mine spared. The village will be without a true healer, an innocent man dead in my stead, his work on my hands. I cannot send Treul to his death, not even for the sake of my labor.* I swallow, shove the sleeves of my dress back. I reach up, slip the lantern onto the hook on the rafters and there is light, and a brush of wind from nowhere throwing the flame into scattered shards. I lift my eyes to the men—the soldiers. "If you have anything outside that you would have sheltered, you would do best to bring it. The storm will be here in a moment. It will not be long now." *The storm, and my death, if he does not survive the next watches. Creator...*

Two of the men are gone, through the door. I move across the room, lift onto my tiptoes beside the shelf. The crocks are scattered across it, the last of last season's herbs and the first of this. *None of these are calvesfoot.* I reach up higher, hand searching the shelf above. *There.* The pot is round, smooth and larger than my palm. I bring it down, turn across the room. *Calvesfoot to draw out poison, and then willow bark will have to be boiled for the fever that will come in more force. Cayenne for the pain.* I pause beside him, lift the wax seal over the crock, and slip my fingers into it. "How many watches since he began to show illness?"

The remaining soldier is standing between me and the fireplace, where he was before with Blått, his arms folded, eyes never straying from me. His hair is a shock of red, eyes narrow. He shifts his shoulders. "A watch. A little more. The poison did not kick in at once, and he rode a good ways on his own before he fell unconscious." I glance up at him again, my fingers sliding the salve over the wound. He lifts a brow, expression dry. "Are salves all that you are going to do, healer?" The last word is a half sneer. "I could have done that myself with a few leaves of the forest. Are you an herbalist or merely a leaf crumbler, kûráh?"

I look down, scrape my fingers against the side of the crock with the unused salve. "How long ago did he receive the cut?"

His eyes half narrow, baiting. "Two watches at least." *Two watches?* My heart sinks, eyes half swirl. I turn away, set the crock down. *The poison will have to be sweated out, if there is to be any chance. Fire then.* I turn toward the fireplace, step past the redhead soldier. He does not move out of the way and my hip bumps the table, pain bursting through it. I grimace, lift a log and toss it onto the fire. I throw another one after it. The flames lick higher for just a moment, settling back down to barely anything more than coals, dark in the deep of the cottage. I drop to my knees, look up at the soldier. "Get his tunic off. I need to be able to reach the wound when I get back to him." He does not move, still facing away from me, shoulders impossibly straight. My jaw clenches. "I cannot move the fabric without cutting through it and do not want to use a blade on the clothing of your officer. I would leave that to you, out of respect. Please remove it." He glances down at me, over his shoulder, annoyance in his eyes.

I lean forward, and puff out a breath toward the fire. The flames lick higher, a spark leaping for just a moment, and it is gone. I breathe again, lean closer, and there are steps across the room, padding against the dirt of the floor, moving away from me. *He is going to tend to the officer.* I breathe again, flames roaring up, leaping around the logs and dying down once more. My fingers grip another log, smaller and drier. I set it in the middle of the rest, flames biting at my skin. I draw my hand back, press it against my thigh. *That will do, for now. The flames will grow given time.*

I turn away, grip my skirts and jerk them from beneath my knees, stand slowly. The soldier is over the unconscious officer, pulling the sleeve off his arm. I move around the table once more, step up beside him. The buttons down the side of the tunic are all undone, arm half jutting out. He jerks the sleeve, and the face of the officer flickers, pain. *The only sign of life since they arrived.* I purse my lips, move up beside him. "Let me. You have freed it. Thank you." He moves, a step away and I step forward where he was. There is blood all down the officer's arm, crusted to each strand of hair along his skin, clotted and dark. All of it is dried, half a day old. *Two watches. Why did he wait so long to seek help? Did he try, before his mind began to fall away?* I snatch a cloth from the bucket of water, only a few steps from me, and dab it on his arm, through the blood. Water trickles down the table, dripping against the floor.

Wind rips through the door and something slams hard—crocks rattling, shaking in their places. My head snaps up. The door slams against the shelf again, wind tearing through the room. I turn back to his arm, my hand still brushing the cloth across his blood-caked skin. *The rain will be here any moment. That door should not be left to swing.* I shift to the side, shielding my eyes with the hair loose from my braid. *There will be no escaping from them, once the storm has arrived.* My eyes burn, color shifting—I push it back, set the cloth aside.

I turn, my fingers snatching up the powder bowl behind me. *Chamomile, sage, and willow root, to fight infection.* I take a pinch of it, turn toward the officer. The soldier is watching me, eyes looking too closely, too sharply. I dust the powder over the wound, turn back. Wind brushes in, throwing my skirts sideways, twisting them around my legs. Wood clatters, the door slamming against the shelf again. I gasp, powder in my eyes for a moment—I jerk back, away.

The soldier swears, words dark. I grimace and my eyes itch, tears leaking from them. I stagger across the room. My hand fumbles with the door, the wind screaming. Figures are moving toward the door fast, pelts of water striking the ground, loud, hard. Two soldiers dart past me, their shoulders bumping mine, and they are inside. I press the door toward its frame, shove it against the blowing wind. Water pelts my arm, and then it is gone, the door snapping shut against the frame. I twist the rope over the notch and suck in a breath, my hands pressed hard against the door. *The storm is come. There is nowhere for them to go now. Nowhere for me to go where they are not while it lasts.* I drag in a short breath, turn back toward the fire. *Creator help me.*

The flames are leaping high, licking at the edges of the chimney stones. I step up to it, lift the poker, and shift the logs in their place. The flames are already high around them, heat curling toward my hands, up my arms. I draw the poker back, suck in a breath. *It will do for now.* Heat is rolling out from it, flames roaring with the winds swooping down the chimney shaft. I pause. *How far out of the fireplace will the flames leap, if the winds gust stronger?* Water sizzles against the fire, droplets spattering from the stones above. I draw my feet under me. *It does not matter for now. If the officer dies, the cottage will matter little.*

One of the soldiers is only a few steps from me, his arms still folded—the red-haired soldier who never left. He is glaring, scowling at me. "Are you planning to burn us down with flames like that, witch? Burn any higher and we'll take you."

I purse my lips, dust my hands across my skirts. "If your officer does not sweat enough of the poison out, he will not make it through the night. This fire is his best chance at living." I half turn away, tucking my skirts into my waistband. "I am sorry for the discomfort. It is the best way to deal with poisonings this far into his lifeblood." Disgust slips across his face, his lips curling. He turns away. I shake my head, and my feet pad softly against the floor, toward the officer on the table. The other man is standing only a step from him, his eyes half watching me, half on the floor, as though he cannot avoid watching, as though he cannot stop his eyes tracking my every movement.

I stop beside the injured man, my eyes flickering to the wound. The powder has set in, the barest traces of red beneath the gray of it. *That is a good sign, for now.* I purse my lips. "What names are you called by?"

The man beside me glances up and his eyes are back on the floor again, flames dancing in them. The wind howls. "Not your concern. Tend his wound."

I straighten. "What am I to say then, when I need your aid with him while you are here?"

He glances at me, his eyes meeting mine for the first time. "And what would you need my aid with, healer?" The word is a sneer again.

I force my eyes down, lift my hand toward the injured man. "He needs to be moved to the cot behind you. I cannot move him on my own. Two of you will have to, so that he does not get jostled. He cannot stay like this against the table if you wish for him to be well." I glance down at the man half across my table. He is long, likely matching the height of the tallest of the other three when standing, his shoulders broad, arms sturdy. *It will take at least two of them to move him. They are not broad men.*

The man beside the fire is watching me, his arms still folded, head half tilted toward the floor. "I am Lieutenant Marc. Move out of the way." He straightens, steps toward me, and I move to the side, away from the table. Wind howls outside, screaming, and the fire hisses in the fireplace. The red-head steps up, matching the movements of Lieutenant Marc. His hands grip the ankles of the injured man, and they lift, standing. They turn to the side, heaving him around the table, onto the cot in the back of the room, feet shuffling, movements stifled.

My eyes flick to the other man. The wind screams and there is a burst of ash from the fire—coals scatter across the floor, knocking into the boots of the last soldier. He looks at them blankly, lifting a foot to smush one of them into the dirt of the floor. I turn away.

Lieutenant Marc steps back to the table, moving towards the door. I glance at him, step up to the injured man. "What name is he called by, Lieutenant Marc?"

The lieutenant looks at me, assessment in his gaze, as if to take in all of me in a single glance. He lifts his chin. "Captain Einion Flint." His voice is slow, uncertain.

I move my eyes back to the unconscious man. "Captain Flint." I slip my fingers beneath my sleeves, roll them slowly back. I look at the lieutenant, at the others. "You all may lay your cloaks over the pegs there." I nod toward the wall where the basket rack is, empty but for one small oak weave basket. "It will be getting warmer in here with the flames this high." Wind howls again, smoke bursting into the room, coals scattering across the floor. The lieutenant nods, not taking his eyes off of me for a moment. Smoke is settling near the top of the rafters, between the half-dried hanging plants and the herbs of last harvest. I grimace. The red-head moves, sliding his cloak off his shoulders, and gold glints along them. I turn away, press my fingers against the captain's arm.

His skin is taut beside the wound, hot to the touch. There is the barest rim of red around it now, where a moment ago there was only the sick purple of the poison seeping into his flesh. *If that continues, he has a chance of making it through the night, though only time will tell if his mind comes with him.* My heart catches, eyes half burning, and I shove back the change again. *Let time tell.* I lift a cloth from the bucket beside me and swipe it across the wound. His hand clenches. My eyes dart down to it.

His fingers are tight, veins stark in the flesh of his forearm. I drag my eyes back to the wound, slowly swipe the last of the herbs off. His hand stays clenched, not slackening or shifting. *By lore, he ought not to be reacting, not yet.* I set the cloth on the rim of the bucket and grab the crock of herbs again, swiping another clump of salve across the open wound. I pause, my hands still on the crock. *There is nothing more to be done. The rest of the poison will have to be sweated out over time, by morning, or he will be gone.* Light dances from the flames of the fireplace, curling too high, wind throwing it in gusts towards the dirt packed floor. The lieutenant is watching it, his eyes on the floor once more, cautious. Only the redhead has taken off his cloak, the pattern of gold on his shoulders simple, barely there. I turn back toward the captain, the loose fabric of his tunic beneath him, the gold glinting in the dancing, curling light.

I bring the blanket up over him, sweat slick and hot on his arms. *Herbs will have to work their way, sweat work its way. There is nothing more to be done but to wait, and to keep my head down.*

III

The Dark Watches

The captain's chest rises and falls, his body still but for the uneven movement. I wring a cloth out over the bucket, my soaked fingers crinkled with the constant fluids. I turn back toward the captain, press the cloth against his forehead. Sweat is slick across his skin. He shivers, throwing his head sideways, and the dark veins in his temple throb. I swipe the cloth down, along his neck to his shoulders, and back to the bucket. The hair on the back of my neck is clinging to my skin, slick, the sleeves of my dress damp against my arms. I draw the cloth out of the bucket, my fingers awkward.

His head tosses to the side, arm tensing, eyes fluttering beneath his eyelids. I swallow hard, my heart sinking. *The fever is rising still.*

"What are you doing, healer?" *Lieutenant Marc's voice.* I turn my eyes down, swipe the cloth across the captain's forehead again.

"Lowering his fever."

There is a soft brushing of fabric behind me, the lieutenant shifting in his seat. *He should be resting, sleeping like the others.* "And is it working?"

I clear my throat. "It is early yet to tell." I draw the cloth across the captain's cheek, trickle water down through his beard to cool his neck. His jaw flexes beneath the cloth. I frown, lower my hand. *I gave him willow bark not so long ago. His fever should be dropping, not rising like this.* I lift my eyes to the willow crock. It is empty, the last fragments of wood scattered across its floor on the shelf beside the fire. I straighten.

Blått jumps up from the ground, his tail wagging, eyes alight. I turn away, toward the door, reach for the knife within my basket. "What are you doing?" The lieutenant's voice is low, an edge to it. The tall, silent man raises his head from the floor, knocking back his blankets awkwardly.

I straighten my neck, tie the knife sheath to my belt. "Going for willow bark. It calms fevers and I have no more in the cottage. He needs it, if his fever is to lower."

The lieutenant grits his teeth, anger flashing through his eyes. "Then should you not have gathered more of it before? Going out in the night watches for plants seems a foolish thing, wench. When you have injured yourself, do you think one of us will be able to care for him?"

I shake my head, slip the basket over my arm. The captain's head tosses, throwing the cloth to the ground. I purse my lips, lift it from the earth. The underside is brown now, from the dirt packed floor, faint in the shadows of the lantern. I set it aside, lift another from the shelf, and drop it into the bucket. *It will not do, to get dirt in his eyes.* "One of you can take up the cloth while I am gone, tend him. I will only be out long enough to reach the nearest willow tree. It is not far from here, and I have gathered herbs on darker nights." I wring the new cloth out, set it against his forehead, and his eyelids flicker again, still closed, tight. His voice murmurs, a fevered breath. My chest tightens. *The night watches have settled in.*

"How do you plan to see the branches to cut, in the dark after a storm? It is like pitch out there, and you cannot hold a lantern and cut. This is foolery."

I shake my head, step away from the captain. "I have only one lantern and you will need that here. I will manage in the dark."

He straightens. "You will not. Tram, go with her." He flicks his hand toward one of the men, an idle gesture.

I shake my head once more. "Gót, that will not be necessary. I have managed often in the dark on my own. I can manage again, and you all should be resting. You have had a long day, and tomorrow will be long enough to match it, if the captain is well."

The lieutenant lifts a brow, expression dry. "Tram. Get up and go with the healer. We will not be losing the captain tonight, not for lack of effort." I incline my head—straight down, forward, acknowledgement and nothing more. He turns away.

The tall man who must be Tram stands, dusting dirt from the black of his uniform. He stoops, bringing something from his saddle bag, where his head was only moments ago. He straightens again, moving toward the fire, and kneels, tilting something to it. The lieutenant is still sitting, his back against his own saddle bags, gaze on the far wall. I grit my teeth, reach for the door, and Blått half barks, lifting his head again, eager. I flick my eyes to him, pull the door open. Tram steps away from the fire, something flaming in his hands. *A torch.* Blått lopes through the door, tail batting against my skirts, and he is gone, into the darkness. I step out after him, footsteps faint on the earth behind me.

I start up the path, tuck my skirts up above my feet, into the side of my belt where the knife rests. Firelight dances on the ground, casting long shadows where my feet step, Blått gone from the ring of light. I move up the path, planting my feet over a root. Something calls in the trees overhead, and a shudder creeps up my spine. A daytime bird call, a mourning dove and a robin in the same breath. *A mockingbird, in the night watches.* I shudder, step around a tree, and the light is gone. Crickets call, the sound of the Frogs of Lív increasing with each step, their song the sound of early growth, of warm nights, and new grasses.

The light slips around the tree and shakes, Tram cursing. His step sounds on the ground behind me, heavy and out of place in the night forest. Blått barks. I shake my head. *That hound.*

He barks again. Tram's step sounds heavy on the ground behind me once more, and the leaves press against the skin of my foot. "Should you not see what he has found?" Tram's voice is low, lower than it seemed a watch ago when he took his rest.

I shake my head, step up a small overhang where the roots of a tree have clustered in the hill runoff. "It will only have been a opossum or something of the like. There is little enough in these woods to trouble a landlot, even in the night watches." He grunts, and the torchlight waivers behind the trunk of a tree for a moment. The Frogs of Lív are calling louder now, their high voices a song through the trees, up from the pond and the creek-beds.

The early leaves of the trees mar the sky, fading into the darkness of the clouds overhead, firelight dancing across the pale greens. A tree curves up ahead, branches long and slender, arching toward the ground in pale green and yellow sprigs like water flowing over stones. I step up to it, draw my knife from its sheath. The growth along the branches is still young, leaves barely sprouting up from them. I slip beneath the branches, and the light dances around them, shadows crawling in. Small branches dot the high limbs, a few small nubs from last season's trimmings. *I will not be able to take more from this tree in this turning. Not until it has had seasons to heal and regrow.* I lift a shoot, only just tanned with Lív, and slice it from the tree. I set it in the basket, turn, grab and cut another one from a second branch.

The light shifts, moving through the draped branches. The soldier mutters something under his breath. "Can you see? I'm not coming in those branches."

I cut through another shoot, set it with the others. "Aye. I will be done in a moment." Light dances on the knife blade for a moment and he mutters, voice carrying something about spiders and frogs. I glide the knife through another and turn back toward the soldier, through the gap in the hanging branches. Tram's brows are drawn together, his face only ridges and shadows.

"Are you done then?" I nod, and he turns, his shadow long over me. The Frogs of Lív are still calling, their chirping song gentle in the night air. *It is late for them to be singing. Nearly the first watch.* One of their voices is sharp, nearby and lonely, far from the creeks and streams.

Tram ducks around a tree, the torch there for a moment and gone again, wavering. I step after him.

The cottage door is open, the lantern gold in the distance through the trees. Tram steps upward, blocking it from sight, and shapes dance out from the torch once more.

There is a bark again, somewhere up the hill, echoing in the hollers and ridges of the woodlands. I glance backward, cupping the basket with my hand to steady it. Branches wave in the breeze, quiet and soft after the storm, droplets spattering against the ground. There is no other sign of movement, only the dark gray beyond the light of the fire and the shapes of the trees rising into the night.

Tram stoops by the doorway, pressing the torch into the earth, and the light sputters and is gone, scent of smoke faint in the air. He steps through the doorway, and I duck in after him.

I lift the stems from the basket, turn toward the table, strip the leaves from the stalks, and they patter against the floor. I glance over my shoulder at the captain. The red-head, Dall, is beside him, eyes bleary, hair standing on end, evidence of sleep. *The Lieutenant must have woken him.* He is brushing the cloth down the captain's forehead halfheartedly, gaze struggling to focus.

I set the branches on the table, pull the knife from my belt. There is another bark from Blått in the distance, and the air is thick, muggy—my skin prickles beneath it. The fire crackles. I slide the blade down the outside of the willow branch, stripping off the bark, and it is white-green beneath, young, new wood. I toss it in the pot, already waiting on the table for another poultice, and grip another, curling the blade down each side of it, the wood strange beneath my water-wrinkled fingers.

"Didn't she say she wanted willow bark?" Tram's voice is quiet, low.

The lieutenant looks up from the far side of the room, his back against the wall, saddle propped behind him still. "Aye, she did. What of it? She's got it, and a buggin' lot of leaves to level."

Tram coughs. "Looks like she's throwing the stems in the pot and leaving the bark. Think she's tired out, ey?"

I shake my head, throw the next branch into the pot. "Gót. This is the way to make the tisane. With the bark stripped off, the branches bare, the wood will infuse the water so that it can aid in healing."

The lieutenant snorts. "She's said many things. Leave her be. If she does not know her work, she'll know it tomorrow when we take her to be court-martialed after he dies."

My hand slows on the knife. I press it down, and it thuds against the table, the strip of bark falling to the side, tapping against the table. I slice off the last strip, toss it into the pot with the others. Eight branches and water. I toss a pinch of rosemary and liquorice root in after it, both powdered, and lift the pot from the table, turn for the water bucket. There is little left in it, the other bucket still beside Dall. The cloth bobs in it as he draws it out again and brings it to the captain's forehead. I pour some water into the pot. Tram is watching, his stance haphazard, almost uncertain in the room. I nod my head to the side, gesture for him to step away from the fire. He shuffles, steps slow now, his hands rolling up the tunic on his forearms. There is sweat on his skin.

I hook the handle of the pot over the flames, fire licking at my wrists. I step away from it, turn back toward the cot. The captain's face is still pale, water and sweat trickling down in lines into his dark beard. Dall's hand is awkward around the cloth, his knuckles pale, gripping it tightly, water pouring from it onto the floor, dripping up the captain's chest and arms as he raises it to his face. *He did not wring it out.* His eyes are still hazy, blinking, brows drawn low. *The man is not awake enough to tend anything.*

I clear my throat, step up beside him. "I can tend him, soldier. Thank you. You may take your rest again."

He stands sharply, dropping the cloth back to the bucket, and it splashes, sending a shower of droplets spattering dark onto the earthen floor. I grab the cloth, wring it, run it down the side of the captain's face. His eyelids flicker, arm slipping off the cot. I lift it, set it beside him again. The room is silent again but for the crackling flames, the faint calling of the crickets, and the Frogs of Lív beyond the window. The lieutenant is speaking in low tones to Tram. There is a grunt, almost a laugh, low and ill humored. I press the cloth against the captain's cheek. *If the veins do not shrink, the fever does not abate, the dawn watches will bring no good tiding. The men seem to care little for this man.*

I swipe the cloth across his forehead. *Creator, please save him. Please spare his life, and bring him back for now, but that he would do no more harm.*

I cannot sing, not while they are here.

•▶|◀▶|◀▶|◀▶|◀▶|◀▶|◀•

The world is blurred over. The captain's head lays to the side, hair tossed across his forehead. I grip his jaw, turn it, and he jerks it back, the tendons in his neck flexing. My teeth grit. I turn his head again, and this time it stays, half limp where I placed it. I lift the rag, twist it, the tea dark between his lips. His throat bobs, arm tensing across his stomach. I twist the rag tighter, the last of the liquid dripping out of it, catching in his beard and on his lips.

I set the cloth in the bowl, the liquid rippling around it in tiny ringlets. I press my hand against my forehead, shut my eyes hard. *Creator, Elnial, please, if this man dies, all my work will go with him, with him in death. All my father's hopes. Please heal him.* I stand, and my legs waver beneath me, the world too light for a moment. I grip the cot hard, press my hand against my head once more. The soldiers do not stir, the rumbling of a snore stark through the quiet. *The night watches have set in, if he fades, it will be now, when the time creeps slowly.*

If he goes, it will be now when life leaks most with the dark watches.

IV

Fear

Something thuds in the room, and there is a bark.

I lift my head and the world aches, groans. Someone is swearing. "Get that fire-slogging hound out of here and shut the door. We have no need for any of this. Blaze of—" *The lieutenant.* His voice trails off, another curse.

Someone grunts and there is a figure stumbling over the floor. "Why does it have to be so blasting hot?" He swears something more, his tunic gone, chest bare and thin. *Tram.* I look down, press my head against the cot. *I should not have slept so long. I cannot control my emotions when I am only barely awake. But they have not glanced at me.* My eyes burn. I shove it back, stand, and the world feels hazy, light cutting through the open shutters. Blått whines, and someone swears once more.

I shake my head, straighten. "He means no harm. Let him be."

Tram looks up sharply, his thick brows lowered, bare chest stark white in the browns of the room. "You'd say that, but orders is orders to me."

I shake my head again, turn toward the lieutenant. "He will not trouble you if you leave him be. There is no need to shut him outside, no need to close the door now. It will only make it warmer within the cottage and we will all suffer for that."

The lieutenant waves a hand idly, his arm draped over his knee. "Leave him be, Tram. Tend to the horses. Dall, start a fire for morning grub." Dall stands, stumbling to his feet, and staggers through the doorway, his gaze squinted, steps uncertain with sleep, hair a thousand strands of red in all directions on his head.

I turn toward the cot. The captain's face is still pale, a bead of sweat trickling down his cheek. His skin is fallow, nearly gray still. I press my hand against his forehead. He tosses his head sharply to the side, eyes darting beneath his closed lids and a murmur slips from his lips. I move my hand with him, set it gently on once more. His forehead is still hot, still burning. My mouth tightens. *There is nothing more to be done, for now, but to make sure that he is drinking water and tinctures.* I tilt my head down, press my fingers against his wrist. Heart beats press against my fingers, strange, off-kilter. *Erratic.* I press my eyes shut. *Creator... let him—*

"Healer. Report on the captain." Lieutenant Marc's voice. It is sharp.

I lift my head, keep my eyes forward, on the shelf above the cot. "He is yet unconscious. There is little more I can say, until he wakes from his sleep."

There is a step behind me, hard on the floor, booted. "Then he had better wake soon. I will not wait all day for your use of heat and herbs to work. You had better try something stronger, if you plan to remain here, unharmed."

I lift my head, turn toward him. *Present no threat. Calm him.* "I can only do what may be done, lieutenant. I cannot make him wake, nor force the herbs to do their work. He may not wake for days yet and will need every moment of his rest to heal. I would encourage you to wait outside, where it is less warm. The heat will have to be kept up, if he is to continue sweating the poison from his lifestream." I lift my eyes to his. He is not watching me, his eyes on the captain's face. "I ask for your patience."

He snorts, turning toward the door, back still sharp, posture the preciseness of a well-trained soldier. "You will be asking for more than my patience, if he does not wake sooner than days from now. We have reports to give. Work faster. The queen's men only wait so long for results." I force my head to incline—respect and nothing more. He lifts a brow. "Someone will stay with you at all times. If you need anything, or think you are not up to this task…" his eyes snap to mine again. "You had better be up to it. If he dies, the queen will require his blood from your hands. It will not be from mine for your failure."

I force my eyes down, incline my head once more. *There is fear in his eyes.* "I understand, and am doing all that may be done. My home is at your disposal while you stay, but I encourage you to wait outside, all of you. It will be less taxing, where there is more air and less heat."

His eyes flick toward me, derisive. "We will wait no longer for him to wake while being outdoors. You cannot make me forget the passing of time. There is a fort to report back to, and our tardiness and the resources of her Royal Grace's military depend upon your work. Someone will stay with you in here, to see if you have need of anything, healer." He moves through the door, his voice cutting out. "Dall. Get inside. You are on watch with the healer. Tram, take over that fire… Don't let that burn…" His voice fades, caught up in the forest and trees, into the world beyond.

My jaw tightens. *I can do less than may be done, if they are here, with me. Oh, stars.*

Tram's eyes are on me, watching, bored. I tap the spoon against the pot, set it aside. I glance over at the sleeping figure on the cot. His face is unchanged, evening light caught across his forehead, throwing lines of the oak branches over it. His chest is barely rising, barely falling.

My throat tightens.

I step across the room, press my steam-slick hands against my apron, and scan his face. His skin is no longer flushed, as in the day.

Perhaps I calmed the fire too soon. I press my fingers against his forehead.

Something snaps around my wrist, and I gasp, my eyes burning. His eyes are open, on mine, unfocused and fever-bright. Confusion washes over them. "Wha—" his hand tightens on my wrist. *My eyes are going to shift. Take control.* I shove it back, shove it down hard, and he is scanning my face, eyes moving rapidly, darting. "Who are you?" *Take control.*

I suck in a breath, pain burning through my wrist. "I am a healer. Eness. Eness Finch. You have been ill."

"Healer?" His gaze sharpens, his eyes dark, his face unreadable, and his hand tightens on my wrist—bones grate against each other, grinding. I gasp, force my eyes shut. *He is going to see, going to see them change. I cannot hide them well in pain.* "What healer? Where are my men, kúráh? Where have you taken me?"

I shake my head, keep my eyes closed, keep them shut, and they swirl beneath my eyelids. "Here. Tram is behind me if you will only look." I quiet my voice, keep it calm, and pain spikes through my wrist. I grit my teeth, gasp.

"Captain Flint." The hand on my wrist does not slacken. "This is the woman Lieutenant Marc found for you, after you fell unconscious. She is a healer, and we are here, all of us. You have been under her care." The hand loosens but does not let go of my arm.

"Unconscious?" I force my eyes open. *They should be gray.* His gaze is hazy again, unfocused.

His hand slips from my wrist. I jerk it back against my chest, suck in a breath. My eyes are swirling, will be a million colors again, not gray. I suck in a breath through my teeth. "Captain." My voice is calm, quiet. I keep my gaze from his, down. *Do not present a challenge, even to a soldier that is ill.* "You have been unwell." I lift the cup from beside the leg of the cot. "You should drink this, if you are able. It will help with the healing."

He looks at me, eyes still fever-bright. "I will not drink that. You may take it away."

I swallow, slow my hand beneath the cup. *Do not tempt him to grab you again.* "Your fever has been rising and falling for more than the last day. Willow root will help it come down and stay down. Please. These are simple herbs, healing herbs." I lift my hand, but he does not take the cup. "They will not harm you but only aid in getting you back to full strength. Please."

He turns his head away, clenching his eyes shut. "Soldier. You are relieved. Report that I am awake to Lieutenant Marc and send him my way. You may remain outside to tend to your tasks there." Tram moves on the edge of my vision, vanishing through the door, and I am alone with the captain. His eyes are still closed, face drawn. "What herbs?" His voice is still brittle, but weaker now.

I purse my lips. "They are only three: rosemary, licorice root, and willow bark. They are all fruitful in fighting infection and in healing, old herbs of the healing scripts. For the sake of your men, please drink." I lift the cup higher, toward him and away from my waist.

He opens his eyes, gaze locking on mine, and his eyes flick over me, studying all there is of me. His face is expressionless, no sign of thought or humor or notion. He takes the cup, in the hand of his wounded arm. I shake my head, draw my hand back. "Please, let me aid you, or use your other hand. That one should lay still."

He lifts a brow, expression dry, and turns his eyes away, taking the cup in his other hand. There are dark rings under his eyes, those gray veins still crawling up his bare arms toward them, up through his neck. He pauses, the cup resting against his chest. "If you have lied to me about this, healer, the consequences will not be mild. There are no sleeping drugs, no other herbs in this drink, no herbs but the ones you have told me?" His voice is weak, but his tone is unwavering, harsh.

I shake my head sharply, force back the burning of my eyes. *He only threatens that which he does not understand.* "Gót. The herbs are all as I have told you, three herbs, all simple, all mild. Sleep should come to you again soon, but not from any of thing that I have given you. Your body is still weak."

His eyes leave mine and he lifts the cup to his lips, throwing his head back. He swallows twice and is done, lowering the cup again. He grimaces, glancing down into its depths. I take it from his fingers, turn back towards the table on the far side of the room. *He drank it quickly, quicker than I have ever seen anyone swallow it down.*

A shadow falls across the floor, over the faint light on my feet. I glance up. Lieutenant Marc is in the doorway, Blåthjortt beside him. The lieutenant is inclining his head in the way they have all greeted each other since they have arrived, only deeper now, toward the captain. The captain inclines his head back. "Lieutenant Marc. I assume everything is in order. How far from the road have you drawn us?"

Marc's eyes go to the ceiling. I glance over at the hound. He is curling up, beside the herb shelf. The lieutenant is speaking. "It is just over the hill. We did not go far. The man on the road knew what he was about, with the cabin in the woods and the woman. It was not far." *Man on the road?* My eyes burn. I look down, turn away, towards the hound. *The traveler. Would they have met him? No one else has been up here, not in seasons, but he should have been long on his way, far from where they came from if he kept to his road. It has been three dawns.*

The captain folds his hands over his stomach, crusts of dried herbs flaking from his arm onto the floor, caught in a glimmer of sunlight from the far window. "How many days have we been off it?"

Marc's eyes are still on the ceiling, back straight. "Only since you fell unconscious, yesterday morn. We will be back on it within a day, is my intention and hope, with only two days lost. We can still be at the fort before the time for reporting has come."

The captain lifts a brow. "What are the healer's thoughts on that hope?"

"This healer?" The lieutenant snorts lightly, his eyes flickering to me. "She is hardly worth the name. If you say the word tomorrow, we can ride. We have only a few preparations to make."

The captain's face turns impassive again. "You left the care of an officer to a healer you didn't trust, lieutenant?" The captain's voice does not change its pitch, its tone, but the lieutenant straightens, his eyes snapping to the ceiling once more.

His posture is now sharper than any man's I have ever seen. "Gót. I just did not assume that you would wait for the word of a mountain healer." He nods toward me, and Blått lifts his head from the floor.

"I thought to scout out another, but there wasn't time. The man did not say she was a healer, but she was a bonus when we arrived, for you would not have made it to another one. She must have some skill, else your wound was less bad than we were led to believe by her, or you would not be awake, captain. She must have been skilled in some way."

The captain's jaw tightens beneath his beard, a fraction of a movement. "So, did you check to see if there was a village nearby, to learn if she was trustworthy, or were you simply content to sit and toy with the life of an officer of the queen?"

Marc's face pales, his eyes lifting higher to the ceiling. Blått's head flattens against the floor once more. "The healer began work right away, and there is no sign of anyone else within a watch's ride. She is the only lot that lives in this cottage. It seemed unwise to venture away on a mere chance of finding another healer, while you were unconscious and our party small. I did not think she would answer truthfully if I asked her of her own skill, or of the layout of the area and the villages near here."

The captain's eyes are still hard. He nods his head, movement barely visible, and folds his arms over his chest. "You wouldn't trust her word, but you would trust her to work with my life?" He shakes his head. "You should have scouted further before settling in, and have watched every move she made, that having failed. This kind of rash action will get you nowhere but the Strife House in the future and will not be tolerated by another captain, nor will it be a second time in my Mark. Is that understood?" The lieutenant inclines his head, low, his eyes leaving the ceiling to the floor. The captain shifts his arms on his chest. "Get the horses ready. We'll set out at first light tomorrow." The lieutenant nods a different motion this time—respect and honor—moving backwards through the doorway.

I fold my hands, press them against each other. *If he travels tomorrow, he will not likely make it two days, not in his condition.* I look down. *Can I let them go, knowing that he will die on the road?*

How many of my people have died at his hands? Would it not be a mercy to all who would cross his path? A soldier less to haunt them, to hunt us down at the Queen's command?

My eyes burn. I lift a leaf from the table, loose and half dried, yesterday's work left discarded. *I cannot let them go, knowing that it will be to his death, cannot have his blood on my hand.* I lift my eyes to the shelves. *Creator, please give me wisdom. If I speak and he stays, will my life be forfeited for his, for one of the Queen's men? There must be another way, they must leave. I will not be able to keep my eyes from them forever.* I drop the leaf back to the table, turn slowly, the dirt of the floor soft beneath my feet. I pause, steps from the bed. "The poison will still be leaving your blood tomorrow. It would be unwise for you to take to the road at dawn, unless a healer may be sent for to travel your way with you. You are still weak and will be for many days."

He does not look at me, eyes on the room, on the shelves and herbs and things that no man has seen in many turnings until only a few days ago. *There should not be this much alertness in his mind, not yet, not with the poison.* "It will be days before one could arrive if sent for. What you are suggesting cannot be done."

I tighten my lips. "If you travel without one, you are not likely to make it to your journey's end. That was no light poison that you came upon. Another watch and you would not be sitting in my home, but in the Bright Halls above. If you can send for a healer from the fort, it would be wise, even if you will be waiting for days yet. I would not advise you to take to the road again without one, for at least another three days. It would be toying with your life."

He is not looking at me, eyes still on the shelves. "And how long have you been an herbalist?"

I flick my eyes back to his face. "I ended my apprenticeship with a healer five Stráles ago."

His brow lifts, just barely. "And you took up a cabin in the woods? Is there a village nearby that you serve, or are you here alone, in an untamed forest?"

I fold my hands before me. "I did. And aye, there is a village nearby. I serve through poultices and salves in Sámling. The healer cannot keep up with the salves and all those who live there at once, not while tending their wounds and infirmities." *Keep him calm.*

His eyes flicker to mine. "What business does a woman who is purely an *herbalist* have tending a wounded soldier? Should the healer not have found an apprentice of his own to make salves rather than utilizing a stray woman in the woods, alone and unchecked?"

I force my eyes to stay neutral, to stay gray. *Do not ask why I am here.* "The poison would not have waited for you to find someone else, as the lieutenant has said. You were at the grave when they brought you through my door. There would have been no more traveling, no waiting. Krevák poison waits for no man. I know my craft, though it has been several turnings since I have openly used it." His face is calm, not a trace of any expression on it. I look away, toward the fireplace. "I am being a poor host. You must be hungry." I move over, toward the fire and the pot hanging over it. "I have a thin soup, until you are well enough to eat something more, perhaps later in the evening."

"How far are we from your village?"

My eyes flicker over to him, hand reaching for a bowl, for the ladle. "A little more than half a watch. Unless you are on horseback. Are you comfortable, on the cot, captain?" I lift the ladle from the pot, pour broth into the bowl, and turn. Steam brushes against my lips. His eyes are watching the door, hazy once more. *Perhaps he will rest again now.* I reach the bowl out, toward him, offer it. He does not take it, his eyes still on the door, not even glancing toward me. The veins in his face are fading now, only the barest traces of the sickening gray and purple beneath his skin. *He is healing readily enough. Praise the Creator.* I clear my throat. *Should I speak again? But what else can I do? Will they blame my labor, if he dies on the road? How long, if they leave at dawn, before they are knocking on my door again?* I shift my hand, look down. "It would be unwise for you all to leave tomorrow. You will not have healed enough to travel well. Your body is still working the poison out of your blood, but do as seems best to you."

His eyes snap to mine, sharp, face void, gaze calculating, the haziness gone once more from it. *He is far too alert.* "What would you suggest then? There is no near healer to be sent for."

I purse my lips, hand still beneath the bowl, holding it toward him. "Then I would suggest that you wait at least another few days, as I have said. Your body will be prone to weakness for days yet, perhaps as long as half a fortnight. It is a wonder that you are sitting up now, but it will come and go, if the poison is the one that I trust it to have been. I would not rush to the roads again if you value your wellbeing, or they will be carrying you once more. You may lose your mind if you do." *Twice now, I have invited him to rest, to stay. If he leaves, they cannot blame it on my head. His blood will be on his own.*

He takes the bowl, without a word, and tastes the soup, only the smallest amount on the edge of the spoon. "Thank you for your advice, healer. I suggest you tend to your tasks."

I nod, turn away.

I have invited them to stay longer. My eyes flicker toward the floor and back to him. *Would they have left me to my tasks sooner, if I had sealed my lips? If I had not spoken?*

I might have let him leave.

V

New Orders

I lift my head, half groan. The world is blurry, caught up with the last of sleep, and the door across the room is open, dawn only barely brushing through it with traces of mist.

I press a strand of pale hair back from my face, push myself up from the cot on the floor. The captain is motionless across the room, his feet even with my eyes. I look back to the door, draw my hair up from my face. Wind brushes in, soft and cool, the world blushed with early dawn, hinting at peach and red in the growing light. *I overslept.* I shove my body up from the floor, grimace. My bones ache, joints stiff.

My eyes flicker to the door, open, tapping lightly against the crock shelf. I press it shut, a shudder creeping up my spine. The air was warm yesterday, but today it is tinted cold, nearly frosted. Something damp runs along my hand. I jerk it back, something moving at the edge of my vision—fuzzy and tangled. *Blått's head.* He looks up at me, hound eyes watching, mouth clamped shut, tongue not lolling like it normally does. I ruffle his ears, running my fingers through his fur. "Time to make breakfast, Blåthjortt." I smile. "What would you have? Deer from last harvest?"

"Do you frequently speak with the hound?" My heart leaps into my throat. *The captain's voice.* I bite back the changing of my irises, keep my gaze on Blått.

"Only when it is fitting. There is not often anyone else to speak to, here, in the mountains." I turn toward the fire. "Are you hungry?"

He glances at me and turns his head away, eyes cast toward the door. "The men have gone to the village for supplies. We will be setting out at first dawn tomorrow."

My eyes flick over to his. I look away, back toward the spoon in my hands. *Praise be to the Creator. They are not staying long then, in spite of my words.* "Then I will make sure that you get all of the herbs needed to aid in your healing today and more for the road. I will show one of the men how they are to be used. You might rest today, while you can. I will help you rise after the third watch to see if you can stand."

"Can you read?"

I snap my gaze back to him. His voice is dry, face still expressionless. *Read?* I set the spoon down. *Tread lightly.* "As a healer it is required, in order to decipher the notes from other healers about remedies and herbal uses. Aye. I can." He nods, toward the table on the far side of the room. There is a paper on it, folded, fully white, whiter than any I have yet seen. There is a seal on it, set in the gold of beeswax with a small leaf beneath it. An oak leaf, still pink with Lív. I lift the paper. "What is this? Can you not read it, sonyá?" I glance back at him. There is a candle beside him on the window shelf, the same beeswax trickling down its side as on the seal. The hairs on my neck stand on end and unease curls in my stomach.

He is watching me, hands folded across his stomach, a satchel beside him. "That is for you."

I look away, sharply. My eyes burn, shifting, and my heart thuds softly in my chest. I lift the seal, the leaf brushing against my fingers, still young, a new leaf. There are words marked across the page, even and sprawling like nothing I've ever seen, not in the quiet scrawl of Aílé nor the notes that she collected from the other healers. A shudder creeps up my spine. There are words that do not match the rest of the script, do not read as written by the same hand. I read.

Eness Finch,
You are ordered upon receiving this message to join the fifth mark upon their leaving your home until they arrive in the Shod outpost. You will be given a task by the commanding officer and

expected to adhere promptly to every order, as given. Upon completion of this task and arrival in the fort you will be compensated for your time as seems fitting to the commanding officer.

In accordance with custom, a guard will be assigned to you from the time that you leave until you arrive back at your home again.

Failure to comply or failure to complete your orders will result in a court-martial at the nearest city to your location at the time of the failure or in punishment at the captain's discretion.

Lieutenant Colonel Langhardy"

My heart stills. *At your captain's discretion. And what if there is no reason behind it, no thought or discretion? What if he decides merely that I am not worth his time to bring me back to my home?* I suck in a breath. *I cannot go with them. How long will it take them to see what I am, out there on the road, rising and sleeping in their presence for many days? One poorly timed glance, one strong emotion and I will be at their mercy, at the power of their wills.* My hand shakes beneath the paper. *I already am. I am under their jurisdiction already, to travel with them at their bidding, to do as they ask of me. I am at the captain's mercy. I should not have told them to bring a healer. They did not need to bring me along, if he is healing this well. They will have stayed an extra day by dawn tomorrow.*

My spine crawls, scalp prickling. *The captain should have eaten already, or he will not be fit to ride, and I will be dead within two dawns in spite of the rest.* I set the letter down and turn, back toward the pot hanging beneath the eave of the chimney. My fingers lift the bowl from the shelf next to it, hand steady. My heart pounds in my chest, tripping. *Keep your eyes gray, keep them calm. It will be impractical for them to bring a peasant healer with them. I am of no account, and they will not want me, within a few days.* "You will be hungry." I lift the ladle, pour the stew into the bowl, barely warm from the small fire of the night watches. I draw in a breath, force it out slowly. I turn toward him, my face calm, hand steady. "You should rest again until a later watch. It would not be wise for you to rise until then." I hand him the bowl. "How many days' journey is it from here to the outpost?"

He takes the bowl and it looks awkward in his hands. "Seven. You will be gone a fortnight at least. You had best get anything in order that needs to be done here today or find someone to tend it while you are away. We will not be back before then."

I incline my head. "And if you are well enough to travel without me, within a few days? If I am no longer needed, may I return to my home?"

He looks down at his bowl, a dismissal and my heart sinks. "Then you will ride on with us. We do not have the time or resources to send you safely back to your home until we have arrived at the fort. Your orders will not change with my health, but will remain as they are stated. Is that clear, healer?" I incline my head again, brush a strand of hair back over my shoulder. It is still loose, the braid all frayed ends from yesterday. I turn away, back toward the door. *There is no one to tell that I am leaving, no one to tend this while I am gone. I could not make it to the village and back and still prepare for leaving, prepare him for the roads.* My stomach sinks.

I look toward the shelves and my heart drops further into my stomach. *The riverweed. It will not wait until I have returned. By the end of a fortnight its season will be over and gone to Sámling. I cannot make the salves as potent this harvest without its juices.* I lift my head and snatch the basket from the hook set in the logs of the wall. "I am going to the forests, then." *What would his reply be, if I urged him to take no one, told him I was wrong, about his need for a healer? Would he not condemn me for false words, for cowering from the orders given?* The hound is lying on the floor beside the shelves, his eyes on me, alert, waiting for me to say that we are going out, heading to the forests. I hum and shake my head. His ears droop. "Blått will stay with you. If there is anything you need, send him for me and I will return as quickly as I may." The hound's tail thumps against the ground, his head between his paws.

The captain shakes his head on the edge of my vision. "That will not be necessary." I glance back at him. He is looking down, arms folded over his chest.

I tilt my head straight down, courtesy. "It would be a comfort to me, if he was here, unless you have ruled against it. I would know that he can come for me if you fall ill again." *They will cause less trouble, with a hound here.* I turn toward the door and Blått half rises. I shake my head, hum again. "Stay. Lie down." His head lowers, ears pasting to the side of it. I slip the basket over my arm, step outside.

The light is early, the world covered over with thin gray clouds, and the wind is soft. I tuck the basket tighter over my arm, move toward the path. The soldiers' fire is smoldering beneath the trees, off to the side, a chain of smoke carving up from it beneath the branches. There is no one around it, not a horse or a man in sight. *Did they all go to the village?* I shift my hand on the basket. *If I go with them at dawn, I will be less able to run, once we are on the road. There will be nowhere to go, not from there. I cannot hide anyway, cannot escape through their grasp when they are so close at all times, as with a traveling party. They would find me if I ran, and there would be only a trial then, before death.* I step forward, onto the path. *What else is there to do, but to go with them? If I hide, stay, they will hunt me. If I run, they will only track me down and the ending will be one and the same. I have no horse to run with, no one to run to for aid.* A bird calls in the forest, echoing in the trees—a sparrow, on a branch, its head raised, voice high.

I glance up the path. Sunlight cuts through the trees, soft, catching in the fog of morning, cutting through the clouds. Trillium is gentle on the hillside, their petals uncurling from night. A new bird calls, another taking up its song, the soft coo of a mourning dove at the daylight watch. *I am of no import, none beyond keeping the captain alive. They will ignore me, if I do not make myself known, do not make myself odious to them. If I keep quiet and keep my gaze down, they will forget I am with them within a day or two. They already care little enough that I am with them, so long as the captain is healing quickly as may be.* I step over a fallen log. There are flowers scattered across the path, the small red blooms of the end of the maple flowers and the deep purples of the redbud tree blending with the branches fallen from the storm.

A fortnight. It is too long to go, without anyone seeing anything, when I know nothing about their mission, about them. But all of these are simple men. They will pay no heed to me, if I keep myself small, keep under their watch and within their wishes. I hid my heritage before, in Guncalk. I can hide it again, before these soldiers.

My heart slows. *The guard. I will have a guard. To what end? What is there to guard me from but them? He will surely pay me the same heed they have, if he is of their ranks. I can make it so, can keep under their sight once more. It has been many seasons since I have needed to.* I cringe, shake my head and the basket sways sharply against my hip, branches pressing against my feet. *There is no other choice. If I stay, it will be to a court-martial.*

I stoop, lift the branch of a pine tree fallen to the earth, needles dark green and long.

VI

Sradfaang

There are men on the slope by the cottage, horses beside them. I lift my chin, step down, riverweed juices thick and clinging to my skin, sticking my hand to the handle of the basket. *Horses. I cannot keep up on foot if they are on horseback.* I tighten my lips. The three men who brought the captain in are all beside the door, tending the mounts, unpacking luggage. Dall is lifting a bag from the back of one of the horses, his shoulders still ramrod straight, head high.

I step down, and there is something moving out from behind the cottage, not the length of a fallen tree from me. It is huge, dark as a shadow, as the night watches. *A horse.* It is massive, black and shaggy, head rising nearly to the roof of my cottage. There is fur around its great hooves, like nothing I've ever seen, and it is large, too large to be here, wrong beside the cottage. Something steps out beside it, tall. My heart shrinks, hand tightens on the basket.

A goblin. He is taller than any man I've ever seen, a strange cloak wrapped around his shoulders, short, almost like a woman's cloak, seamless, the pattern of it dark and simplistic. His hair is corded, bound back behind his head, his features large and sharp at once in his green-gray skin. *A goblin. None of them should be here, not this far away from the cities. They bring only death, at the queen's bidding. Swipe heads from shoulders at a moment's notice, bodies cleaved in two. They bring only death and destruction, broken homes, and screaming women. He should not be here.* My heart shrinks. *They do not belong this far from her direct word.* The men are moving, setting aside things, the goblin approaching their place. His eyes are focused on them, body lean and tall like every one of them I have yet seen.

I straighten my shoulders, step down the slope, keep my eyes on the ground. *Keep control. Do not lose it now, from his arrival. He will leave again soon.* My eyes will be burning, yellow. The goblin slows, clicks to his mount, and it halts, shifting its massive, hairy feet. He turns away, moving back beside it to lift something from the saddle. I step close to the trees and Blått is loping up the slope from the cottage toward me, his tail wagging, thrashing at the branches around him. He bounds up beside me, and no one is looking, no one watching the hound. The black horse snorts, tossing its huge head. Blått's nose lifts, his body slowed now, standing still before me. I nudge his shoulder, move down the slope, move for the door. The soldiers are ignoring me, goblin out of sight behind the massive horse. *Praise be to the Creator, it is gone for now.*

I duck through the doorway, and the basket taps my hip, the scent of riverweed and pine strong for a moment. *The goblin will be dropping something off, a missive or a report. Goblins do not travel with lower-ranking officers, the likes of these men in my home.* I set the basket down, my hands wrapping around the stalks of riverweed and pine branches, their heads heavy at the end of them, mud still clinging to the stalks from the water, dried now, crusted. Blått nudges my arm with his head, fur warm against my skin. I glance down at him. His mouth is shut, eyes watching me, watching the riverweed in my hands, bright.

I glance over my shoulder toward the captain's place, strands of pale hair over my eyes. I brush them back, mud staining my fingers dark. The captain is on the cot, reading something on a scroll. *An old-fashioned mode of communication.* His bad arm is resting against his chest, the bandage thick on it, green near its center. I clear my throat, set the basket on its hook, dried mud cracking from its rims. "Will the goblin rest with the men tonight, or will he be on his way again at once?"

He looks up at me and back to the scroll in his hands. "His way is ours."

The world stills. I swallow. "With us? Is there concern for safety?"

He lifts a brow. "There is not. However, there are rules and customs to be heeded, and he is your guard." My heart drops into my stomach. *Goblin. Not a goblin.* I look away sharply. My eyes will be a hundred colors. I cannot speak to any of them right now. I snatch the bundle of herbs up, draw the pine from it, set them aside. *They will need to be washed, the riverweed chopped and readied for salves before nightfall, before tomorrow's departure.* I grab the knife and an empty pot, set them against the table. *Goblins do not guard landlots of low rank. I am less than nothing, to them, even as a healer. I am out of practice, a poultice maker of the woods. Would they set someone of such high skill to guard a healer from the wastelands?*

"Will that be an issue?" The captain's voice is even, void of any tone as his face is of emotion. *Careful. Testing. He is testing me.*

I swallow and lift the first bundle of riverweed. "Gót. I am only surprised. There are not usually goblins in our lands, in these parts, unless there is trouble. Why would his way be with me?" *They only came to my home when death came to our village, with soldiers and goblins, swords, heads gone from shoulders.* "I thought they worked in larger cities, doing hard jobs for the Queen, not small tasks like the watch of a peasant healer." Her name sticks in my throat. *The Queen who ordered those deaths, all of them, all those villagers gone to blood and bones.*

His eyes are on me and I can feel it. The hair on the back of my neck prickles. I lift the bundle of riverweed, stoop, dunk their heads into the bucket of water beside me. Paper rustles across the room. "Those that I have known usually do, or they work in the south. It is an honor for him to be guarding you. He rarely guards anyone who is not of high rank or status."

I pull the stems out, shake the droplets off, and they splatter against the water and ground below. "Then perhaps he would be better suited guarding someone else? I can travel without a guard. You are not expecting trouble, on the road?" I lift my voice, curve the question gently.

He lifts a brow. "We are not. He is traveling our way already and was due to meet our mark at the post if we had not met with trouble. He would not have been tasked with you otherwise. And you will have a guard. We will not break that custom. It is there to keep more than just you safe, healer." His voice is hard, low.

I set the stalks against the table, wrap my fingers around the knife handle. I tilt my head down, my lips pursing. *Goblins. They are said to pay more heed to the actions and movements of those around them, the goblins of the guard ranks. Their reputation has spread, even here, to these mountains. Heightened sight. Heightened smell. 'An honor to be guarded by him.' An honor, to someone not in hiding. An honor to someone who's blood is not hunted by his Order. An honor to someone not fleeing the sword of the same Queen that he serves.* I bring the knife down and the bulbs roll away from the stalks, thudding against the wood of the table. A shadow looms over the doorway light. I lift the bulbs, toss them into the pot, and they clatter, scattering about its surface. The shadow has barely moved, still over the light that should be faint on the floor, even with the shifting clouds of the day.

I turn. *The goblin.* My heart stills. His eyes are on me for only a moment, then they turn away. I snap mine down. He is taller than the door, stopped just this side of it, with his head in the rafters, higher than the stalks of my herbs from last Sámling. His gaze is scanning the room at the edge of my vision, taking in all that there is of it in only a moment, all of my space and home.

The captain looks up, lifting a brow. I turn toward the riverweed stems. "Sradfaang. You might have brought a less auspicious horse."

The goblin lifts an eyebrow, his face dry. "He is the only mount within at least six leagues with any sense or size about him. I'll ride one of your uncomfortable mounts when they have at least half a mind to watch for holes along the way. I don't care to be thrown." His voice is strange, like he is speaking through his nose, and low like the caves of the earth at once. He grins, the barest turning-up of his mouth at the corner, canines sharp. "You look like a stuck hog, Flint." The captain grins, setting aside the scroll. *They are friends.* The goblin's hand is resting near his sword, idly, like that is where it always rests. He drops his back against the wall, eyes half watching the room, half watching the man. I lift the knife, grip the stalks once more, and slice through them, scattering sections across the wood. He glances at me, then away again, back to the man on the cot, folding his arms beneath his strange half cloak. "Did the bandits go down with you? Were they part of the cult?"

The captain glances at him. "They were not bandits. I do not believe they were maa'eulé either. None of them were marked and they do not usually deal in poisons. They made no claims to be of them and they are usually loud about that, as you know. These were a few dissenters. A small band. Most of them escaped cleanly into the forest. It was a brief fight on uneven ground and we only injured half of them, at most before they turned back." *The maa'eulé. I do not know that name.*

The goblin lifts a brow. "Maa'eulé are dissenters. Was it not an unfortunate fight, if you came out of it like this?" He shifts his arms, leaving only faint lines beneath the cloak on the edge of my vision. I toss the stalks into the mortar, my hand reaching for the pestle.

"It was a short fight. The man should not have gotten as close as he did and it will not happen again. I can assure you of that." The captain's voice is clipped, hard.

The goblin snorts, sound low in his throat. "I am surprised it happened this time. I have never known you to be wounded, not off the field. Perhaps we should get you a guard. Maybe Brewn?" He glances at the captain again, a mocking glint flickering in his eyes. The captain gives him a side eye, only half looking at him, and the goblin smirks. He shifts his hand to his sword hilt again. "Do we set out at dawn?"

The captain nods. "That is the intention." His gaze flicks to me. "Sradfaang of the Goldtide. This is Eness Finch, your charge for the next fortnight. She will abide by your word. She has been helpful and accommodating since we arrived and has caused no trouble so I expect you to have none."

The goblin's eyes shift to me, almost glinting green in the shadows and a shudder runs up my spine. "It is a pleasure." His expression is passive, voice passive like it. His eyes flick over me, taking in all there is of me in a moment, and he looks away. He inclines his head just barely, respect and nothing more.

I incline my head, the same movement, but fully done—no slight in it. I press my hands against my skirts, the juice of the plants thick on my fingers as it clings to the fabric, bites into it. "It is an honor, and I trust your task will be a simple one. I am neither known nor wanted." *Not known, but aye, wanted.*

He glances at me again and lifts a brow. "I trust it will as well, and that you will have little enough to worry about with the captain. I have never known him to be down for more than a day. Your task should be easy, easier than mine within two dawns."

I look away, down toward the half-crushed stalks in the mortar. "I hope that to be true, but his wound was not a slight one. It is a wonder that he is not in the grave now."

The goblin makes a strange noise under his breath, his feet adjusting on the floor. "That is not what the soldiers told me. Perhaps it is best that they do not know the trouble they almost put you in by straying from the road."

The captain looks up, his gaze sharp, fixed. "They strayed from the road?"

The goblin nods. "I followed your trail when I left Barchot, out of curiosity. After you fell, they left the trail and took to the woods. They would have come upon a village half a watch before they arrived here if they had merely stuck to the road. They had been off it for more than a watch when they arrived in this place. Lieutenant Marc is a fool of a man. A tracker that I would not trust to guide a pack of swine through the Wourthing gate."

The captain lifts a brow. "I will speak with them later, to see what reason they give for lying to me, but that is not for now. Get yourself settled for the night, Faang. It will be a long journey for the first few days." *A courteous dismissal. One of equals.*

The goblin nods and shifts his legs, moving toward the door. He inclines his head toward the captain—respect and equality. "Rest yourself then. There will be time enough for scrolls on the trail. There is nothing between us and the outpost but trees and a few hills." He snorts, ducking through the doorway, and is gone around the cottage.

I turn toward the captain. He is watching the door, his eyes half glazed. *The only sign he has given in more than a watch that he is still weak from the poison.* I step forward, hands tucked into my skirts, fabric clinging to my skin. *What if the goblin is right, and the poison was not as harsh as I thought?* I shift my hands. "You should drink more water and then rest, if you have a mind to. There will be long days of travel ahead, as you have said, and I would see you well." I turn toward the water bucket, and my hands are steady, firm but my heart shakes in my chest. *What if he is healed, before we even leave? What reason, then, for opening my lips to stay them from going? I asked for this, told him to bring a healer. I have sealed my own journey.*

I hand him the mug, water dripping from its side.

VII

Departure

The captain's weight presses hard on my wrist, his hand gripping my forearm, his legs supporting far more of him than they ought to be able to. Yesterday, he could barely get to his feet, could not take more than a step, but today he is nearly completely upright, like a drunk man walking, only a faint sway to his steps, and not the collapse of before. *He is healing fast, strangely fast.* He slows by the horse, dragging his feet to a halt, a breath catching in his throat. I tighten my arm beneath his hold.

Tram looks up from the reins of the mount, lifting a brow. "Do you need help, Captain Flint?"

The captain steps away from me and I grimace, moving after him. He places his foot in the part of the saddle that hangs down and easily swings his leg over and up, onto the horse. He looks down at the soldier and inclines his head, taking the reins from him easily. *He moved smoothly for one nearly unstable, swaying on his feet.* I turn. My pack is not on the ground by the door. I glance around. Dall is moving it toward a horse, his shock of red hair barely visible in the half-light. I move after him, step widely around the back of the captain's mount. It sidesteps, sharply, and my heart leaps into my throat. I snap my eyes down. *The shadows are too dark for them to see eyes this early, but it is unwise to test the sight of the goblin, wherever he is.* I draw a breath, move after Dall. "I will carry that with me."

He glances at me, hoisting my bag up, onto the side of the saddle. "That's what the horses are for. And you'd not keep your saddle, carrying a pack on your back. You'd fall off at the first slope and we'd be slowed early."

My eyes snap to his. "Saddle?"

There are steps—a horse's—behind me, moving closer. I sidestep, but the horse has stopped, hooves not far from my feet, nose snorting. "You will be joining us on horseback." *The captain.* "We will not wait for anyone on foot. It would double our journey's duration to do so. Will that be a problem?"

My heart shrinks. "Gót."

Lieutenant Marc is striding by, his gait even. He looks back at me, his brow raising. "Have you not ridden before, wench?" There is humor and derision in his eyes.

I shake my head. "Gót, and I am not familiar with the animals. Could I not keep up on foot?"

The captain's horse side steps, and his hands shift the reins in the dark. "You will ride. It does not take much skill to follow on horseback and you can learn over the day. There will be no keeping up on foot. Mount up. The sun is nearly here."

My teeth clench.

Dall glances at me, his face unimpressed, eyes darting over me. "Do you know how to mount, kúráh?" His voice matches his expression in the dark, tone nearly mirroring the derision of Lieutenant Marc.

I shake my head. "Which animal am I to ride?"

He nods toward the one next to him. "Place your foot in the stirrup—your left foot—and swing your right over the saddle while gripping the horn. I do not know how tricky it is in a skirt but you'll have to figure it out before the captain leaves. I'm not getting left behind with you."

My eyes flicker to his. I grip my hands together. "The stirrup?"

His widen, disbelief, and he scoffs. He moves around the horse, towards me. He points sharply to the strap on the saddle that the captain stepped in to swing up, and his voice is curt. "That there." The strap the captain used to swing up is shorter on mine, closer to the belly of the animal, higher from the ground. I step up to the horse and there is something pressing against my hand, furred and warm.

Blåthjortt. He looks up at me, tongue out, eyes faintly shimmering in the shadows. I purse my lips. *Horses. I do not do horses, do not do animals beyond hounds. The rest are unpredictable.* I move my foot closer and duck my head, drag in a breath. Blått's head nudges my hand, and there is a snort, another horse. *It is now or never. They will ride and it would be unwise to wait for their patience to wane while I tarry.*

I step close to the animal, plant my foot in the thing called a stirrup. The horse is tall, shoulder above my head, standing perfectly still. It lifts its head, ears pricking. I purse my lips, slip my fingers under the saddle. *How do I get my leg up?* I shut my eyes, jerk my body upward, and something moves beneath me, the world shifting. I gasp, drop back to the ground, jerk my arms back from the animal. My breath puffs, eyes burn. *Curse it.* I ball my hands against my side, fix my gaze on the ground. *Take a breath. Take a breath.*

"Not like that." Tram is beside me, his face nearly scornful at the edges of my vision.

I keep my gaze down, shake my head. "I am sorry. I haven't the faintest idea how to mount, nor what a horn is. Perhaps I had better walk?" *Would I be punished for failure, for not mounting, if I cannot?*

He shakes his head, gesturing, impatient. "Gót. You will not make the first watch marching. Put your left foot in the stirrup." *It is the same thing the Dall said, nothing different.* I lift my left foot, slip it in, and the leather is cool beneath the skin of my toes. He half points, the gesture crisp. "Grip the saddle on either side to get your balance and swing yourself up, your other leg over. You cannot reach the horn. Dall should have seen that." He snorts, the sound less pleasant than the horses' noises. I grip the saddle again, swing my leg up, and the horse does not move this time, does not sidestep away. I release a breath, my hands pressed hard against the top of the saddle. *I am up.* The horse steps beneath me. I flail, grip hard at the thing jutting up from the saddle. Tram nods on the edge of my sight. "Grab the reins and relax or you'll be sore within the first half-watch. We do not have time to stop for saddle sores. And you have the horn, there." He nods toward my hands.

I nod. *Saddle sores? Does he expect me to be trouble so soon?* I bend slightly forward, and my breaths are fast, short. The leather strap that must be the reins is looped over the part of the saddle that sticks up, twisted around it more than once. *I will have to let go with one hand to unwind it.* I grit my teeth. *Creator, let the horse stay still.* I release one hand and pull the cord of it free, and they are now long, loose in my hand, curling down the side of the horse. *I do not know how to use these. What use can they be for holding on, for staying atop this beast?* The other horses begin to move and my head jerks up. The captain is in the front, his back straight, moving fluidly with each step of the horse. *I can watch him then, from further back, see that he does not fall. So long as I do not fall.* My jaw tightens, fear flickering in my chest. I look down. My mount is not following, its feet still motionless. *If my horse follows. I cannot make it go.* I stare down at it, and the horse flicks its ears, eyes ahead. *Can it see what it carries on its back, tell the difference between a landlot and a satchel?*

Dall clicks to his horse, and it is moving after the other two. The world moves beneath me. I gasp, grip the thing jutting up from the saddle again, the reins awkward, twisted around my hand. The steps of my mount are fast, jolting me with each movement, back and forth. I tighten my hands on the saddle.

Something moves behind me, huge beneath the shadows of the trees, like one of them, but darker, thicker. I flick my gaze over my shoulder, my hands clutching at the hard piece of leather. *The goblin and his massive horse.* He is speaking to Tram, strange cloak still around his shoulders, his eyes alert, glimmering green in the gray of the dawn.

I turn forward, and the horse snorts, tossing its head. I grit my teeth. *Why would anyone voluntarily ride one of these, when they could walk on their own feet?* Something moves beside the horse, blue-gray and trotting. *Blåthjortt.* He lifts his head, tongue lolling, eyes at ease, calm. I squeeze mine shut, clutch tighter at the saddle beneath me. The trail is rolling out, down the slopes to the road and up over the hills where no one treads, beyond the blue ridges of the first mountains.

⋅▶│◀▶│◀▶│◀▶│◀▶│◀▶│◀⋅

The air is only barely warmed beneath the branches of the trees, flicking at my skin, leaves swaying with the soft breeze. My body aches, each movement of the animal beneath me awkward, and my hands are stiff around the leather straps. I roll my neck to the side, muscles aching, throbbing. The captain's back is still straight, framed by the soldiers in front of me, his shoulders squared, movements matching the horse's, swing for swing. *He should be worn thin by now, exhausted from the day's travel. Dusk is not far away. How can he go this long, after his nod to death?*

His head is tilted to the side, no longer fixed ahead, no longer straight. *Perhaps he is better at hiding fatigue than I gave him credit for.* The sun has gone behind pale gray clouds of Lív, trees with only the barest traces of green on them here, near the top of the Glycall ridges. My body aches. I tighten my hands, glance down. My fingers are clenched around the piece of the saddle still, reins threading around them. I stretch my fingers out, and the reins move with them, my skin red from clasping. They are stiff, joints rolling.

Blått lifts his head beside my mount, his tongue lolling, head half-bowed, tired, like these men should be. Their heads are still up, backs still straight, though all the daylight watches are nearly over. My eyes flicker through the party. The men at the front are watching the road ahead, the gazes of the two men in front of me on the trees around us, careful. *They never look back. Have not glanced back even once throughout the entire day.* I lift my head. *I could ride the entire fortnight like this, if we can make it dawn to dusk without any of them looking my way for more than a moment. They will have no occasion to see my eyes, not with the riders behind me the only ones to ever glance my direction, and they can see nothing of my face. I could make it home again, in safety. I could continue my work in peace, once more.* Hope bubbles in my chest. I press it back. *I have not even made it through the first day. Let hope stay quiet.*

I shift my weight and my legs ache, sore. I grimace. *Let them ride until dark has fallen, Creator, please let them ride on until night.*

They cannot see the sign of my heritage in the dark. The captain's back ahead is straight, his gaze on the road again, head fixed forward with only barely a tilt in it now.

Something whistles ahead, slight and faint amidst the creaking of leather, the treading of hooves against the dirt and stones of the road. The horses are slowing. My heart sinks.

I glance up, Dall moves to dismount before me. I press my hands against the saddle. *Everything aches. But it is not yet dark.* I slip my leg over, and my feet hit the ground. Pain spirals up my calves, pain from my legs, from my sides, from my hips, and I gasp, press my head hard against the cool of the leather. *Curse it.* I lift my head, shift my leg to the side, and pain bursts out from it again. I gasp, still my leg. I press my eyes shut, press my head harder into the saddle. *My hands are still holding the reins.* I drop them.

The world shifts. I jerk backward away from the horse, my legs stumbling beneath me. I gasp. The horse lifts its head, watching me, its tail snapping out behind it, like annoyance. There are men moving everywhere, lifting things, pulling saddles from the other animals, their steps even and steady. I press a hand against my thigh, turn. The captain is standing not far from his mount, watching the men, giving orders to Tram, his voice quiet. I press my hand harder against my leg, hobble forward, and my legs burn, the pain lessened where my hand presses, but everywhere else, it is ripping at my joints, at my flesh. I grimace, cast my eyes down.

The pain will fade. I flick my gaze around, keep my eyes lowered. There is a tiny clearing, not more than an opening in the trees, where grass has grown tall, thin and sparse like the hair of an aging man. There is a patch of light upon it, cast upon the head of the captain, the haze of the cloudy sky low, thick on the branches of the trees. Metal rings against metal, a small sound. I turn. Lieutenant Marc is lifting the saddle from my mount, his eyes on me, unimpressed. He lifts a brow, hoisting the saddle. "Can you not move?" He starts off, his back to me again, not looking for a word of response.

I turn. There is no goblin in the camp, his mount riderless like the rest, the saddle still on. The captain is leaning against a tree now, his face pale, hair half falling over his eyes. His arm is pasted against his side, across his waist, stiff. *The only sign of pain he has given all day.* I step forward and my body protests, screaming. I grimace, force my leg forward, press my hand hard against my leg again. *He needs to be seen to, should have been helped down, not allowed to dismount on his own. I should have moved to him sooner.* The captain glances at me, eyes impassive. I slow, a few breaths from him, lower my eyes to the earth. "Captain Flint. Will you sit? The day has been long." *Do not make him feel weak. He will be strung out.* "I would like to check your wound before the light has gone. Is it troubling you?"

He angles his arm, the movement slight. "I will not take a seat. You may check it as you wish, healer, but I am not sitting now."

I purse my lips. "Your body will be worn, from the day of riding. I am tired, and I am not recovering from illness. Please captain, take a seat." My legs ache, joints ache. I lift my chin but keep my eyes lowered. *Do not pose a threat.*

"I have given my answer. You may tend it here or move on, healer. There is other work around camp to be done." His eyes are on the camp, on the movements of horse and man around us in the growing shadows.

I press my hand harder against my thigh, muscles tight and pulling. *He ought to sit, to rest. That is my task, to see to him, to see that he heals, not to the other events of the camp.* My lips tighten. "You will have to slip your arm from your sleeve, or I cannot tend it."

He does not look at me, his eyes still on the movement of the men. He moves sharply, and his arm is out of his sleeve, slipped beneath his shirt, only his shoulder and the top of his arm exposed from it. "Is this sufficient, healer?" His voice is curt, eyes still ahead and I step forward, nod. I slip my fingers into the bandage, pull it free, and flakes of herbs flutter to the ground.

The veins have faded out, no longer the black they were at dawn, nor the faint purple of yesterday, but gone back to the pale blue-green of life. I lift the bandage further. The wound is nearly gone, closed and clean, only deep red with a ring of dark crust around it. *The goblin was right. The wound is almost healed, almost gone. Nothing heals that quickly on its own, not by natural means.* I flick my eyes toward the ground. *In another day, there will be no more need for me to tend him, to be here with them at all. And they will not send me back, will not send me home until nearly a whole fortnight has passed from now. One day I was needed. Tomorrow, no longer. I should not have spoken to him. That was rashness.* My head swirls. *But it should not have been. He ought to need a healer for days yet, more for the harshness of the riding.* I shift the bandage. "It is healing well. There will be little need for me, after tomorrow." *Would he change his mind, if asked, if I begged him to send me home again?*

He glances down at me and off toward the camp. "You have checked it. Gather wood for a fire before the light is gone completely. All hands will help around camp as they are able."

I incline my head, tuck the bandage back into place. *I cannot challenge him twice in one evening. That would be unwise, in every sense.* I step away, a limp. "Please sit, captain. Today was a long ride, all the daylight watches. I would see you still healing tomorrow, and not regressing back into fever." He does not look at me, does not show any sign of hearing. I purse my lips, turn away.

The three men are moving, each of them at task, hands working beneath the fading clouds of evening. *Where is the goblin?* My eyes flicker over the beginnings of the campsite. Dall is stacking the last saddle, besides the goblin's mount. Lieutenant Marc is starting a fire, kneeling on the earth, his hands cupped over his mouth, breathing on the beginning of a flame, smoke curling up from it in puffs. Tram is carrying buckets, moving out into the forest. *There will be a stream nearby, if they chose this site. He will be finding water, for the evening.* I step forward—my leg hitches, tightening. I suck in a breath, rub my hand over the muscle. *Lands, that hurts.* I brush a hand down the side of my leg, the muscles tight beneath it, bunching in my skin. I grimace. *That will not have worn out, by the time we mount again tomorrow. I will start again sore, in the saddle for thirteen more days.* I grimace again. *I did not bring a salve for aches, for the soreness of muscles used strangely.*

The hairs on the back of my neck prickle. I glance over my shoulder, the captain's eyes flickering toward the darkening trees. *He will want to know if I will obey him.* I force my legs forward, hobble toward the trees. Something strikes my toes—I stumble, hand colliding with a tree. Bark rips at my palm. I glance down, clutch my hand to my chest. *A fallen log.* It was hidden in the grasses. I reach down, wrap my fingers around it. My hand protests, stinging. *I will have lost skin to that tree.* I pull the log up, and it is long, longer than the height of a man, dragging into the grasses beside me. I drop it against the tree, step by it. *There will be others to carry, and this one is near enough to leave for later.*

I step forward, lift my head, and there is something moving in the trees, a shadow. I still. It steps into the light, tall. My heart slows in my throat. *The goblin.* I step to the side, move into the trees and shadows.

"What are you doing out here?" The goblin's voice is sharp.

I pause, keep my eyes forward. "Gathering firewood."

He grunts, a strange noise, low and humorless. "Do not stray far. I do not want to come find you." He is gone, moving through the trees, something slung over his shoulders.

I lift a branch from the ground, and another, and turn, back toward the campsite, my hands filled. I grab the other branch from the tree side, the one I stumbled over and tuck it under my arm, pull it through the grasses. *The storms must have been harsher here, higher on the mountains. The ground is littered with many branches, though the trees look no barer against the twilight sky.* My legs ache, protesting. I hobble forward, heave the slipping branches higher on my hip. There is a small fire in the clearing, Lieutenant Marc still leaning over it, encouraging the flames up with his breath, the fire casting lines and caverns across his face. Smoke curls upward, gray in the faint blue of the fading light.

Captain Flint is sitting on the ground, his back against the tree he stood by a moment ago, his legs crossed. I stoop by the fire, drop the wood into a pile. There is a cluster of branches there already, larger than the ones I carried, and they are already broken in pieces, ready for use in the flames, many of them coated in moss and debris from the earth. They are all thick, thick enough I could not break them without the use of an axe, their edges white in the night. I turn. Dall is gone, the saddles stacked and left behind Lieutenant Marc, the horses no longer standing in a line, but off together with their backs to us. I flick my eyes around, step slowly toward the tree line. There is no movement of the hound, no blue-gray fur in the campsite. I look away, toward the trees. *He will be off on the trail of something small, chasing it after the watches of marching at pace with us. I do not think a season of marching would wear out the life's vigor of that hound.*

Tram lifts his head, stepping out from the trees, a log over his shoulder brushing the branches behind him. He lowers it, grunting beneath its weight. "Ey. Marc," his voice is strained, evening out as the log hits the earth, "you think we ought to make a stew tonight? I got a couple of mushrooms from the back. First night on the road again. Tradition and what? What'd your girl say?"

Lieutenant Marc looks up from the fire, his brow lifting, unimpressed. He sets his hands against his thighs, the shadows of the fire stranger now across his face. "I wouldn't trust a 'shroom you found if you got a healer to check it. Chances are, we'd still be seeing things by last watch. And that was only kúráh talk: fancies. I wouldn't put faith in it any more than I would put faith in star theory."

Tram snorts. "*You'd* be seeing things. I know this one. I grew up eating it, and I'm still here, ain't I? Wouldn't harm a carvéh."

Lieutenant Marc's brow lifts higher, a smirk tugging at the edges of his lips. "Then I *know* I do not want to eat it. Especially not now that you got your muggy hands all over it. Where they been these last few days, I'd want to know?"

Tram lifts the end of one of my branches, planting his foot at its middle and he jerks upward, a snap resounding in the forest. He grunts, tossing the piece in his hand to the side, into the stack. "Better places than that fire has now been, with you breathing on it. What you planning to do, love it to life with that breath of yours?"

Marc grins, the look feral in the firelight. "I would say it was more my smile. I've won lots of kúráhs over with it."

Tram brushes his hands off, turning back toward the woods, and I move the other way, toward the woods on the opposite side. He calls back, over his shoulder, kicking at a stone. "The only thing your smile will do is wither it. Try it on that healer civ if you do not believe me. I'd bet she'd be scared witless." I grimace, keep walking, my head up.

There is a figure at the edge of my vision, the goblin, moving from the trees, his stride even toward the fire. "Try it on the healer civ, and you will find yourself being led along by your horse tomorrow, on foot. I would have thought your captain's rule to keep clear of civs on the road would have been enough, soldier, not to mention your knowledge that I am her guard. That seems like a place you do not want to put yourself." His voice is sharp, even. The lieutenant's head shoots up.

He inclines it, courtesy and apology. "We will be trying nothing on her. Tram only intended it as a jest, sonyá." He half laughs. "That civ wouldn't know what a smile is, living the way she has. It wouldn't be worth the effort to try and amuse her. I bet she'd just stare."

I step behind a tree, stoop for a branch. I lift it beneath my arm, look toward the sky. *Praise be they have already decided I am not worth an effort.* I half shudder, tuck the broken branch beneath my arm. *Their language is tamer than the men who came around the herbalist shop, back when Aílé was still well and thriving in Guncalk, but not as tame as the words of a hound these last many moons.* There is laughter again in the camp, a sharp bark of it from lieutenant Marc, joined by Dall's strange, breathy laugh. I turn further into the woods, the branches heavy on my hip.

VIII

The Mountainers

The flames are high, crackling and snapping beside my skirts. I turn the spoon, the soup swirling around it, tubers bobbing in and out of sight beneath the surface of the liquid. I press one against the side, catching it with the spoon, and it starts to mush beneath it, slowing near the middle. Still barely hard. I tap the spoon out, set it on the hook of the cooking frame, and the fire crackles, droplets from the rim of the pot vanishing into it with each snapping flame. I turn away.

The captain is motionless at the edges of the circle, a quill and paper in his hand. The soldiers are at the far side of the firelight, dice rattling together between their hands. I drop against the ground at the side of the fire, fold my legs beneath me, and there is warmth against my skin. A light flickers, dancing in the forest, faint and gold. *A firefly.* I smile, wrap my arms around my knees and something warm brushes my arm. I glance up. Blått is standing, his head over mine, drool lit by the light of the fire on his lips, his tongue lolling. He nudges my shoulder. I smile, brush my hand over his head.

The goblin steps out of the darkness beside the captain, his form sudden and strange, dropping to the ground beside him, his face unreadable. He throws back his half cloak, his arms folding, legs crossed, and he breathes out something, low, to the captain and the captain responds, their faces both impassive in the light of the fire. A firefly flickers above the goblin's head.

I turn away, comb my hands through Blått's fur. He drops sharply, lowering himself to the ground, a sigh rattling through his throat. His eyes are on me again, waiting. I run my fingers along his head and there is a grunt from the men, dice clattering together again as one of them scoops them in his hand, dust settling with them. *The rain did not reach the ground here, or else the sun has dried it faster than it does in the mountains below.*

The goblin nods at the edge of my vision, his head low, closer to the captain's now, though he must be a full head taller when standing. He is slouching, and I cannot pick up a trace of their words, though their lips are moving beneath their beards. *What do they speak of, in tones so hushed? Of wars and hunts? Of the next task given by the Queen on that blood-rimmed throne?*

I stand, tug my sleeves down my arms, back into their places. My legs ache, and the air is strangely chilled for this late in Lív, flames only half warming where the darkness does not reach. I step forward, grip the handle of the spoon, and dip it into the soup. The root is soft beneath the tip of the spoon, halving easily into the broth, nothing catching at its center. *It is ready enough.* I drop my voice, leave it soft in the quiet of the camp. "The soup is ready, if you all will take it."

The soldiers look up, and they glance back at their dice, marking something in the earth. One of them laughs and swipes his hand across it, making a new line in the earth. The other snorts, writing it back into place, and they stand, Dall shoving Lieutenant Marc in the shoulder.

Lieutenant Marc turns, a scowl creeping over his features. His eyes meet mine and he nods, reaching for the bowl in my hand. I extend it to him, lift the stack from the earth, and he is there, too close, serving himself from the pot above the flames. He glances at me, hands still moving. "Have you tended the captain this evening?"

I meet his gaze, keep mine steady, Blått's head pressing beneath my hand. "Once, but it will be done again after he has eaten. He will not be neglected."

His mouth tightens, brow lifting. "Oughtn't you to have done that before sitting on the ground uselessly? Seems like with your life on the line, you might have done more than not neglect him, if you valued it. But then, it is not my neck that will be rolling." He turns away. My lip twists. *He would not have spoken to me if I was not so close at hand. I ought to have stepped away or served the captain first to avoid his notice.* My eyes flicker toward the captain. He is still sitting, speaking with the goblin, their voices muffled beneath the breath of the wind. *They will not wish to be interrupted, not for food, not now when they are yet speaking.*

The captain says something and the goblin stands. I step forward and lift a bowl from the stack in my hand. Dall snatches one from it, turning away, the ladle in his hand. He steps away, Tram still gathering something from the earth where they sat moments ago. I grab the ladle, pour the soup into a bowl, and there is someone beside me, their presence heavy. *The goblin.* Firelight leaps over his face, his eyes on the men. I step backward—my heart thuds in my throat. I duck my head, move away, the stew sloshing against my fingertips. My eyes burn. *His steps are silent, movements too quick. I cannot keep away from him, keep him in my sights, when he vanishes and slips through the shadows like night and walks so that no man can hear him. I did not see him move, did not notice him come.* I pause by the captain. He is watching the flames, his eyes focused somewhere beyond them, unseeing. His hand reaches out, toward me. I place the bowl in it and incline my head, courtesy. "May you continue to heal with the night watches, captain."

He does not acknowledge me, does not look up from the crackling flames, and there is a laugh behind me, Marc, high and brash, blended with Tram's sharp bark.

•▶|◀▶|◀▶|◀▶|◀▶|◀▶|◀•

The horse stumbles, and everything jolts, protesting. I press my hands against the pommel, half lift myself from the saddle. The horse snorts, throwing strands of hair back at my hands, lashing at them, red with the last light of the setting sun. I grimace, brush them off my knuckles.

The men are silent. Horse hooves are loud on the rocks of the road, stones clattering together on the high trail, the first path we have been on since we began. Blått's steps are silent beside me, his head still up, as though we have not been walking for three days now, as though his body does not ache with every step. *Is it strange that there is a path here, where the tallest of the Glycall mountains wind higher than any I have been in? Should they not have taken the road through the smaller ones?* Evergreen branches brush the tops of the men's heads, too high to reach mine, even atop the horse. Lív has only barely touched the branches of these trees, leaves small, if there, only the redbuds and small white flowers of the nallias are blooming, and the occasional glimmer of a dogwood tree. *Lív is nearly half done, down in the valley.* Out over the ledge, red is brushing the tops of the highest trees on the mountain side, lighting them with the last of the sun. I press my hands against the saddle again, shift, and it barely alleviates the pain in my legs, the sores on them. I draw a breath. Blått's head bumps against the side of my foot, with each step of the horse.

My eyes flicker up. The sky is a dusty blue behind the emboldening colors, the clouds soft against the evening sky, lit with traces of pinks and gold. I half smile.

There is a whistle ahead, short, sharp and a single word that I do not catch. *The captain's order to make camp.* The captain's horse is leaving the trail, moving under a hanging of high branches. He slips off his horse, taking up the reins, and starts forward on foot, vanishing under the branches of an evergreen. I purse my lips. *He should not be driving himself as hard as he does, not even with the wound mostly healed. He is not so beyond the poison's reach, the weakness of the fevered nights.* I glance back over my shoulder, at the red light against the tops of the trees, and it is gone, hidden behind the branches of the evergreens.

Dall follows the captain's lead, dismounting from his horse. I slip off mine, my legs protesting, and go after him, under the heavy branches. Everything aches. The horse is stepping behind me, its ears down, breaths slow. Men duck their heads before me, tucking under branches that are too high to reach them, as though they think they can. A smile pulls at my lips. The air is cooler in the forest, licking at my bare feet, and at my hands and face. Moss is soft between my toes, leaves still crumbling from seasons gone. Blått presses his nose against my arm, his eyes lifting up to my face. I half smile, flick my hand to brush his head.

The captain pauses, barely visible over Dall's horse before me. He turns toward his mount, loosening something on his tack. "Make camp here." There is a ring of small trees beneath a young oak, branches already long and twisting upward toward the evening brushed sky.

I stop, the horse slowing behind me, a puff of breath brushing the back of my neck. A shudder runs up my spine. I step away from it, glance back at the beast. *Why does it follow, when it could go any way it chose?* It is standing still, as though it were tied, legs motionless, eyes watching me, vacant and lackluster. I drop the reins, turn away.

Blått is no longer beside me. I glance up. There are feet in the air, on the far side of camp, Blått's, his back against the earth, rolling in the leaves beneath the young oaks. I tuck my skirts up, into my belt, move forward into camp.

Tram is already stacking branches, logs that were piled from other travelers in the center of the ring. A small flame licks up from beneath Marc's hands, and I turn, back toward the mounts. The captain is moving the saddle off his horse, his shirt gathering around the bandages on his arm as he lifts, moving the saddle down. I purse my lips, twist the loose strands of hair back from my face. *He should not be doing that yet, any of that. Are these not the soldiers' jobs, and not his?* I stop behind him. He sets the saddle down, turning back towards the horse. I clasp my hands before me—respect. "Captain. I would look to your wound, before the last of the light is gone. It is fading now, and I do not wish it to wait until morning again."

His hands are busy with the straps of the next mount, his back toward me. "The light is gone. You will check it in the morning." He pulls a strap free, glancing at me. "Gather wood."

I force my hands to stay relaxed. *I did not tend it this morning, could not clean it last evening with the light gone. There may be infection, after days of riding, if it is not completely healed by now, with sweat and dirt and the hair of horses working into it. He is putting strain upon himself too soon.* I lift my head. "Captain. It has not been cleaned this last day. I would tend it this evening, by firelight if need be, but I would wish to clean it tonight, as soon as can be. I would not have you get infection, after so much healing. You have come too far for that."

He does not stop, hands still working over the mount, tending it, though he is right: night has already settled into the forest. The shadows are longer now and stars will be showing themselves soon behind the fading colors of the sky. "I have given you my answer. You will tend it in the morning, by daylight. Find firewood."

My eyes burn. I turn away, my steps fast, harsh, and move past Blått. He is on the ground, his head between his paws now, eyes watching me. He whines, high, short. I slow my steps. *They do not need to know that I am troubled by him. But they are not looking, are all tending their tasks.*

The goblin is gone, the horses with him, saddles off the ones on the far side of the ring. I step through the trees, everything in the circle fading with their branches. I move sharply around a stone. *Curse him. Could he have not listened for a moment? He is healing, healing fast, but it is not fast enough to mean that all is already well. And if he is infected, the blame will not fall on his head.* Something pricks my foot. I ignore it, step around a tree, tall and slender in the dying light. There are shadows ahead, dark, thick, evergreen trees in the midst of the forests. The wind brushes, cold, and a shiver creeps over my arms. The scent of the trees is heavy on the wind, thick with the smell of upturned soil.

I stoop, grip the edges of a branch. It is long, trailing beneath the evergreens, the smell of them strange, sharp, not the pines of home. *Cedars. They do not often smell so strong, unless they have been disturbed by something.* I lift my head, pause. The shadows are thick around me, shapes no longer visible in the darkness dancing before my eyes. I step backward and another shiver creeps up my spine. *I have strayed too far. I should search closer to the camp, tonight.* I turn and something snakes around my mouth, clamping over it, alive.

A hand. Breath brushes close to my ear and panic bubbles in my chest, air caught, hot and clammy against my lips.

"Move, and I snap your neck. Savvy?" I freeze. The hand on my mouth tightens. Breath brushes my ear again, hot, and his voice lowers. "I said, savvy?"

I nod, and the hand loosens only a fraction, but there is air again, air to my lungs. I suck in hard, and another hand snakes across my stomach, pinning my body fully against his. He steps forward, his thigh pressing hard against mine, shoving it forward with each step. His voice snakes past my ear, low, breath damp on my skin. "Move faster, or it's the blade." I step forward, his legs pushing against the back of mine, shoving me through the evergreens, away from camp. My lungs burn, heart drumming in my ears. A stick snaps, sharp beneath my foot—the man swears. "Keep your steps quiet if you value your life. I'll have no trouble snapping that pretty neck as promised." I nod, his hand moving with the motion, and his leg shoves harder, knee thudding against the back of my thigh. I suck a breath between his fingers.

His leg stops, jolting me to a halt, and he stiffens, his hand on my stomach tightening, pulling me further against him. He swears. His leg slams into mine, shoving me forward again, and he is pushing me through the trees. There is a stick, snapping somewhere beside me, and another figure faint in the darkness, his eyes white. His face is dark, blotched by a beard, a hat pulled low over his brow in the increasing shadows.

"Kawn." The voice comes from beside my ear. The second figure stops beside him, and the air reeks of old sweat and something fouler. "Shikes you gave me a scare. Tell Reul I've got a wench from the party. Bringin' her back for information. And be prancin' quietly about doin' it. You're louder than a mawbear. That camp's closer'n I thought they'd be." His voice is low, no longer brushing my skin.

The figure beside me nods. He turns away, vanishing into the trees, steps silent as they go. My heart sinks. The man behind me steps forward, his knee shoving against mine through my skirts. He freezes again and his hand jerks my face—my head snaps to the side. I gasp, my breath caught.

He does not move, hand clamped across my jaw. My breaths wrack against my ribs.

A voice cuts out, sharp, low in the trees. "Move, and this goes through you." *The goblin.* My heart slows, eyes burn. The man is motionless, his hand stiff across my stomach. "Let her go, and step away."

The man swears, voice high and his hand moves up toward my face. "You had better step back, or I'll break her little neck. I've got my hands—" His voice cuts off and he is limp, his hand sliding from my face, from my body, gone. I stagger and there is the sound of something thudding against the earth. I spin, step backward sharply. The goblin is standing over a shape on the ground—the man, motionless. I suck in air, lungs aching, face damp.

"You are not wounded." The goblin's voice and it is not a question. He turns to me, eyes glinting in the darkness, the man motionless on the earth by his feet. *Did he kill him?* I step forward and something wraps around my arm, jerking me to a halt. "Gót. He is not wounded. We are leaving."

I shake my head, stumble. "Then why did he fall like a man dead?"

The goblin makes a sharp noise, annoyance and my stomach twists, dread. "He is unconscious. Now move, healer, or his friends will be here and they will not be."

My eyes burn. He pulls my arm and I stumble again. His steps are long and fast, too fast for me, and branches catch at my feet, pulling at my skirts. My heart pounds, eyes burn. There is a ring of light ahead, beyond the trees, the fire and men, and we are inside it, the goblin's hand leaving my arm. He steps away. I force my eyes down, suck in another breath. *Calm your eyes. Calm them or they will give you away to no end. The men of the forest will not disturb a camp filled with soldiers unless they are desperate.*

The goblin is speaking. "..There are eight at least that I can scent, not likely any more if it is a scouting party. Which it is. They are not known to send more on a scout than that." His feet are at the edge of my vision, turning toward the soldiers.

The captain speaks. "I scented them." *He scented them? How could he have scented them from here?* I lift my eyes and he grins savagely toward the goblin, his canines sharp, smile sharp with them. *A cavene. He is Cavene. Curse it, I should have seen it sooner. The people of the iron north, with blood that heals quicker than men's, senses heightened like that of the goblin kind, and teeth sharp like the hounds they raise.* His eyes flicker to mine, then away, focused on his men. I jerk my eyes down. *Curse it. What did he see, when he turned toward? I have never been so lax before, did not school my eyes.* The captain's voice rings out. "Draw your weapons and move into position. Healer, get down. Stay with the hound. They are already here."

I drop down into a crouch beside the log, set my hand on Blått's head. He nudges my hand, his head low. The men are all facing outward, each of them with a weapon in their hands. The goblin's is huge, a strange, thick sword with markings down it that gleam in the firelight. He turns his head sharply, nods toward the far side of the ring, and Blåthjortt growls, low in his throat.

A man steps out of the trees, fluid in the shadows. He is covered in a dark cloak, long, longer than any man's I have ever seen, the ends of it reaching his ankles and the hood of it drawn over his face. He lifts his head slightly and his eyes glint in the shadows of the hood. I suck in a breath, force my eyes to calm, to still. He pauses, his eyes sizing up each of the men in turn. "It was not wise," his voice is thickly accented, the tongue of the mountain folk, "of yo' to travel through these mountains wit' no extended guard and only th' five of yo' for protection. These mountains are not kind to those wh' come trespassing, even when they are not soldiers of a traitor queen." My heart slows.

The goblin moves just barely, lowering his sword to the top of my vision. "It is bold of you to enter the camp of four of the queen's soldiers and a Knoc'gnori warrior with only seven mountain men at your back. I have taken on that many on my own with my eyes shut, sonyá." *Knoc'gnori?* My eyes sting. I look away once more.

The man straightens, the glint of a smile on his lips in the shadows. He raises his hands, throwing back his hood and his face catches in the firelight, pale, work-heavy and thick, like those of the mountain folk who visited the village once. He lifts a brow, appraising the goblin and there is a fleeting smile beneath his beard again. "Your senses are better than we gave yo' credit for, sonyá." He inclines his head toward the goblin, respect alone. "I am Ruel. You are trespassing on my people's land, and we ask that yo' leave by sunrise. We will offer you th' courtesy of our woods for the night, this time. But if you leave your camp like the civ did again, yo' will not find us lenient a second time, sonyá."

The goblin bares his teeth, his sword motionless in his hand. "If your hands do not touch my ward, then I have no quarrel with you. Mine was only with your man who laid hands on that which wasn't his."

The man—Ruel—lifts a brow and steps forward, an easy, fluid motion. "The girl was wandering, and she seems a strange charge for a warrior of your ranking, goblin, if yo' are Knoc'gnori. Tell me, is she royalty or have yo' taken t' protecting commoners on the road? She does not look like our royalty."

The goblin flashes a dry smile, shifting the sword in his hand. "That would be the business of the queen that you insulted and none of yours. I go where I am bidden. If your men keep clear of the camp, I will have no quarrel with them or you. We will not touch your lands and will leave peaceably."

The captain steps forward, his back straight, sword tip pointed at the earth. "I am Captain Einion Flint, of the queen's Mark. We accept your offer, Ruel the Scarlet. I have heard of you and your people and we would not have crossed into your lands if we had known we were near them. Our path will not take us this way again. If you grant us peace for the night, we will leave your borders tomorrow at dawn. I make no threats to you and offer only a return of the courtesy that you have extended tonight."

Ruel flashes a smile, and it is brilliant, confident. *Is he not a bandit, a commoner? How has the captain heard of him?* He bows, just a small inclination of his neck and waves his hand toward the forests. There is the snap of a stick, somewhere. A shadow moves in the trees, fading out. *A man, standing down.* Ruel's eyes flicker back to the captain. "You will likely have heard of my father, and not myself. Rothbar has had far more fame, trailing these parts than I. But I accept, for my people. We expect yo' to depart at your word, and it is an honor t' meet you, Captain Flint of the Mark." He bows again, that flourishing bow with neither respect nor courtesy in it and turns, his cloak swishing behind him and he is gone.

The captain moves and I flick my eyes toward the ground once more. He sheathes his sword, lifting his head. "Settle in. Dall and Tram, gather the rest of the wood we have already and stack it. We will do waybread tonight with the rations we have in our packs. Move." The men scatter, moving for the forests that were just occupied with the Wandering Men. I press my head against my hands. My face is dirty, the man's hand a ghost on my mouth, skin still damp with it.

A shudder creeps up my spine. Blått presses his nose against my arm, his eyes watchful, wide still and he whines. I brush my hand against his nose. Fire crackles, snapping upward, and there is a call in the woods, the sound of an owl. I shiver.

The captain turns toward me. "Healer. You were not wounded?"

I keep my head down, run my hand along Blått's muzzle. "Gót. I am well."

He turns away. "They would have let you go, once they had the information they needed. You were never in danger. Ruel is known to be an honorable man, even if he does not heed the law of the land and the Queen's rule." He starts away. "Settle in for the night. We depart before dawn." His steps are even, silent, along the camp to the far side of it, to the shadows where the chief of the Wandering Men stood heartbeats ago.

IX

Flames and Fire

I lift my head, grip the ladle. The fire is high, flames bright, battling back the last dampness of the rains of the day. My hair is still clinging to the back of my neck, cool with the evening winds. Warmth bites at my legs, hot. I glance down and my heart trips. Flames are licking up my skirts, nearly to my knees already.

I drop toward the ground and the flames curl higher up the side of my skirts, out from beneath my knees. I gasp and there is a shout, somewhere off in the camp, echoing in the wood. I smack the flames, heat searing at my hands and the flame are growing higher. A hand snakes past mine, large, covering all there is of the fire licking up my legs in a moment, and there is only smoke. A trail of it snakes up from my ankles, from the smoldering fabric, dark edged now.

My heart thuds in my ears, eyes on the hand beside me, green-gray. *The goblin's.* He drops his arms over his knees and straightens, the movements silent. I draw in a breath.

Someone is beside the goblin, next to me, boots dark and soot coated. "Are you burned, healer?" My eyes snap up, meet the captain's. *I do not know what color my irises are.* I rip my gaze away, stumble to my feet, my skirts clutched hard in my hands, still hot from the flames.

I swallow, stoop, lift the bowl from the dust where it dropped from the stack. "I am well. I will be more careful with my skirts, in future days. I should not have let them get so close to the flames tonight. Thank you." *What color were my eyes, when they met his a moment ago? Surely he would have spoken at once if he saw them, if they were not what they should have been. That is how traitors of the Queen were always brought in by soldiers before, when I was a child.* I turn away. "I should not have gotten so close. Food is ready, if you are, captain." I swallow and grip the ladle, the soup swirling about it.

The goblin snorts, moving away. "Aye. We do not want to have to take you back to your village charred as coal. You would not make a very good start to tomorrow's fire. Nor a very good Dark Thing."

Dall snorts. "She would not become a Dark Thing. They only come from warriors and the ill blooded who die by fire. She is as plain as a butter crock on a holy day—nothing that would call to become a Dark Thing. She would only be the same as she is, but burnt out."

Tram chuckles from the far side of the camp, lifting his head. "*You* might become ash, Dall. You aren't any less plain, for uses. Barely out of recruitment training, aye? Not much of a warrior..." He laughs, throwing back his head and Marc joins, nudging his ribs.

Dall flushes, standing. "At least I passed the blade tests at the first attempt. And which of you two has actually seen a Dark Thing in person? Not living where you came from."

I turn away, tighten my hand on the ladle. I shudder. *I should not have stood so close to the fire. One glance at the wrong moment, and the captain would have known.* I glance up. He is gone, moved away. *He will not have noticed any color in them, or they would have me tied, to wait trail by now. The fire light that betrayed me, may have masked the change tonight. Gold light, to mask the gold tones of fear.* I flick my eyes up, to the captain across the flames, my legs hot and cold in the night air. *Wouldn't it?* He drops against the tree, silent, his eyes on the earth and I can read nothing in them, can read nothing of his gaze. His hand rests against his leg, forming three shapes distinctly, quickly. *Signs.* My eyes flicker around the camp and slow. The goblin. He is watching the captain, watching the signs of his hands. He signals something back, over his leg where I cannot see.

They are speaking with words that cannot be heard. My hand is white against the bowl, white against the ladle in the stew. *How long have they been speaking this way, in the long watches of the campsite?*

If they did not see, then what do they speak of, with hands?

They spoke in whispers, before. Spoke in whispers these few last nights.

My heart settles in the pit of my stomach, swirling. *Creator. Help.*

X

Flagroot

The captain is striding across the camp, morning light catching on the shoulders of his tunic where the gold trim runs. The captain is striding across the camp, morning light catching on the shoulders of his tunic where the gold trim runs. His face is a mask, his eyes fixed, no trace of last evening. "Tram, Dall and Marc, get ready to depart. I expect you all to have my message to the Lieutenant Colonel by the third day as ordered." *Depart?* Dall snorts, and the captain's eyes snap to him, still vacant of emotion or sign. "Or I can report more on the incidents of this trip than you want on your records. Is that understood, soldier?" His eyes snap to Lieutenant Marc as the man straightens, Dall following his movements. Tram's back is already straight, as it always is, his eyes on his work and not on his officer.

Lieutenant Marc inclines his head, his eyes forward. "Understood, Captain. We will be there at the time appointed and keep to the roadways as you ordered. There will be no delaying this time." The lieutenant bows the stiff, full body inclination of a soldier to a commanding officer.

Another figure is leaning against a tree at the far side of camp, a man I have never seen before. I start. His face is unremarkable, a pale man, slight and short in stature. His dress is that of a tradesman, the simple garb of any man off the streets, not the neat black of a soldier, nor the leathers and tans of a guard nor the swirling cloaks of the mountain men.

He bows, the same formal bow as the soldiers toward the captain and steps away from the tree. "Captain Flint." He moves toward him, his steps as silent as the goblin's, meeting the captain at the middle of the camp ring. I set the clean pot down, dried, keep my eyes on the men to the side. "Are you confident about this? Would it not be better for you to keep your guard, if you have been unwell and the goblin is tasked with another charge?" He glances my way, and I turn my eyes to my work. He speaks on. "I can deliver the message and be back to my post inside half a fortnight for the next report. I am quick, and these are your men. I can deliver it, if it would give you more ease, sónya. Lieutenant Colonel Sprene would not be well pleased if you did not arrive in safety." There is meaning behind his voice, crouching behind each word. I keep my hand upon the half-dried dishes, dew heavy upon them.

The captain shakes his head. "Gót. Lieutenant Marc will see your report delivered. I need you back at your post in the event that anything suddenly changes. You are known there and I do not need to explain the importance of that to you, Lieutenant Chole. You cannot be spared. They can be. Lieutenant Colonel Sprene will be even more displeased if you are missing at your post when trouble arises than if I return with another bruise. It is fortunate we met you." The captain nods at him, a slighter version of the bow he was given a moment ago. The stranger inclines his head and he turns, his eyes flickering over me for just a moment. He nods at me, the barest movement of his head and turns away, not waiting for a reply.

The goblin steps out of the trees, mounts saddled behind him. The man—Lieutenant Chole—mirrors the movement he made to the captain toward him, a low bow, and swings up onto a waiting mount, plain as the man and he is gone through the trees, vanishing back up the trail. I turn my head away, set the last dish back into the sack. The men are moving quickly through the camp, gathering their sacks, tying them to the backs of their mounts. The captain's eyes flick to them, watching their work.

Dall swings up onto his mount, his eyes forward, a strand of red hair brushing over his nose. *I am not like to see them again, if I understand the captain's words. They are off to a different fort, with orders to stay. Praise be to the Creator.* I turn my eyes down, my jaw tightening. *But what import would the report have, that it would be sent so swiftly, leaving an officer without guard?* My hands are tight on the sack. I force them to loosen, purse my lips. *There will now be less men to pay heed to me in camp, in the days remaining. If he suspects me, there will be less men to help him find out for certain, what I am.*

But he may not need them.

I slip the bag over my shoulder, stand, sunlight cutting through the camp with the exit of the men.

•▶|◀▶|◀▶|◀▶|◀▶|◀▶|◀•

Wind whistles through the trees, a moan, soft, and it is quiet in camp without the three men playing dice on its edges. The fire snaps and I lift my head, glance at it. It is still high, stoked, flames dancing above the pot. There is steam rising and twisting into the curled whisps of smoke. The captain steps toward the flames, his actions relaxed like I have never seen them, posture calm, shoulders even. I tighten my arms about my waist. *Was it the men's presence that made him on edge, or merely his wound? Or is he playing a part?* He stoops, setting three mugs on the ground and straightens, gripping the pot with a cloth to shield his hand from the heat. "Healer." I lift my chin, keep my gaze low. He does not look my way, hands intent on his task, pouring the water into the vessels below with skill I cannot match for all my seasons at the art. "Will you take tea?" He glances toward the goblin. "Sradfaang?"

I blink, fold my hands together. *Tea?* I swallow, glance down at the mugs on the earth. *He has not made teas before, through all the days until this. It would be unwise to offend him, to reject what is offered. Is there something I am missing? He can hide something, in tea, easily enough.* I incline my head, slowly. *Do not offend.* "Aye, if it would not be a trouble to you."

The goblin shakes his head. "I do not care for it."

The captain loops the pot handle back over the hanger and stoops, his hand pulling out a small pouch. He dusts something dark from the bag into the cups—tea leaves. Steam curls up from them, lit gold by the flames of the fire. I pull my shawl further up my shoulders, fold my legs beneath me. He stands, moving towards me, a mug in each hand. He offers one to me. I take it, incline my head slightly to the left—appreciation. "Thank you." He nods back, his eyes still not on mine, always away, always ignoring.

I press my hands around the mug. The stone is still cool beneath my fingers, the scent of sweet melissa, lavender and grouse weed wafting up from it, pleasant and warm. I sniff again. *That was kind of him. Strangely kind.* I wrap my hands tighter, lift the tea and draw in another breath, of the steam. There are no hints of any herbs beyond those three, three simple herbs, easy to identify, calming but not relaxing. I lift it to my lips, smell one last time. *There is no trace of anything beyond them. They are not strong enough to mask it.* I take a sip.

The taste is sweet, water hot but not scalding. *He did not wait for it to boil, but poured it early, as you should when dealing with the herbs he chose.* I glance at the pot still hanging above the fire and curl down further into my shawl. The night air is only barely cool, mid Lív weather now that we are down the mountains, the first crickets calling off in the forest, echoed by the frogs-of-Lív. I sip the tea again, long and slow, calm heat spreading through my chest. My fingers tingle around the cup, warmth from it creeping into my palms. A firefly darts in the trees, light here and then gone again, and there is another, and another, like stars in the darkness of the woodlands. There is no moon tonight, no trace of light from above, the clouds thick. I take another sip, long and slow, and something chirps, an insect somewhere within the camp, its call soft.

The captain speaks, low to the goblin, and goblin snorts back. "Not if you value your legs. They'd take them off in a moment." The captain laughs, low and nearly silent.

I turn away. *My lips feel numb.* I frown. *It will be the heat of the water in the night air. That can cause them to feel off.*

I take another sip and my eyes half burn, twisting.

My heart sinks.

No. That cannot be right, unless it is only the smoke and not a shift in my irises? I tilt my head down, focus on the grass beneath my feet. My heart twists in my chest, eyes watering. *I will have imagined it. I was calm, I am calm yet.* I draw in a breath, force is out slowly. I take another sip of tea, keep my eyes down, on my feet, bare on the leaves and grass that are broken from many steps. There is silence in the night air, but for the captain is speaking to the goblin, their voices still low and far from me, on the other side of the camp where the fireflies flicker. The fire snaps, sending sparks upward.

Trees groan, wind blowing through their branches, its voice eerie with the sounds of night. A frog calls out again, nearby, closer now than it was before. The night is calm, quiet, the men across camp quiet with it.

I lift the mug, draw in a long sip, glance down at it. Leaves swirl just beneath the surface, already more than half gone, steam still curling up and brushing against my cheeks. The fire crackles, voices across camp gone for a moment beyond the sounds, and they are back, the captain's voice alone.

I settle my legs down, breathe in, and my eyes burn, shifting into colors.

I snap them shut. *No.*

They do not shift for no reason, do not change without cause. That is the curse and blessing of our blood. They show emotion, mirror it, but do not change on their own, never on their own. None of those herbs should have caused this, could have caused this. I have used them all a thousand times, know them all, their scent, their taste, their feel. My eyes bite again, shifting, burning and I shove it back, bite back the shift and it isn't slowing, the feeling almost dull, changing, changing still and I can hardly feel it. *I can barely feel it.* I set the mug down, keep my head low. *No. No. This is not how this works. I will not die from a foolish shifting in my gaze. Not like this.* I glance at the men, keep the fire between us. *They cannot notice, if they cannot see me clearly through the smoke haze.* Neither of them look up, their voices soft, still speaking words I cannot hear. I turn my head, move toward the forest.

A voice cuts out—the goblin's. "It is late, to be wandering."

I slow, my foot barely against the earth. "Aye. But I am going to relieve myself." *Let him not catch the lie in my voice. Let it slip by him.*

"Do not stray far. The woods are dark tonight." *Praise Elnial.* I nod, turn away through the trees. A branch catches at my hair, pulling it and my scalp screams. I jerk away, and there is no burning in my eyes, no shifting. *They should be shifting, with the tug of pain.* I draw in a breath, stumble. The slope is before me, curving down sharply with only a few trees across it, if my sight is true in the thickening darkness. A firefly glints, steps from me and it is gone again, leaving a hole in the darkness of my vision. *The goblin was right. The night is deep. I cannot see the bottom of the hill, though it is not far, was not far half a watch ago when I last came down here for wood.* I draw in a breath. My head swirls, eyes water, but the burning is gone, gone to nothingness. *I cannot feel them change.* My heart sinks, dropping into the pit of my chest. *Do they still change, or have they gone silent at last, gone to nothing?* I grip my skirts. *I cannot tell, will not know unless they tell me.* My throat is dry.

If I turn in, if I lay down for sleep, will they ever know if they have not already seen? I could speak nothing to them. I have done it many nights before. There would be nothing strange, in that, in lying down to rest silently without glancing their way.

But if tomorrow comes and I still cannot control it, cannot feel when it changes, what will come with morning light? I cannot stifle that which I do not know, cannot control that which I cannot feel. If they are changing tomorrow, I will not know until it is too late, the sign giving me away. They changed for no reason now, before it faded out. My throat constricts, my nails bite into my arms. The shadows of the trees are large, dark, lights of the insects dancing between them faintly. *I cannot return and wait to be found out.*

I tighten my hands on my arms, fireflies flickering out in the trees before me. *If I go back to camp, tell them I found an herb in the woods, how long until they come searching for me? How far could I run, with a goblin and a cavene tracking my scent? How many counts would they wait before they were after my trail, hunting me down? I would not make it a hundred paces before they caught me again, and my life would be over as surely as if I stayed to be found out.*

I draw a breath, my hands shaking on my arms. *Creator please.* The firelight dances behind me between the trees, orange and bright and too close yet. *The captain will not likely be an excellent tracker, unless he was in his life before he joined her majesty's military. The goblin perhaps will not care to follow, if I make it far enough to keep it from being an easy prey for him. I can mask my scent, use herbs to slow them down until I have put enough distance between us for them to leave off. If he cannot scent me, he cannot find me easily in this darkness. It is dark tonight.*

Creator, please help me. I swallow, turn and my eyes are still swimming, still watering and they should be burning, should be a hundred colors now. *There is no time. The night watches will be guarded by one of them. It is now, or it is never and tomorrow will be too late to learn if this lasts until the sun rises. Creator, help.*

I drop my arms, turn back to camp, duck beneath the low hanging branches, the darkness is rolled away, light spilling onto the grasses, yellow violets half-closed and broken sticks blended together beneath the trees. My eyes burn, but with light, sudden and real, flames dancing. I duck, move toward the saddles. Shadows play across the earth, mine coiling in the twisting of my skirts around each step, away from the shadows of the trees. I kneel, lift my saddle bag and my cheek feels damp. I brush it and my finger comes away soaked. *I am crying.*

"Healer?" The goblin's voice. *It has not been his custom to speak with me so often in the days gone.*

I clear my throat. *Let my voice not betray me.* "I found herbs in the woods," I clutch the bag in my hands, straighten. "I would beg permission to harvest them."

"Now? Do you intend to pick them by starlight?" *The goblin's voice.*

The fire crackles, and the captain's voice speaks. "What herbs?"

I lift my head higher. "Bitterroot." *Poison. That is not harvested this time in turning. Curse it.* I tighten my hands on the bag over my shoulder. *They will surely not know when it is harvested or what it is known for.* "I do not wish to beg for time to gather it in the morning. Tonight will cost us no time, on the trail, slow us down none tomorrow. I have done this before many times in the dark, but it will take some time to dig for it."

"Do not stray far." The captain's voice once more and they are speaking again, voices low, even.

My heart lifts, feet moving on their own. I nod, turn, a tear slipping down my cheek, and I do not swipe at it. I duck beneath the branches into the dark. *They will ignore me, the way they have so far for a spell, before my absence runs long.* I dip beneath the branches and roots press against my heels, and then the ground is soft again with the earth of the deep woods, heavy with the leaves of last harvest. A tears spatters damp against my foot. I lift my eyes. *Down the slope, herbs from the bag and then where from there? I do not know these woods, do not know anyone in these hills, not for leagues in any direction and I am wanted. There will be a price on me for more than just my bloodline, when they realize I have run, if they care enough that I failed to complete my orders to put a price on it.*

I am on foot. Herbs and then where is there to go but aimlessly into these mountains? I cannot go home. There is no safety left there. I know nowhere else.

Would it be better to be lost in the forests, or to find death at the hands of the Queen's men? I swallow. Leaves skid on the slope, sliding beneath my feet. I snap my hand around a tree, and my shoulder jerks tight. My arm throbs. The woods are dark, world swirling beneath the liquid in my eyes, blurring the faint light of a few glimmering fireflies. My throat tightens. I step down, and the slope fades, trees thicker, world darkening below.

I slow, drop down beside a large dark shape—a great tree, fallen. I drop the bag from my shoulder. Crocks clatter, cloths between only barely muffling their fall. I jerk the flap of the bag open, slip my hand inside and my fingers fumble on a crock. I pull the wax off and breathe in sharply.

There is nothing.

No scent. No smell. I bring it higher, breathe in sharper. There is nothing at all, not even a trace of the scents that should be there, of herbs or the rich scent of tallow or the faintness of beeswax and lavender and dandelions. I jerk my head back, suck in a breath through my nose.

There is no smell in the forest, no hint of the earth of the woods, no scent of trees and Lív and life. *Nothing. I cannot smell anything.*

My heart thuds in my chest, hand shakes, trembling in the grays and shadows. A firefly flickers, here and then gone before my eyes. *No. No no no.* I shove my hand into my bag, pull free another crock, my fingers prying loose the wax and it is off. I shove my finger into it, the salve cool, soft on my skin. I lift my finger, just beneath my nose and draw in a breath. There is nothing, no trace of any scent in the air, no hint of disturbed salves.

I lower my hand. My heart slows. *I do not know which is which, in the darkness. Their colors are masked this far from the fire light. I cannot hide if I do not know which will mask and which will tell where I have run with certainty.* I swallow, the bag slipping from my lap. It thuds softly against the earth, crocks clanking together.

Then I will run without the cover of herbs. I slip the wax back over the pots, stumble to my feet. Lights flicker in the darkness.

The goblin knew how many men there were, from scent alone, knew that Ruel had only seven with him. It will be no struggle for him to find me, his senses unhampered in the darkness.

But there is no other choice. If I wake tomorrow and it has not faded, I will be dead within half a fortnight at the latest, turned in for a price and trial at the hands of the courts. At the fort, there will be nowhere to turn, nowhere to run. I turn—the world churns and my legs cave, the ground falling away.

I gasp and my hand strikes something. *A tree.* My throat bobs—I lift my head and the world churns sharply, twisting in the dark. I gasp. "Stars." I swallow hard. *Creator, please help.* I press my foot forward and the ground is not there, not beneath my foot. My hand collides hard with a trunk, fingers snaking around it and the world jerks to a halt, spinning around me. My heart twists, thundering. *Am I ill so quickly, that I can no longer walk? Illness does not onset so swiftly. Stars. This is no illness.*

"Healer?" I jerk my head down and the goblin's voice is close, *too close*. He is barely two steps from me, a shadow in the churning dark. *He should not have come for me so soon. I have barely left camp, have been gone only a breath. I did not hear him coming.* "You are not well." There is no inflection to his words, a flatness in them that was not there before.

I look away, twist my hands against the bark and the world swirls again. *He already has me, if he chooses. Five turnings of hiding, five turnings of living alone and I am caught without running, taken without a fight.* I lift my head, draw a breath. "I—" the world jerks, tree falling away. Something slams against my side and the world is still moving, swirling around me, the sky falling away into nothingness. I cry out.

"Healer?" The goblin's voice is above me now and there is something on my arm, moving, my feet twisting beneath me, catching in something heavy and thick. My eyes flicker toward my arm, a shape around it. *A hand. His hand, on my arm.*

I look up, jerk away—the world falls again. "I am sorry. I am alright, only—" I look away, force my eyes down. *Can he see, in the dark?* The world jerks and there is his hand, pulling it up short once more. I gasp, press my head against my shoulder and something clatters on the earth beside me, pottery against stone. *The bag. The crocks. They will have broken, from that fall. Curse it.* The handle of the satchel is around my arm, pulling me downward. "Pardon. I do not underst—" I stoop, hand fumbling with the earth and there is nothing there, no bag, only the dirt and leaves and ground. I drop into a crouch and the satchel clatters. I press my hands against my eyes and his grip is gone from my arm. *He should not have come to look for me so soon. Where has the bag gone?*

There is a step above, a form moving over the faint traces of light from the fire. "Sradfaang. Is all well?"

There is no response. *He must have nodded to him.* The goblin's foot moves beside me, into my sight. "Can you walk?"

My throat tightens. "If you will let me rest for a moment, I will walk up. It is only a sudden dizziness. It will pass in a moment." He snorts and my heart sinks in my chest. *What will he do with me, if I cannot stand, cannot follow him?* I shake my head and the world tilts again, gone. I press my hand hard against the earth. *Curse it...*

A bird calls in the forest, the sound the high and clear shriek of a nighthawk.

"It is time to move." The goblin's voice is curt. "If you will not walk, then I will carry you. That is the end of it. You will not be idling here, in the dark."

I jerk my head up and the world jerks. I am against the ground again, my hand caught beneath me. I gasp, pull back, pain through my wrist. "Gót! Gót. Leave me a moment. It will pass. Please, it will pass and I will come up when it does." *If he doesn't leave me, then in a breath, they will know. Fár, I'm failing at last. They will find me out.*

Branches crunch, leaves crumbling into nothing beneath his foot. "As I have stated, it is time to move. Your choices have been laid out before you. Choose one, or I will have no choice but to make that decision for you. Is that clear?"

I tighten my hand on the stone beside me, my head whirling, fireflies swirling away in my sight and my heart sinks lower. *I cannot stand. The world will not hold still for long enough.* I swallow hard, lift my chin. "If you will carry me, I will go, but my legs will not support me enough to follow you."

He moves in the dark and his arms are pulling me upward. I stiffen, my legs wavering and his shoulder meets my stomach. He moves and I am in the air, over his shoulder, the world tilting upside down. Blood rushes to my head—I gasp. There is a cacophony of shapes everywhere, all moving by quickly, too quickly. The trees are blurring by, will not stop swirling. I gag, turn my head away.

"Please," I drag my hands up, press them against my eyes, bile raw against my throat, against the roof of my mouth. "I will try again to walk if you will set me down. Please." My voice is slow, sluggish, the world not sluggish around me.

He pauses and there is light dancing on my skin, through my fingers, orange and white. He stoops. My feet brush the earth, plant against them. I stagger and the world falls away again, tumbling over. It stops. There is something steady on my arm, lowering me to the side where the ground shouldn't be. *I cannot tell which way is up, and which way down.* Voices twist together beyond me. I press my eyes against my hands, the ground underneath me shifting, something damp and hard against my back. *A boulder.*

"Is she well?" *The captain's voice.*

"She is unable to stand, as you see. I do not think she knows where she is, at the moment." The goblin's voice sounds far away, muffled in the rushing in my ears.

"Had she run, or was she only preparing to?"

My head snaps up and the world goes with it. My throat constricts and I gag again, the light blinding and shapes are everywhere across my vision like a nightmare. I press my hand hard against my lips, against the bile swirling there. *Oh stars.* I squint through the light, the shapes barely taking form.

The captain's eyes are on the goblin, at the edge of my vision. His expression is focused, calm or maybe it is only the light, only the swirling, ragged world. The goblin inclines his head. "She was barely down the slope, meddling with these. She had not yet run." He lifts a pot, the wax only half on it, tiny in his palm. It is blue stone. *I had the right one. A calming salve, hardly potent, but gentle and useful to help mother animals bond to their mislaid offspring by blocking the scents of those that have touched them.* I curse, under my breath. The captain's eyes snap to mine.

Something moves across them. *Confirmation.* He nods and I jerk my eyes down. My heart thunders out of my chest. *He knows at last. And I have failed. There will be no more running. No more working to aid my people. Creator...* "Healer." The captain's voice is low, measured. "You should rest for the night. The effects of the tea will have worn out with the dawn."

"Tea?" *The tea was all what it should have been.* "I do not understand."

He drops down in front of me, half kneeling, too close now. I press myself away, against the stone behind me. "There was flagroot in it. I put more in it than I should have. You are smaller than I gave you credit for, but I had to be sure it would work tonight. As you know, it will not harm you, but will confirm something for me."

Flagroot. Stars no. I clench my hands together against the ground. "There was no scent of flagroot. I have worked with it before, and it is strong, pungent. You do not miss its taste or its smell."

A dry smile flits across his lips. "It was frozen in the north, to remove the scent and taste."

My eyes snap up, meet his. He is watching, nothing in his eyes but careful guardedness. I look away. *Flagroot. He laid a trap, and I walked into it, eyes open.*

But this was only to confirm. He already knew. Was it the fire, or was there another time, when I did not guard my gaze, shield my eyes? I shake my head, tilt it toward him. "You know then. Do with me what you will, only do it swiftly. Please. Do not draw out my time needlessly, to watches on end. I will not struggle against you, if you will be swift and not make my life linger." The world jolts and my hands slam against the ground, catching me. I press my eyes shut, shut out the swirling, the churning of the world. *Flagroot is not supposed to do this, even to Fians. It did not when I tested it before, and it was a large dose often, larger than he likely will have given for mine was boiled down.* "This cannot have been only flagroot. It does not make you ill, does not make the world churn and spin like this."

A leaf crunches. "The dizziness that you are feeling is the kúráh's bonnet flower. I could not have you running, before I could be sure of my guess. I apologize for the effects."

I press my hand against my head, the world thick. *Kúráh's bonnet.* "Wolfsbane?" *Poison. Toxin. Used for confusion and then paralysis. He has already carried out the sentence before he knew what I was for certain.*

"Aye. Wolfsbane. And I am not going to kill you. I have worked with the plant many times. It is only enough to make you stumble, and you will have expelled most of it by now. The rest will wear off with sleep." The captain moves to his feet, the air shifting with the motion. *A trick. Will it not kill?*

My eyes are burning, but not with turning colors. They swim with tears against my eyelids. I lift my head. "Please then, finish what you have begun. I am here, and you have me. Let the goblin finish me, and do not leave me to the poison or trial." *Heart slowed, and then death. Is that not how this poison kills?* I bow my head, the world swirling around me.

"Gót." His form is moving away from me.

"Gót?" I lift my head, strands of hair clinging to my face. The goblin watching from beside the flames. The light plays through his eyes making them bright like a Dark Thing and his arms are crossed, huge, over his chest, his face emotionless, impassive. I straighten. "Are you going to leave me to die then? I have expelled none of it. All that you gave me is yet in me, and is it not your right to end my time here, in this woodland? Please. Do not let me die in this way. Do not let this stretch out to endless watches. I beg that you would put an end to this and not take me in to trail and the slow death of the courts at the hand of the Queen."

The captain sets a log on the fire, not turning toward me. Sparks fly upward, above his head, scattering into the wavering branches of the trees. His movements are slow, precise, maddeningly precise. "The Queen does not carry out sentences. You would not be taken that far. But I am not," he straightens, turning toward me once more, "going to end your life. Neither will the poison or Sradfaang. His job is still to defend you, and he will, until his orders are fulfilled. The poison was not enough to kill a child. It was measured with many turnings of experience, I can assure you of that, healer."

I scoff. "'To defend me?' My life is forfeit in my bloodline, or did you not know what you were doing with that herb, when you uncovered my lineage?" My heart sinks in my chest. I drop backward. "If you are laying a trap, I beg that you would not or I…" I swallow, swallow back the emptiness of the world and it's too big. "…I can end my own timestring. Only give me a dagger and I will do it. Do not drag me to stand before your courts. I have heard the punishment of those who seek their favor, their pardon, of what has become of my bloodline there. Let not my days be stretched out to that end." The goblin's eyes flicker to mine and there is silence, only the echoes of the fire snapping in the air.

The captain turns slowly, his eyes finding mine. "No one is taking your life on my watch, Eness Finch. Rest. I will explain the rest in the morning when your mind has cleared of the toxin. I know you are afraid, but you will be safe here. Rest tonight."

I stare and the world is off balance. "Our queen holds us as less than landlots and you will let me live knowingly and tell me I am safe? For a game? For sport? For gain when tomorrow comes and I walk in willingly to your fort and to my death? Do not meddle with me, as a lynx with their prey. I know what is done to those under suspicion of the Queen's men. End my time or let me go, but do not toy with me, Captain. I beg that you would not."

His eyes are on me, earnest now and it is worse than when they showed nothing at all. "I do not toy. I would not have done what I have the way I have if I had known from the start what you were, but I intend to take you somewhere safe. You will not be at the fort for any longer than can be helped while we give reports to our overseeing officers. If I could spare you entrance there, I would but it cannot be avoided so late in the journey. I am sorry."

I stare at him, my eyes a thousand colors in the dancing light of the flames. "Would you have left me, had you known? Would not your men have drug me in? I was safe, in the forest. If you would take me somewhere safe then let me return the way I came, alone. Let me go my own way and never enter within a league of you or yours again. If you wish for my well being than let me leave."

He shakes his head, a fractured movement. "Your region is no longer safe for anyone in hiding, much less a Fian woman, like you. I would have ordered you to come with me if you had not nearly signed your own life to it by insisting that I needed a healer. I saw your notes, knew what you were working on in that cottage. It would not have been safe for you to stay, even without your heritage." I stare at him. He continues. "There is a road being constructed, one for military travel between Fort Barchot and Jennings. Your cottage will be right along it inside of two turnings at the latest. In another three moons, there will be soldiers traveling back and forth to begin the work on it. I would not have left you there to be found and gathered in for your work."

I press my hand against the ground, hard, drop back against the stone. *He saw my work, in the cottage, read my notes? When? When did he have time to read them, when he was not nearly at death's door? Oh stars.*

I swallow hard, firelight still curling upward, as if nothing has happened, has changed. I swallow again and my throat will not clear. "Are you certain a road is coming? That area would be impractical, for military to cross. There are…many hills. Many hollers to cross and creeks to traverse over. It would be a long and winding way through the Glycall mountains."

The goblin snorts. "All ways through the Glycalls are long and winding. There has been an uprising in activity from those who claim to be for freedom not far from you. The area has already been designated as a point to combat the uprising as well as further travel between forts. I saw the papers more than a moon ago in the hands of one of my charges. He speaks the truth, healer."

The captain stands. "I am sorry. You could go back, but I cannot guarantee your safety there. There are already troops using the highway, before it is formed, and there will be more to come as I have said. Many of the colonels have been made aware of it in the last moon. The men will have to stray only a little from the road to find you, like mine own did. You are good at hiding, but how long will that last if there is a man who is no respecter of boundaries at your door, in your cottage? There are enough of them in the Queen's men. You will not be ignorant of that—I am not. If they were to find the work you were attempting, even with as cryptic as your notes were, and guess at what you were attempting, your death would be one longer and more drawn out than you can imagine. I brought you out when I thought you were attempting to aid a friend in this. If it is known that you are of them and attempting to shield them from the Queen, her generals will not be kind to you and you will be taken all the way up the chain. Your ending will be violent and it will be public. Your best option, is to trust us for now."

I clench my hands. "And what would you do with my life?"

I look up and he is watching me, his eyes settled, quiet. He drapes his hands between his knees. "I would take you to a hiding. I have told you all I can. It would not still be safe if it was told to every wayfarer in need of a haven. But I can guarantee your safety there, if you will trust us. It has been a safe place for many men seeking a quiet place until they can turn to their own homes. Sradfaang will take you there and see to it that you are settled. You are his task, whatever you choose, but if you go back to your home in the hills, only death awaits you there. It is only a matter of days before there will be more soldiers knocking on your door, and I do not think you will want to try avoiding them twice. Nor are you likely to be able to."

"A haven?" I look up. There is no lie in his gaze, no sign of a falsehood. *What soldier, would offer a woman sanctuary, when gain is offered at the hand of his monarch? His ruler? What reward would he be given, for turning in a fian who had studied ways to shield others from his order?* I look away. "And my home will be left then, gone to time?" *Herbs wasted, notes wasted.*

He shakes his head. "It may become a stopping point along the road, when they find it. Or your village may fill it with another healer, an herbalist to take back up your task, but not your work. I burnt your notes, before we left. I am sorry. And the haven cannot be avoided, unless there is someone else you would trust to go to. If there is, Sradfaang will take you there, but it would not be wise to go back to your home."

Burned them? The world churns sharply. My shoulder thuds against the boulder, my head pulsing and there is a pinprick in my palm. I grimace, press my eyes shut. *Someone else? There is no one else.* The world aches for a moment and it is gone, the pulsing gone. I peel my eyes open, slowly, keep them on the ground. "How? When did you burn them?" *Full turnings of labor, gone. Five turnings. Burned.*

He drops into a crouch once more, not far from me. "I am sorry, Eness Finch. I would not have, if there was another choice, but we could not leave them to be found, and it would be unwise to take them with us. There are random searches on our baggage in the Mark, especially in outposts like the one we are traveling to. I hope to the Creator that something good comes out of it. You have had enough toil without the uprooting you gained by tending my life. How long were you there?"

My head throbs. *What good will it do, to speak on this? Creator, please help me. Save me again by Your Might.* I lift my head. *I cannot think tonight. Cannot think through any of this. He asks for trust, and burns full turnings of work.* I press my hands under me. "I am sorry. I will take my rest, if you will excuse me. I am sorry. I will bring up all that I have in me if I speak any longer. The world is churning."

He stands smoke drifting over his eyes for a moment. "Aye." He half bows, a gesture of respect, the smoke clearing around him. "You should rest. The herbs will still be watches in wearing off, which I apologize for. If there was a way around it while assuring your safety, I would have done it, but I became aware of your heritage too late on this journey. You guard it well. I thought you had a friend to help you with your research, not that it was your own blood that you studied. The mirror was a wise thought." *I did not guard it well enough.* I nod. *I will not go home again. Not go back to the cottage, to my notes and the hills and flowers. There will be little left, if I ever return, nothing worth returning to. There is nowhere to run to, if I could escape from them, before death knocks.* He inclines his head. "You should move. You will feel better if you empty your stomach of the toxins."

My throat is tight, eye twisting in a hundred shades behind the veil of herbs. I turn my head away. "I thank you." He turns toward the goblin. I crawl forward, the world still swirling and my knees grind hard against the earth. I slow beside my bed roll, press my head against my hands. His hand flashes on the edge of my vision, a symbol, toward the goblin and there is a sign back, words lost in signal. My skin crawls.

Why do they sign if they have already spoken to me? What more do they hide, if they mean no harm?

XI

Fort Barchot

Something is rumbling, quiet in the darkness. I press my head down, sleep heavy, frogs chirping in the night.

There is silence for a moment, and then a voice, low as the earth. "…if she does not settle down?"

"Then we will cross that river when it rises. It is the same, Srad, as with the others. She will settle or we will handle it as need be. They are not unprepared."

There is a grunt, the goblin's voice. "She is the same, but will also be a higher risk to all of them and I would have less risk there, now with what he is looking to attempt as I understand it. We need more time, if we are going to be successful. He needs more time, and with each new lot we bring in, the time may be shrinking. I do not care for this idea."

"If there was another place to take her, we would, but it would slow you down by more than a fortnight to take her to another haven, any of them, on the chance they will take in someone of her bloodline. Would you spare the time on a chance?"

The goblin snorts. "It would be foolhardy to take her to another. There are few havens left that would take in one of her bloodline. Sikkerhet will, to their detriment. I do not like him taking this risk."

I force out a breath, slow and easy. The captain speaks again. "Would you have him not take in those that ask for help, those that need it desperately?"

"She is not desperate, Einion, not yet. She would have run to her own safety, if we allowed it. If you had not drugged her, I think she would have been gone by now into the dark." He snorts. "Not that I could not have found her. That hair of hers stands out like a beacon in the darkness and she reeks of herbs. I could follow her trail in a cave at full dark."

There is movement, fabric against fabric. The captain laughs, the sound light. "You have followed many lots in the dark." There is silence again, for a moment, the fire snapping. "It would not have been to her own safety, Srad. She knows nothing of the world at large, not as it is now. We cannot have her running off to nowhere. You would have tracked her down and that would have put us more days off trail, which would cause problems on other fronts. I do not like the amount of lying I have had to do of late. Keep her safe, until she is settled. Keep her there. She may yet be useful, to Eerol and Ciaran and the cause. There is much that she could do for it, with her skill. Keep her there."

There is silence, long and sharp, no longer the chirping of frogs, no longer the snapping and crackling of the fire. *Useful, and they know nothing of my gift. If they learned, what use would they put me to? I cannot stay with them. I have gone from being hunted to being ready to be utilized by those within their supposed safe haven.* My heart sinks, and the captain's voice fades out. Silence curls in, long and thick.

"She is no longer sleeping." The voice is quiet, the goblin's. I keep my head down, my back to them, and there is quiet across the camp, the fire no longer crackling, the crickets and frogs the only sounds of night. I shiver, skin warm beneath the blanket and night air.

•▶|◀▶|◀▶|◀▶|◀▶|◀▶|◀•

My head throbs.

I press it against my palm, press it down into the earth. There is movement down past the end of my feet, the goblin, twisting a log into the dying embers of the fire. Smoke churns up from it.

The captain steps into my line of sight, lifting my saddle from the earth. He straightens, glancing at me. "Would you speak now, or wait until we are on the road once more?"

I drag my body upward, incline my head. *He is asking, not insisting upon speaking. That is a curtesy soldiers are not known to offer. He will likely not offer it again.* I clear my throat. "It will be simpler now. I would hear what you have to say."

He inclines his head, setting the saddle down again and kneels. "There is a safe haven, not many days travel from here. It is deep in the heart of the Glycalls, the location well-guarded, for the safety of all those that hide there. You will be welcomed there, given a place to live, if you choose. There are not many safe places left in this kingdom, as I am certain you have been aware. They will keep your secret and ask in return only your work as a part of that community, offering your skills to help make it a comfortable place for others. It is to there, that I am sending you with Sradfaang this evening. He will see to it that you make it there in safety." His eyes are earnest. "What questions do you have for me? I will answer what I can."

I turn away, shove back the swirling of my eyes, and it works, the burn fading. *Praise Elnial.* I swallow hard. *What questions do I ask, a captain I little trust?* Words in the dark creep back into my mind. I nod my head. "I have no questions at present. I am sorry. Thank you for speaking with me." *A safe haven. Who would offer a safe haven to those hunted by the land? It will only be a matter of time, before my place there is betrayed. It has happened before to many of my blood who thought they found safety in their community. It has happened to many others, not of our blood, not exiled.*

He lifts a brow, his expression dry. "Then I will leave you to gather yourself. It is a short ride to the fort. Barely a watch. Get yourself ready." *Barely a watch. Less time than he said yesterday, when we halted for the night.* My stomach is tight, head still throbbing. He stands, moving away across the camp, my saddle held in his hands.

I turn toward the open sky, dawn already come.

The captain adjusts his grip on his reins. "You will speak to no one." His horse side steps, prancing like a cat in a milking room. "The soldiers there cannot require you to speak if you are under the protection of a higher officer, which you are. Two. Remember that if anyone tries to speak with you. There will be no occasion for them to, but if something changes while you are there, you will remind them of that. If you mention either of our names, they will leave off any questions and see to it that you are left alone. Is that understood?" I incline my head. *Ride into the fort, ride out again. A simple task. An easy trap, if they wanted to do me harm. But it would have been simpler for them to have bound and hauled me this last night. I pose no threat, that they should play this game. But what gain is there for them, in bringing me out again safely, in risking themselves to see me to safety?*

My eyes flicker to the goblin. *How high is his rank, that I would have to answer no questions at the bidding of those in this fort? Captain is a mid-ranking officer at the highest. I know little of the Knoc'gnori.*

The captain turns his mount back to the road, mine following. He glances over his shoulder, toward me. "Sradfaang will have you out of there within a watch. Keep to yourself and keep the hound beside you. He will not be free to roam here. There are no hounds at this fort. Sradfaang will give you instruction once I am gone and again when he comes to get you. Is that understood?" I incline my head, and he nods back at me. "I am sorry to put you through this, but you cannot be left in the forests. You would be found by patrol and brought in for questioning. There are many bands like those we met in the mountains who are no friends of the fort. Soldiers would assume that you are one of them and bring you in. I am sorry." He glances back at me once more, and away. "This will be the cleanest way to get you to where it is safe again. I ask that you keep your head down and listen to orders as you have done so far."

My stomach swirls. *Have I listened to orders? Did I not try to run in the night?* The captain's horse starts into a trot and mine follows, the movement rough beneath me, throwing me up and down. I tighten my knees and force them to relax again. I am slipping forward, the saddle sliding beneath me. *Pressure will make her go faster.* I draw in a breath, pull back on the reins, and I am slipping further in the saddle, gliding toward her head. *Do not push the horse forward, do not lose the pace.* Blått is beside me, his gait matching hers easily, like it is nothing. I tighten my legs.

There is a building ahead down the slope, through the trees, a tower beside it. It is only the bare bones of a structure, logs bound together with ropes and a wooden platform in the trees. There are men on it, all wearing the same black cloaks, though the air is warm today. There are men on the ground, soldiers scattered through the trees. All of them are dressed in the same dark garb, some of them in dark sleeveless tunics. *There are more than fifty of them. We are walking into their center.* I bite back the swirling of my eyes.

The captain's horse is rapidly drawing close to the soldiers, to the clouds of dust kicked up by their feet. One of them slows, his eyes catching on the captain. He nods, a half bow, formal—the respect of soldiers. He bows again, this time to the goblin behind me, and the others are all halting their fights, repeating his motion, courtesy and deference in their movements, their bow deeper toward the goblin. *He is known here. Known and respected.*

The captain bows back to them but he does not slow his pace, following the road into an archway in the low stone building. The air is cool beneath the arch, and there is sunlight again, dappled on my skin through the branches of the great tree in the courtyard, at its center. There is an open yard past it, all dirt, men wrestling on the ground in the same black tunics, dusted with the gray of sand and no longer the red of mountain clay. A short man is standing in the midst of them, watching, his cloak touching the ground like the mountain man Ruel, but his is charred black, the same as any of the soldier's. His face is watching every motion of the men on the ground, calculating, gaze sharp like the captain's.

His voice barks out. "Again." The men separate, moving to their feet and each of them shift to the side, approaching a new man. The small man barks out a word and they all step forward, grabbing each other, one man on the ground in an instant, his body smacking the earth.

The captain's horse halts, mine slowing behind him. He throws his leg over the side of his mount, and I drag my eyes away from the wrestling men. He slings his cloak up onto his shoulders. I slip my leg over the side of my mount and my feet hit the ground, hard. Pain burns up my leg. I turn away from the animal, brush my skirts back into place. The captain turns toward me, a small bag in his hand. "Sradfaang will show you where to wait, and he will come get you when it is time." He nods at me, a half bow and turns away, gone, no time given for a response. He is already moving across the training grounds to the far side of the structure.

I swallow and glance toward the goblin. He is waiting beside his great shadow of a horse, face passive. The small man's voice rings out once more, "Again!"

The goblin steps around the horses, his feet kicking up dust on the dry sand of the yard. I move after him, Blått chasing at my heels. He steps through an empty doorway and the air is cold, the world dark. I blink spots out of my vision, and the ground is cool stone beneath my feet, nails tapping against stone beside me. They halt, Blått blinking up at me in the darkness, his head lowered.

"Healer," The goblin's voice is hollow in the hallway, "this way." I start forward. There is light ahead, faint and growing, and it catches on Blått's coat ahead of me, catches on the goblin's strange cloak like the sides of a tree, dull and dark. He turns at the end of the hallway, shadows long, and there is a window, light pouring in. He pauses beside it, twists a doorknob on the wall beside him. There is a tapestry beside him, gold and small, the cloth of it simple make, the symbol of the rearing stag of Auvridal. *The war emblem.* The stag is not etched in green but in red, the threads of the cloth gold even in the shadows.

He pushes open the door, stepping back. "Wait here. I will return for you by the end of a watch."

I step around the corner, into the room. It is sparse, tiny, almost taken up by a thin cot, pressed against the wall. *What kind of room is this, that I am putting myself in?* I turn back toward the goblin. "How far are we to travel tonight, once you have completed your report?" Blått is beside him, odd in the hallway beside the towering goblin.

The goblin shakes his head, glancing impatiently over his shoulder. "Until dark, as we have done." He turns away, and Blått steps into the space, the room too small for both of us together. My legs bump the cot. I press them hard against it, and the goblin draws the door shut.

Blått whines, lifting his head, his back against my stomach, tail thumping the wall.

The room is all stone like the hallways beyond, all but the wooden cot pressed against my leg. I glance out the window. *It is glass.* I step forward, press my finger against the surface. It is cool, waved like ice in Gråsving. *What kind of fort is this, that they took the time and expense to import glass for it?* The panes are thick. I can see nothing through them, gain nothing of the outside world through its cloudy surface but shapes and shadows. I drop onto the edge of the cot, curl my legs up beneath me. Blått whines, pressing his nose against my cheek. I brush my hands along his head, push his snout away.

One watch. The captain said it would only be one that we are here. But it would not be the first time, nor the last, that a soldier lied to someone in their care. How long should I wait, before testing these halls, to see if I can creep through them, to escape unseen? If I walk quietly enough, keep my head down, how long would it take for a soldier to stop me?

I will not be questioned, if I use their names. He told me that.

Unless they have given orders for me to be apprehended if seen beyond the grounds.

My eyes flick to Blåthjortt beside me. *If I run, if I make it from these walls, I will not be able to take him with me. He would be left at their hands, for them to do with as they please. A hound would be out of place walking these halls. But I will be just as out of place, a woman in a fort of soldiers, with no village nearby, no call for me to be here, unless I am under watch. How long will it take for me to be found and brought in, by either Wandering Men or scouts of these soldiers, if I run?* My stomach tightens, eyes dart to the window. The sunlight is still warm through it, the full bright of morning.

If they have lied and the goblin does not return, there may be no other choice. I will not wait here to be killed in their time.

Creator, let him return. Let my death not come at their hands.

•▶|◀▶|◀▶|◀▶|◀▶|◀▶|◀•

The wood grain of the wall is strange, deep as old wood, and there is no variation in the color of the panels. I shift my hands, press them against my crossed knees. *It has been too long.* I stand and my chest nearly strikes the wall across from me, my feet trapped beneath Blått. I suck in a breath, turn, drag my feet from beneath him. He looks up, his eyes reproachful. *This room would not fit a man without him turning in a ball, or even a woman only a little broader or taller than I. There is no space for movement, no space for walking, only a door and a cot. You could lose your mind in a place like this, if left for too long to gaze into nothingness.*

I step forward, pause, and turn, back towards the cot. Blått's tail flickers at my feet, strands of it brushing against my toes. The glass of the window is tinted bright gold halfway up, the light of the sun striking it. It is beautiful, dark and light meeting in its center. *It has been more than a watch. How long does it take to give a report? How long should I wait, before attempting to get out?*

I glance toward the window. *Would it be better to try and escape after dark, when the soldiers surely will be about their own activities? What men will they have on watch, to guard a camp filled with soldiers? Their best or their worst or all the men in between?* I draw in a breath, glance down at the hound by my feet. *How long will they leave me, before deciding what they intend to do?* I turn, grip the doorknob. It does not turn, does not move at all in my grip. My heart sinks. *It is locked. I should have tried it as soon as I entered, before I thought of an escape. If the goblin does not return, the captain does not come for me...*

My eyes flicker back to the window. *If I run, it must be through the glass. I have heard that glass is loud when it breaks, but it shatters with ease. It would be heard, as readily as pounding on the door to get out. There will be no escape through those panes. I would be caught in a moment, in a place like this, if it is as loud as the stories say.*

I turn back toward the window, and Blått's head lifts beside me, his nose pressing against my fingertips. The darkness has reached further up the panes, light fading out into the blue gray of evening and the late watches. *How late will it be now? The fifth watch?*

Blått's head spins around.

A step falls in the hallway, soft, barely a breath. *There have been many steps in the hallway, since the leaving of the goblin. But none of them have been soft.* The doorknob shifts and the door swings open. The goblin is standing on the other side of the frame, his head blocked by its wood and his legs gone behind Blått's standing form, only his chest and waist visible. I press to my feet, smooth my skirts.

"Healer." He steps to the side, head still gone behind the door frame. "Gather your hound. We are leaving."

I step, move past him, into the hall. He fills it, his head brushing the ceiling as it did at my home. I click to Blått and he is already turning, moving up the hall after the goblin. His steps are nearly silent on the stone floors, movements quiet, a strange, practiced sound as though he were permitting his feet to make noise. We are moving up the hall, away from the doorway that we came in through this morning.

I purse my lips, move around Blått's high back. The hound is stretching, movements labored, lazy. *The goblin is outpacing us.* I pick up my steps, start after him. He ducks through a doorway. There is a long room before us, tables pushed to its edges, lining every wall, and a long scrawling mark carved into the center of the stone floor. I cannot make it out, the design too far away and deep in the stones. My feet echo on the stones, the room empty but for three papers, tacked to the far wall, and the tables pushed to the side. The goblin steps through a door and there is another hallway, many doors lining it, all closed. He grabs the first doorknob, pulling it open, and there is sunlight, cutting in, bright, sharp. He steps through and the light is gone for a moment. It flashes back, full. I shield my eyes, step after him, pulling the door shut behind me. Blått's nails are no longer ringing on stone.

The goblin strides across the yard, his back straight. His great horse is standing ahead in the shadowed ring between buildings, saddles already on them, the horse strangely large, even in this place. *They waited to bring me out until the last moment, until they were already prepared to leave.* There is a horse beside the goblin's mount, one I have not seen before, though it is brown, like the one I have ridden these last days. The new horse is solid brown, but for a white line across its face like the sheep hounds of Guncalk. The goblin steps up to his great horse. "Mount up. The captain will be seeing us off and does not have much time to spare."

I step up to the horse and it does not shy away, perfectly motionless in front of me. I plant my foot into the saddle, and jerk myself upward, and the horse doesn't move, doesn't even sidestep as the other always did. My leg barely clears its back, skirts bunching, catching on my ankles and shins. I shift in the saddle, smooth them down, and the horse moves, half whinnying, the note high. My feet slide against the horse's sides—they do not reach the stirrups, only my left planted in one, the other hanging useless.

A soldier is offering me something, the reins. He glances at the stirrups, and he steps forward without a word, his back ramrod straight, actions precise. He grips the leather beneath my leg, pulling upward, the gold on his shoulders glinting in the sunlight. It is a simple pattern, the same as Marc's. *A lieutenant.*

The goblin snorts. "Not the same saddle." It is a statement, made to no one. The soldier steps around the horse's head, and he grips the other stirrup, knocking my bunched skirts out of the way. He jerks a strap and the stirrup is pressing against the sole of my foot, as it should be. I incline my head to him—appreciation and respect. He turns away, gone, face a blur in the cooling shadows of the afternoon, unremarkable, unmemorable. RUTABAGA

Sradfaang glances back at me, and he is off, wordless, up the road, clicking to his mount. Blått is moving beside him, his feet kicking up dust in the late-watch light. I click to my mount, but it is already moving, feet even on the packed ground of the training rings. There is the sound of hooves ahead, but everything else is quiet, no noise of training, of men at work, only hooves and the distant murmur of voices somewhere off in the fort. *Do they halt training so early in the day?*

Sradfaang ducks through the arch, another mounted figure moves up beside him. The captain swings his mount ahead, taking the trail ahead of the goblin. I press my hand against the saddle horn. *What kind of farewell does he need to give, that he would see us off?* The horses are trotting up the hill, dust churning up behind their hooves, swirling around the furred feet of the great black horse.

The outpost is to the left and then gone again through the trees, men nodding and bowing from the heights toward the men ahead of me. There are only two men visible now in the outpost, two men whose eyes never even flicker toward me. *Do they ever look up, at those that pass through the gate, and back out into the roads? Is it by order or choice that they keep their eyes down? Or is it so common a thing to see travelers here, that they do not wonder at it anymore?*

The goblin's horse crests the hill, and for a moment the captain's mount is visible beyond it, and then it is gone again. The road rounds off, turning off toward the higher hills, back toward my cottage and home, and we are past the last of the men, past the last of the soldiers of the fort. *I am out again. Past the guards and into the lands again.*

The goblin is reining in his mount and the captain has already turned, moving back up beside him. His horse is facing me, its feet prancing.

Captain Flint glances at me, eyes flickering between me and the hound beside me. "Healer." His eyes settle on mine. "I apologize for all the strife of this. I am not blind to your sacrifice on my behalf, nor the hard position you were in in my camp these last days." He inclines his head toward me, respect and honor in its tilt. "I pray this will turn out for the better, where you go now. Death only would have awaited you where you came from, if not now, then in the times to come." My eyes burn, and I bite back the shift. *What awaits for me where I go but that, longer, more stretched out, with their own aims and goals blended in?* He nods at the goblin. "You would do well to listen to Sradfaang. There are few men more loyal to their task in all Auvridal, or the Fresh Isle itself. He will guard you well until you reach your destination and see to it that you are seen to once you arrive. Do not let his council fall on deaf ears while you take the road with him. He has never failed to serve well."

I nod—respect and nothing more, and his eyes stay on me for a moment longer, calculating, judging. I hold his gaze. His chin lifts, just slightly, and he turns, toward the goblin. "Tell the Swan I will be there as soon as I can, that this delay should not be much longer, and give Eerol my regards. You know the rest." *The Swan?*

The goblin nods, bowing the low bow of honor and friendship—his left hand down by his waist. "Good roads to you, Einion. May the Light see you where you are bound and back to your place in safety. Until we ride again."

The captain nods, reflecting every motion of the goblin, though his carries less grace. "And you, my friend. May the world carry you on your way and back in safety, until we ride again."

The captain clicks to his mount, the slightest sound, and he is off down the road, the goblin moving past him. My mount starts after the goblin, Blått's gait is easy beside me. My horse's steps are slow, listless, the goblin's easily outstepping it. I swallow. *Then we are off again. To walls and trees and to supposed safe havens, and all that will come with them.* Trees twist away toward the sky, and the goblin drops back, his horse moving behind mine. I turn back toward him.

He clicks to my mount, the sound even. "Keep to the roadway. We will not leave it until today has passed."

I straighten, my skin crawling once more. *He is behind me. He intends to remain there. I can keep no eye on him, while he hides back there, cannot know what he is doing or thinking.*

That did not trouble me before. But before, it was not only me and him, and the endless hills of the Glycalls. Before, there were others.

Blått tears off into the forests, his head high, bark snapping out, the white tail of a rabbit ripping through the undergrowth in his wake.

I turn my head away. *I will go with him. They have honored their word thus far. I will follow him. And I will leave, once we have arrived and there is a chance. There will be no safety found within those walls. Not for me. If there are landlots dwelling there, it would only be a matter of time before it would no longer be safe, one of their secrets betraying them, or one of mine.*

It would only be a matter of time, perhaps of days.

I cannot give up my work so willingly, so plainly to sit idly and wait for death to find me, and all those of my blood.

I have failed, and they have burned my work. But I can begin again, somewhere, somehow and find a way out of this. Creator, please watch over us.

XII

Wolves

The goblin's head is lifted, the tips of one of his pointed ears just visible over his coiled hair. It is pricked up, alert as it has not been all day. I press my hand against the saddle, shift myself further onto it. *Do I ask, what it is, or do I leave him be? He is not often one for speech.*

His horse moves forward, a little faster now, and my mount mirrors his, steps increasing their movement. I flick my eyes out toward the trees. *Where in the woods does he see trouble? Or does he hear it?*

There is little change in the forest but in the foliage, oaks replacing the poplars, ash, and spruce of the last few miles, ground apples getting thinned out over the earth. Trillium dot the hillsides, the purples and blues of larkspur beautiful beside the bright whites of the trillium, bees humming faintly around them. *Nothing to alarm in the flowers or hills.*

Blått's ears are lowered, his movements sluggish, slow. *Tired.* I purse my lips, glance at the goblin. *Perhaps I am misreading him. The dog has not scented anything, or he would be off and away, barking.*

Unless it is a man. The goblin's ear pricks up, just the barest motion, but there is no other movement, his horse still ambling forward. I drag my eyes away, flick them toward the sky. The branches are swaying above us, their movement gentle and serene, the last of the light bright red across the tops of their branches. A bee flutters, moving in and out of the branches, small amid the red of the sunlight, sharp and fading. *I have barely seen any bees this Liv. They have not reached my mountains yet this season, had not reached them when we left them, seven dawns ago.* I flick my gaze back to the trail. The goblin is beside his horse, his hand reaching for his saddle bags. *I did not hear him dismount no slow.*

I press my hands against the saddle, flick my eyes to Blått. The hound is still walking slowly, down beside my mount, his tail still, head lowered. *No sharpness to his gaze, no warning bark. What does the goblin sense, that the hound does not?* The goblin's hand is pulling a bag off of his saddle, small and lightly colored like the leather of a rabbit skin.

I lift my gaze from the hound. "What is it you scent?"

He moves away from his mount, not glancing my way. "Nothing for you to be concerned with." He flips the bag open, drawing a pouch from it, and Blått's head shoots up.

My hands tighten on the saddle, eyes snap back to the goblin. "What is that?"

His hands have not stopped moving, lifting something small from the pouch. "It is for the men who have been tailing us this last half league. We are not stopping. Stay atop your horse and keep the hound back. You will not want him running through this once it is down, healer."

My heart slows in my chest, eyes stay on him. He is stooping, dusting something on the ground. It is powdered, pale and nearly the same color as the red hued clay of the road. Blått barks, moving forward. I grip the reins, click to him and he slows, looking up at me, eyes pleading. I shake my head, click out a command. Blått drops onto his haunches.

I keep my gaze on him. "What is that, that it would trouble the hound?"

The goblin's movements are careful, measured, pouring the powder in a line across the road behind me. "Ulvestunr."

My eyes snap to him. "Wolvessong? That herb is forbidden. And will it not trouble the wolf kind alone, and not men of the forests?"

The horse under me shifts, sidestepping and I grip the saddle, click to it. It ignores me.

The goblin glances at me, straightening, and his eyes glint, catching in the faint red of the sun. He turns away again, toward his horse. "It is not forbidden for Knoc'gnori." He catches his horse's bridle, pulling it back to the road, away from the line in the dust. Blått follows, his head up, eyes alert now, sharp. He continues. "When they walk through it, they will carry the scent of the powder with them into the woods. There are enough wolves in this area to keep them busy and off our trail, if they are smart enough to realize the wolves are tracking them before they get close at hand. It is time to go." The hound glances backward toward the line of powder, fading into the dirt of the road. *How long will it take the wolves to be on their trail, to hunt them?* My heart tightens. *And what kind of lot is the goblin, that he is willing to throw away their lives so easily, to toy with them like this?*

I nudge my mount and it follows the goblin's, hooves nearly silent on the fresh branches of a fallen tree over the road. "Who are they?"

He glances back at me, and his eyes trail over to the trees. "Woodland bandits. They will be looking for an easy prize." I grimace. *They should know better than to track a goblin, without knowing his status. They should have heard the stories, of all the villages torn by his kind. They do not often travel so far into the hills.* My throat is tight, eyes burning, shifting. A memory flashes in my mind, heads rolling, death and blood-soaked leaves. *Goblins' work, in the name of the queen. Is he the kind to do the like, this goblin soldier? He has traveled with us peaceably, but there is no reason, no call, for that not to change. He is willing to toy with the lives of these men, as though they were nothing.*

And they were willing to toy with ours, tracking us so far. How long, before they decide to close in, to their own deaths? Do they think they could take a goblin warrior, or do they not read him truly?

His sword hangs on his horse, in easy reach, a sure mark of what he is. *Do they not draw close enough to see?*

My eyes flicker back, toward the trail behind us, the horse rising and falling beneath me. *Wolvessong. How long until we hear the hunting call of the wolves? I have not heard it, not since Blått came to my home. They ceased to haunt my hills, once he was there. Even the coyotes ceased to come.*

The goblin's head is high, as it always is, his gait steady beside his mount, movements like a shadow in the forest.

How long has the goblin carried that powder on his person, for a time like this?

My eyes flicker over him, his form swinging back onto his horse. I swallow hard.

Somewhere in the forest, a bird calls.

A howl sounds, high, eerie. My head snaps up, my heart catches in my throat. The call is echoed, another, higher, twisting together and echoing in the trees.

"They will not bother us. Be calm." The goblin's voice is curt.

My eyes flicker to him. His back is against a tree, a blade on his lap, hands working over it, sharpening or cleaning, I cannot tell. I set the satchel down. "How do they not scent what you carry with you, to hunt you in the forests?"

"How do we not scent what you carry with you?" His eyes flicker from the blade to me. I meet his eyes, look away. He snorts, turning back to his work. "Because it is in a tallow sealed bag, made with beaver hide and bees wax. I take no risks with it. It would be especially foolish in town." I nod slowly. His eyes move to me again and away, expression dry. "If you are worried, they will not kill them."

I draw a plant from my bag, roots still hanging from it, dirt crumbling down from each one. "Do you know wolves so well?"

He runs the cloth over his blade, the sound hollow. "These wolves are not big enough to bring down a man, unless he is on his own. Those men will not be. They are smarter than that, even in these forests. But they are big enough to make a nuisance of themselves until the men retreat back to their own homes. They will have dealt with them before and are not likely to be harmed by them. Unless they are foolish."

The fire crackles, sparks flying in a sudden shower upward. I shiver, press my back against the stone wall behind me. The goblin's gaze is back on his work, his hands moving slowly over the blade, and I can no longer see them in the shadows behind his crossed legs.

The air is cool, damp. *It tastes of coming rain.*

Blåthjortt's head is up, his eyes on the trees, watchful in the dark of the night. *He is never watchful. Never alert.* I set the plant in the pouch and twist up the laces around its shoots, the leaves jutting out, and there is a howl, the hunting call of a wolf. *Will we hear them, when they draw close to the men?*

I lift my head, the air cool now, damp, brushing strands of hair across my skin. The howl is echoed by the shout of a man, off in the forests, catching in the hollers and crags of the hills. I shudder.

XIII

Falling Rain

"Healer." The voice is low. My face is damp, the darkness slipping away. My back is cold, something pressing against it, hard and chilled. I drag my head upward. *A stone. The stone at the back of the campsite.* The voice speaks again, low hollow. *The goblin's voice.* "Get up. It is time to depart."

I drag my body under me, glance up. The air is dark, fog curling through the branches of the forest, eerie and soft in the early morning. My arm shakes beneath me, my body aching. The fire is gone, not even a breath of coals on the earth, only smoke, pale and faint in the shadows. I shiver, pull my arms around my waist. Everything feels off in the dark before dawn, the air heavy without the welcome of light. *Why do we rise so early, if there are men and wolves about?* "Is dawn near?" My teeth chatter against my jaw. I clamp it shut. There is dew across my skin, damp and cool.

"Near enough. His voice is quiet, muffled and too sharp, like the shadows before dawn. "Get ready for the road. We will not wait long." He straightens, his figure vague, and I cannot make out his expression, anything of his face or posture in the dark and fog. He turns away, starting into the trees and fog.

I press my arms under me, and my bones are cold, the world dull and too close. I stand, my shawl slapping against my skirts, against the stones, the sound too loud and sudden. I pull it away. Frogs call in the forest, crickets gone with the morning watches. *Are we to second watch yet, or before?* I shudder. There is a shadow on the far side of the circle, sidestepping, shifting in the dark. *A horse.* I move forward, and a figure looms out of the dark, sudden and large. *The goblin.* I stiffen, draw my arms about myself. *The horses are already saddled. How long did he sleep?* I press my legs together, bones chattering. There is a shadow moving around the horses, smaller, colorless and soft, its movements awkward. It looks toward me, slowing its gait. *Blåthjortt.* He starts toward me, his tail is wagging, moving oddly in the predawn shades. He barks, softly, a welcome sound. I click my tongue, hold my hand out toward him, my shawl slipping off my shoulders.

He bounds toward me, his mouth a vicious grin in the mist. His head presses against my hand, tail thumping hard against my legs. I brush his head, move for the horses. The woods are silent, the mid or last watches of night. *It is strangely cold for the first of Sámling.*

The goblin steps back around my mount. I swallow, shift my feet. He does not glance at me, moving toward his horse. "Mount up." I turn away, grip my saddle and everything feels too big and small, aching in the dark.

Something calls, off in the forests, a opossum, or a fox, high and eerie in the early black.

•▶|◀▶|◀▶|◀▶|◀▶|◀▶|◀•

Rain spatters against my head, droplets fast and hard, and the goblin's shape is hazy in the lines of the falling rain. I swipe a hand across my brow, water trickling into my eyes, trickling down my spine onto my saddle and skirts.

Thunder cracks, lightning flashing through the trees, illuminating trees for a moment and it is gone.

My eyes burn, shift. *We should not stay out in this rain. The storm is drawing closer, rain falling quicker. You do not stay out in a storm that may bring wind.* I cannot see the goblin, only his horse in the pounding downpour. A droplet spatters into my eye, clinging to my lashes. I swipe at it, fling the droplets from my skin to the side. Thunder cracks again and there is no flash, no change in the pressing gray of the woods. I choke, water running into my mouth, and press a hand above my nose, turn my head away. Blått is faint on the ground beside me, his head down, ears alert. I click to him.

The horse jerks, the world jolting sideways, stumbling. I gasp. My hand fumbles with the saddle and it's slick, leather skidding beneath my fingers, throwing me toward the side. I press my knees together and it does not stop, my skirts sliding over the leather. I gasp, the horse still plodding forward, each jolt throwing me further down, toward the feet and rain.

I jerk forward, press my chest into its neck, and it snorts, throwing strands of hair toward my skin. Rain pours down my cheeks, trickling along my neck into the horse's soaked mane clinging to my skin. I tighten my hand on the saddle, my fingers clutched under it, clenched. I lift my head, just barely, brush hair from my eyes with my shoulder. There is no shape ahead of me, only the everlasting rainfall, a sheet of white, and it batters at my skin, bites into my scalp. I squint, strain, and there is a tree and nothing more ahead, only white droplets, and shadows. I grimace, drag my body upward and the horse grunts, sidestepping. I swipe the water from my eyes, squint into the darkness. There are only faint outlines of branches ahead, trees in the roaring of the rain. My eyes flicker down. There is no Blåthjortt beside me, his shape lost into the dripping gray. My head snaps up.

I cough, tense my grip on the saddle, water trickling through my lips, down my chin. "Sonyá?" My voice comes back to me, caught in the sound of a thousand falling raindrops and I can hear nothing over it, only a thousand tiny spatters. Thunder crackles and there is a flash, lightning, and nothing once more.

I shield my gaze and the rain pelts my hand, burning into my skin. My eyes shift, stomach sinking. "Sradfaang?!" My voice is high, ripping from my throat. There is no response but the crashing of rain against the branches and leaves, my voice muffled back to me. I click to the horse, nudge its sides. Its pace does not pick up, steps still sluggish, head bowed away from me, water running from it in a trickle to the leaves. I click again, press my heels in, and the horse snorts, head throwing strands of hair stinging against my hands. *Move horse.* I grimace. *I do not know this land, do not know this place if he is gone. What way was the trail, before the rain stole the world away?*

A heavy drop bites against my skin, more following, the rain pelts increasing. I lift my head.

I could leave now. Leave him here. There will be no tracking me, in the storm, no following where I go in the rain.

But I know nowhere within leagues of here. If I run, there will be nowhere to go, and there will be nothing more for me but the lost reaches of the far Glycalls.

I swipe my hand against my face and there is a tree ahead, the shape still faint but growing. *The world is a little clearer, barely, the rain lighter again.* I click to the horse, and there is another tree in the thick white-gray. Something is standing not far ahead, moving between their trunks, and it is gone again, fading out. The horse has not quickened its pace, its head still down, steps slow on the sloshing earth. *I can hear each step now, the world quieted.*

I click my tongue again and there is water between my lips, strands of hair running with it, catching on my tongue. I draw them away, and there is a branch, running along the top of my head, gone again into the storm. I swipe my hair back from my face, brush back the trickle of water. My skin is heavy, limbs heavy. I scan the trees, scan the haze between them. There is nothing but the trees there, nothing but branches around me. I pull the reins, turn the horse to the side. *If the goblin has gone, how can I follow? He cannot have brought me out here to leave me so late. That would have been a foolish ruse, when he may have left me many times before.*

"This way, healer." The voice is sharp, cutting beneath the thunder's clap. My head snaps around, heart pounding. The goblin is only a pace from me, sliding off his horse. He plants his feet on the earth, stepping backward, face obscured by the darkness beneath the boughs of the evergreens.

I clear my throat, water falling from my lashes. "Would it be wise, to wait out the downpour here?" I shout over the rain.

He glances over his shoulder at me, face barely visible through the shadows. "You will be better off on foot for this next stretch. We will continue."

My lips tighten. I slip my legs from the saddle, and they jolt against the earth. My skirt slaps my knees, clinging to them. I tighten my jaw, swipe the trickling water from my skin. I reach for the horse's reins. It jerks its head back, snorting, tossing it high above my reach. I step forward, reach for the bridle, and it snorts again, its feet dancing, skidding on the spongy, soaked earth. *Curse it.* The goblin is watching, his face all in shadows beneath his hood. I snap at the reins, my fingers grazing them, catch on the edge, and I pull down, jerk. The horse yanks its head again, pulling against my arms. I grimace, step forward and the goblin's hand snakes out. I flinch. His hand is on the reins beside me, stilled. "I will take these. She will only slow your pace."

I draw my hand back and he is pulling her away, starting up the slope beneath the heavy evergreen. My hands feel empty, brittle, water slipping from my fingertips. I turn, step down the slope. Blått is running across the ground, moving through the underbrush, his head still down, fur tangled, catching in every loose branch.

The trees are thick, like shadows along the hillside. Something brushes my shoulder and there is a spattering of heavy droplets joining the rest, fast and hard. I swipe a hand across my face, brush back the branch and the stick pulls strands of my hair free. The air reeks of dampness, moved earth beneath the new rain. The ground snakes beneath my feet and I gasp, arms flail too late. I jerk my arms in, wait for impact, but something grips my shoulders, tight. *I am no longer falling.* I blink, lift my head and my eyes burn, swirling. The goblin's face looks down at me, his hands arms extending to my shoulders. Raindrops splatter in my eyes from his shoulders. I pull my feet back under me.

"Watch your feet." His voice is plain, dry. I turn toward the slopes, grip my soaked skirts in my hands, half bow—appreciation. He quirks a brow. His eyes dart toward the shadows of the forest. "Move along. This slope is no good place to stop."

I turn back toward the trail. There are streaks in the ground, where my heels slid and stopped, the earth showing orange beneath the leaves. I step around them, plant my feet against the stones at the edges of their tread. The way down is slick with leaves trees small and clustered along the slope. My hands grip branches, feet half skidding again on the trails of mud. *There will be no need for the goblin to catch me again if I fall fast enough. In this rain, I may.* My toes grip the roots, mud squishing up between them, soft and thick, and I plant my foot on the ground, leaves crunching beneath it once more. The earth is leveled ahead, curling upward on the other side of the narrowed holler. I grip my skirts. Water trickles through my hands.

A horse snorts behind me, rocks clattering beneath hooves, and there is another snort, soft and high. I grab at a branch, pull myself up the path ahead. Rocks slip beneath my feet, skittering down the slope, and I clench my jaw, jerk myself upward. I grip the next branch, breaths heavy in my chest, pull upward. *How long, can the goblin go, in the rain? The air is not the warm it should be, in Stråle, spatter of droplets cold. Will sickness set into his bones, if he stays wet for many more watches?* I glance back, over my shoulder. The goblin is easily moving up the slope, his eyes on the horses behind him, speaking softly, low. *He does not even seem to be wet, in the shadows. Maybe a trick of the half-light. No one could be out here and not soaked through by now. But how long, can a goblin last?*

My foot skids. I gasp, grip a branch and my hand burns—it twists. "Healer? Do you require aid?" his voice is dry, unimpressed.

I purse my lips, wrap my toes into a root. "Gót. I am well." My voice is tight. I wrap my toes further into the roots, heave myself upward. My fingers fumble with a higher branch, grip it, slipping on the water-skimmed bark. Rain drops spatter against my head, heavy, large, cascading from the boughs of the evergreen beside me. *The goblin must have nudged it.*

Something shifts in the trees ahead, the barest movement. My head snaps up. Water trickles down my face. I drag in a breath, search the shadows. The forest is still but for the dripping of rain against leaves, against my skin.

"Sradfaang." The voice is loud, not five paces in front of me. I shift my grip on the branch, eyes wide. I cannot see anyone there, but the voice is a woman's, low and full. "We were not expecting you yet."

She knows him. We have arrived. It is nearly time for me to leave, then.

The goblin snorts and a horse echoes it, sound muffled in the dripping woods. "You rarely are expecting me. Ciaran should have been; I am not early for what he was informed of. Though I have a kúráh and she was not planned for, as you see."

Something moves on the slope above us and a figure steps out from behind a tree, her face obscured by branches, but there is something strange to it, dancing beneath the rain. She shifts her stance. "That is a woman? You might have stopped sooner, before she looked akin to a half-drowned mink. I've seen dead muskrat look less sorry."

A rock thuds dully below me, the sound soft. "And then we would still be sitting in it. Show her the trail. I do not care to be in this rain any longer than need be."

The woman nods her head backward. "This way." I dig my feet into the mud, drag myself up the slope again. She is standing still, only a few breaths from me, her arms folded, collecting a pool of water that glints in the faint light of the clouds. There are lines on her face, pale, like tears pouring from her eyes, their markings stark against her dark skin in the shadows of her hood. *A praor woman.* I swallow, wrap my hand around a tree. *People of mark and color. I have rarely seen any of them, since we moved from Blackwater turnings ago. I have never seen marks akin to hers.*

She nods and I can feel her eyes darting over my skin. *She will not be able to make out much in the storm-coated light.* She turns away, sharply. "This way, kúráh, unless you would like to stay in this rain." She steps across the ground, leveled out at the top of the hill. My legs are aching, the world unsteady. She is moving beneath the branches, the last gray of day faint beneath the low clouds, rain still pouring in steady streams. I pick up my skirts, the fabric pulling my fingers, lift my eyes. There is nothing ahead, no sign of the woman.

I turn, search the trees. *She will be just beneath the evergreens ahead, lost to shadows. She cannot have gone far.* I step forward and the pine needles are cool against the soles of my feet. I shiver, step quicker over them. There is movement ahead, the woman. Her figure is a haze in the darkness beneath the trees, barely there. I squint, move after her, and there is a rustle behind me, horse hooves clattering on stones and gone again.

Something is looming ahead, dark on the mountainside, not the cluster of trees, its presence heavy. The air is thick, everything hinting at shades of blue and black now with the failing of day. The woman is vanishing in and out between trees, her cloak swirling between steps. I move beneath the trees, branches brushing at my scalp, pulling at the strands of hair. A stick snaps, ahead, the sound slight in the soaked forest. I move that way, the woman's shape lost to the trees and darkness again. Rocks press beneath my feet, thicker now, clustered together. *A path.*

There is darkness ahead, no sound coming out of it, no movement in the air before me. *Something huge. Motionless. What is this?* I suck in a breath, my eyes burning. I step backward, and my back presses against a branch—I stare up, the thing all in shadow on the side of the mountain.

"This way." The voice is ahead, and it sounds strange, as if catching on something solid. *A building, or the mountain itself? A cliff face?* I step forward and my skin creeps. The forest is silent, nothing beyond the continual dripping of branches and leaves. I glance down, backward. *There is no sign of Blått.* I duck under a low branch and there is a figure next to me. She reaches out her hand, and a knock rings out, the sound echoing, solid. *Wooden.* Something shifts and there is a bright square of light, opening before us. I step backward, my eyes burning. There is a hand on my arm, voices that I do not know speaking around me. I step backward, and the hand pulls, guiding me forward. The light is bright, too bright. "Where did she come from?" The voice is a man's, not far from me. I do not pull away, stiffen my shoulders. *Discover what they want, why they are here. Do not resist, not yet. Give them time. It would be unwise, not to shield your gift and your life.*

A voice speaks, another man's, solid like the walls of a fortress. "…They will have it. Who is this?" I blink into the light, keep my gaze tilted down, away from it. It is sharp. A man is looking at me, his eyes creased at the edges, kind. He is bearded and it is dark, grayed at its edges, his face only half lit by the light of the door behind him. "You look to have been a long ways in coming to our home, I think. Come in, civ." I draw back the changing of my eyes but he is not looking, stepping away into the room. Light flashes against my face, brighter again for a moment. *A lantern.* I shield my eyes with my hand, turn away and there are figures moving around me, voices again on all sides. I glance behind me. *Where have the horses gone? The goblin? Blått?*

Voices catch on the walls of the building, more of them, muffled, and the air is warm ahead, biting into my skin. I step forward, after the man, his hand still on my arm. My skin crawls, damp and wrong in the warmth and brightness of building.

Figures are moving everywhere, seven or eight of them. "Fetch Ciaran. Sradfaang has brought in another one." The voice of the first man.

I force my eyes down, heart thudding in my chest. *Brought in another one? Brought in what? A lost woman?* Figures are moving about the room, the woman from outside speaking, drawing soaked gloves from her hands. Her eyes are on the man with the grayed beard, face eager. "… She might have been. I did not ask him where she is from or how he came upon her…" *Where she is from.* Figures are moving about the room. My eyes dart back toward the door. "He said he was bringing her in for Eerol." *I did not hear him speak to her, about me, about anyone here. When could they have spoken?* My skin crawls. I glance back toward the door. It is still open, branches of the soaked evergreens glittering through its breadth. *There will be no time to run later, if they are not who he said they are.* I glance around the room. *No one is watching. To run will be without Blått, but I cannot guard my gift in a fort of this size, not alone.* I step toward the door.

"I would not do that." The voice is low, a new man's.

I glance at him, force my eyes to stay calm, gray like the skies outside. He steps away, not close enough to reach me if I run. *He cannot grab me.*

I bolt through the door. Branches slap at my skin, pull at my hair, and there is only darkness and the falling of rain, slapping my soaked skin, my skirts pulling heavily at my legs. Someone calls behind me, and there is the bark of a hound. *Not Blått.* I grimace. My feet skid and there is something pulling across my waist, yanking off the earth. I grab at it, gasp, and my hands hit skin and fabric. *An arm.* I grip it, pull at it, and it does not release, does not loosen, pulling the air from my lungs. My feet scramble, back, hitting something solid. *Stars no.*

"Be calm." *The goblin's voice.*

A shudder runs up my spine. I jerk at the arm, push his skin, and my eyes burn, twist. *He found me in a moment. I barely made it twenty paces from the door of the fort before he caught me. Curse it. I failed.* I heave my foot back, and he does not even grunt, my heel throbbing with the impact of his leg. I slacken my grip, his arm pressing harder against my stomach, the air leaving my lungs again. I choke in a breath. "Let me go, please."

He moves, a puff of breath against my hair like the bandit who grabbed me in the forest. He speaks. "Come back inside and let them explain. No one here means you harm. They were ready to welcome you, to see that you are safe."

My skin crawls. I jerk away again and he sets my feet on the ground. I stumble away. He is watching me, at attention, his hand not near his sword hilt, but ready to grab me again if I run. I clench my jaw, my eyes burning still. "Let me go, goblin. I am not going to hide here to be used, to become a tool or a weapon in the hands of a fortress or resistance. The country is not silent about what becomes of resistance. We have seen it in every village and city these last many turnings. I will not stay to become a danger or a tool."

He puffs out a breath, the sound like a sigh, longsuffering. "And what will you do, if we let you go? If you take to the forests alone, you will be dead inside two days. If by some miracle, you make it back to your cottage in the hills, what do you think is awaiting you there? A welcome? The captain spoke truly, if you even could find your way back there is nothing waiting for you there. You have found one of the only safe havens for your kind in this whole country and you are running from it before you even catch your breath to see what kind of place it is. I have known cats with more wisdom than you."

I straighten. "There are no safe havens for my kind. They are being rooted out, one by one, and have been for many turnings since the prince died. You know well, and if you do not, you should know well the trouble and damage that has been done across the kingdom." Rain spatters against my head. "I do not know these people, nor what they stand for. I will not risk my life to find out. Safe havens will be as day old molasses to flies, a target for the Queen's men. Give it only a few moons and her men will be at this doorstep. I will not add to that danger."

He hisses through his teeth. "You know nothing of this place, nor how long it has stood. Get inside. Listen to them. Ask a question or two. I am not letting you run away to become worm food because tonight because you would not stay to see. You may cause trouble as you please once you are not my charge but tonight, we are resting. You are in no state to be making these judgments."

The rain mists across my skin, light and cold. "When should I make this judgment? You have seen the destruction that comes to those who harbor my kind in their home. If this is a safe haven, I will only endanger it by coming here. This choice should be made now, before anything is risked or said or done. I do not know or trust these people."

There is a gleam above me, a flash of white teeth, and it is gone. "You do not trust the captain or I, and yet you were willing to travel this far to come to this place, for reasons I will not pretend to know. Einion told you this place was a safe haven. If you did not believe him enough to try, you should have tried to escape sooner, before you were leagues from everything you know. It is foolery to run from here, when you know nothing of the area or people. Foolery that I do not intend to stand idly and watch. Get inside."

I wrap my arms around my waist, and my skirts cling to my skin, to my legs. "You would have found me inside half a watch if I had run while on the road. I know little of the Knoc'gnori, but I know your skill. How many of my kind are here, in this safe haven?"

His eyes glint in the shadows of the trees. He shifts, his hand moving to rest beside his sword hilt. *Habit.* "I cannot force you to trust me. But I can promise that I will protect you for as long as I am here and will see to it that you are safe. That is my task. This is a haven for far more than just you, and it is secure, as secure as any fort I have seen in this country. You will gain nothing by running, and lose little by staying. There is little chance you will ever find an opportunity for safety like this again as long as the war on your blood-kind wages on. Make a choice, healer. I will not stay in this rain and wait forever."

His eyes settle on me in the darkness, waiting. *As though I have a choice, as though he has not already told me that the choice tonight is not mine.* I look down, keep the border of my vision on him. *If I stay, where will they take me, in this fort? There will not likely be an escape, once I am inside. Not from a fort of that scale, not if it is secure, as he has said. I will be taking my life, giving it up. My task will be finished at last, failed. But there is no other choice. I cannot run from him.*

Creator. Help me.

I swallow hard, incline my head. "I will stay tonight, to hear what they say."

He inclines his head. "So be it." He gestures with his hand, up the slope, back toward the darkness and the muffled hillside, where the fort dwells. I step up it, rocks and leaves pricking at my skin.

He moves past me, his hand reaching out, pulling the door open, and there are stones under my feet, voices muffled by warmth and wood. He gestures for me to step in, a bracelet gleaming on his arm in the light of the door. *I did not see that on him before.* I step past him, into the fortress, and the door shuts.

"Ciaran." The goblin's voice is quiet. There is a fire, glowing in a massive stone built fireplace, and a table before it, spread with papers. Men are around it, speaking in low tones, their voices not carrying through in the space around them. The goblin is speaking to one of them, bowing lower than I have seen him bow, a posture of respect and difference, his head tilting down to his chest at the end. He nods toward me. "This is Eness Finch, a healer, sent by Einion. I will tell you more of her coming once Fitzclaste has returned." I step toward him, stone grating against my damp feet, skirts hugging my legs, the last of the rain trickling down my scalp.

The man speaking with the goblin is tall, well over two handbreadths taller than I, his head held like a noble man's, face strong, eyes on me, gentle. His hair is crowned by a ring of firelight, catching in the golden strands like a king of old. He nods at me, head inclining, and a scar glints on his cheek. It is faint, paled with seasons, though he is not yet old. His eyes look old, though he is not, cannot be, but a few turnings further in life than me. He reaches out his hand toward me. It is gloved, black. I bite back the burning of my eyes. Every part of him is clean, perfectly kept. I am soaked, muddied from the road. He lifts my hand, gripping my wrist—respect and welcome. "Eness Finch. You are welcome in here." I lift my eyes, meet his, barely grip his gloved wrist back. He is watching, his eyes warm and kind. "I am Ciaran." His hand releases mine, carefully. He turns toward a man behind him. "Ask Iris to find her some dried clothes. She will want to change." The figure nods, moving away.

Another man steps down the stairs, moving toward me. He grips my wrist in the same way, but his hand is ungloved. His eyes are gentle, features dark, the man who tried to welcome me in before. His beard faintly graying, eyes crinkled at the corners. "Eness Finch. I am Fitzclaste Jornamn. Welcome to our home." He smiles, releasing my hand. He steps back. "I pray your stay here will be one of rest. My wife will help you find a bed. She will also help you find dry clothes before you are settled, as I am sure will be welcomed, after the days you are like to have had on the road. I gather they were long from the little I have heard." The gray at the edges of his hair matching the graying of his beard.

I nod, swallow hard, and my eyes are burning faintly. I shove it back, glance away. "Thank you." My voice is low. "I am sorry to be of trouble, in coming this late in eventide. You are gracious to welcome us into your home, and your evening."

He shakes his head, eyes still warm, bright. "Sikkerhet is built to be a safe haven to those in need. We begrudge no one, their arrival, and gladly we welcome you, Eness Finch. Healers are doubly welcome, for the skill they bring with them. Let me bring you to find dry clothes." The other men do not look up, do not even glance at me as Fitzclaste turns. *Is it so common a thing, that they bring others in* here? Do they not worry or wonder about those brought through the door? If this place is safe, should they not wonder, who might bring trouble?

Fitzclaste moves toward the stairs he came down only moments ago. I glance at the goblin. He is speaking with the golden man and another, his eyes lit by the fire, green-gold and unearthly. I turn back, step onto the stairs. He has already started up, his eyes half on me. *Deeper into the fortress.* My heart tightens. My feet are cold on the stones, mud still clinging to my toes. My eyes flicker upward. The torches are large, more than fifteen of them lining the way up the stairs, carefully high, sputtering smoke into the shadows blinking on the walls where the rocks are stained dark with soot. The stairs are cut into the stone of the earth, clean and carefully carved, intricately made.

I slow at the top of the stairs, step after Fitzclaste. The hall is neatly made, rugs lining the floors, ornate and beautiful, low seats along the wall in a style that I do not recognize. *I have never seen a home this ornate. What kind of safe haven is this, that they have made it so luxuriously?* He speaks, glancing over his shoulder. "How far did you travel today?"

He is striding ahead, his gait comfortable like the hall we are in, boots clean. My skirts are heavy with water and dirt, water dripping to my feet from them. I clutch the fabric, lift them above the gentle rugs and floor, above my mud-stained feet. "I do not know the distance. It has not been my custom before to travel on horseback, as I have done these last many days."

He pulls open a door, the wood of it heavy, decorated with a simple design. "Did you travel with a mark, or Sradfaang alone? I would be surprised if it was not far." He pauses, voices echoing up the halls. I glance at him. *He is waiting for me to move through the door first.* I step through, pulling my skirts away from the frame. The carpet is strange under my toes, dirt grating between them. He steps forward. "This way." He is nodding, toward a hall beside me. I step into it.

There are fewer torches here, only one further down, flickering against the dark wood on the walls. Fitzclaste pauses by a door where the hallway ends, pulling it open. There is a glow from inside, voices murmuring together. I step backward, away from their sight. *Women's voices, all of them.* "Teja." Fitzclaste is standing just inside the doorway, his eyes on someone beyond it. "Will you come with me for a moment, love?" There is a murmuring again, and step falls in the room.

A woman ducks through the doorway past him, her dark eyes large, hair gray across her temples. She is tall, of a height with him, her face kindly like the man beside her, lines at the corners of her eyes, curls clinging to her cheek. Her lips purse, and she sets her hand on his arm gently. "Fitz. You might not have drug her so far from the rooms. I could have come to her." She steps forward, her hand reaching for mine.

I draw back, shake my head. "Please, do not trouble yourself. I am soaked with the storm and elements. I will soil your hands."

She inclines her head, eyes flickering to her husband, as if looking for something. He half nods his head, moving for the door. "Sradfaang is here, below. I have brought her to you to get her settled. She will be staying for a while, and I think we have a room she'll be well in?" He inclines his head toward me—courtesy. "Tejan, this is Eness Finch. Eness, this is my wife, Tejan, the lady of this house. She will help get you settled."

Tejan inclines her head at me, waving a hand toward the door. "Of course. It is an honor to meet you, Eness Finch. We have a bed for you, and dresses enough to spare to get you settled for the night watches." She lifts her eyes to mine. "Would you care for some food, before you settle, lai? You look a little tired out." She smiles softly. *Lai. A foreign word. Woman?*

I glance back at her, wrap my arms about my waist once more. Her eyes are on mine, patient, dark in the shadows, like the woodlands. "I am well. Please do not trouble yourself. We had food on the road."

She shakes her head. "It would be no trouble. Do not worry for that. If you are hungry, Fitz or I will fetch you something. It is no trouble." She slows her steps. Fitzclaste is pushing a door open, the place beyond it dark. Tejan smiles. "This will do for you. There are two other kúráhs in there, whom you will meet in the morning. Are you certain you need nothing from the kitchens? They are not far from here, and storms make the soul hungry, I think."

I shake my head. "Do not worry for me. But thank you, kúráh." She nods, and glances at her husband.

"Thank you, love. I'll see her in. Did you send someone to tell Iris where we would be taking her?"

He nods. "She may have already been here. You'll see inside. I'll be below. We have a meeting to finish." His hand reaches for hers, catching it for just a moment, and he steps away. "Goodrest to you, Eness Finch. I trust our home will be a comfort and safety to you in the time to come. If you have need of anything, you need only ask. What we have, we give to you."

I incline my head, a little lower, to the left. "And to you. Thank you, for your kindness, Fitzclaste Jornamn." I step through the doorway after Tejan. The room is dark, only a single light in it, a candle in Tejan's hands, on a strange metal holder. *Metal holders. If they are part of an uprising, here in the woods, they will not be part of the dark cults. They abhor the use of metal, do they not? They have used metal in their door knobs too.*

She glances at me, setting the lantern holder on the shelf. The light flickers for just a moment, and steadies itself, a small flame in the darkness. "There is a night dress there that should fit you, lai. Iris has already come. I will bring you a day dress in the morning, or send it with one of the others, depending on what calls on me." She is moving across the small room, her hands lifting something, setting it to the side. Her hips wide, like a woman who has borne children, figure comfortable and hair streaked with far more gray than I thought before, still black beneath the strands. Grayer than her husband's. She glances back at me, slowing beside a bed. There are three of them in the room, two stacked on top of each other, strange, leaving space for two to sleep easily where there should be one. The other is a cot, low to the floor like mine back home. But this one is rich, with wood and blankets, set within a room that matches it, tone for tone.

I wrap my arms around my waist. Cold clings to my skin. She turns. "The girls are still in the great hall, but I will warn them to be silent when they come in." She half laughs, stepping forward, and the sound is like warmth, like comfort and blankets. "I am sorry to have to settle you at night, when things are long and strange, but you will do well, I have no doubt. If you have need of anything, please let us know." She half inclines her head, respect. "For the Jornamn family, I welcome you to our home in the mountains. If you have need of anything, please find me or ask someone. We will find what we can." She inclines her head again, half to the side. *A welcome. They have uttered many welcomes, since we arrived.*

I swallow, incline my head to the left, then right—respect and honor. "Thank you, Tejan. I am sorry for your trouble and am grateful tonight for your hospitality to a stranger in your home."

She half smiles, stepping toward the door. "We are a safe haven, Eness Finch. It is a joy to have a way to serve in times as dark as these, and we are glad to welcome you, a stranger to our home. I trust you will soon no longer be a stranger." I flinch, eyes burning sharply. Her eyes quiet and she straightens. "Fitz has not seen sign of your blood yet, has he?"

I look away. *Curse it.* "I cannot say. But I will leave at your request. I am aware of the danger that comes with harboring one of my blood. I will leave now, if you ask it."

Her eyes are scanning mine, soft. She shakes her head. "We are a safe haven, Eness. It does not change, for your blood or for any other unloved by our country or queen. We have no others of your heritage here, but I welcome you just the same, and pray that you will find peace here, and not strife. There have been others of your line here before, and they have all been welcome, before they went on their way again. I pray it will be the same with you, and that you will find quiet within these walls." She steps away, moving for the door. She pauses by it, glancing over her shoulder. "Everyone here will see to it that you are welcomed. Do not fear. In the morning, I will come see to it that you make it to the hall. The girls rise early, and you should rest as late as you can. The road was long, I believe. There is no need to rise before you are ready, now." She nods toward the far side of the room. "There is a pitcher and basin there, for you to wash. If you have need of anything, come find me. I will be in the room Fitzclaste found me in."

I shake, eyes half burning once more. *They know of my blood, and still welcome me?* "Gót. Thank you, Tejan. I am well." I incline my head again. She smiles, a gracious thing, half lit by the candle on the shelf.

"Then I will leave you to your rest. Goodeven to you, Eness Finch. We are glad to have you with us." She steps through the door, pulling it closed behind her.

I breathe out slowly, steady my hand against the wall. The world is dark, light dancing from the candle onto the items on the shelf - a set of unlit candles, a jar, a flower, dried and bent, and a stone, engraved with small lines of script. The room is too large, nearly the size of my whole cottage, three beds within it, blankets and dresses everywhere, at least five of them. There is a chest on the far side of the room, a pale garment over it. *The night dress she gestured to.* My hand shakes. *I should wash, before I touch it.*

I glance around the room, and my hand shakes. *I should not be here, not in this place. It is a haven, wealthy, comforting and I am covered with dirt, with days and mud. I should not be in this place.*

They welcomed me, knowing what I am. Knowing the risk. Would they plan to sell me, these people of the mountain fort?

I step forward, dunk my hands into the water of the basin. It is warm, pleasant on my skin. *How did they know, where I would be taken? When did Fitzclaste have time to go for someone?* My head aches, the water swirling in gold and black around my hands. *When he went upstairs. He knew the goblin would bring me back.* I swipe the water up my arms, the coolness of the rain water slipping off, slipping away. *Warmed water, carefully made rugs and blankets and furniture made with detail and care. What is this safe haven, that it is lavish, that it is ornamented so delicately, with detail put into every part of the places I have been? What are these people, that they would have a fort, so lavish in the woodlands?*

XIV

Sikkerhet

The door groans, faint in the darkness, a light dancing across the dark of the room. There is a figure, moving through the light, and another. I keep my head down in the blankets around me, force my eyes open. *The women, or someone else?*

The figures move toward the shelf, placing a lit candle upon it, their movements slow, sluggish. One of them glances at me, her eyes barely illuminated by the candle. She scans over me and looks away quickly, loosing the laces on the side of her dress. *A woman. They must be the two the woman spoke of, Teja.*

I do not move, force my eyes to stay half-hooded, dark in the night, furs pulled up to my head. The light goes out, movement fading out with the creaking of the cot frames across the room.

Blått. I do not know where they put him, when we arrived.

•▶|◀▶|◀▶|◀▶|◀▶|◀▶|◀•

Something is shifting in the darkness, cloth against cloth or skin. I roll my shoulders and my body aches, sore, warm. There is the barest of a whisper, light and soft, across the room, a voice I do not know. *A woman's voice.* My eyes are blurry, something on the edges of my vision. I drag my body up, pull the blanket with me. The air of the room is warm, motionless, and I can see nothing in the darkness, not even movement to match sound.

There is silence for a moment.

Something shifts across the room, and there is a creak and a small square of light—the door, open. Someone moves through, blocking the light for a moment, and it is gone, the door pulling shut softly behind them, the square of light gone. The room is silent. I swallow, wrap my arms around my stomach. *What time do they rise?*

I press my back against the wall, blankets shifting around my legs, soft and light. I tighten my arms. The darkness is gentle, thick with the closed-off room, no movement of air like home, creeping through the heavy shutters or the open door. I glance down, across the room. *Could I find my way out, if I left this room?*

I press the blankets down, off the thin gown over my shoulders. *I do not know this place. If I left to wander its halls, I could not make it back to the room before. The goblin was right. It would be foolish to run out into the night, into the forests without an idea of where I am going, of where my path will take me or where one is.*

My lips tighten, hands tighten around my arms in the dark. The room is still, lifeless. *There are no windows in this space, nothing to let in light or air. How do they know when to rise and when dawn comes?*

•▶|◀▶|◀▶|◀▶|◀▶|◀▶|◀•

Something is knocking, somewhere in the haze.

I bolt upright, press my hands against my eyes. There are faint sounds coming from somewhere. *Landlots.* I swallow, glance across the room. It is still dark, only the barest trickle of light on the floor beyond the foot of the bed. My head is heavy, eyes foggy. *Was the knock for me, or another?*

There is a knock again, faint. *On my door.* "Eness Finch?" The voice is familiar, a woman's voice.

I throw my legs over the side of the bed, push the blankets from them. "Aye?" The doorknob creaks, and there is a flood of light, blinding. I jerk up my hand, shield my eyes, and there is a footfall on the far side of the room. I stand, move backward, put my back to the wall.

"A pardon for the light." *Tejan.* "I did not know this room stayed so dark after daybreak, though it is near the heart of the building - I should have known it would."

I incline my head, lower my hand from my eyes, slowly. The light is sharp still, casting lines across everything in the room. "Do not apologize." I clear my throat. She is holding a candle, pushing the door closed behind her. I swallow. There is something over her arm, cloth.

She sets the candle upon the shelf next to the one from last night, another strange holder around this one. The candle stem is deep yellow, not mud-colored like the ones from the village or my home. I brush my hair forward over my arms, cover my shift. "Thank you for coming this morning. I am grateful for your time on my behalf."

Her eyes flicker toward me, and it is hard to see them, with the light of the door gone and the candle behind her. She half-smiles, the lines of her face softening, like an eldermamé. "My task this morning is to see to it that our newest arrival is settled in without too much worry or trouble for her. So I am glad enough to come. My husband and I enjoy the opportunity to welcome all those who come to our home."

She offers the cloth to me. It is a small square, woven, coarse. She nods at it. "So that you may wash your face, again, from the dirt of yesterday. You will likely want to feel clean, after all those leagues." She smiles, gesturing toward the hook on the wall where my dress once was, something not mine now hanging there. "That dress is for you. Iris has your old one, and she will clean it for you and return it later."

My eyes widen. I shake my head, press back the changing of my eyes. "She does not need to trouble herself. I can tend to it."

She shakes her head, eyes meeting mine. "Iris is part of the group of women who do all the laundry. If everyone did their own, nothing would ever be done here. You are free to do yours, if you choose, but I think your skills will be greatly appreciated elsewhere, from the little Srad has told me."

I fold my hands. "Which skills?"

She smiles, inclining her head. "Your skills with herbs. We have a healer here, but he does not love the herbal work, and I know he would appreciate the assistance, should you choose to give it. There is often more work than I think he can tend to in a day, though he does not say as much. He has not had an apprentice in many moons now." She shakes her head. "You will be free of course to choose what task you would like to take, but I would imagine you would be most comfortable where the work is your own occupation."

She steps backwards, her hands folding in front of her, mimicking my own. "I should let you get ready for the day. One of the girls will meet you in the hallway in a few moments, to show you to the hall, for breakfast. If you need anything, please let my husband or myself know, and we will see what may be done." She smiles.

I nod at her, low, respect. "Gooddawn to you, Tejan Jornamn."

She turns, moving back through the door. I glance at the dress on the wall, the light from beyond the door on it for just a moment, and it is gone again. I step toward the dress, my arms over my chest. The fabric is simple, a gray-green color like oleaster leaves or perhaps blue, dyed with some skill, even across the whole of the fabric even by candlelight. I lift the garment, the feel of it fine beneath my fingers, intricately made. It would have been made on a loom finer than my whole home. I fumble, pull it over my head, and it slips into place, smooth on my shift. There is a small amount of embroidery across the chest, a sash to tie it into place. I twist the fabric, tuck it into itself, out of the way, and it no longer hangs. The fabric swishes around my feet, easy, the pleats hanging neatly.

I step toward the door, twist my hair back into place, and there are voices outside, loud, laughing. I pause. *Women's laughs. The women Tejan has sent to find me, or others. I do not know how many lots live in this place.* I draw in a breath, pull the handle open and there are two women, talking in the hallway just across from me, the space lit by the light of day pouring down it from far away. The first woman has pale markings on her face, lines, white against her bronzed skin, like moonlight on water, or tears. *The woman from the woods.*

She glances up at me, a smile across her face, almost sharp. She scans over me, no welcome in her gaze. The woman she was speaking with looks up at me. She is short, shorter than me by half a hand's breadth at least, her hair dark, eyes dark, smile light. "Eness Finch?" I incline my head and she bows, the smile brightening like a ray of sunlight. "I am Anna. It is well that you are with us. Would you like to find some morning hash with us?"

I frown, my eyes half-burning, and I bite it back. She does not blink, does not look away. *My eyes will not have shifted, or she would have shown some sign of it.* I incline my head, acknowledgement. "I do not know what hash is, so I cannot say if I will join you. But if you know my name, I will imagine that Tejan sent you to find me and I will gladly come." The woman with the tear-like markings is watching, her eyes flickering between the two of us, hair bound back in many braids sharply twisted into a bun at the base of her neck, the style like a man's.

Anna laughs, amusement dancing in the faint creases around her eyes. "Hash is something Nellie comes up with, a blending of whatever she has on hand when morning comes. I think it is simple to make for so many people, but I do not mind. It almost always has potatoes in it, and that is a treat I will not turn up my chin to. Potatoes are better than kings' feasts in my mind. This morning's is quite good I hear. Arda says it has spice in it." She starts down the hallway, gathering her skirts into her hands as she moves.

The other woman steps after her, her eyes not even flickering toward me. "Was your journey long?"

My eyes dart toward her, past Anna, whose head is only at my nose. "Only part of it. But you will know that from the goblin."

She glances at me, eyes strange above the markings, and half-smiles—it is sharp once more. "You are a village healer, I heard last night. Where are you from, Eness Finch?"

Anna turns the corner and there is one of the doors I was brought through last night. She pushes it open, nodding for us to step through. I move through after the praoran woman, glance back at her. "I am from nowhere, and aye, of a kind. I mostly work in salves and rarely in wounds. I am more herbalist than healer." I lift my skirts, stepping off the carpet as it ends, on to the smooth wood of the floors. "Is this your home?

She grins at me, flashing that still-sharp smile, and this one is wry, wrought with a hundred meanings. "It is when I choose for it to be. I am not often here."

Anna glances over her shoulder, grinning. "Aorla is a messenger, mostly. Despite her unusual markings, people rarely look twice when she goes places, where they are suspicious with men. She looks common enough when she does her hair poorly."

The praor—Aorla—gives her a dry look and glances away. "You have not told us where you are from, Eness Finch. What brought you here? No one is from nowhere, especially not here. And everyone has a reason to come, to flee here."

I look up at her—she is taller than I am, her eyes looking down at me. I turn away. "I am from a small village, not one you will have heard of, and I had not lived there long." *I will not risk the villagers by telling strangers where I have dwelt. Soldiers have killed for less than living near a traitor.*

I glance up the hallway. Anna is gripping the knob of another door, a larger one, uncarved and dark. "I was brought by the goblin, Sradfaang, for reasons that are my own, but you will have known that. You met us in the dark of the forest last night. I recognize both your face and voice this morn."

She glances at me, her eyes calculating like a falcon in the sky. She raises a brow. "I know many small villages, and your sight is better than I gave it credit for last eve. You seemed too exhausted, and perhaps worn, to have known me today."

I nod, turn my head away. I half-smile. "I do not often forget a face, and yours is memorable. There are few praors where I come from."

Aorla lifts a brow. "Then you will not have come from anywhere near Blackwater or Forester."

Anna heaves the door open, and there are voices, murmuring together in a cascade. Anna gestures for me to step through before her. I incline my head, step forward. I am standing at the side of a great room, ceilings high, shafts of logs carefully exposed running along it. The floor is taken up by tables, end to end along it, three rows of them, a few more pressed against a wall, large pots on the first one.

A woman is lifting one of the pots, setting it against her hip as though it weighed nothing. She is speaking with another woman who is carrying a stack of bowls, moving slowly, her eyes tracking the words the other is saying. There are only a few lots in the room, together on the far side, beyond the women, not the cascade of voices I had thought. *How many could a room like this hold, if they chose to fill it, for a feast day or a call to arms?*

How many do they have in here, day to day?

Anna nods toward the tables on the far side of the room, where the pots and dishes are. "There is breakfast, if you are hungry."

Aorla is no longer standing beside us. I glance up. She is stepping away, towards the tables across the room, toward a cluster of men, speaking and laughing. Anna looks up at me, her eyes waiting. *Waiting on me.*

My face warms. I step forward, incline my head back to her. "Thank you for your guidance, Anna." I slow. My eyes flick back to her. "Do you know where a hound would be placed?"

She blinks, shoving her hands into the pockets of her apron. "Hounds?" She tilts her head to the side. "Aye. On the far side of the fort, the roadway door, out to the hunting forests I think. They are kept in the stables. That is where the ones for hunting are kept."

She glances over her shoulder, toward the men and the praor. "I'll wait for you to finish your breakfast. Tejan asked me to see you to the meeting rooms when you are done, to speak with Fitz and to make sure you do not get lost. There are many halls, and I need to speak with Baldwin about something anyway, so I will wait here." She is already moving across the room.

I move toward the pots, the room too large around me. There is a ladle, tucked against the side of a great dark pot, something like potatoes caked to it in chunks. *Bits and pieces, like Anna said. Hash.* I grip the ladle, glance into the pot. The mixture is of potatoes, herbs and something else, slightly orange in it. *Do they still have carrots, this far into the growing moons? Their storage for root crops during the dark seasons must be impressive to hold enough to have them this late.* I lift the ladle, dump the hash into the bowl waiting beside the pot. It clings to the ladle, thick and caked there, cooled. I brush it out with the side of the bowl, drop the ladle back into the pot.

There is a stack of spoons, further down it. I step forward, grab one, and there is a shadow beside me, huge and looming, a person.

My head snaps up, heart leaping into my throat.

The goblin stares back at me, his brow raised, a wicked smile on his lips. I look away, down toward the bowl, keep him at the corner of my vision. My eyes are burning, shifting. I lift the bowl. He steps to the side, speaking. "Is it your custom to be that unaware of those around you in places you do not know, healer? I thought you were wiser than to pay so little heed to your surroundings."

I wrap my fingers tighter around the bowl, shake my head. I step toward the table nearest us, keep him in my sight. *My eyes have stopped burning, will be gray once more.* I lift them to his face. "I did not hear your steps in the room. That, I believe, is more of an honor to your skill, sónya, than a discredit to my watching everywhere. You have much skill in keeping quiet, as I have seen this last near fortnight in the woods."

He lifts a brow, his face dry, arms crossed over his chest. "I walked straight towards you across the room and made little effort to be quiet. You ought to have seen me before I arrived, ought to have heard me. You were paying no attention to what is around you. To whom is around you. Strange for a woman who has spent so much time avoiding others and aiming to be alone."

I purse my lips, drop onto the bench beside me, and set the bowl down. The goblin does not move away, nor does he move to sit, his form towering over the table. I look up, quiet my expression. "Are you in need of something?"

His eyes flicker to mine, back across the room, scanning it evenly, as though by habit. "I have orders to take you down to the healing rooms when you are done with your meal."

I lift my spoon, tighten my hand around it. "Is Anna not to show me to speak with Ciaran and Fitzclaste?"

He does not look down, eyes still scanning the room. "I have a message to give Eerol, and since you did not come from an especially war-torn part of the country, it was decided that you would be better going to work with him at once. They have other things to tend to, and Tejan and Eerol can tell you anything you need to know about this place. If you do not choose to help in the healing rooms, you can speak with Tejan, after the day is spent. She will find you somewhere else to serve here."

I slow my hand on my spoon. "Then there is little need for Anna to wait here."

I move to stand, but he starts across the room toward the lots on the far side, ignoring me. His steps are still silent on the floor beneath the echoing voices. *I could not have heard him coming if I had tried, if I had listened with all that I am worth.* I grimace.

I take a bite, glance towards the door. *Where is the far side of the building, where the stables will be? Before I am anywhere, I should find my hound. He will be into trouble, if left alone for too long.*

My eyes flick to the floors. The wood of it almost glossy, worn down. But not scratched, the way all the wood flooring I have seen has been, worn with the treading of animals and of children dragging objects where they go. *They must not have their hounds indoors. What was this place, before it became a safe haven? This building is far older than the turnings since the wars began. The floors are evenly worn, beams stained dark with smoke above the fireplace from turnings long gone. It was not built to be a safe haven for this war that began with the death of the king. What then, did they build it for?*

A step falls beside me. I jerk my eyes up and there is the goblin again, scanning the room. I take the last bite of the hash, swallow it, and glance back at him with the corners of my gaze. His gaze is calm, the roaming of his eyes like a habit, not like a wakefulness, for fear of trouble. *He is not worried, here.*

"Are you ready, healer?" He does not look toward me, the braid on his beard all that I can see of his face.

I stand. "I would tend to this bowl, first."

His eyes flicker down to me, dry. He takes the bowl from the table, sets it over beside the spoons without a step and turns back, toward the massive doors. "This way. I want to explain to Eerol your stay here before I am called away again."

I blink, step after him, his gait too long for mine. *Is he expecting to leave again so soon after we have arrived?* My heart lifts. I keep my eyes on my steps. *If he is not here and I can find the door out, I can leave and take to the woods, should there be a need. I have only been asked to stay as long as he does.*

He pulls the door open and stops, waiting. I step through the door, and he is behind me again, close. "Left." His voice is curt. My skin crawls. I duck through the hallway on my left and there is another hall stretching out, many doors along its length. It ends with another turn, another hallway, and the goblin has not slowed his pace behind me, this hall less furnished than the others. *How great is this building, that it would have so many twists and turns?* He steps ahead of me, turning at the end of the hall, his stride long, easy, not the watchful gait of the woodlands. There is an opening at the end of the hallway, lit by a torch—wood meeting rock in a cave-like staircase leading down into the earth.

XV

Eerol

The goblin ducks through the opening. His head is hunched as he moves down, the ceiling of the stairs too low for him. *It is far above my head.* The ceiling is smooth, carved out by skilled handwork and not damp like the caves that I have found before.

I move onto the last step, my eyes on my feet, and the goblin straightens, turning to the right. There is a warmth in the air here beneath the earth that is strange. The air smells comforting, floor smooth and cool beneath my feet. *It's familiar, down here.* The goblin strides through a circular archway, carved of stone like the walls, and there are shelves ahead, lining each side of the room. There is a fireplace and a fire crackling in it in the corner, large, flames licking at the walls of its confinement, and there are herbs, herbs on the air, the scent of them heavy and warm. Crocks of all colors sit on the table before us, knives strewn across, their blades tinted green and herbs flecked. *Like home.*

There is a rustle of fabric and a man steps through the circle of the far archway. He is neither tall nor short, his eyes sharp and dark, nose large and hooked. His graying brows are bushy, heavier than I have ever seen on a man before. They jut out, hairs gnarled, crooked at angles, like he tried to smooth them out.

The goblin folds his arms, his hand resting near his sword, as it always does. "Eerol." His voice does not echo like it should in the stone room, flat and even like a home.

The man turns, raising an eyebrow at the goblin. He casts a shrewd glance at me, his bushy brow still raised. "Srad. What needs doing?" His brow lifts a little higher, eyes scanning over me. They lift back to the goblin, the man's hands reaching to rest on the table, his forearms tensing, thick. "Is she injured? I see no wounds. Nor do I recognize her."

The goblin's lips twist, wryly. "She is the herbalist Einion sent. And she is not wounded."

The man's eyes flicker to me, scan over me once more. His face blank now, almost derisive, no longer the cool scanning of before. His other brow lifts. His eyes stay on mine. "Ah, then. You have much experience in the field of herbalism, I would assume, or you would not have been sent by the captain?" There is an undertone to his voice, calculating, his eyes on the crocks he is moving over from the table. But they are still watching me, with the corner of his vision.

I incline my head toward him—deference. "I have worked in it for more than twelve turnings. Only half of those have been in the field. I have worked in herbalism alone for another healer these last few gråsvings, since I finished my apprenticeship."

His eyes flick to the shelves and he straightens, crocks stacked under his arm. "Well then. Make a sleeping tea." He turns away. "If you do that correctly without anyone dying, you can stay." He glances at the goblin, setting the crocks down one by one into the wash basin. "Is there anything else, toa?" *A Menantian term of respect.*

Sradfaang nods, folding his arms. "Aye. She is here to find safety and has secrets that will pose an issue if they come out. I assume you will know what to do with that knowledge. Einion sends his regards." My eyes flicker up, throat tightens. *What does he intend to ask of the healer, with those words?*

The healing man nods, reaching his hands back to adjust the leather bands twisted around his hair. "When is Flint due back? Another few dawns I'd have thought. The man never seems to keep his appointments. Causing trouble across the countryside, ey?"

The goblin shifts, turning for the doorway out. He half-smiles. "I cannot say. His plans changed with his orders back at the outpost, as you will have heard." He steps through the archway and is gone, up the stairs.

I turn back to the medicine man. He is already watching me, his eyes careful, calculating. "You are young, civ."

I fold my hands before me. "I have told you of my history. And aye, I have not seen many seasons."

His brow lifts again, hooked nose twitching. "You have told me nothing but that you have worked in herbs and that you apprenticed. That is little of your life. Make that tea. There are the shelves." His hand waves vaguely toward the walls, his fingers bent, crooked.

My lips tighten. I force my eyes to stay calm, to stay gray. *There is a trap in his words, in the saying of them.* I lift my eyes. "How would you make your sleeping tea, sónya? To aid a child or a man?"

A smile brushes at the edges of his lips, tightening his eyes. "Va. That is the question you would be asking then. Good." He nods, gesturing a thick hand toward the shelves. "Make it your own way, one for a grown man, and one for a child. I want to see what you know of them. Keep them separate."

He half-smiles again, a gruff thing, and lifts a pot. *The smile is half-sharp, like the goblin's.* It clears from his face, heavy brows settling. He picks up another crock. "So." He turns away. "Why have you been brought to our fortress in the mountains?"

I lift a crock from the shelf, keep my eyes forward. "Is this not a refuge?"

He nods, rolling up the sleeves of his tunic. "Va. It is. But there must be a reason to need a refuge to come. Healers do not show up every day. You are the first in all my time in this place to come, to show up here. Though, whether or not you have skill remains to be seen." There is the sound of something hitting water, another crock in the wash basin.

I pull the lid off the crock in my hand. The leaves in it are large and dried, whole and browned near their edges. *Echinacea.* I set the lid back on it, place it back on the shelf. *I usually only use the blooms for salves. I will have to ask what use there is in the leaves. Aílé did not use them.*

I reach for the one beside it, a tan one. *The healer is waiting for a response. He will keep waiting until I speak.* I clear my throat. "I am here because my life was thought to be in danger."

He lifts a brow on the edge of my vision, his arms crossed, face stoic. "How unique. The differences between the tale you have told and the tale of the others that came before you to this place is astounding. Riveting." His voice is wrung with sarcasm, with wry tones.

My back stiffens, hands lift another crock. I keep my voice even. "I was unaware that I was to tell it for your amusement, healer. But I apologize. My tale is my own, and I would keep it as such."

"I am not surprised that a fian would want to keep her story a secret, especially to protect the captain who aided her. Well done, Eness Finch."

My eyes snap to his, half-burn. I bite it back sharply.

He grins, a savage thing, all edges. "And as I thought. A fian herbalist in my ward. There's something I have not yet seen." He nods at me. "Srad might have told me of your blood, or Ciaran last night. It would have saved me some assumptions and sticking my nose in where it is not wanted. Did they not think I would figure it out, or do they not know what your bloodline is, Eness Finch?"

My heart tightens. I lift my eyes. *He cannot have seen, cannot know if he was not told. He is testing, once more.* "They do not all know. And I am glad he did not tell you. It would be a secret best not spread, if it were true. Having one here would be a danger, would it not?"

His brow lifts again at the side of my sight. "If it were not true, I would not have seen that yellow cross your eyes only moments ago. Fear does not cross my eyes the same way. But you need not fear me. I have kept secrets for those in greater peril than you, and I have no use for gold or soldiers or even queens. You have nothing to fear from me."

I lift my head, keep my eyes forward, on the crock. "Nothing to fear? That people has something to fear from everyone, Eerol of

Sikkerhet. Lots are being sold out across the country. We all have something to fear, today in Auvridal. And there are few in this world without a buying price. What would you sell to keep your loved ones safe?"

He snorts. "My loved ones are far from here and have been fighting this war longer than you have known it existed, lai. I have no use for gold or soldiers, so long as they get out of the way of the prince when the time is right. Make that tea. I will tell your tale to no one, as long as you are here. And loyal."

'...Out of the way of the prince?' My eyes flicker to him, scan over him. He has turned away, but his eyes are still half-watching me over his shoulder, eyeing me. *As though he knows I am watching him. He figured me out far too easily, learned my secret far too quickly, with only a guess at my heritage. What life has he lived, that he could guess so easily a secret I have well kept?*

My hand grips the lid of the crock and I pull it open. "What prince would you claim as yours, Eerol of the healing rooms? The one who lost his life running from his mother? From the queen who blames that people for her husband's death?"

He looks at me, only a half-glance over his shoulder. "Va. The prince of Auvridal. The only prince left. The only royalty half-worth being loyal to, whenever he makes it to the throne."

I lower the crock, set it back on the shelf. My eyes burn. *Are there conspirators for a dead prince in this place?* "He is missing, is he not? Presumed dead, so the tale has gone, these four turnings at least. Have not these death tolls been the result of his death? Punishments sent out for the crime of many with the ending of his life?"

He laughs, a strange, grating thing. "Missing, va, so the tale goes. Turned by the Maa'eulé to their side. A traitor to the throne, to his mother, turned to the side of those who killed his father. So the tale goes. Our poor prince, lost before his coronation day. If he was not safe, who then is? Are those teas done yet?" His eyes cast over his shoulder and he turns, expression as unreadable as the captain's or goblin's.

I glance at him, fingers barely brushing the edges of the leaves in the crock before me. *Lemon balm.* "I have not yet found—" I press the lid back onto the crock, set it on the high shelf, my toes against the floor. "—the rest of the herbs needed. They will be done. What do you mean he was turned? Who are the Maa'eulé?"

He grunts, shuffling his feet. "You do not know them? And you are checking crocks one by one, ey? If you do not ask questions you struggle alone. Struggle she will." He shakes his head, moving through the doorway into the second room beyond.

I stare at him, a new crock in my hand. My face warms, eyes burn. *Did he think I would ask him where every herb was, when he sent me to find them on the shelves? Am I not to learn where he keeps each of them, so that I can utilize them, if I am to stay?* I watch him. He is moving pots around, swiping out the inside of them with a cloth. *Ignoring my question.*

There is a humming from the healer in the room beyond, more grunt than song.

XVI

Hall Song

A tap sounds on the staircase, familiar, repetitive. *Hound nails on stone.* I lift my head. A voice speaks. "Come along, hound. Just down the stairs. Stop sniffin' that." The voice is a man's, not one that I know, but it is good humored. There is a shuffling of steps, Blått's against the stone of the stairs, and he barks.

The steps pick up, there is a blur of blue-gray fur, and something crashes into me, knocking into my waist. I stumble back, catching his head. He barks, lifting his nose toward my face, and barks again, tongue out, eyes alight, feet scrambling up toward my shoulders. I shove him down, smile. A man steps down the stairs, a smile on his face to match mine. He inclines his head toward me and is gone again, stepping back into the staircase.

Someone swears.

"What in the hot blaze of Hartwool is that thing?" I turn my head, Blått's tongue lapping at my hands, his tail wagging furiously. Eerol is standing in the archway, a towel stilled in his hands, his face red, beads of sweat across his brow. His eyes are on Blått, and they are wide, stunned. "Oh, I'll have that goblin's head. That's not a hound for healing rooms..." He leans his arm against the door, eyes still staring at Blått.

I shake my head. "He has worked in mine all his life. It will have been quieter there, than here, but he listens to given commands." I click my tongue, three times, and Blått drops onto the ground, his eyes still wide, eager, tail still whipping against the floor.

Eerol's eyes flicker to mine. "Worked in yours, ey? What'd he work on? And how'd he do with children, when they were brought in, crying and unwieldy?" He shakes his head, wringing the towel through his hands. "I'll not say he cannot stay, but one wrong move, and he is out. I do not need a creature that large down here throwing hair in my salves and knocking crocks over. He is more the size of a horse than a hound, I should think. Definitely not one a random healer woman would have."

I run a hand along Blått's ears, smile. "In the mountains where I am from, hounds this large are not uncommon. Are yours so small here?"

He laughs shortly, shaking his head. "I do not mean that farmers cannot have a hound that large, only that he looks to be more suited for taking down an elk stag than resting by a fire. He may stay. Probably useful that you had him, given where you came from."

He looks down at the hound, half-crouching, and Blått tilts his head that way, tail smacking hard against my legs. "You couldn't have barked those soldiers away, ey?" Blått's tail slaps harder against me, and Eerol chuckles, straightening again. He turns away, moving into the other rooms, and the hound follows. His eyes glance back at me for a moment, then he is gone, sniffing through the room.

I draw in a breath. *He has taken to the healer, then.* I lift the spoon, set it back on the hanging rack, and lift the dish towel, the cloth damp in my hands, reeking of lavender and rosemary.

•▶|◀▶|◀▶|◀▶|◀▶|◀▶|◀•

The room is bustling with noise, crowded, landlots everywhere filling it fuller than a market square at harvest. My heart sinks into my stomach, eyes burn faintly. *How many landlots are here, living in this fort? There must be more than fifty heads, more than I have seen in one place outside of town squares.*

The healing man grunts beside me. "Well, Tren is back on his feet. The lump. He was supposed to be off them for another night. He better not smile or that girl will get an idea about him." The man beside him grunts in return, almost a chortle.

I fold my hands together, turn away. A woman is laughing not far from me, her head thrown back, eyes dancing. Her curls are dark, long, and she is speaking with a man who is holding a bowl, his face relaxed, skin pale, almost pallid.

Eerol is still standing by the great door, his head cocked to the side, watching the room. *This will be life for him, where he goes in the evening to learn of all that has gone on. For how many turnings, is this what they have done? How many turnings have these people been at this place? Do they gather every evening, for food, for fellowship?*

Eerol glances at me. "Are you not going all the way in?"

I nod, my lips tightening. "I am only watching first. Much seems to be happening, here." I brush my hands against my skirts—there is something caught on my fingers, soft. *Hound fur. He was quiet about staying below, beside the fireplace.*

Eerol grunts again. "This is less than normal. If you wait for it to calm you'll be here all night, I should think. Go on in, healer." He steps into the room, moving around a man and between two others that are speaking, greeting them both. The woman laughs again, the same gentle, high laugh.

I swallow hard, lift my head. *They will pay little attention to me here. These people have many things to do, besides paying attention to those they do not know here.* I step in, move along the path that Eerol took, through the moving arms, and waving hands, toward the tables on the far side where the food has waited at the meals earlier today. The noise is loud, strange in my ears, voices laughing, talking, blending together into a wave of sounds, all foreign, all unknown.

I glance down at the floor, duck under an arm, and a man laughs above me, the sound rough. Another joins him, slapping him on the back. There is a chuckle from another, only a step away from me, their eyes on each other, laughing, speaking, as though they have been at it all night. I turn toward the tables.

Something bumps my shoulder—I pull back, spin. *A man.* He is still moving forward, his stride unbroken, a bowl in his hand, un-spilt. I turn, step toward the wall. I press my back against it, my jaw tightening, and three more men walk by, all laughing.

One of them glances at me, smiling, and he is gone again, off into the crowd. I press my back harder against the wall. *That is only one lot that has acknowledged me. I can blend in here. Perhaps over time, the noise may even seem quieter, with the aging of this place, if I can stay long enough to know it.*

My ears ring, the sound of the voices still crashing together, a chorus. *A few of them are fading out.* The laughs are gone, a quiet falling over the room. Everyone is looking towards something, toward someone on the side of the room farthest from me. The murmuring sounds are gone.

A voice rings out, catching over the hush. "You all will be ready to eat?" There is a laugh, voices mixed together and rolling across the room again, heads nodding. "Then I will not keep you long." The voice is familiar, but I can see nothing of the speaker. "I only wish to give thanks."

The silence deepens and there are heads around the room, bowing, lowering as though royalty were present in it. The voice lifts again. "Creator, we thank you for this bountiful food you have provided and for the safety You have given all those hidden here today. We ask Your blessing on this food and that You would deliver our country from the hands that have sought to rip it apart. By Your grace, and through Your Hand."

My heart drops into my stomach. There is a murmur around the room, landlots moving again, voices picking up, laughter resuming. I look away. *"...the hands that have sought to rip it apart." Do they understand the treachery in that prayer? The danger of it, in a place filled brimful with souls?* My eyes snap around the room. There are more than sixty lots here, more than sixty minds with their own loyalties, their own thoughts and intentions. *Do they not question that one of them may betray them all, for a price? Villages have been torn up for less, homes left shattered and minds left broken.* Voices have taken up again, sounds rippling in waves through the room.

A woman steps up to me, smiling. "I do not think we have met before." Her eyes are bright, hand reaching out for mine, for the grip of new trust. I accept her hand, grip her wrist lightly, and she pulls it away again, smiling once more. "I am Iris Meivah. I think you came in late yesterday even? I think we share a room."

I incline my head, force down the unease in my stomach. "Aye. I am Eness Finch. It is an honor to learn your name. I believe Tejan mentioned you last night, or this morning."

She smiles, a laugh breaking from her lips. "She like as not did. I work with the seamstresses, and so they often come to me to find garb for anyone who comes in need of clothes. I have your dress now, if I am not mistaken. It is in the sewing rooms, at the back. You will have to come visit some afternoon, if you have any handwork. We always love having others come to work for the afternoon with us, on your own work."

I half-smile. "Nearly all of my work is handwork, but it does not take to being moved to side rooms. I think I would slow down your labor, were I to bring mine in. I am an herbalist."

Her eyes brighten. "You are the new healer too?" She claps her hands together. "I ought to have known. We rarely get two people together who are not related. Was your village in danger from the queen, or did you come alone as I have guessed? Who brought you in?"

I blink at her, bite back the changing of my eyes. *Do they speak so openly of the queen, of her treachery everywhere here?* I swallow, shake my head. "Gót. I do not live near a village. Did not live near a village." I meet her gaze. "How many of you are there here? I have had little time to ask questions but of Eerol, who does not seem to care for them."

She laughs, glancing at me again. "Aye. I doubt you will have learned much from him, other than his own thoughts on life and the world. He is a wise old man but a stubborn one." She shakes her head. "Stars. I do not know. There may be more than seventy of us now, with the children. It seems there are always new ones coming and going, it is hard to keep up. Lord Fitz or Ciaran would know."

I swallow hard, turn my eyes away, force a smile to my lips. "Do you not know, then, all those who live here?"

She shakes her head, her eyes wandering. "Not all of them. I cannot keep up with them all. I spend most of my days in the sewing rooms at the back. There are not many lots who come there but the women and children, and they come and go, so I do not get to know them all much."

I incline my head. *They do not know all those who live here, but still they speak freely? Stars, that is unwise. Does she not wonder who will repeat the words she has said? Who will take them and recall them in the days to come? Is our country not at war in its own lands?*

I force a smile. "How long have you been here, Iris Meivah? Many turnings?"

She shakes her head. "Gót, not more than one. I came not long after Dan returned, if you have met him. But you likely will not have. I forgot he left again a few fortnights ago. There were a few less of us, then. We have been growing by leaps and bounds these last few turnings. I think we may actually have a marriage in the next moon or so, if things continue the way they have. That may be a first. It is for my time here."

I draw a smile to my lips, force back the changing of my eyes. *Rapid growth. That is asking for disaster to come. This is unwise, all of this. Do they regulate the growth, or have they become so confident in their hiding that they would leave off caution? How do these men regulate it?* I glance at her. "Are all those here in hiding, from the queen's men?"

She inclines her head. "Aye. I think that is true. I confess though," she pauses, "I am truly not certain. I have not asked most of the men."

There will be others, who know each reason for each person. But can they shield, when speech is given so freely? When words are not tested nor tried? Where others come and go? Are we not yet in a quiet war that deals in words given in secret and searched out?

I incline my head toward her. "Pardon, Iris." I move to step away, toward the door. "I would find my hound. I left him elsewhere and I would find him again. It was well to meet you."

She inclines her head back, straightening, and her voice is a blur. "…it was well to meet you. May your search be…" She steps away and I turn. My eyes scan the room. The talk has not slowed, voices churning together, faces slipping past.

A woman's eyes meet mine, dark and watchful, wide. They do not leave, studying, and she inclines her head. I incline mine back, turn away. Her eyes are watching too closely. I step to the side, duck around a man. He is laughing, speaking with the men in front of him, a bowl in his hand. I move toward the door, duck under an arm, and there is another, across my path, a woman talking wildly, eager in a story, her arms flailing. I move about her, step faster towards the door. *I cannot think here. This place is too loud. I need to return to the healing ward, to space, if I cannot have air.*

I push the door open and it is heavy, wood thick, and my arms strain. It swings and I am through, the noise nearly cutting out as it shuts behind me. There are voices in the hallway, somewhere along it, moving off somewhere behind me. I spin away, toward the healing ward. The halls are large, the air cool with evening and loud with stories. I pick up my pace, up toward the healing rooms. There is no one around, not a trace or sign of anyone, not a voice but those back in the hall, echoing. *I cannot stay. Not in a place that risks itself so freely, in prayer and voice and word.*

My foot slaps stone and I draw in a breath. *They speak too freely, for those that do not know all that are nearby. Can they trust those they cannot account for? Even those who seek Elnial, as the prayer says they do, have been known to turn each other in. Do they question no loyalties, have no uncertainties about those around them after fifteen turnings of war, fifteen turnings of betraying lives for gain and wealth?* There are steps, further down the hall. I pick up my pace, start down the stairs that curl down into darkness.

I swallow, my eyes burning. My feet slap the stairs. I grab a torch from the wall, carry it down. *How many turnings have they lived like this, hidden in the mountains, traded their own stories, spoken ill of the queen?* I step off the steps, into the healing rooms, and Blått stands, stretching, his movements easy, calm. I turn, set the torch into a cage hanging from the ceiling. *How long do they expect to go on, with so little care given to what is said? How have they survived this long?*

I pause, scan the room. The healing wards are quiet, not a sound in them. *There is only one exit from these rooms. No way out but upward. It is all stone, beneath the ground, solid as the earth, unless there is a room I have not been to, down here.* I turn, glance toward the stairs and the opening behind them. *I have not looked there, to see what is beyond.* The darkness is thicker there, away from the torch. *A passage or a tunnel? Perhaps a second way out, in the event of trouble. It would not be wise to have no exit from a room like this.*

I swallow, turn toward the table. *There will be no hiding of secrets here, and I have secrets to keep of my own. These lots take risks that I cannot, not with my gift, not with my life. Eerol guesses things far too easily.*

It will only be a matter of time before the queen's men find out where they are. All tongues in a place of this size cannot be accounted for, all words, all voices. This is what I have stayed away from, what we have hidden from. They should have already been sold out by now. It is a miracle they have not. Or they have a deal with a queen's man.

I glance at Blått and he is watching me, his eyes lifted, tail wagging. I lift a bag from the table. He steps forward, eager, his eyes alert, steady and half-hidden by the last of his coat from the dark moons. I suck in a breath, set my hand gently on his head. "They asked no oath, that they would trust so completely." I run my hand along his ear and his tongue lolls out a little. I shake my head. "Perhaps we should go."

There is a step behind me, soft, the barest brush of the floor. My heart leaps into my throat. "Healer." *The goblin's voice.*

My eyes burn a million colors. I swallow, force my back to stay toward him. His feet are barely visible on the edge of my vision. "Sradfaang." My voice is calm. *The sound was to warn me he was there. He did not intend to surprise.*

He shifts his feet, just behind me. "You left the room suddenly. Was there trouble, that you would run so soon? Consider leaving?"

I swallow, keep my head down. "Gót. I only wished to find a moment alone. It has been long since I have been in a place with so many landlots gathered in one room."

There is a strange noise, somewhere between a laugh and a snort, derisive. "You did not intend to run, then?" There is an edge to his voice, a tone to it.

I swallow hard, turn slowly. My eyes flicker back toward the hilt of his sword. His arms are crossed, his poncho gone, thick markings across his bare shoulders where they meet his tunic. Its style is strange, one I have not seen before, the gold trim of it thin, more intricate than the dark lines marring the shoulders of the soldiers. *What rank is he, that his gold is so thin and so carefully woven?*

My heart thuds. *His hand is not close to his sword. But it could be, at a moment's notice, with a breath. I have seen him use his speed and strength together.* But *he wouldn't need a blade. He took down the man in the forest without force.* My eyes burn. *I should never have come down here. He would not have entered my room to find me, if I had gone there.*

I lift my head. "I came down to check on Blått. Why have you come? I only came away a moment ago."

He lifts a brow, face expressionless. "You did not come to check the hound." I turn my gaze down again, but he is continuing. "What was said, that you would flee? Did you worry for your eyes, or your safety?" He steps to the side, pacing toward the wall. *But he is still watching, watching me.*

I shake my head, my eyes forward. "I worried for nothing. I came to be where it is silent."

He slows, standing still. "Then why was there fear in your gaze? Nieave said there was panic written in your eyes, and she does not overstate. What did you see or hear that you would consider running? Do not lie to me. I will know it."

He heard the words I spoke, only a moment before he came. My eyes burn. "I have told you why I left. My reason has not changed."

He turns, his expression dry. "And you are a terrible liar. A half-truth is still not a truth. You are better at adapting than you let on, better at controlling your mind and eyes. I saw you hide your ancestry for half a fortnight before it was rooted out. I do not believe for a moment that you are startled by too much noise, nor do I believe that you were not getting ready to run. So, tell me, what made you consider taking to the forests? I heard your words."

My eyes meet his. He lifts a brow, dry, and all humor is gone from his face. My stomach sinks. I bite back the eye change, force them to stay calm. A humorless smile spreads over his face. "That is what I thought. It was not a passing thought, to leave."

I shake my head. *He will not understand.* "I did not plan to run, but to consider it. There are many parts at play here, as you know, Sradfaang of the Goldtide. Excuse me. I would turn in for the night." I step toward the door.

"You are not leaving until you tell the truth, or I will follow you through this building. I do not plan to hear tomorrow morning that my charge got herself shot by an arrow beyond these walls because she tried to sneak out while my back was turned, nor do I plan to be tracking you through the dark and rain again. I will wait."

I lift my eyes, meet his gaze. He is watching, something calculating in his eyes. *He means what he says.* I clench my jaw, incline my head. "If the words spoken within these walls were to get back to even one ear beyond these walls hopeful of gain, this place would not stand to meet another dawn. I have not been here long enough to have earned their trust, yet already they speak openly, toy with their own safety. It is unwise to speak that way in any company now, much less company that is mixed by many minds and unknown loyalties. There can be little trust, where so many voices abound."

His arms fold over his chest, eyes watching me. "Did you not intend to ask questions of their protocol for determining who is here, who comes and who goes, and where they are allowed to go to before you ran?"

I lift my head. "No. And I had not decided to run today. But I do not need to take the word of someone I do not know or trust, on people they cannot control. I would rather be where I know I am safe."

His expression goes drier. "And where will you find safety? Alone?" I purse my lips and he scoffs. "You have a plan for where to flee to then?"

I tighten my hand on Blått's ear. "There would be time to decide later, where to go and where to stay. I am not leaving today."

He folds his arms. "When then, do you plan to go? Did you intend to seek help or just run out into the wilds and hope for the best, in bandit-infested mountains?"

I shake my head. "I will not run aimlessly. Nor do I intend to leave tomorrow, but the words spoken tonight were—" my voice trails off.

"Treasonous?" A smile glints on his lips, harsh, mocking. "Is that what you intended to say, healer? Many of their words are treason, but you are not asking questions of those who watch out for the welfare of this place and all those who live here." I turn my eyes down. He shakes his head. "If you take to the woods on your own, where will you go? You do not know these hills, or any of the landlots within five leagues of this place I am certain. If you leave here, and you are not caught by the first soldiers you see as a prisoner of the crown, you will be found by wandering men and misused or dead within half a fortnight. There are many wandering men in the forest of these woods. Not all of them are half as honorable as the ones we met. So where would you go? To starvation and abuse at the hands of the men you are fleeing from?"

I lift my head. "I do not know, Sradfaang of the Goldtide. There are questions I would ask, but if I am a danger to this place and words are flippantly used by those that come and go as the woman above said, then it is better to find my death out there than risk the lives of those here and my own by staying. Will not my blood be a greater risk to them, to those that are new here, whose blood is not as deeply hunted by the queen? They cannot all be sought by her men, not all their wives and husbands and children. If there are whole families here, I do not want to further their danger by adding my blood to the crimes heaped against them. If I am found here, their deaths will be harsher. You know the work I intend to continue. That is treason beyond their words. It would only be adding to them."

His jaw tightens, hands adjusting on his arms over my head. "You are using your mind then, *good*. They are not all hunted, gòt. But you have still not asked enough questions. Question Tejan and Fitzclaste. They will tell you more about this place, about the people here and those they let in. No one within these walls was lightly chosen, nor gathered here without thought. Not even you, healer. The man who chose you is not one to make decisions lightly. You would be wise to not throw away the place he gave you on a whim. Even one based in treason." He turns away.

I turn my head away. "I do not run to throw away an opportunity, but I will stay to ask questions, at your bidding."

He nods. "Good. I do not want to be chasing you out into the dark again."

I shake my head. "If I left, you would not need to. You have seen me to safety."

His brow lifts again. "My orders were not dependent upon your safety, but upon time. I was to see you back to your home or to complete a fortnight and a half of duty, whichever came first. Those were my orders."

I drop my hands from Blått's head. "Then can I not release you from your orders? Mine were fulfilled. Should not yours be also?"

His lips twist, wry. "You cannot. And was not and am not bound at your word. There is more at play here than you. I would be honor bound to see you back for the safety of this place and its people, even if I was not your guard. You may not expressly know anything, but even idiots can be dangerous without knowledge. If you run, rather than leaving at the word of the lord of this place, I will hunt you down for their safety. As you have said, there are many lives at stake here."

My heart sinks in my chest. I grip Blått's fur. "Then I will stay and ask questions. But when I leave, I will not take others with me. I will not be a continued danger where I cannot be a help. But I will stay for as long as is reasonable. You have my word."

He inclines his head slightly. "So be it. Goodeven, healer, and good rest to you." He inclines his head and turns away, moving beyond the shadows of the room, into the staircase.

Blått's head nudges my hand. *So be it. And when tomorrow dawns, and they still speak the same, speak in words foolishly spoken, will I regret my word?*

It is given. I will not run. I will not leave.

XVII

Kúráh Talk

Blått pads beside me, his steps soft on the rugs of the floor. There is a voice ahead, rumbling in the hall, a man's, deep and low. Another answers it, higher and clouded, a woman's. Two figures round the corner ahead, and Blått lifts his head, eyes eager.

The man is of average height, his frame slender, hair darkened red and he is young, perhaps in his twenty-second or twenty-third turning. The woman is alike in age, her hair dark, coiled, face paled and her voice is familiar.

She smiles at the hound, a laugh breaking through her lips. "I had heard there was a hound with you, but thought it must have been a myth when I never saw him in the rooms. He is a good hound."

The man's eyes meet mine and he inclines his head, his face flushing. "Goodnoon to you, kúráh." His voice is deep, low, rumbling. He looks down at the hound, placing his hand on Blått's head. Blått's tongue is lolling, his eyes no less eager, but content now, tail thudding against the bench by the wall, a rhythmic tapping.

I lift my eyes to the woman. She extends her hand, a greeting. I offer mine, take her wrist and she clasps it shortly, her hand is callused against my skin. "I am Tollah, and I believe we have shared a room these last few nights. It is well to finally meet you." She inclines her head, honor, her hand releasing mine. *Tollah. The second woman I share a room with.*

I incline my head back. "Tollah. It is well to meet you. I am Eness, and you have met Blåthjortt now. We are bound for the outdoors, for a moment of air." There is a step behind me, solid.

I turn. There is another man, taller, broader. He inclines his head at me, and at Tollah, then back to me. "Healer. If you would, I am heading the way of the forests to speak with the men in the stables. I can take the hound with me, and you can return to your work below, if you would like." There is an undertone to his words, as though something were unspoken in them.

They have sent someone to take the hound outdoors each time since we arrived. Am I not free, to come and go as I choose? To walk where I please while I stay, so long as I do not go far enough from the walls to cause trouble?

I scratch behind Blått's ear. The man's eyes are earnest, dark and deep-set. I look down, toward the hound. "That would be well. I will return to the healing rooms, and you have saved me some trouble." I incline my head, and there is relief in the corners of his eyes. He inclines his back, clicking to the hound.

Blått is still standing between me and the first man, his head lifted. I click my tongue once, nod toward the man, and Blått's eyes meet mine, waiting, excited. I half-smile. "Go. Blått. Follow." He steps forward, toward the man, eyes still on me.

The man is speaking to the blushing man, his voice easy. "Oy, G'moy. That game last night wasn't finished and does not count. I never counted an unfinished game yet and we will not be counting that one. I was only one head behind. There was more than time for a comeback, or for you to make another foolish move, I'd 'a said. I've seen you do worse." He snorts.

The deep voiced man—G'moy—grins, his face flushing high on his cheekbones above his scuffed beard. "I'd say a game is a game, but we may yet finish it, if you would take off duty for once and come to the hall."

Tollah laughs. "He'd do that if there weren't stories on watch when Ågë is there. You'd be like Tren, if you ever had a guard watch, G'moy."

The man standing next to Blått—Tren—laughs, a short, breathy thing, and inclines his head, but G'moy shakes his sharply. "I might, if he wasn't so buggin' light lipped. That man speaks more fluid words than a Saying Woman, even in his sleep. I'd not bunk in his room again for all the South Lakes combined, with their hunting. I'll keep to the gardens."

Tollah laughs again, glancing back over her shoulder. She turns toward me. "Eness. I will walk with you, if you are moving toward the healing rooms. I must return to the kitchens anyway." She glances at G'moy, inclining her head. "I hope that you are not stationed next time a tale is told. The last one was one that will not like to be forgotten. He has gained much skill since I think you last heard him. It makes the days go swifter to have a story to ponder, or a song. You should not miss the next one."

G'moy smiles, inclining his head. "Aye. I hope the same. Goodeven to you, Tollah. Healer." He inclines his head toward each of us in turn, and is gone, moving past Tren.

Tren moves wordlessly by, Blått following at his heels.

Tollah turns toward me, and she starts up the hall. "Healer. I assume you have been given some guidance or a tour of Sikkerhet, so that you are not entirely on your own here?"

I force a smile, incline my head toward her. "I think I have been shown all that was needed, but I would care to see more of it, once I have gotten my bearings of what I do know. I should like to know the rest of the ways outdoors."

She throws her head back and laughs, sharply. I start. She shakes her head, still laughing. "By that I think you will mean that you have been shown where you are working, your room, the hall and nothing else. You were shown all the essentials. I am sorry. We have been busy of late and I imagine no one was asked to show you the other rooms. There are many of them, and a soul could get lost if you wandered into the wrong hall. The hills know that I did, when I first arrived with my brother."

She glances at me, her smile softening, eyes uniquely blue against the pale of her skin. "If you stay for as long as you may, you will want to know what is here, beyond those few rooms. There are many useful ones here, many for sewing and gathering and afternoons when things are quiet and conversations are long. It makes the time gentler, when the days are passing slowly, and makes for good conversations, when the older women gather with the younger ones. I would not miss one of those afternoons for all the gold Auvridal has to offer."

I glance at her. "You are like a village then, here in the mountains? Do your older women teach the younger old skills, or is it only for conversation that you gather?"

She shakes her head. "We talk about many things. About the war. Some days, they will bring their handwork and we will share skills. Some days, they will tell tales about life before the war. When the dark months grow long, we gather there more often. We used to gather more, that is, before we grew. There is less time for fellowship, now that there are so many of us. And there never have been many older women here."

We turn around the hall and there is a woman stepping up it, a basket on her arm. She inclines her head to both of us, stepping past and I glance back at Tollah. Her gaze is forward. "Do you ever leave these walls?"

She glances at me, her look curious. "Gót. Not often. I have once or twice since I came, but there is little reason to leave. My only blood in the world is here. I have been here too long to desire to leave, until the land is at peace again. This is my home."

I slow my steps. "You do not miss it, then, the world beyond these walls, or you know that it is better, here, where you are safe?"

She glances at me, slowing to a stop beside the mouth of the hall. "Neither you nor I, I think, are old enough to miss the days of peace. But I do miss the peace of childhood. That as it is, I do not miss the fear of the villages. It is better to be where my brother and his family are safe, and where I can watch their children grow, until the times are better. This is what we have."

I nod. "Excuse me. I have asked too many questions. I should return to my task and I believe this is where our halls split. You work in the kitchens, I believe Tejan said?"

She nods, her smile soft. "I do. And it was well to meet you, Eness Finch. That was not too many questions. I will see you this evening, at gathering time, Creator allowing. And it seems that you already know your way around better than many of us did when we first arrived. You may find your way around on your own, I think, if you are watchful enough and given time to see."

She smiles again, and pulls the small door to the hall open. There is a puff of air, scented heavily with savory things; the smell of hot lard and something more, spices. The door shuts, leaving the taste of warm bread on the wind, and herbs in the air. I step up the hall, fold my arms around my waist. There is no tapping of Blått's nails on the wood of the floor, the sound gone, only the constant, quiet murmuring of the halls, of voices in rooms I have not yet seen.

I start up the hall.

They dwell in quiet here, like their own village caught up in one building. Do they forget in bits and pieces, the happenings of the world beyond? Can they forget, when they speak so freely of them here, safe in these walls? I step into the hall, the end of it curling down into the earth. The voices behind me are nearly gone now, leaving the heavy quiet of a building.

What man can lose his home and not fight for it? What woman can give up her life and not seek to gain it back, or rebuild? Are they free here, or are they trapped, beneath the orders of those who command this place? Can they be content to stay? I step onto the stairs, the stone cool beneath my feet. *Can there be peace, in giving up on the world beyond, by hiding away until the turmoil is gone, another generation or turning come?*

I step onto the floor and there is the laugh again, a child's laugh. I turn the corner and Eerol is framed beneath the stone archway, facing away from me, a broom in his hand. A child is standing before him, laughing, a woman clutching her hand. The little girl grins. "Heal-E, you is a silly man."

Eerol grunts, shaking his head. "A silly man?" There is humor in his voice. "Am I a silly man for saying that dandelion tea would serve better for burning your clothes, with a flavor like it has? Have you tried it out, for tastes alone?"

The little girl giggles and then stops sharply, staring at me. Eerol glances back, his brows drawing low. He lifts one. "Where is the hound?" The little girl blinks up at me, half-hidden behind the woman now.

I smile at her. "I was asked to let another take him out."

He snorts, turning toward me, a hand planted against the table. "Asked, were you?" He shakes his head, lifting a bag from the table and turns toward the woman. "Maylah, give her a cup of this every evening before bed. It will help with the ringworm."

The woman inclines her head. "Thank you, Eerol." She turns toward me, inclining her head. The woman beside her glances over, smiling softly. "You must have just arrived." She inclines her head. "I have not seen you here before but it is good to meet you." The little girl is still staring at me behind her mother's arm, eyes wide and soft brown.

I smile, incline my head toward them. "It is well to meet you. I hope you feel better, little kúráh." The little girl hugs closer to her mother's legs and Maylah smiles, an apology written in it, moving toward the stairs. Their steps slowly fade.

Eerol grunts, spinning sharply away. He shakes his head, lifting the crock from the table. "You might ask why you are being kept indoors. Do they fear that you will run, or that you will get lost? You don't seem easily lost."

My eyes snap to his. I shake my head sharply. "Gót. I have given my word to the goblin." I glance at him and turn my eyes away. "I know of no reason they keep me within. They may not be. It may be only kindness that they yield in offering to bring him out."

He snorts, setting a hand on his hip. "And you may also be blind."

I lift my apron from the table, slip it around my shoulders. "Do you know these people, here?" *Does he know those that lead here, know them well?*

He bobs his head. "Oh aye. I should know most of them." He turns away. "I'll speak to Sradfaang later. Or Fitz. He will know why, if there is a reason and not just the practicality of the thing in keeping you inside. You would be better served in your effort to not need so many breaks for a prancing hound." He glances down at the hound.

"They might worry more about something else. That hound is about as much trouble as a wet rag. Only a problem if you step on it."

I half-smile, twist the apron straps into place. "You need not ask them. I will speak with them, when I have the chance."

He glances at me, lifting a brow. "Oh eiy, will you?"

I incline my head and turn for the wash basin. I tighten my lips. *If they would have me trapped away inside while I am here, I can wait.* There is the sound of the straw of the broom against the floor, high and sharp, and Eerol grunts, about orders and watches of the day.

XVIII

The Harper

Eerol is laughing, the noise high and strange like a woodpecker call. He nods to the man next to him, the sounds of the great hall rumbling, his laugh only threading through it for a moment. I lift a bowl from the table. The healing man is still standing beside the table where the pots are, talking. I half-smile. *He will not like to be moving anytime soon, not now that he has entered a conversation.*

I glance toward the edge of the room, and a man steps around me and off into it, laughing, the one who always speaks with his hands. *I do not know his name.* I tuck back a smile, move by another man, standing beside the wall. There is an instrument tucked under his arm, small and intricately carved. *A harp.* I incline my head toward him, step around a child ducking around my feet.

I step, dump a ladle of stew into the bowl in my hand, and turn away.

"Lai." *An old man's voice, weathered.* My eyes flicker back. The man with the harp is standing by the wall, watching me with a single eye. His other is covered by a patch, white and leathered, a single tree carved roughly into it. His hair is white, white like the midday strále sun, his skin showing seasons beyond knowledge, wrinkles by his eyes, by his grinning lips.

He smiles brightly, a missing tooth a black hole on the edge of it. He nods. "I thought that would be you." He steps toward me, and he and I are of a height, his eye at a level with mine. "I have been looking a long time for you, little kúráh. It is good to finally know your coming."

I force a smile to my lips. "We have not yet met, lede, but I am honored to know you today." I bob my head, bow. "Who are you looking for? Kindred perhaps? I will help you look, if you have lost someone."

His eye sparkles, and a laugh clear and even breaks from his lips. His hand shifts the harp under his arm. "I am looking for no one. And of course we have not yet met." He chuckles again. "Do you take me for simple, lai? I have been waiting all my days for the Blood Sparrow and I know her when I see her. I have had many dreams in waiting for your arrival, for you to stand here, in the hall of kings, to catch sight of your coming."

I bite back the burning in my eyes, shake my head. *Blood Sparrow. Gót. No one has spoken that title in more than a decade.* "I am sorry, lede, but I am not the one you are looking for. I am a mountain healer, and we stand not in the hall of a king, but in the safe haven of a lord. May I help you find your seat, find someone that you know?"

He grins, the brow over his one eye raising. "You take me for lost." He laughs loudly, shaking his head, his grin spreading. There is something sharp like knowledge behind it. "A mountain herbalist, lai? I have heard of your voice, in visions. Seen your song in tales. What you carry is powerful, little kúráh, and the time is near at hand when it will be called upon and you will stand before nations, wielding your gift, ancient tunes not given by your own mind or heart. I have seen it. Elnial does not mis-gift, and He will strengthen what He has given, in the humble and diligent. I have seen your gift."

My heart plummets into my chest, eyes burning, burning. I turn my head away and an arm waves over it, a man standing too close. I step to the side, away from him, I turn my eyes back to the harpist. "I am sorry, lede. You are mistaken. I am not who you are looking for."

How could he know? I have not spoken of my voice, not in turnings upon turnings. Those who knew of it are in the grave now, all fallen to death and decay by time and war. I shake my head again. *Someone spoke of that poem once, spoke it over my name. Turnings ago, when I was a child.*

I incline my head, respect and honor. "I am sorry, lede. I ask your pardon. I have overstayed here and must go." My eyes flicker around, figures close, all talking, all speaking with each other, eyes on each other and not us, not him. He makes no move to leave. *They will not have heard the words. Old words spoken by an old tongue, words silent for turnings. They cannot know.*

He should not know, should not have spoken to me.

But he knows. Unless he is guessing in the dark, he knows.

I lift my eyes to his one, and it is already on mine. He smiles again, soft and rueful, his hand strumming the strings of the harp. "Do not fear, lai. They do not know what we speak of, even if they were listening. How could they? The Sparrow has not sung, not for them, but the time will come and is now when you will have to choose, whether to stand or to hide. Your gift has not been seen in ages. Perhaps it was for this reason you were brought to this place, little one." He inclines his head, his eyes scanning me over. "You are shorter than I thought you would be."

My brows twist, heart slowing. "Brought here? I was brought by the goblin, lede. The reasons will have been Elnial's alone, for I know them not, not yet." I force my voice down, force it low, but no one is looking, all of them talking around us. The bowl in my hand is heavy. "The goblin knew nothing of my voice, lede. I have not spoken of it to anyone." *My gift. The song. I should have never thought I could stay. I cannot use it here. To use it would be to open the door to danger for all here.*

He smiles, and it's gentle. "For whose safety, would you run?" He tucks his hands into his sleeves, the harp still beneath his forearm. "Are not lives woven together by Another's hand? You cannot say why you have come, as if the goblin's or your own hand were the only ones at work, your wills the only will. Have you not seen in your days, how Elnial has used our works and times for His glory, or have you hidden so far away that you have not even seen that working?" He shakes his head, that one green eye watching me from beneath the string of the patch. "The Swan and the Sparrow. The Corvus has not yet flown. Will you flee again or will you stand now? You have a place where you might be free to aid. Will you run?"

There is a shout, across the room. I half-turn, my eyes burning. I look down sharply. A man is standing on a chair. He waves his arm, a flourish, a grin on his face. "Harper! Will you favor us with a tune? We've had the noise of these lots long enough and we would have a tale, if you will grant us one, in the new fashion of these days beyond these walls." I swallow hard, turn back toward the harper.

He is nodding, eye on the crowd, a grin on his weathered face. "You call loud enough and I hear you, Eon. I will play if you will but eat and be still. I do not play for churning cattle, nor for rushing seas or waving winds. But I will play for a quieted Sikkerhet, if they will lend me their ears for a spell." There is a chorus of laughter around the room, voices joining the one from the chair in cheering, in jests, and murmuring an agreement.

The harper smiles, a soft thing, his eye moving back to me, and the crowd is mulling, moving—figures taking seats and talking once more. "Your time is coming, Eness Finch. Let your voice come and use it or hide away somewhere further up and further out as you have done for many seasons. But you cannot hide on the fringes of this war anymore. The choice is yours, but the consequences will stretch out far beyond your grasp, for good or ill, in wisdom or foolhardiness. This choice will be yours, to death or life for more than just your own body."

He steps forward, pressing my hand with his. It is soft like only the very aged, calloused around his fingertips. "Do not choose lightly, little Finch." He bows slightly, tilting my hand sideways, and he is gone into the crowd, his form vanishing into its waves.

A familiar bow, and one of respect and courtesy. A bow to someone of higher rank. There are cheers again, louder than before, ribbing and jests and laughter chorusing together into a ruckus of sounds.

I turn toward the wall, the voices raising. *Blood Sparrow. The voice that spoke that long ago was wrong. They spoke, and their words faded out, into endless turnings. Into endless deaths. The words they predicted then with never came to pass, the ground broken and unsettled in that village where my family fell, where death claimed them.*

I step toward the door, duck, and something warm sloshes against my thumb. I glance down. *The bowl.* I am still holding it, my fingers clutched around it, stew damp on my thumb. I slow, noise churning, laughter crashing, and there is the single note of a harp string. I turn toward the crowd.

The harper is on a chair on the far side of the room, the people of Sikkerhet settling into seats, only a few still moving. His eye is fixed on them, a smile still across his face, always there.

He grins. "This song is an old one, a prophecy spoken more than a hundred turnings ago, as a queen of this people lay dying. It has yet to come to pass. There will be a day that it is seen, but for now, I offer it to you all, a quiet song for a quiet night. Will that suit your minds?" There is a cheer, mugs lifted into the air, and the harper draws that single note again, the strings of his harp humming.

He smiles, lifts his voice, his hands already working over the strings of the harp.

> "Auvridal, of the high plains and low valleys.
> Auvridal, lost to shadows.
> A child will come, a man in his time.
> And the hope will dawn, with songs of life to a people long in darkness.
> Songs of healing through the Sparrow, the Blood Sparrow.
> Shadows will cry out and new voices will join,
> Voices from a people not your own."

I step back toward the door. Someone grins down at me, a man. He glances back at the harper. "This tune is one I know." His voice is low. "It used to be the tune of a lullaby my tâ sang."

The harper's voice is still rising and falling beneath the words of the man, light and simple across the room.

> "...Cruelty shall end in freedom, gold shall be wrought,

The Corvus shall guide, and these darkest parts will at
last see light.
When the North Spring freezes and shadows draw long,
The highlands shall come down and bring arms.
Hope from the hills. Strength to a dying land.
Auvridal, of the war-torn people. Auvridal of the sold.
Days will come when you seek life,
And Life has sought you first."

I turn toward the door, nod to the man beside me, and the Harper's voice rings out the last notes, the last words.

"Let the red rim flow, my brothers!
There is light where the Dark once dwelt.
Let the red rim flow, my brothers,
At the Hands of Joy is sorrow's song gone."

XIX

Desperate Light

I step up the hall, press the door open and there is sunlight. The last rays of it glint over the wooded hills, cutting through the trees, all pink-gold and warm. The words of the song ring in my head, words only half-spoken all those seasons ago. *The woman only knew half of the prophecy, only spoke in broken pieces when she uttered it over my head. My fár told her to leave.*

The wind brushes, a cool note in it. I glance backward, toward the fort. There is no one nearby, no sign or sight of guards or watchmen. I start forward. My skirts swirl about my legs, caught in the wind, the leaves of the trees dancing. There is pink on the oak branches, nearly faded out. *Lív is almost done in these mountains. I could not tell, in the rain when I arrived.* I wrap my arms about my shoulders. 'Blood Sparrow', *a bird of death or of life? If that title is mine, do I bring death, through failure? Through seasons of failing to cure my people, to hide their sign, the swirling tones of their eyes?*

'..*songs of life to a people long in darkness. Songs of healing through the Sparrow, the Blood Sparrow...*' *A bird of death, or life?*

A bolt of sunlight cuts in shafts through the trees, spearing through the deep clouds, gold and fire bright. It catches in each plant along the hillside, in the small green leaves of the new life there, late larkspur flowers starkly purple beneath the fading sun. The clouds are edging red, red beneath the pink-gold of the light. It brushes each branch of each tree dancing over the shifting leaves.

Blood Sparrow. My skirts swirl, snap softly in the winds. *I am no Blood Sparrow. I have failed my people for long enough. Five turnings and more. The seasons my fár waited. Now, another fortnight is lost, since the soldiers came to my door. Another moon half gone of the warm times, the times I can fight for them.*

'Keep this hidden, Eness. This tends only toward death.' My mother's words are sharp-edged in time.

A gift toward death, or life? A song of healing, for only a few? I have hidden this longer than the queen has been on the throne, longer than the prince has been gone, the king slain. A song of death, or life?

I tighten my arms about my waist, lift my head, and the sunlight is bright across my eyes. "Creator." The air is still. "Elnial, please, grant me wisdom. I have hidden this. Have I hidden it in vain, in selfish gain all these months?"

The wind rustles, blooms of the larkspur swaying in the reddening light. "Will You save my people? You Who made them, please bring them back from the brink of death and redeem their blood. I can do nothing if You do not open the way. My efforts have all fallen on empty lands, and You have seen each one die. Please," My voice cracks, wind ripping through the branches. "Please save them. Please bring me to somewhere that I can help and not hide away for my own life, and show me if I am to use this gift or to tuck it away into darkness. I have hidden it. Have I hidden it in vain? Have I failed by hiding it, failed Your people?"

My throat is thick, the sunlight fading in the trees, a cloud rolling over the sun. My eyes flicker through the trees, burn. "I will offer my life up, if only You show me the way that I should go. Please, save this people from the hand of death. Save my people, for they are Yours. Have they not always been? Redeem this country from the hands that rip it apart. Please, Elnial, redeem these peoples. All of them from this darkness."

The wind whips again and my skirts snap, the trees only half-coated in pale reddening light. I glance down the hill. Something pale moves, between the branches of an elm tree. *A doe.* She caught in the light of the trees for a breath, her head lifted, eyes alert. She flicks her tail and is gone, stepping forward into the long green shadows.

"Excuse me." My eyes snap over my shoulder. There is a man, standing not three paces from me, hay caught in his hair, his eyes warm, uncertain. Strands of hair have fallen over them, over the smudges of dirt on his skin. "I do not intend to intrude, but it would be wise to turn back inside." He twitches his hands, the movement nervous. "I do not recognize you, so I imagine you might not want to be out in the woods after dark, if you do not know the way around them well. A pardon if I am wrong. I just wanted to offer advice, if you are."

I glance back out, over the hills, and the doe is out of sight. The light is nearly gone, clouds still churning red and dark. I incline my head. "Thank you." There are steps behind me, fading out.

I turn. The man is gone, door to the stables open, a light inside. There is a voice in the distance, humming a song, off key and strange. I step toward the fortress. The wind whispers through the trees, gentle with evening, but there is a note to it that tastes of storms. I grip the door, pull it open. Wind rips sharply, pulling at it. I step inside, drag it shut.

Voices catch in the hall, speaking in even tones not far from me. I glance up.

Fitzclaste, the gold man, Ciaran, the goblin, and another man whom I do not know are all standing not three strides from me. The goblin is near the back, his eyes on the men beside him. *Not on me.*

Fitzclaste looks up. "Healer." His brow lifts. "Did you not stay for the music? The harper is a renowned one, skilled in his craft and in lore. He is more than worth the evening. You might head back that way now. I thought you would have stayed to hear it, if you were there."

More than worth listening to. I incline my head, a bow, press a strand of hair back from my cheek. "I wanted some air before the sun set. Today was long, below the stairs. I am not used to being cooped up for so long below the earth."

Fitzclaste half-smiles, bobbing his head. "I am glad to see you outside. I had some concern that the guards might have troubled you.

I had heard there was some confusion about whether or not you were to be allowed outdoors." He nods again, turning back toward the conversation. "If you will excuse us. We have some matters to discuss."

I bow, toward the circle as a whole, and step away, up the hall. The goblin is ducking into a room, the shelves beyond lined with something small and oddly shaped. *Books. And scrolls.* I step past, and the door swings shut, their words gone with it.

My eyes widen. *Books. I have never seen so many in one place. Not a quarter so many. There must have been fifty, just on the shelves I could catch sight of through the door. Will they have any of the healing scripts?* The door shuts.

There is a woman moving up the hall, her steps even, eyes alight. *Anna, small and bright.* I turn away, start up the hall toward my quarters.

XX

The Blood Sparrow

There is a woman, standing in the doorway, a cough wracking her form. She presses her hand against her lips, looking away. I lift my head and she turns back, her eyes watering, hand on her chest. She smiles at me, a watery smile, stepping forward into the room. "Goodeven."

I smile. "Goodeven to you. May I help you?"

Her pale skin flushed below her watering eyes, her dark hair falling out of place, half-down. She inclines her head. "I was looking for Eerol. Is he here?" Her voice is high, hoarse, like someone torn by the cold seasons. *It is past time for this kind of illness, with the growing moons so far come.*

I set down the pot, dust my hands upon my apron. "Aye. I will find him for you, if you will but wait a moment. You may take a seat." I gesture toward the chair beside the arch, and turn. Eerol is behind me, only a step away, moving through the doorway of the second room.

He half-smiles at the woman, the corners of his eyes crinkling into a thousand lines. "Nellie. That cough again?" *The name is familiar, has been spoken often here.* My eyes flicker to her. She is young, not more than a few turnings my senior, if any. Her skin is pale, eyes dark, face soft, her frame slender. There is a puff of flour, pale against the dark fabric of her skirts.

She is nodding, smiling sheepishly. "La. I did not expect it so soon but I'm wondering if the trees didn't get to it this mornin'. They always make it worse, when they bloom." She smiles ruefully, stepping further into the room. *She is tall, taller than the healing man.*

I step backward, move toward my work, and lift a crock from the shelf. I pull the lid from it, and the sweet scent of lavender drifts out. *Her accent is strange, foreign, thick.*

Eerol nods, his head bobbing up and down. His gaze flickers toward me. "Eness, would you grab that soothing tea, there?" He gestures toward the shelves, a wide, vague movement. I glance at the shelves of teas, beside the fire. I grab a tall, slender one and set it on the table beside him.

He steps up beside me, a small bag in one hand, shoving back the sleeves of his shirt with the other. He shuffles, lifting the pot from me, pouring it sideways into the bag, and turns back to Nellie. His hand twists it closed. "This with a little honey should do, as you know. Is your throat alright today? You did not let it get bad this time before coming down?"

She smiles, nodding again. "La. I came down before it got worse enough for that. I'm hoping the tea helps keep it from getting bad this time. I do not want a repeat of last strále. And I know you'd be havin' words if I did." She inclines her head. "Thank you, Heal-E." She takes the bag from him and inclines her head, appreciation. *Heal-E. The name many of the children call him.* There is familiarity in her humor toward him.

The healing man nods back, smiling. "What are you all making up in the kitchen for tonight? Stew again, ey?" *Making. She is the woman Tejan said on the first night tended the kitchens, made the food for each day. They have spoken of her much since.* I glance at her. *She is young to have full charge of them, unless she has been here for many, many moons.*

She shakes her head, moving backward, and her steps easy and light. "Gót. I'm making another hash tonight. One I made up a few days ago, and I think you'll like it. The rosemary and basil are high enough to use now and we harvested some new onions in the fields.

I am hopin' to use those, to mix them with some fresh ginger for th' potatoes."

Her eyes flicker to me. She inclines her head, a small movement, respect to someone unknown. "You must be the new healing kúráh. I am Nellie." She extends her hand.

I set the herbs down and take her wrist, grasp it. "Eness Finch. And it is good to meet you. You do your task well, kúráh."

She smiles, something like pride flickering through her gaze. I withdraw my wrist. "Well, thank yo'. It is a good task, keeping the kitchen runnin', and an easy one too with so many hands eager to aid. The others, I think, do more of the work than I. I only manage and make plans."

She smiles again, softly, and turns toward the archway. "Thank you, Heal-E, Eness. I will look for you in the hall at the next watch. Goodeven to you." She steps through the archway, vanishing into the staircase, the tea bag held in her hand.

Eerol glances at me, shaking his head. I wait. He shakes his head again, his smile gone, pressing a hand to his leg. "I'd bet it'll rain today."

I frown, pick up a pinch of lavender, and drop it into the mortar. "Does it look to, or does your leg tell you of it?"

He grunts, grinning toward me, a savage grin. "Nie. A civ with a cough tells me that we will have more visitors, and my back tells me it will rain. My leg tells me only that I am old." He grins again, turning away. "It never rains, but it dumps, and this last half a fortnight since you arrived has been far too quiet. Watch it. There will be others today, some of them mud coated, if I am not mistaken." He grunts. "And I'm not. Doing this far too long to be wrong today. Nellie is always the harbinger, though a sweet one. She is too kind to me." He grunts again.

I half-smile, my eyes flickering toward the fire. "I will watch then." The flames are crackling beneath the pots, the two of them hanging together over the fire, both heavy with thick green juices of plants long dead and revitalized. I flick my eyes back to the healing man. He is pulling cloth strips from a basket, measuring them with the length of his arm. I lift the lavender crock. "Do you not go out for new herbs when lív comes in? It is fully here now."

He glances at me and back to his work. "Aye. I do. But we've had a quiet one so far. Plants are slow to grow and I am slow to move. I'll move quicker when they do." He glances up at me again, beneath his wiry, large brows. "Are you wanting to get out there, or are you ascertaining my actions?"

I pinch up the ground lavender, dust it across the bowl. "I am doing neither. I am only surprised to see you so much indoors, when the seasons are alive. I did not get a good sight of the world out there, but it seemed to me that your season of lív cannot be much behind ours back home, and ours was nearly in full stride, like a deer at run. When I was out last even, yours seemed to have come. But you will know these woods better than I do."

He grunts, slicing through the strip of fabric. "You can go out tomorrow, gather some, if you like. I will speak with the goblin."

I look up. "With the goblin?"

He glances at me, grunts. "Oh, aye. He asked to be told before you are sent outside." My eyes burn. He looks up, his eyes softening. "Just in case something happens to you, lai. You are free to go, from their word, they only ask to know. I forgot to tell you, I spoke with Lord Fitz and Sradfaang last evening. They said you are free to roam, but that there had been a misunderstanding with the watchmen and Lord Fitz."

I half-smile. *Is it still freedom if the goblin or someone else must be told each time?*

He lifts a brow, setting the fabric to the side, strips cut. "Is it the outdoors or the herbs you miss, lai?"

I half-smile, and it twists on my lips. "The wind. But I have missed harvesting also. Will that still be asked of me, when the goblin leaves for the ranks?"

He shakes his head. "I do not know. But I think he plans to stay a while longer, something to do with Ciaran and orders with you. There is always something to be done here, always something for him to do at least. He is a strategist like no other and Ciaran likes to make use of him in the rare time we get him. Fitz has had a time of it getting him here, and I trust that now that he is, he will stay a spell or two whether he wishes it or not." He snorts, and looks back up at me. "But from what he said to you, I gathered he will not be due back at the ranks for another half-fortnight. That is plenty of time for them to cook up a scheme or two. If he and that captain have not already done so."

I set the lid back on the crock. *From what he said to me?* Eerol glances at me. I lift a brow. "How did you hear him speak with me?" *He spoke with me while the others were at supper, in the hall above.*

Eerol inclines his head, turning away. "I came halfway down the stairs before I realized you were speaking and it was not a conversation I wanted to overhear. But I did learn that you would be staying, for now at least. And that he was assigned to you and did not just bring you in at random. That's a story I'd like to hear."

He snorts again, laughing. "A Goldtide officer getting assigned to a peasant is something I'd like to have seen. That would have been a funny order for an officer to have to give." My eyes twist. He lifts a brow. "If it is the conversation you are worried about, I don't repeat to anyone the words I hear anywhere, unless they prove useful, and those weren't. I am glad you are staying for as long as you will, healer. I already knew of your heritage and reluctance. There was nothing new in the words spoken."

I force a smile, look down to the carved stones of the floor. There are leaves across them, fallen from the table, broken, crushed into the stone. Fragments of them are scattered across it, tiny bits.

Eerol is humming to himself. I slow my step across the floor. *Humming the song of the prophecy, the poem.* A shudder crawls up my spine. I turn away, step through the archway, into the room beyond, and the notes of his humming follow me. '*…Cruelty shall end in freedom…*'

•▶|◀▶|◀▶|◀▶|◀▶|◀▶|◀•

A step falls on the ground behind me, hard. I turn, the pot in my hand, speak. "Eerol—"

A man is just inside the threshold, his blood-soaked hand against his side, his eyes glazed, unfocused. He steps forward, staggers. *He is going to fall.* The pot crashes to the table and I lunge forward—he sways. My hands barely grip his arm, barely pull him up. I stagger, and he is pulling me, dragging me downward, his weight heavy across my arms.

My knee slams against the floor, the man draped over my legs, his head lolling back toward the stones.. There is something slick against my leg, damp. *Blood. Creator help.* My eyes burn, swirl. He is murmuring, speaking words, jumbled, and slurred together. "...Eerol, Eerol... it wasn't meant to... blades...I fell..."

I press my hand against his side, and there is blood, thick against my fingers. *If I lift my hand to inspect the wound, he will continue to lose blood. This is too much. But if I do not, I cannot tend to it anymore than this.* I press my fingers down harder. "Do not move, sonyá. Eerol is not here." Blått barks behind me.

The man shakes his head against my knee, his eyes rolling back. His hand goes limp beside mine.

My eyes snap to his face. He is pale, too pale. *Unconscious.* I slide him down, against the ground, my heart thudding. My hand is coated, blood oozing through my fingers from his side. I lift it for just a moment, pull back the fabric from the wound, and my heart slows.

I press my hand back into place. *A blade wound. If it was a knife, it should not have been pulled out, not until help was near at hand. Not until it could have been staunched immediately.* I draw in a breath and my heart pounds in my ears. *This man is bleeding out.*

I lift my head, lift my voice. "Eerol?!" The word is muffled in the room, moving nowhere against the stone walls. I suck in a breath, my hand heavy on the wound, his form heavy against my legs. There is no sound, no steps. No aid. *This man is dying.* Blått barks again, still steps away from me. "Eerol?!"

There is no sound, but Blått's scratching and the man's heavy breaths.

I can save him.

I bow my head, my jaw tightening, and my heart slows, the world slowing. *"The time has come..." Creator, please help me. If I wield it, let no one know.* My eyes flicker to the man's face.

What else can be done? I cannot take my hand from the wound. I can save him. He was too far gone before he walked through the door for anything else, without aid. '..the time is yet at hand...'

I lift my voice, curl the note of the song upward, high, clear. It rings along the pots, along the walls, echoing like no words do here, below the earth. I curve it down, press my hand harder against his side. His head tosses, eyes fluttering beneath his eyelids—I drop the note, bring it down further, and it drifts along, slow, quiet. I keep it there, lulling it, trilling it, and his breath is gentler, chest no longer rising and falling like the end of a death race. *Heal only enough to save, sing enough to heal.* I curve the song, and my hand is shaking, neck aching. I lift my head, swing off the last note, the end where it should be, and there is color in his skin, in his face again. I draw in a breath, breathe it out. *He is healed enough, beneath the red.* I end the last note. Silence echoes in the room. My breaths slip.

"Oh, lands." *A voice.* I spin hard. Eerol is only a step behind me, a broom in his hands, stilled beside Blåthjortt. His eyes are wide, on the man on the ground beside me, his aged hands tightening against the broomstick.

I shift the man toward the floor, gently, move toward my feet—the world swirls. My hand snaps around the edge of the table, palm digging into it. I press my eyes shut, pulse hammering in my ears. "Eerol." I force my eyes open, and the world is still curling at the edges of my vision with darkness. My skull throbs. "He..." *He was dying?*

His eyes are on the man on the floor. He swears sharply, dropping to his knees beside him, and his hands prod at the wound, slowly, as though it may bite him. He swears again, eyes hidden beneath his brows. "What did you do to him?"

I shake my head. "I... It was..." the world is curling at the edges again. I drop onto my knees. My hands are shaking against the table, blood coated. "Creator..."

"Healer?" I force my eyes to open, and he is looking back at the man again, worry written across his features. He shakes his head, swiping a cloth across the wound beneath the torn shirt. The blood smears, the wound closed beneath it, a dark red rim around its edges, where it once was.

He hisses out a breath. "You did this with a song? With your voice? Could you not just have been a normal healer? A normal woodland woman come to stay?" He shakes his head. "But of course you did not choose this." He looks down again, tossing the cloth to the floor. It slaps dully, loud in the room. His eyes lift to my hands, to the floor, and the blood-soaked puddle upon it. "This is a cursed lot of blood. Lands filth."

I swallow, press my hand against my skirts. It smears there, leaving a trail of blood. "Who will you tell?"

His eyes snap to mine beneath his brows, his head lifting. "Tell?"

I nod, drop backward against the floor. "Aye, tell. The soldiers..."

His eyes sharpen. "Soldiers? The soldiers of the queen are the last lots I'd want to speak with about this. I wouldn't like to know what the queen would try to do with this gift, if she knew of it. She's the bloody last person I would like to inform, Creator take her." My eyes burn and he is still speaking, kneeling by the man in the pool of blood. "I have told you, I tell no one what I hear, and I am not going to tell anyone this, lai. It is your secret to keep, and I would not like to imagine what any of the rulers would do with you, if they were ever to catch you. I will not tell a single soul." His eyes soften, and mine burn, heart easing. He looks down at the blood again and swears. "Shadows of the west. You healed him with a song?" His eyes lift back to mine.

I incline my head, swallow hard. *How long has it been since that last one? Seven turnings?* "Aye. Creator help me, aye."

He nods, his eyes wandering back to the man on the floor, his face pale. "He must have, for this to have been done. This is not a gift that has been seen in..." His head shakes. "Lands filth. Does the goblin know of this? Fitz? The man can keep a secret from the north winds if he chose to..."

I shake my head sharply. "Gót. He does not and does not need to know. There is no call for anyone beyond this room to know. I would keep this secret, if you will give me that."

The man stirs on the floor. Eerol looks up at me, dropping back on his heels, his hand coated red with blood. "This thing, you might consider trusting someone with, civ. This is the kind of thing that could change kingdoms, move the tides of war. A gift in healing has not been seen in time unmemorable, since the ancient days. Elnial has rarely gifted those. But you will have reasons to keep it silent. This has not been seen since legends... Snakes in shoes...."

He shakes his head again. "I would not like to see the queen get her darkened hands on you, either." His eyes meet mine, head shaking. He presses his hands against his knees. "I will not tell anyone without your bidding, you have my word, and it is gladly given."

He nods toward my hands. "Wash those and help me move him, if you can. If not, I will get a man from upstairs to get him to a cot. Lands filth." His head is shaking, eyes on the wound again. "We will need to bandage the wound..."

I nod and shake my head, and I do not know what I'm doing. *'Cruelty shall lead to freedom...'* The world is spinning at the edges. I turn, move toward the fire, and my steps sway. *'...until the Blood Sparrow sings...songs of healing...a people long in darkness...'* I press my hands hard against the rim of the water bucket, slow the swaying of the world. My breaths slow. *No one has known in seasons long gone. Not since the death of my family.* I dip my hand into the water, scrub it against the side. The blood drifts off in dark flecks, swirling in the water. It tints pink. *My eyes will be yellow now, gold around the edges.*

The healer huffs out a breath behind me. "What in the stars…" I half-turn, hand still in the bucket. His eyes are on the wound, a cloth in his hand, wet. "This red ring…" his hand is tracing something around the wound. "Is this from the wound? It's not from blood. It has not had long enough to settle like this. It is not coming off."

I shake my head and grimace at the movement. "It has come with every wound I have healed in that way. The red rim. It comes with the healing."

He raises a brow, his head tilting half-sideways. "And you have healed many this way? How did you plan to keep this hidden if you have used it?"

I shake my head, turn toward him sharply. "I have not used it more than five times. I have lived alone, as I said, for many turnings now, and I have tried to keep it quiet, keep the time I used it few and far between." Water spatters against my feet. I look down. It is dripping off my soaked hands. I cup them together, continue. "It would not have been wise to let word of it get out, not even to a few. There have only ever been three that knew. Those that I healed were always unconscious, always near death." I set my hands back in the bucket, keep my gaze on him.

He glances at me. "As he was?"

I incline my head, swallow. "Aye. As he was."

He puffs out a breath, setting his hand on his knees once more. "Aye. That will not do. You will keep your secret. But the course you have chosen may not have been wise, these last few turnings. Living on your own in a war-torn land may not be the wisest choice with your bloodline if you are intending to keep this secret in the long run, until it is over, unless you planned to take it with you to your grave to hide it. It will only be a matter of time before they find you again, and one, if not the other of your secrets will be found out. Then your gift will be used, or it will be futile. You would be better off trusting someone with it, to help to guard this. Someone would be wise to tell, but hiding a gift of the Creator seems a foolhardy thing."

I tighten my lips, set my hands against the side of the bucket. "In the telling, there is a greater chance that the word will slip, that another will know, and how long will it take to get back to someone who would abuse it? It was not by my own reckoning that this was kept silent, though the council is old. If the queen were to find out, she would not merely use me. I would become a weapon in her hands, keeping her soldiers alive while others died. I would be as a chained hound, doomed to wait out my days at her bidding. There is no wisdom in sharing it that I can see, not even to share it with you."

He looks up, his eyes sharp. "Then you will keep it. I have given you my word. My mouth will speak of it to no one, not without your bidding. But I also give what advice I have. Secrets grow heavy with the hiding, and this one will grow to effect more than you in the keeping, or in the sharing. The choice is yours."

He turns away, swearing again. "We will have to bandage this wound for at least half a fortnight, if not longer, to keep questions from being asked. He is not cavene for the quick healing of his blood, so we cannot blame it on that. Shikes, that is a lot of blood. Nor on any herb or drink that I know of that can heal to match this. He will have to be kept from seeing it until it is healed further."

I nod my head, press my hands against my apron. "Then we will keep it bandaged." *I should have sung for less time.* There is still blood across the tan of my apron, smeared against its fabric. *'Cruelty shall lead to freedom…' And now the Sparrow has sung again.*

Eerol stands, and the man on the ground groans, his wounds healed.

XXI

Pounding Feet

There is a sound in the hallway, steps, fast and sharp.

"Eerol?!" The voice is alarmed, a man's voice. My eyes burn, head spins. Eerol's hand is already moving, pressing a cloth over the wound. He turns toward me. "Grab the wound staunch powder. Quickly. Go." I spin toward the shelf and my hand snatches at the crock, blue for wound care. It is slick, slipping through my water-damp fingers. I clasp my other hand beneath it, turn toward Eerol, and there is a figure bolting into the room.

Eerol snatches the crock from my hand, and the man's eyes snap up from the floor, to him. "Skies to heavens. What has happened here? There is blood from the armory room—" his voice cuts off. "Tulé. What did he do?" Some of the panic leaks from his face, his hand relaxing on his sword.

Eerol shakes his head. His hand is still on the wound, pressing as though it were still bleeding, as though it could still bleed. "We do not know. But the healer was quick and he will recover well enough. Some of this blood is water from the basin there, so it is not so bad as it looks." He shifts his weight. "Jons. Help me lift him. Since you are here in a hurry, you might as well be some use." Blått moves to the side as the healer speaks, walking away into the rooms beyond. He stretches out beside the fire and drops down.

The man—Jons—glances at me, his gaze sharp. I twist my hands into my apron, dry them. He steps forward, his hand moving away from his sword hilt. He is tall, broadly built, his eyes dark, figure moving with the sharp precision of a soldier or a hunting man. He stoops, slipping his hands beneath the wounded man's shoulder, and Eerol grunts, moving to his feet slowly. He grips the unconscious man's ankles, and they stand together, moving slowly around the table, into the room beyond, and the cots waiting there.

I stoop, lift the staunching crock from the floor, and the world swirls, jolting. My hand snaps around the table, grips it. I press my eyes shut. *Stars.* The world slows and there are voices in the other room, Eerol and Jons, speaking in even tones, about blood and weapons and an armory room. *They keep an armory here. I should have guessed, in a fort this large.* I glance over the table.

Jons' face is impassive in the room beyond, his eyes fixed on something behind the door frame beside the head of a cot. His arms are folded across his chest, jaw set. "Where is the weapon? I'd have that, before I look into this and report to Lord Fitz. Knowing Tulé, there was likely no foul play."

Eerol steps around the bed, his hands working against a darkened cloth. "Eness. There was not a blade?" He lifts a brow, then shakes his head, swiping the cloth across his palm. "Of course there wasn't. You would not have pulled it without hands here to help. My apologies." He starts to turn and pauses, pressing a hand against his leg. "Was he holding one?"

I shake my head, straighten slowly. My hand is still tight on the table's edge. "There was no knife, that I saw with him. I imagine he will have dropped it above, before he came down, or in the hallway." I swallow hard. "What do you mean, no foul play? This man was soaked with blood when he came in."

Jons' eyes snap to me. He turns, his arms folded over his chest. "I mean that Tulé has more than a reputation when it comes to wounding himself."

Eerol nods. "The wound would not have been inconsistent with a fall, if he was in the armory. Who let the man on that duty anyway? Tulé is clumsier than a wet rag. I would have thought someone would have noticed that and put him to work elsewhere, where he wouldn't do harm to himself or others. Tulé in an armory is like a child in dried basket reeds."

Jons' face is still impassive, expression present nowhere around his sharp eyes or his thinly pressed lips. "I do not know. But he was not assigned to it. I know the list of men who are and he is not among them. Havard is not foolish enough to put an unskilled man on the task of cleaning blades."

He shakes his head. "I do not like conjecture. I will look into it and you may ask Fitz about it later." He inclines his head, respect and dismissal, and moves forward, past me. His eyes never flicker my way, never glance down toward the blood slicked puddle on the floor where Tulé once was.

Eerol grunts, stepping through the doorway. He presses his hands against his hip, rubbing it. "Raining. I said it would be pouring." His eyes meet mine and they soften. He turns toward me. "Do not be troubled, healer. Your secret was kept. Jons will give the report as he finds it. It will be as we have said and it will be well. They will discover what happened."

I flick my eyes to his. "And of the wound? I agree that the angle could be accidental, but I have never known a wound that severe to not be intentional."

Eerol grunts, shaking his head. "That is because you have not met Tulé. If that was done by a man, it was clumsily done. I do not think Jons was off in his guess, but he will look into it and be certain. He is a dogged man in his intentions and looking into things. He will make certain there was no foul play and seek council before he decides what likely happened, and by then, Tulé will likely be awake to speak for himself."

He shakes his head, sets the cloth down. "If you had seen the wound, you would likely agree with the thought we had. It was poorly done, and that man has a third leg that trips him when he is not looking, I'd grant. He nearly took out three women at a dance last harvest and I thought I was going to have to set ankles. But, they will look into it. There are many skilled men here when it comes to reading signs." *My song was called out by a wound of accident? One that could have been avoided, in a breath?*

I incline my head, turn back toward the table. There is blood still clinging to the crevices in my fingers, damp and dark. Eerol is moving to kneel on the floor. I shake my head. "I will clean that. You tend to your salves, Eerol."

He snorts. "I am not so aged I cannot clean a floor. You tend to yourself. Or tend those salves yourself. I will clean this floor."

I turn my head toward the stairs. There are voices echoing down it, hurried and hushed.

XXII

Harbinger

Eerol lifts his head, the knife in his hands moving across the gnarled roots. He lifts a brow. "You might put that spoon down. There is no need for it just now."

My eyes flicker toward the fire beside me, I swirl the spoon through the pot. Steam rolls off the brown liquid inside, herbs coiling beneath the surface with each turn of the spoon. "I enjoy stirring it, and it is a good passage of time."

He glances at me, shifting his legs. "Suit yourself. But when your arms are sore tomorrow, you will not be complaining to me. Blasted hot flames…" I swirl the spoon again, steam clinging to my skin. The fire crackles.

I turn my gaze back toward the healer. His head is bent, hands working at a blade in his hand, shaving down the ends of a root. His eyes are focused, brows low, heavy, nearly covering up all that there is of his sunken eyes.

He lifts a brow, gaze still on his work. "Are you staring at my head or my work, civ? Either way, do not tell me. I quite enjoy the attention once and awhile and saying something would spoil it."

My back snaps upright. I shake my head, a laugh pulling at my lips. "I was staring at neither, only wondering how long you all have dwelt here. I am still trying to piece together this place."

His eyes lift to mine, a heavy brow raising. He grunts. "You'll be piecing together for a while, if you only ask question by staring at men's heads." He turns his eyes back toward the knife in his hand, slicing through another root, his cut faultless. He tilts his head. "Dwelt here, ey? Several turnings at least. Cannot quite recall. It's been a spell, and blast it if the days do not roll together down here into one."

I brush my hands against my skirts, swipe the moisture from my skin. *So long that he would not remember, or is his memory so bad?* "What brought you to this place, so far from anywhere known?"

He lifts a brow, eyes meeting mine slowly. "It is not so far from anywhere known. It is only far from anywhere large enough to be a bother. That is the work of it." He lifts the fabric for another cut. "I do not think you want to be troubling about my past, civ, unless you would like me troubling about yours. Best keep to safer conversations." He grins, a twisted grin.

I fold my hands. "There is little about my life that I would not tell, that you do not already know, healer. What safer conversations would you keep to?"

He looks up sharply. A grin pulls at his lips. "Lai. There you go. I don't know. But there is still little about my life that I would tell you. It is best left to its own. How is Tulé today?"

I shake my head, wring my hands through my skirts. They are still damp, cooling now from the steam. "I have not seen him since he left his cot, two dawns past. Shall I seek him out now?"

He lifts a brow, slowing the knife. "Well, the bugger didn't come like I told him to. I'll be finding him at mealtime next and he'll get a word or two. Or maybe I'll just watch him. That'll get him thinking fit enough to stop him from staying away from where he ought to be. I'd like to watch him squirm in his seat for a few breaths. Tarnish it, he should have gotten that wound checked." He mutters something low, knife still working at the end of the short root. He lifts his head. "Or we could set the hound on him." He glances at Blått. Blått's tail knocks against the floor, his head still between his paws, excitement in his eyes. Eerol snorts. "The hound would like as not just kiss his hand. Not setting that hound on anyone." He mutters something.

I laugh, lift a cloth from the table. "Has Tulé seen the wound yet, that you have seen?"

He looks up at me once more, hands working again. "If I have not seen him, I could not know to tell you." He snorts. "I told the bugger not to take the wrap off, but I also told him to come see you this morning. He could have tossed aside both instructions as likely as one. I doubt he will have taken off the bandage though. Do not worry. I am only a tart old man. If he has seen the wound, he will not know what it means other than that it is a good excuse to not come see you or I. He'll think he got lucky."

My eyes flicker back to the pot, jaw tightens. I swipe the cloth across the table, brush the scattered remnants of leaves into my hand. *And if he does know enough to ask questions, who will he question about the sudden healing? Eerol or I? Or will he only speak of it to those he knows, the word of a miraculous healing floating around these halls. That is how rumors begin, and how they grow. I have sown out the seeds for both and cannot check it, not now. I would not have ended his life to keep them back.*

I brush the leaves off faster, the pile in my palm growing. *Curse it. He should have come back down or stayed. There is nothing to be done for it now but to wait again. To wait and see what word will have spread through these halls.*

•▶|◀▶|◀▶|◀▶|◀▶|◀▶|◀•

I move to step onto the stairs and freeze, my eyes widening. There is a woman, high on them. One of her hands is clutching her swollen stomach, swollen with child. There is another woman beside her, one that I have seen before. *Nieave. The woman who sent the goblin after me all those evenings ago.* I plant my foot back on the floor, Blått's head nuzzling damp against my elbow. "Is her time here?" I ask.

Nieave looks down at me, her braid neatly falling over her shoulder, hands supporting the other woman. "I believe so. She is near and she says her pains have become regular just in the last half a watch. We have come for Eerol."

I step onto the stairs, pause. *There is no good way for me to help her here, but to make sure she does not fall.* I take another step up the stairs and I am just below the woman with child. She straightens, only a little, her hand still cradling her stomach. "You must be Eness. I have heard much of you." Her voice is tight, a small smile brushing her lips. Her eyes are alert, bright.

I force a smile to my lips, incline my head. "I am. Would you like to come down?"

She grimaces, shaking her head. "Gót. We were to do this in our own rooms, upstairs. I should not have tried to come alone, but I wanted to get Eerol upstairs before they became as regular as they have, and it seems I am too late. I should have called someone sooner to go…" Her voice cuts out and she grimaces, looking down.

I lift my eyes to Nieave, and look back at her. "Has your water broken?" She nods, her lips pursed. I flick my eyes up the staircase, slip my hand slowly underneath her arm. "How far are your rooms from here?"

She shakes her head. "Just two halls over. But I cannot tell how close we are to the child coming. This is my first. Where is Eerol? Is he not here?" There is fear in her voice, her eyes brighter now, alarmed.

I shake my head. "Gót. He is upstairs, in a meeting room, but I will fetch him. Can you make it back to your rooms, with Nieave's help?" She nods, moving her hands again along her stomach.

I glance up the staircase. *It would be unwise to leave her here, on the steps with only one woman for aid if she falls.* I tighten my grip on her arm, drop my voice. *Let it be soothing.* "Let us get you to the top of the stairs and then I will run for Eerol, and you may head back to your rooms to prepare and rest before the child is here." She nods, her jaw tight, and half-turns back. Her steps are awkward, shuffling on the stair. *Creator, let the child still have time left in the womb today.* I keep my hand beneath her arm. She plants her foot on the floor of the hall and I lift my eyes to hers. "Will you be alright now?"

She nods, and Nieave is echoing it, her gaze steady, firm. "Aye." Nieave hands are gentle, both on the woman's arm now, supporting and helping, watchful. Careful. *Is that her nature, to be always watchful? Sradfaang said as much.*

I move away. "I am going for Eerol. Will he know the way to your rooms?" She nods again, turning. I glance at Nieave, and she nods. I look back down the stairs. The hound is still at the bottom of them, his tail wagging, eyes alert. I shake my head, click my tongue. "Stay."

Nieave lifts her head, her eyes meeting mine as I turn. "Her name is Amalie. He knows her time is near. I will stay with her until he arrives and as long as I am needed." There is warning in her eyes, hurry. I incline my head, turn up the hall. *Eerol said he was going to the meeting room, beside the library. If he is not there, then there will be someone to ask for directions to the healer before her time has come in force.*

I pick up my pace, move up the hall. A man steps to the side. His eyes follow me, curious. "Is all well?" I nod back at him, move around the corner, and he is gone. I clutch my skirts in my hand, move faster around the next corner. There are two women in the hallway, another man behind them, carrying something. I angle past them, keep my eyes forward. The women say nothing, barely moving to let me by, their conversation still flowing, murmurs in the hallways.

The door is ahead, dark in the shadows of its frame. I stop beside it. The door is shut, voices faint beyond it. I knock twice, sharply.

The voices halt. There is no new sound beyond it, no sound but the voices of the women in the hallway, beyond the corner, and the steps of the man, heavy on the floors.

I press my hand against my skirts. The door creaks, opens, and there is a man—Jons of the impassive face. I step to the side, foot moving around him. His shoulder swings out sharply, blocking my way. I step back. His brows lower. "What do you need here? You cannot get in that way." His voice is sharp, hard, his brows dark lines.

I draw back, raise my eyes to his. "I am looking for Eerol, and it is of some importance, or I would not trouble you. You know my task here. I would not come here idly."

His squared jaw tenses, form not moving from across the doorframe. A voice calls out. "Let her through, Jons." The voice is clear, even, that of Ciaran. Jons raises a brow, his eyes still on me. He steps to the side.

Eerol is by a table, Ciaran and Fitz beside him with two other men I have only seen in the great hall and Sradfaang. The table is spread with papers, conversation quieted. Many of the papers are maps, maps of colors and threads and skilled work.

I keep my eyes away from them, on the healing man. *I have not come here to snoop.* "Eerol, Amalie is asking for you. Her time is near. She is heading back to her rooms now to wait there."

He lifts a bushy brow, hand still on the table. "And can you not sit with her for a spell? You have delivered children before, I would expect. I will be done here as soon as I am able, but in the meantime it would be well for me to continue."

I incline my head—respect. "I have delivered many children, but she is anxious for you. I am unknown. It has been turnings since I last delivered a child, as you will imagine. I can go to her, but she may not have long and this is her first. She has asked for you."

His jaw tightens and he turns toward the golden man beside him. "It is and she mayn't. Ciaran, I am asking your leave. We will have to finish this later, or you will have to go on without me. That may be the better option. I do not want to leave the civ in a lurch, and I do not know how long she may be. It could be many watches for a first time."

Ciaran nods his head, his hair shifting, bound at the base of his neck. "Go. We will do what we can, and the rest will wait a few watches for you. Amalie will not." A half-smile pulls at his lips. "Wish her well from us. I'll send someone to get Caj off of watch duty and send him that way." He nods to one of the men on the edges of the room and the man starts off, slipping past me through the doorway.

Eerol grins, lifting a bag from the floor at the edge of the room. "Well then, we crave your prayers, and if all goes well and she is as far along as the healer thinks, I will see you in the hall tonight for whatever Nellie has cooked up."

Ciaran half-bows, a smile drawing at his lips, and the goblin mirrors him behind his shoulder.

Eerol turns toward me, his steps quick now. I move through the door, behind him. He pauses in the hallway, glancing back at me, and he angles the strap of his satchel against his shoulder. "You will keep an eye on the healing rooms while I am gone, aye?"

I nod. "Aye. But I will follow you first. I would know where her rooms are, in case you have need of anything in the time you are there."

He smiles, appreciation in his eyes, and his steps start up the hallway, faster now. "This way then." He turns.

I glance at him, my steps struggling to match his stride. His steps are quick and long, though he is not tall. I lift my skirts, over my feet, pick up my pace. "Have there been many children born here in the time since you arrived, all those turnings ago?"

He laughs, bobbing his head. "Na. Six or seven these last four turnings. A few of them you have seen running around in the halls in the evenings. Their families have been in hiding for a long spell, usually over guarding someone like you." My eyes snap to him, burn. He inclines his head, turning up a hall. "They are here for that, among other things. I cannot tell you all. I do not know all, nor ask why everyone comes. I only look to their well-being when they come to me, so as to how many, if you want to know, I do not know. You could ask."

I shake my head, lower my voice. *Words do not echo much in these halls, but it is better to be safe.* "Do they know that they hide one now, by dwelling here, with me?"

He shakes his head, his eyes focused on the hall before him. "Nie. They do not. But do not worry yourself over any of that. We have our orders, and there is just as much risk for others that are hidden here as you, and they are aware of those, most of them. Their punishment would already be great, were they found out here. You can add little to it."

What could they be hiding here, that their punishment would be no worse, for knowing a fian is in their company and not turning them in to the queen's men? Do they not fear her men? Fear the reach she has extended to the far corners of this land?

He turns up a hall, his pace slowing to pass a woman, with a small child beside her. It is a little boy, his eyes wide, seeming to take up all there is of his face. He stares up at me. I offer a smile. Eerol bobs his head beside me. "Gooddawn, Norla." He calls backward, toward the woman, his stride unbroken.

"Gooddawn, Eerol. On your way to Amalie?" She calls back to him, and he grins over his shoulder.

"Aye. That we are. Be praying! Another wee one to join the protest tonight, ey?" We turn another corner, and they are gone. I step up beside him and he slows, slowing to a door. It is only a little ways down from the one I share with Iris and Tollah. He pauses, knocking, and there is a voice inside—Nieave's, low and calm. "Come in."

He steps through, nodding to me. "I will send someone if I need you, and you may come if you have need of anything, even a question. We will like as not be sitting for a while, as you know." He grunts. "Though I doubt you will have any questions. However, it never rains but it dumps, so you may need help, and if you do, do not hesitate to find me." I nod my head, and the door closes.

My stomach sinks, dread welling in it. *Something is off. Is it for the child that I fear, for the woman, or for something more?* I move away, back up the hall toward the healing rooms, my steps slow.

I turn the corner and the woman with the little boy is near the end of the hall, walking slowly, a basket on her hip that I did not see before. I step up beside her and the child looks up at me, his eyes still wide, still taking up all of his face. I half-smile. "Gooddawn to you."

His eyes widen further, but he does shrink back, does not move toward his mother. He speaks. "Is yous the new healer?"

I half-nod, and his mother smiles. "He listens well in the meeting hall. Will you tell her gooddawn, Jørn?"

The boy half-nods. "G'even. Did you help Tulé? I seen him and hims says you did. Him said it was a kúráh and you is a kúráh."

I force a smile to my lips, incline my head. *Pray that he has said nothing more than that I helped him, that he recalls nothing more.* "Aye, some. Along with Eerol, whom you know, I think."

He nods, hair bobbing. "Aye. I knows him. But I like prettier healers better because they does not has fat eyebrows."

His mother checks his shoulder with her hip. "Jørn. Do not say rude things about the master healer." She glances over at me, her smile tighter, a long-suffering tilt to it. But there is amusement there too. "Your name is Eness, is it not?"

I incline my head, return her smile. "Aye. And yours is Norla?"

She grins and nods. "Aye. I have heard many things about you. Tulé is my husband's brother, and my husband is in the stables. He says you have a hound and that you came from the southlands? The mountains?"

I nod, force the smile to stay on my lips. *They will have been speaking of me. That is what happens in villages when newcomers arrive.* "Aye. I do. And Tulé is healing remarkably well from what I have heard, praise the Creator."

She smiles, nodding her head. "Aye. He seems to be. And he says something similar to what Jørn has just said, so it seems you will have a following here. A comely face to see goes a long way, I think, when someone is in pain or ill." She laughs. "Or at the very least, far after the seasons of Eerol's terse remarks." I half-smile and she turns to start up the other branch of the hallway. "It was good to meet you, Eness. Gooddawn to you at your work." Jørn's hand lifts, and twists to the left, a farewell of friends.

I nod back and step up the hall, back toward the rooms below. "Gooddawn to you, at yours."

XXIII

Bloodsong

Blått presses his head against my leg, his eyes watching my hands over the fire. I shift the spoon, lift a chunk of herb and press it to the side, crush it. Blått's eyes are pleading, large, the deep brown soft. He blinks at me, eyes wide and waiting. I bring my free hand down to his head, run it along his muzzle. "What is it, Blåthjortt? Do you wish to go outdoors?"

He stares, no noise, no movement, just those eyes, watchful, pleading. His tail is motionless on the floor. I look down at him. "What is it?" Dread tightens in my stomach.

There is a footfall, by the stairs. I glance over my shoulder and Blått does not move, does not stir. I press my hand hard against his head, lift the spoon from the pot into the steam above. There is a man standing beside the stairs, his hand on the wall, posture almost casual. "Eness Finch?"

I incline my head. "Aye."

His face grim, his eyes rimmed with the darkest lashes I have ever seen on a man. *Eyes like Amalie's.* He lifts a brow. "Can you ride?"

My heart stills, eyes burn, just barely. I bite it back, turn my gaze toward the pot. I hang the spoon on the rack. "Aye. But if you are looking to make a long journey, I do not think I am the one you are looking for. I have little skill in that riding, and do not wish for a long journey."

"I am not looking to make one." He steps forward, the movement exact and easy, like every move he has made since he entered the room. Dread twists tighter in my chest. "I was sent by Lord Fitz to find you. There is a scouting party missing. They are asking for a healer to travel with the men looking for them, in case there was an injury, or anything worse than that. Eerol is occupied. Will you come?"

My heart sinks, swirls. I press my hands against my apron, slowly. Blått's head is against my side, his eyes watching the man now. I turn fully toward the man. "Let me find a bag, and I will be with you." *How many bandages should be brought, for an unknown number of wounds on an unknown number men?* I move toward the bandage basket beside the shelf. "How many men were in the party?"

The man shakes his head, the gesture almost impatient. "There is a bag in the stables kept stocked. They will have it on your mount by the time we get there. Come along." I swallow, my eyes flickering toward him. His arms are folded, eyes to the side, as if listening up the stairs behind him.

I incline my head and slip the apron up, over it, the ties dragging along my wrists. I drop it against a chair and turn. "I am ready when you are. What name are you called by?"

He glances down at me, dark lashes thick. "Ágë. Ágë Holht." He inclines his head, turning away. He starts toward the stairs, his steps fast, long.

I nod, click to Blått, and he lifts his head, watching me from beside the flames now. His eyes are pleading, still wide, as if he knows something that I do not, as if he senses something I cannot see. I click again, a command. "Stay, Blåthjortt. Stay." The hound drops his head, curling up by the flames, his eyes on me, until they are gone behind the archway.

I turn back toward Ágë. He is starting up the stairs, his steps even, taking them fast, and he is at the top long before me. I clutch my skirts in my hands, push my steps faster. *There will be need for hurry, if the men have been missing long. I do not know how many watches they have been gone for.* I step up, into the hall, and he is already moving again, halfway up the hall. I move after him. There is laughter up, catching on the walls, a woman's laugh.

I lift my head. "How long has the party been missing?"

He pulls a door open, gesturing for me to go through. "Half a watch."

I step into the next hallway. "And how long have they been gone?"

He pulls the door shut, stepping by me again. "Two and a half watches. They were on patrol, were to be gone two full watches. The rest you will have from Havard." He steps around a corner, pulling another door open ahead of us.

I blink, darkness ahead where light should be, outside of Sikkerhet. *The stables.* The air reeks of dust, of aged grasses, and something heavy and earth toned. There is a shaft of sunlight, bright, cutting through the crack of a shutter tied haphazardly closed. Dust dances through the light beam, wind calling, and the building creaks beneath it. A strand of hay drifts through the light, gone again into the shadows.

Ágë is moving forward, cutting through the stream of light, his steps sure in the sudden strange dark where no torch stands. I step after him, around the edge of a stall. There is a snort—a horse—and the whine of a hound dog, many steps tramping somewhere deeper in the building. Ágë steps around a corner, and there are voices ahead, precise, sharp. He pauses and my eyes strain to adjust in the dark.

A figure turns out from the rest—Fitz—a small shaft of light catching on his eyes. He glances at me, and moves his eyes to rest on the other man. "You are ready and she has come then. Good." His eyes meet Ágë's. "I am sorry to ask this of you today. We can find someone else, if you would stay to be near at hand. You may trade posts with one of the men on watch upstairs." There are several men moving behind him, lifting saddles to horses in the darkness of the room.

Ágë shakes his head sharply. "I will not shirk from my post. You have asked. I will go. Amalie does not need me near. She has Caj."

Fitz inclines his head again. "If you are certain. Your sister will be well cared for while you are gone."

Ágë nods again, and Fitz turns away. His sister. Why do they ask this of him, that he would go to the woods while she is in labor? Could not another man go in his stead, if there is danger in this?

A figure moves behind Fitz, stepping out of the shadows of the stalls. *The goblin.*

Fitz steps forward, around us, and his stride does not break. "Then follow me." *He is shorter up close than I remembered, head only just above the shoulder of the man beside me.* Ágë turns, following him back the way we came. "You will stay in a group until you see some sign. Splitting up is not like to do any good, and it increases the potential for more casualties, if there are any. I will send out another party if we do not see you within a watch." Ágë nods, the motion sharp. *One watch. There will be barely that much light left in the sky, by now.*

Fitz's eyes flicker to me. "Sradfaang informs me that you only recently learned to ride. Will you be well enough on a mount again? I trust that Ágë told you where you will be going."

I shake my head, stepping after him. "He informed me that we will be looking for missing scouts. And I am not fond of animals, but aye, I can ride well enough to go where need be."

He nods, the movement short, and his hand is pushing against the wall. Sunlight streams in, sharp, blinding. I throw my hands up and my eyes burn, shafts of light cutting through them. I slow, but the men are still moving, steps certain, voices continuing on, speaking of a plan, of woods and places and landmarks I do not recognize. I lower my hand, my eyes watering. *It is clouded. The light should not feel so bright.*

The goblin is stepping up beside Fitz, blurred through my narrowed sight. He speaks, his voice low. "Something is odd. I do not like the time, nor the light we have left with a clouded sky. I do not like this." His voice is hushed, words intended for only Fitz.

Fitzclaste nods, glancing out over the horses. There are many of them, already saddled, ready, their feet stamping. "I do not either, but there is nothing that can be done. They have not been seen close enough to be trouble, so we will go as planned. I am glad you are going with them, for extra caution. But there is nothing else that can be done. If you scent that anything is off, get them out of there. These are not soldiers."

The goblin shakes his head, glancing out toward the woods, to the sky. "That does not mean that they will not have come closer in the last watch. The last outing was not as careful as they should have been, and I do not like how far they have been traveling of late. I will pull them if I sense danger." His eyes snap back to Fitz. "Everyone will be kept indoors and quiet until we return?"

He nods. I step forward. He is speaking again, quieter now. "They will be kept in until we see you back or send a party after you. Sound the horn if you need aid. I have a party getting ready as we speak, men that will be spared if need be. Dark will likely fall fast when it comes tonight, as you know, and we will remain prepared until we see you again."

His eyes flick toward the sky. The clouds are low, hanging like fog not far above the trees, misting their branches. The light is dim, dimmer than it should be, though a moment ago there was a shaft of sunlight cutting through the darkness of the sky. *The clouds are moving fast then, like a storm coming.*

The goblin's jaw clenches. "That stretches us thin, Jornamn. But it will have to do. Wait longer than a watch. If they have gone as far as they did two days ago, it will take us more than that to get there and back without looking for sign of them."

Fitz nods again, turning to face the men before him. "So let it be." He lifts his voice. "May the swiftest feet guide you on your way, and may you return before the day is out and dark has come. The Creator keep you on your way." He inclines his head, like a blessing, and turns toward me. "That mount is yours, there. We thought it best you have a taller one than your mare for the trails you will be on today. There is a stool there to help you mount. You will be on your own if you ever need to get back on it in the forests, but a man can aid you if you ask."

I bow toward him, glance at the horse. It stamps its foot. "The healing bag is on it?" It snorts.

He nods. "Aye. All is in readiness. Keep to the middle of the party. We are not looking for trouble, but it bears to keep watch, and I would not have you wounded." He nods toward me and turns back toward his men.

I turn, step toward the horse before me—high and almost blue in its sleek coat. There is a box next to it, small and roughly hewn. I step up onto it and plant my foot into the stirrup, the leather slick beneath my foot. I swing up over the horse, and my skirts catch tight, jerking against my legs. I grimace, force myself up. The fabric cuts into my skin. I pull it up my calves, jerk against it, and it barely shifts, skimming my skin. *There is no time to change, was no time to have thought of it. My skirts will be as they are. Too short.*

The goblin snaps his reins, the sound small and familiar in the winds swirling through the trees. There are horses being led out of the stable, men mounting them as soon as they are on the small patch of bald earth beside me.

One mounts up, just near me, and his eyes flicker over, nodding beneath a shock of blond hair. *The only other landlot I have seen that is not dark haired, since I arrived. Him and Ciaran.* He turns, toward the goblin, watching, waiting, and the others are up, filing in behind us. *I am already in the center of the party. I need not move anywhere.*

The goblin clicks, and the horses start forward, nine men around me and the goblin at the front on his great black mount. His eyes are forward, head lifted into the drifting wisps of clouds above the trees.

• ▶ | ◀ ▶ | ◀ ▶ | ◀ ▶ | ◀ ▶ | ◀ ▶ | ◀ •

The slope curves down, horse heads bobbing with it, steep. I lean backward, my hands white against the saddle horn. The air is dark, sky nearing the last of the light beneath the low hanging clouds.

One of the men behind me grunts, the sound quiet. I clench my jaw, soil and branches sliding beneath the hooves of my mount, and my hands tighten on the saddle. *I do not think a taller mount was needed, not for this trail. It is steep enough, without aid from height.* The ground is far below beneath the feet of the horse, earth and rocks skittering upon it.

The air is thick, trees dark and short, all cedars and new spruce. Voices murmur together from the front, low, lost to the tramping of hoof clatters. My horse slows, and the goblin's voice rings out. "Fan out. There is sign on the ground." Horses move, and the goblin is on the level ground below, kneeling, his horse backed away. He looks up, toward the men. "Stay in pairs and do not get beyond earshot. This is blood."

The last man in front of me nods, moving away into the trees, off after another horseman at a signal between them—eye contact and the barest hand motion. They vanish into the growing dark.

I purse my lips. My horse prances, hooves clattering onto level ground, and it side-steps, moving away from the goblin's. I pull the reins gently, draw it back. My eyes flicker to the goblin. He is watching the men, his head alert, ears pricked up in his coiled hair. His head moves, just slightly toward me, eyes staying on the woods before him.

A horse pauses beside me, hoof striking against stone. It snorts, roughly, and my mount draws its head away. I glance at the rider. *The man with the blond hair.* He nods at me, eyes watchful on the forest. My horse side-steps, lowering his head. The goblin nods toward the blonde man, straightening. "Do you see anything, Nevak?"

Nevak glances at the goblin and he draws his horse back, reigning it in. "Nothing yet. Track anything with the blood sign or is it only a spot?"

The goblin looks away, his horse shifting its great feet toward the trees. He moves forward on foot, the horse moving with him. "It's half a trail. A footprint. Landlots. They will not be far from here."

My stomach swirls, eyes burning. *How much blood did he find?* The goblin moves off through the trees, into the branches of the evergreens. I nudge my horse after him, Nevak's mount's steps soft behind us.

The goblin ducks beneath a branch of the last of the greening trees and he is cast in shadows, gone. The ground slopes, pine needles skating across the earth and muffling the foot falls of the horses, sounds strange, eerie, steps ringing out in other parts of the forest.

But not here. The air reeks of pine, and there is something sour, something foul beneath the pressing air.

The goblin figure looms for a moment and he steps forward, half-hidden behind his great horse, and he stoops again, vanishing. I click my mount forward, branches brushing against the top of my head. There is a smell on the winds that I know, metallic and still faint. Nevak's eyes flicker between the trees, alert in the dark.

"Dismount." The voice is a breath, the goblin's.

I flick my eyes to him, but he is still kneeling, still gone behind his mount. I glance down, and something glints in the darkness, tucked into the fallen pine needles. *A sword.* The blade glints as the branches wave. Wind rips through the trees, throwing my skirts against the horse's neck.

I slip my leg over the side of the horse, and the ground slides, needles skittering beneath my feet. I grasp the saddle, straighten sharply. The goblin is standing again, moving forward, the horses following him, and the wind cuts through the trees, snapping in his poncho, throwing cords of his hair into darkness. My arms shiver, skin prickling over my neck. *It is colder now than it was a breath ago. The sun is dropping, nearly gone, taking light with it.*

A whistle cuts through the trees, high and clear from ahead. I spin toward the goblin. He is dropping to his knees, his movements fluid, hurried.

His voice rings out. "Healer." It is sharp, sudden in the stillness of the forest. I dart forward, my steps skidding on needles, and I slow beside him. My eyes burn.

There is a man on the ground before him. His face is a death mask, ashen gray in the shadows beneath the pines, a dark spot, bloomed outward against his clothing. The air reeks of bile. I move forward, and the goblin's head shakes sharply, his hand blocking my way. "Gót. Find and check the others. He is not near saving. Move." I stumble to the side.

My eyes shift again, flicker between the trees. There is another shape, laying on the ground between two trees, his face the same death mask, a limb jutting out beneath him. *Two men. Two more.* The wind howls, ripping at the branches, throwing my skirts against my legs. I move forward, kneel, drag the man out, his face down into the earth. I jerk his shoulder over, and his face is a grimace, hand held over his chest. *But he is not the same deathly pale, not the same mask of time lost.*

I shift backward and his eyes snap up, wide, bleary and rolling back in the fading light. Something glints further down the slope. *A sword. Beside another man.* There is another, beyond him, down the slope and another, their faces pale from here, white-green beneath the trees.

My heart sucks into my chest, catching. They are going to fade. All of them. I cannot help more than one at a time, cannot help more than one man here, and the rest will fade away. How many of them have families, uprooted for my people, waiting at the fort? Uprooted for helping those around them? My heart pounds, mind thunders, eyes swirling. They are going to all die before we can help more than one of them. The wind rips through the trees, tearing at my hair, throwing strands across my eyes. "Cruelty shall lead to freedom…"

"Healer!" The voice is sharp behind me. "Are you going to do nothing?" *I do not know the voice—not Nevak or the goblin.* One of the men on the ground shifts, just barely, a groan, lighter than the breath of the wind, and I press my hand against this man's arm, his wound seeping.

I have never healed so many at once, never sung long enough to try. But I cannot leave them to die beneath the trees.

My hands clasp against my skirts.

"Healer?" The voice is insistent, high.

My life be forfeit. I will save them if I can. I press my hand against the side of the first man beside me. Creator, please help me. Strengthen that which you have given, and let not these men die.

"Healer." The goblin's voice now, low, a command.

My life be forfeit, I will help them.

I lift my voice, curl the song upward and level out the note, carry it. The sound is steady, and the wind rips, tearing through the branches, tearing through the coming darkness. Hair lashes across my face.

A footfall sounds in the needles behind me, soft. "Is she just going to sit there and—" I lift the song higher and it pierces, curling.

The man beside me sucks in a sharp breath, his hand gripping tightly at his leg, and I bring the song down, press my hand against his. *Wounds closed, eyes opened, breaths steady.* I curl the song upward again, shift the notes, and they carry through the underbrush, carry through the softness of the evergreen into the shifting clouds.

The song slows, gentle now, my head pulsing, neck aching. I grip the tree beside me, twist the notes again, curl them downward, toward the earth. *Wounds closed, eyes open, lives steadied to tomorrow...* My head drums. I grip the hand beneath mine, grab it. *Creator, please let me finish. How many men?* I force the song up, force the notes, and they carry, high in the night. *How long is enough?* My head pulses and I curl off the last note, stagger to my feet. My hands are shaking, the man before me blinking up into darkness, his eyes unseeing. *Dazed. He is dazed.* I grip the tree beside me.

The world is silent, achingly quiet, and there is a man standing by me, staring at the figures on the ground. I shake my head, point down the hill, toward the men below. My grip on the tree tightens. "See to those men. They should be…"

My voice catches, the world swirling for a moment, and my hand slips on the trunk, gone. I press my head against my hand, stumble, my shoulder catching on something. *The man at the top of the hill should be checked, needs to be seen to. It may not have been long enough for him. Not long enough to draw back the death mask from him.*

I force my eyes open, stumble forward and there are shouts, voices ringing out, a few men moving through the trees. I stagger around Sradfaang's horse, and the ground shifts beneath my feet, golden needles slipping. My hand snaps around a branch. The wounded man is beside me, on the ground. I drop to the earth beside him.

His face is still pale, so pale, his side a bare glint in the growing dark. *The sun has gone. I can hardly see his face, cannot make out enough to know if he will make it, or if I have failed him.* I press my hand against his side and it is slick, cold, fabric sickeningly damp. The air reeks of bile and metal—of blood.

My fingers brush over the wound, and there are two sides to it, the center soft. *It is not yet closed.* His breathing is shallow, wheezing with each heave of his chest. *He will still not make it.* I grimace, press my hands against my knees. *Night is already here. There is no time to try anything else, to staunch it. He may not be the only one. I cannot see well enough to tend anything with a needle and thread.* I draw in a breath. My hand shakes. *Creator, can I sing longer? Will You help this man, please, see him through?*

I lift the first note of the song, and it is weak, weak and flat in the night. I curl it upward, and the world blurs together, the man's face a line of white streaked across my vision. I force the song to raise, level it out, and my hands slip against my knees, against his wound. *A little longer. Creator, please help.* I press my hand hard against the wound and curl the song higher, a voice echoing in my head. *"Careful child. You do not know what this voice does yet." Ailé's voice, more than eight turnings ago.* I lift the note higher, toward the trees, and the wound pulls together beneath my hand. The world swirls at the edges, folding in with darkness.

The notes trill, weak, and I drop them, with the end.

Something presses between my eyes and the world is gone in darkness.

•▶|◀▶|◀▶|◀▶|◀▶|◀▶|◀•

A hand is on my arm. There are voices somewhere off in the distance, something howling, moaning. *The wind.* I drag my head up and it aches, drums. Someone is speaking, speaking, their voice raspy, low and high. There is a moan again, from beside me. *A man.* I lift my head, and something is slicked to my cheek, my hair clinging to it, damp.

My hand fumbles with the side of the man before me, presses against the wound. *Fully closed. At least as much as I can tell in the dark.*

A hand grips my arm, beneath my elbow. My gaze flicks down. *Fingers long, off colored in the shadows.* I shake my head and it pulses, the world falling sideways. The hand tightens. "Be still." *The goblin.*

I press my hand against my forehead and it is sticky, damp with something thick and cool. *Blood.* I do not move my hand. "Are they all healed? Can they travel?"

"Yes. Do not try moving."

I draw my arm back, shake my head. My eyes shut on their own. "They still need tending…" I half-move, and his hand tightens on my elbow, keeping me in place. I pull my eyes open, and they are heavy, barely obeying.

His gaze meets mine. "They need tending by someone else. You have spent your energy and the men are tending them. Sit still." His voice is curt, but there is a strange note in it, one I have not heard in it before. *Fear?*

A shadow looms behind him, wind curling for a moment, and I shudder. "You healed them with song?" A man's voice, questioning, low. *Low with awe.*

I shake my head, press my hand against it again, and the world slows its swirling. "Gót. It is a gift…"

"You sang and their wounds were closed. You gave your strength that they might be healed." His voice is stronger now, awe gripping it fully.

I press my eyes shut. "Gót. If it was truly my strength I would have died. It is a gift. The Creator blends my life with the song. It is not wholly mine." The world darkens for a moment. I suck in a breath, press my head against my knees, and my skin clings to the fabric, everything too big and too small at once, pulling at the edges. My head pounds.

The goblin's hand is no longer on my arm. I should stand, should check the others. They will need help, if I can get to any of them.

I force my arms under me, force my legs to move, and stand slowly. The world pulses, darkening around the borders once more. I suck in a breath, press my hand hard against something. It is rough, too rough beneath my forehead. I grimace. *Tree bark. Why does it feel sharp?* My head swirls, the world too large for the space. My eyes flicker toward the ground. The man is no longer there. His body is gone, the needles indented where he should be. My eyes burn. *Was he not there a breath ago?* I stumble backward, hand slipping from the sharp tree.

"Healer." I lift my head. Nevak is standing an arm's length away, his eyes careful, hand out as if to catch or stop me.

A wind cuts through the trees, tearing at my face, pulling at my skirts, and something strikes my skin, cutting against my cheek. I swipe at it, and my knees cave, wind howling—my knees crash against the ground.

The wind stills, gone.

I lift my eyes, slowly. There is another figure beside Nevak, taller. It turns toward me and there is a glint of green eyes, glowing for a moment like a Forgotten Thing. I suck in a breath, and his eyes do not flicker toward me, do not move. He is speaking to Nevak, and I can hear no words they say. Nevak nods and moves off through the trees. I lift my knees, press my head against them.

A foot drops into my sight, faint and shadowy in the last of dusk, a knee following it to the ground. "Healer." *The goblin.* I do not lift my gaze, keep it on his knee. *I do not want to see those eyes again, do not want to see them glow.* "It is time to move." *Move.* I draw in a breath, breathe out slowly, and the wind brushes through my hair. I shiver, press my arms tighter about my sides. He does not turn away. "Can you move?"

I lift my head, stare up the slope. Shapes move, uncertain, shifting between trees and shadows. I tighten my jaw. "Then I will carry you." He moves forward.

I jerk back, my breath a hiss, and my eyes meet his. They are no longer glinting, and I can barely see them in the shades of night. "Gót. Gót, I can manage, in a moment." *The men need to get back to Sikkerhet, to be tended. There will not be a long enough moment.* The world swirls.

Something twitches in the shadows of the goblin's face—an eyebrow cocking. "Night is coming and you cannot walk. What would you do? Wait here?" His voice is dry, straight forward.

My chest tightens, eyes burn. *The men need to get back. There is no call to slow them with my pride.* I tighten my jaw, incline my head.

"If you will help, I will try to walk. I cannot get up on my own." He moves forward again, and his hand grips my arm. I move my legs under me and he pulls—my legs wobble, cave.

I snap my hand around a tree branch and the world sways, pine needles skidding beneath me. I gasp. The hand on my arm tightens.

Nevak's voice cuts out. "Healer, you cannot walk. Slow down." *I was not moving fast.*

I shift my hand on the branch. The goblin inclines his head, looking down at me. "We will bring the horse to you." Nevak turns, already moving up the slope.

The world pulses. I press my head against my shoulder, and there are steps, faint and approaching. A voice calls out from above, somewhere beyond them. "Sradfaang. We need your aid with this one."

The goblin's hand shifts on my arm. His voice rings out. "Ágë. Come help with the healer. I am going to go aid them with Tollak. It is time to move out of here." Another hand replaces his, and he is gone, a figure shifting at the edge of my vision.

Ágë glances down at me. "Your horse is here. I am going to help you up, when you are ready."

I incline my head. "I can be ready now." My strength will wane as long as I am standing. Stars, the air is heavy.

Ágë's hand barely moves on my arm. "I am going to lift you onto the mount." He grips my waist, lifting, and I am up, sliding my foot over the side of the horse and into place. I grip at the pommel, and the horse shifts to the side. My stomach clenches, the world moving with it. *I am going to hurl.* I squeeze my eyes shut, and the world shifts again, swirling harder, faster.

There is a grunt, up the hill, and a 'praise be', breathed out from a man somewhere far up the slope. The goblin clears his throat, near me. There is a silence in the trees, voices that I didn't know were murmuring, gone.

The goblin's voice rings out. "As far as anyone in Sikkerhet is concerned,..." I sway, the world swaying, and a hand grips my arm, holding me in place. "...The healer is exhausted from tending the wounds of this many survivors." *A half-truth.* There is a presence beside me, and my head is heavier. The horse shifts forward, and I draw my head down, press it hard against my hands, against the saddle horn.

"Will she be able to ride?" *Nevak's voice.* There is a pressure, between my brows, and I am falling, everything swallowed with darkness, and someone gasps.

XXIV

Darkfall

*T*he world is swaying.

Back and forth. *It does not slow, moving like a cradle; like a tree branch in the wind. Like a horse's gait.* Something moves behind me, pressing into the middle of my back. I drag my head up and my cheek is stiff, aching. My hair is pasted into it, catching with each movement of my head. The world is dark. It's still swaying, back and forth.

Something moves beneath me. "Carefully, kúráh." *A familiar voice, low.* Something scratches against the side of my face—rough hair. I pull my head back. *Fitzclaste's voice. He is not supposed to be here, wherever here is.* His voice speaks again. "You are still on horseback. Do not move too much, or we may both go down. I would lie still if you can."

"Go down?" My voice sounds far away. *Back and forth. I am leaning against him, then. His arm is holding me up.* I shift, drag my eyes open. "Where are we? You were not here before."

He shakes his head, breath brushing the top of my head. "We met you on the road not long after you went unconscious. No more than that now. We are nearly back."

There is something faintly flickering ahead of us, a light beyond the shifting shapes on the road. Wind brushes. I shiver. There is something around me, heavy and thick. It does not reach my feet, bundled around my legs. *A cloak.* I press my arms tighter against my chest and Fitz shifts, his arm angling on my back, moving back into place.

I swallow. *The men. Are they still well, after the ride? I was out for more than half a watch, if we are nearly back.* There is nothing over his shoulder but the shifting of tree branches back into shadows.

A horse nickers, up the way. *The wounds were not wrapped. No one will believe the half-truth that I am merely exhausted from tending them if the wounds are not dressed, men half conscious.* The light is growing, gold from somewhere up the path. Figures move, shapes darting between us and it. Light is brushing the first of the horses, lighting up their manes in a halo of gold in the night.

Someone is standing, solitary above, not moving with the shifting shapes, not a running shadow in the darkness and torch light. "How many wounded?" Ciaran's voice rings out. There is a warm hue to the light caught in his hair, still bound back. We are pulling close to him, his features sharp for a moment in the light of a passing torch.

Fitz draws the mount up to a halt beside him, his voice over my head. "All of them. The healer did her best, but there are some in sore need of aid and rest in the healing ward, inside, where there is light. It was too far gone when they were found to do much."

The horse's head shifts beside my hip, lowering. Fitz draws the reins up. I can no longer see Ciaran, only the bright lines of the branches in the forest visible now. Fitz looks down at me. "I will call one of the men to help you inside."

I shake my head, draw my arms up. "I can walk now, I believe. I will at least try before someone is called to me. There are others to help."

He lifts a brow, doubt written into his features, but he says nothing, his lips a thin line through his graying beard. I look down. *I cannot get off, not with my legs across his the way they are. Not without falling.* He turns his head, back over his shoulder toward where the golden man was. "Will you help her down, Ciaran? She is overdone and was unsteady on her feet when we found them." My face warms, eyes burn.

A figure steps around the horse, face lost in the shadows and he looks up at me, eyes barely catching in the golden light. They meet mine, waiting. "Are you ready, Eness?"

I nod my head, and his hands wrap around my waist, lifting. I flinch and the world blurs by, my feet on the ground. I stumble, my hand clutching for something. It hooks around a strap. *A horse lead. Fitz's mount.* Fitz drops down, beside Ciaran, dusting off his clothes. I sway, tighten my hand. The world feels heavy and light, pressing against my mind. *I cannot walk to the door on my own. I will not make it that far. Curse it. It has been long enough.*

But I have never healed that many before. I have not lost consciousness from it like this, not since the first time I wielded this gift. Fitz is speaking in low tones to the man beside me. "—she may be able to, once they are inside but I would bid that she wait to report. She is spent and the men have already been bandaged as well as they can for the time being. The rest, Eerol and a few extra hands can tend to. Let her go to her rest. She is spent." *They bandaged them. Praise be to the Creator.*

Ciaran nods, his eyes catching in the light of the torches once more, and he looks over the horse's back. He lifts his head, calls out to the ring of light and men. "Get those injured inside as quickly as can be. This is no place to tarry with night here."

The world sways, the horse head moving just barely, and everything shifts with it. I gasp, press my eyes shut, hands tightening on the bridle. My hand is slipping, moving down the leather. *Curse it. I am going to fall.* The horse jerks its head again, and I grimace.

"Healer?" Ciaran's voice cuts through the haze. I force my eyes open and I am wavering against the horse, barely standing beneath its head. Wind brushes, throwing hair across my cheeks. He is beside me, his gaze over the horse's back again for a moment. It moves back to me, veiled so I can read nothing of it, veiled as it always is. *But there is kindness in his eyes, gentleness there.* He inclines his head. "I can aid you to the door, if you can make it to your rooms from there. Can you move?"

I incline my head, my eyes burning and my hand slides further downward on the bridle. "I—" A hand grips my arm, gentle, careful. *Gloved.* "Eness, let go."

I pull my eyes open, step sideways and the world swirls, plummeting. I screw my eyes shut once more. His hand shifts on my arm. "Are you alright?"

I incline my head. "Aye. Only the world will not slow its swirling." His hand angles, his grip steadying my arm, and the world churns less behind my eyes. I drag them open once more.

He inclines his head, his eyes catching in the firelight. "Are you ready?" I nod, and he steps forward. His steps are measured, even and small to match mine. The ground grows with the pool of light before the fortress doors. My legs catch in my skirts. His hand tightens on my arm, angling once more. I tighten my jaw.

We are near the doorway beside the stable, the one that leads back into the great halls toward the healing rooms. *The long way down to the healing rooms. But the short way to the wing where mine are.* He draws the door open and light spills across the earth, sharp around my toes and the swirling ends of my skirts. I press my eyes shut. Everything swirls again, bright and heavy. I draw a breath, step away from him. *He has things he should be doing, greater things to do then see me steadily to the door.* I turn my eyes up toward him. His hand does not release my arm.

I bob my head. "Thank you for the trouble you did not spare. I will make it from here."

He inclines his head, shifting his hand on my arm. "It was no trouble. Are you certain? I cannot go with you now, but I will go for someone. Your legs are unstable, Iai." I shake my head and he inclines his. "So be it then."

He glances over his shoulder. "G'moy." A man steps out of the movement beyond us, his head inclining toward Ciaran. Ciaran nods toward the door. "Walk with the healer a ways. Tell Tejan that Aorla will be helpful to Eerol downstairs, if she can be spared."

I look up at him, my eyes burning. The other man nods. Ciaran looks down at me. "I would like it more if you would humor me, and let him walk with you as far as the kitchens. I would be sure that you are not harmed after a trek like the one you have had." He inclines his head again and draws his hand away, stepping back into the moving shadows.

I look up at the other man—G'moy. He glances down at me, gesturing to the open door.

I step in and my legs drag, catching on the earth. Everything hums with the heaviness of night. I draw in a breath, lift my head. Steps pound in the hall, voices all murmurs and sounds in the humid air.

A step sounds sharply in the hall, and a man darts around the corner ahead of us. His steps are fast, nearly a run. He turns, and his eyes lift to mine. He slows. "Healer." His voice is familiar, but I cannot place his face, not now. "G'moy." He nods to the other man, stepping by him. *Tren. I met him before, days ago, in the halls, walking with some of the women.*

I move around the corner, and there is the next hall, long. Voices catch in it, soft and low, hurried, women's voices. I shuffle my feet, move slowly. G'moy's pace is even. A head juts out of a doorway, a woman's. It is dark haired, as they all are, her eyes soft and slanted. They find mine at once. She steps out, folding her hands against her waist. "Healer." She scans my figure over and her face changes from the soft lines of worry to concern. Her eyes dart to G'moy. "Do you need aid? A chair or ale? They can be fetched, either of them."

I press my hand against the wall, straighten my back and everything feels slowed. "Gót. I am only overtired."

G'moy glances at me, and then to the woman. "Ruidún. Do you know where Tejan is?" *His voice is low, strangely low for a man so fair faced.*

She shakes her head. "Gót. I would check the healing ward." Her eyes flicker from him to me. "The men… Our men…We have heard no word of them. Have they returned? All of them…?" her voice trails off, words unasked.

A smile soft at my lips. "They will all mend, Elnial willing. They are well enough. And aye, they are here, from the report I was told."

She releases a low breath, a prayer in it, and her eyes move down, to the child beside her. *I did not see him before. Jørn. Norla's son.*

She smiles at him, and lifts her head, shaking it. "You should be sitting. You are not fit to stand. G'moy, draw her a chair—"

I shake my head, force a smile back to my lips. "Gót. I will sit where I can aid. Do not trouble for it." She looks up, uncertainty in every line of her face. I step forward, half a step. *I should be down there, now, helping. I can aid from a chair, should aid. Eerol will have questions to combat and eight men to tend.* My eyes meet hers once more. I lift my chin. "Is one of the men yours?"

She nods, her lips tightening. "La. My husband. His hair is very dark and he is bearded, in the way a Grioran man." *One of the men halfway up the hill.* I incline my head. "He is well. I will send someone for you when you are able come down, when they are settled in the healing rooms. Do not fret. They will mend." Relief cuts through her face. She inclines her head—respect and appreciation - and turns, back into the room, urging Jørn before her.

I step forward, turn at the end of the hallway and G'moy nods to me, turning away toward the kitchens. I start forward and there is the staircase leading down into the healing rooms. I slow at the top of them, voices echoing up from below. My hand grips the edge of the wall where it changes from wood into stone. A step sounds below, on the stairs. I snap my gaze up. There is a man, standing near the bottom of the staircase, his eyes on me. He steps backward, away from the stairs, gesturing for me to come down.

I shake my head, tighten my grip on the wall. "You would be better coming up first, if you have a task. I am not quick, not as I am now and you will have much to tend." *He looks familiar, another face I have seen before, somewhere here.*

He half-smiles. "I will wait. It is no trouble, and my task is no longer urgent."

My face warms. I look down, plant my foot on the first step and my legs ache, ache with riding, with walking, with time. "I am grateful, but please. There is no call for you to wait here."

He shakes his head. "I will wait. After what I heard you do tonight, healer, I would not complain though you took a full moon to come down those stairs. But I was sent to ensure that you are alright, so in that, my task is already complete by finding you." He smiles again, a good humored thing.

My heart stutters in my chest. I purse my lips, lift my head. "You may be waiting a full moon then, for this will be slow. Do not speak of that, sonyá." *The stairs are long. It did not seem so far, this morning.*

He steps forward, up the stairs in two easy strides, his hand reaching up toward mine. "Let me." I grip it slowly, and he grips my hand, guiding me down a step. *It is easier, this way.* He guides my hand down again, and we are at the bottom step. He draws his hand back, his head inclining. "I am off to find Lord Fitz. Thank you, healer, for what you did out there. You saved many good men this evening. I will not speak of it again, but we are grateful. More than you know."

My eyes shift, prickling, and I incline my head, bow toward him. He turns, gone up the stairs. *Many will know now, even if he does not speak of it. Many will know after seasons of working for silence, of leaving this idle to keep it there, in the dark. Creator, let their lives far outweigh the risks to them, in what I have done tonight.* I turn.

Men are moving everywhere, lifting things, lowering half-conscious bodies onto raised cots in the farthest room. I step forward, move between two men carrying a stretcher over their heads. One nods towards me.

Eerol is pacing around the second room, his hand pointing every direction in sharp motions and his voice barking out orders. Blåthjortt is beside him, his head up, tail wagging faster than all the moving steps around him. A bandage in Eerol's hand flaps idly with each motion of his arm above the hound's head, brushing barely over his nose.

Eerol's voice rings out. "Anyone who does not need to be in here at this very moment, get out. There are other things to do, other things to tend." I step toward him, stop a few breaths away. The world is swirling a little less, a little more steady around the edges now. Eerol's voice has picked up again. "…Get his shirt off so I can check that wound and rebandage it. And wash it out while you are there. That blood will need to go and the leaves in it. Don't mess with the wound itself."

I lift my eyes to his. "What would you have me do, healer?"

His eyes snap to me and narrow, his movements slowing, hand ceasing its movement in mid air. "Goats at harvest time." He swears, reaching out sharply toward me, and his hand snaps around my arm, the bandage still between his fingers. "You are whiter than the flanks of Eusebus in stråle. You should not be standing. Blaze of—," He pulls, tugging me toward the chair on the side of the room.

I shake my head. Blått is wagging his tail at me, his eyes alight, following Eerol. I pull my arm back. "I am here to help. That is my task and I will see it done."

Eerol's eyes narrow. They flicker across the room. Two men are building a cot in the corner, hammering wooden legs into place against a frame of thick logs. There are men on the cots next to them, their hands bound, clothes black, gold trim glinting upon their shoulders.. My stomach swirls. *Soldiers. Were they with the others?* There are three of them, all wounded, all tied down. One of them is glancing around the room, his eyes on all that is happening, but they are half-glazed, his head movements awkward. *Wounded.* I snap my gaze back to Eerol. *Did I heal the queen's soldiers?* One of them has a haphazard bandage around his shoulder, a bandage from the woods, like the other men. *I healed them. If they were there, I could not have chosen which to heal and which not. Their wounds will bear the mark of the song, the mark of my song.*

Eerol barks something above my head and his eyes flick back to me. His hand grips my arm once more. *Far too many men have done that tonight.* He points toward a cot. "Go tend the man there. He has a head wound that needs some tending immediately and you can sit while you tend it. Landslides, you are pale as dust. Were you not to rest?" He points again, toward the man nearest the door. *A man of Sikkerhet. One of ours.* I step forward, shuffle toward him, and Eerol is barking out orders again.

The wounded man's hair is dark, beard dark, cut short and full. *This will be Ruidun's husband. The woman from the hall.* I pause beside his bed, lift a crock from the shelf. He glances at me, and his eyes are not focused, not blinking as they should be. They stare beyond me. I nod at him and my legs shake. I lift my hands to his head.

"I am going to tend the cut on your temple, if that is well with you." I glance down at him again.

His eyes half-focus, moving to me. They are narrow, by blood right and not by suspicion. He drops his head back against the pillow propped up behind him. *I can no longer reach his wound.* He looks away swiftly. "Gót. This is naught but a scratch. It should be worse– was worse, I could have sworn... There was blood..." He looks down at his hands, staring at them, eyes unfocused again. "There was the scent of blood..."

I drop onto the edge of the bed. The cut above his left brow is thick, caked with dried blood and dirt and crusted with leaves. Blood has trickled down his face, crusting along his eyelashes and smeared across his skin with an attempt to remove it. *Smeared to give him back his sight. That will have been gone when he awoke, with it crusted fully over.*

Eerol's voice is barking something across the room, over the noise of men talking and the clatter of tools and crocks and hammered pegs. I turn to stand, and there is a man beside me, a bucket in his hand. He bows to me, setting it down on the floor by the bed. He straightens. "Eerol said you would be needing this for Severin's wound." He nods toward the man, turning to go.

The man on the bed—Severin, as his name must be—sits forward halfway, his face twisting in a grimace, arm wrapping around his ribs. "Raf, wait." The man with the bucket pauses, and Severin continues. "When you go back upstairs, let Ruidún know I am well. She will be worried." The bucket man—Raf—nods and turns, marching away.

I grab the cloth from the bucket, wring it out, and the water splatters against my skirts. "She has already asked about you and has been assured that you are well enough, but it will not go amiss for her to be told again." I half-smile.

His eyes flicker to mine, focusing and unfocusing again. "You were with the scouting party?"

I nod, dab the cloth over the wound on his temple. It is deep, but half healed, the red rim of the song around it, by the dark rim of half washed blood dried to his skin. "I was there. Where else were you wounded besides this gash?" He grimaces, his hands still clasped over his ribs. *Shielding them from pain. That will have been a bad wound, by the blood soaked into his clothes. It may still be.* I purse my lips. "I am going to check your ribs now, if you will move your hands."

I grip the edge of his tunic and he looks down at me, eyes bleary, glazed. They squint. "My ribs?" He looks down, lifts his hand from his side. The space beneath them is blanketed with dark blood, still slick. *New. He is still bleeding, after the song, after the ride. I did not sing long enough for all of them. This wound is still open, pouring out his life.*

I lift his tunic and call over my shoulder. "May I have bandages here?" A passing man nods, off toward the shelves. I peel Severin's tunic fully back, the wound long across his ribs, deep in his flesh and still weeping blood. *Internal wounds will have closed. But I did not sing long enough for him.*

XXV

The Night Watches

"Is Eness here?"

I lift my head. There is a man, standing near the middle of the room, speaking to Eerol, words that I cannot hear. *Nevak.* He turns, following Eerol's half-gesture. *It is late. The man should be in bed, not coming down here where the torch lights have settled and the fires have burned low.* I shift my back against the shelf and my knees press against my chest. I draw my hand from the bucket on the floor. The water in it is beyond use now, dark with debris from many wounds.

Nevak's steps tread the floor, light under the near silence of the room, the snoring men the only other sound. He pauses in front of me, and his eyes scan over me, just a moment. I lose my grip on my knees, my fingers slick with water against my skirts. His eyes meet mine. "Are you able to walk?"

I lift my head. "Aye. Am I needed?" He inclines his head. I tuck my hands under me, and half-rise, my back aching. A hand wavers in front of my face—his. I take it, and he pulls; the world sways, jolting around me, his skin strange against my water-soaked hands, damp from the bucket. His grip releases, and he steps backward, watching me with the side of his eyes, as though I will fall. *I may yet.* I incline my head. "What are you in need of? I cannot go far." My voice is high, and it sounds wrong above the welcome sounds of the men snoring in the quiet of the room.

He shakes his head, gesturing toward the stairs. "The lords wish to see you, in the library, for a moment."

The lords? I lift my head. *What will they need, this late in the night watches? What could not wait until dawn has come to be spoken of, or is someone else wounded?* My heart sinks, legs shake beneath me. I press my hands against the wall, steady my steps. "Will I need bandages?" He shakes his head, moving toward the stairs, his gaze still half on me, arm alert as though he will catch me if I fall. *No wounds. It may be the song, then.*

Nevak turns toward the stairs, and he slows, his pace adjusting to mine. My steps waver, legs stiff and aching. *I am still not grounded on my feet. The song took more from me than it has before.* I press my hand against the stone of the wall and start up the stairs, my steps slow, heavy. But the world is not swirling, not moving around me as it did when I came down. I draw in a breath, and it is heavy. I move onto the top stair and my chest heaves. I pull in another long breath, keep my eyes down. He is quiet, his eyes on the walls of the hallway.

I start forward again.

He turns at the end of the hall, a little before me, face outlined in the shadows of the torches. I pause by the library door, and his hand reaches out, pulling it open. He inclines his head forward for me to go before him. I glance up, incline my head. "Thank you, Nevak." He nods and I step forward, into the room beyond.

It is glowing soft orange with a torch near the door, another mirroring it across the small space. There is a third in a cage on a shelf, far from the scrolls and books, high on the wall. Scrolls line the room, books across only one wall, a wealth of them.

I flick my eyes toward the men at the center of the room. There are four of them. Fitzclaste is in their midst, seated, Ciaran beside him. Sradfaang has his back toward me, head lowered and there is another man beside the goblin, a man I have seen before. *Havard, I believe.*

Ciaran's eyes move to mine. "Healer." His voice is low. "Please, take a seat. You do not need to stand for this." He waves a gloved hand toward a chair, his manners careful, as they always are.

I turn towards the chairs, settle into the one nearest me. None of the men move to sit, none of them move away from the table, Fitzclaste alone already seated. Havard is speaking to him, his voice hushed. He nods toward Ciaran, quieting into the silence of the rest.

Ciaran steps from behind the table. He leans against its side and stops, eyes flickering to mine. "I am sorry for the lateness of the watch, but what has been said this evening is better confirmed now while time is on our side to safeguard anything that needs to be safeguarded before the morning watches come. I apologize for that. If you have no mind for this tonight, then you may turn in at a word. We will respect your wishes."

I shake my head. "If it is the woods that you would speak of, it will be well to do so in the dark watches, when there are few to hear."

He nods, settling his eyes on me. They are watchful, giving away nothing of his mind. "Very well then. You healed them with song?"

I swallow hard, turn my head away. *Seasons of hiding it, and now it is known, known to at least ten men, likely many more.* "No one can do such a thing, not of their own skill. It is a gift, from the Creator, but aye, a gift that I have wielded."

His eyes do not waver on mine. "It is in your voice then, or a song you sang? I am trying to understand. A gift of the Creator like this has not been seen in many turnings, back before the memory of any of those living, if history is correct."

I incline my head. "Aye. It is in my voice, not in song. I do not know rightly how to describe it in a way that will make any more sense to you than that, my lord. It is a melody that I know, but not one that can be replicated by any other that has attempted, though a few have." Havard shifts, surprise, and something more in his expression.

Ciaran is quiet for a moment, his eyes thoughtful. He lifts a brow. "Einion would have had no inkling of this when he withdrew you, or he would have given some sign of it. You would not have wielded it out in the open. Did you use it on him, in your home?"

I shake my head. "Gót. The soldiers would not leave my side while I was tending him. I would not sing in front of them, not with the risk of it. I do not speak callously when I say that his life was not worth that."

Havard's brow lifts, just barely. "So, you would rather have died, than have a few low ranking soldiers know? I am not ignorant to the position you were in by having those men in your home, and neither was the captain. It would have been death for you, if he had passed under your care. Would that not have been worth it, to have protected your life? If not then, then when have you wielded it before?"

I set my hand against my leg. "What would have kept them from bringing me to their superiors, if they had known? Soldiers have sold out people all over our country for things of less worth than this. I would have been brought in, sold or traded to the highest bidder, become a tool. I would not have this gift fall into the hands of the queen, or her men, not for my life."

Havard tilts his head, an uncertain expression in his eyes.

Ciaran speaks. "And you have had this all your turnings, carried it with you through them?"

I incline my head. "I have carried it for most of my memory. I did not become aware of it until I was nearly nine turnings, after an accident with a woman when we were on the road." I lift my head, scan each of the men, meet their eyes. *None of them hold greed, hold gain in their expressions.*

My throat tightens. *It might have been well, to build a home here. But it is too late now.* "I think, for the safety of all here, it would be wisest for me to leave if this cannot be kept a secret. I sang in front of many tonight. If there had been another way, I would have done it, but this gift is known now and with it comes a high risk. You were aware of my blood, and the price and hunt that goes with it. But I do not like to imagine the damage that would follow in my wake, were the queen's men to get a whisper of this, as they have tonight." I glance at Fitz. "Were not those soldiers in the woods, when I sang?"

He inclines his head. "Aye. They were." He presses his hands against his legs, leaning forward. "I understand your concern for this community and appreciate your tenderness for their wellbeing. With that said, I do not understand where you intend to go if you leave, healer. A cottage could be found, but in a country intent on tearing itself apart, there are few places left within our borders that a woman could live by herself and not be found. It seems a great risk for you to go. If this gift is given, there must be a purpose to it in the turnings to come, and that will not serve if you are off, alone and likely dead, in the woodlands."

I incline my head. *The edges of the room are turning dark.* "But that risk would be for me only. There is no one to trace my presence back to, where I am alone, no one to be punished if I am found and my existence near them known. I understand your concern, but I also do not pretend that you have not seen the damage done to this country on the words of a few when it comes to the connections of homes— a family to a village, a woman to a community. Cities have burned for a few idle words. I will not put you through that, not now that the risk is greater with the knowledge of this, not so long as I have a choice. You all have shown me kindness and I will not show you this in return."

Fitz shifts his hands on his knees. "Let me ask another question, then. I have been told that you were working on an attempt to help your bloodline shield the sign of their heritage when they came upon you. Do you intend to continue this, when you leave? I have heard nothing of it since you came through our door."

I fold my hands against my knees. "Gót. I had intended to continue here but have not re-begun yet. I lost all that I had before, when the soldiers came. I will continue it where I go, when I can."

Sradfaang is facing me now, his back against the wall now, face impassive as Ciaran's. *I did not notice him move.* He lifts a brow. "How close were you before the captain came, to finding anything?"

I look down. "I had found nothing that had done anything more than dampen the shifting of shades. Where I go, I will try again, but it may not be soon enough to help any of my people. It will not likely be soon enough, if the raids continue as they have these last turnings."

Havard lifts a brow. "If you are living alone, far from civilization, it will likely not be. Without others to help, you will not be able to disperse your knowledge to others to let it be utilized, especially not on a country-wide plain. Did you plan for that, when the day comes, for a way to disperse it?"

I shake my head, and the edges of the room curl in. "Gót. That was a question I had no answer to, and will not have, even if I were to live in a village again. I would not tell them what I am working on. You will understand that. The danger would be too high."

Fitz tilts his head. "If we are to find a cottage for you, how do you intend to survive alone? If you are near a village, the risk of discovery will remain, though the price on your head will remain less than if word of this were to get out, I grant you. But if you are truly alone, you will either have time to attempt to survive or to tend your task. There are not enough moments in a day to do both, not alone, and you will have no protection, no defense in the event the queen's men show up at your door again, or Maa'eulé. They have shown signs of taking to raiding villages in the last few moons."

Ciaran inclines his head. "Would there not be some security in knowing that it will be harder for you to be found out here? That others would fight for you, if the time comes for it, and that you would not be alone to face what is to come?"

I shake my head, let my eyes shift, let them change with a hundred colors that I do not know, and lift them to his. "Is there security, in knowing that in your safety, others are placed in danger? How many men live here? How many women and children? Can you vouch for the words and loyalties of them all, when pressed?" I turn my head away, grip the edge of the chair. "Can you promise that this fortress will not be sold out, to the ending of the lives of all those here? You all are already at risk for the work that you do. With this gift here, I increase that ten-fold, if it is valued as highly as I think it will be by the queen's men, if ever they learn of it. That is not a danger I would put anyone in. I have hidden away, for that purpose. More than for my blood, it was for that."

Ciaran lifts his head. "And what if we told you the risk was already great and accounted for, and that we could vouch for the loyalties of those here?"

I glance at him. "You could vouch for thirty men, for sixty people from lives that vary?"

Fitz looks from him to me, and nods, slowly. "We can vouch for each person here. They are carefully chosen before they come, and if there is concern after they arrive, we work to help them to leave."

My grip on the chair tightens. "Will they not then sell us out?"

Ciaran shakes his head, his arms folded over his chest. "We ensure that no one knows rightly the way here, or the way out. It is a precaution that has been taken since the early days. They will not know the way back."

Fitz inclines his head. "Aye. We have taken that precaution since the early days. There are few who know the way to and from this place, the villagers nearby not even among them." *Villagers?*

Ciaran's eyes have not moved from mine, his expression steady. There is silence for a breath, the room humming with the deep quiet of the night watches. Ciaran shifts, adjusting his arms over his chest. "As I see it, you would be wisest to stay. I do not trust the odds of you staying out there on your own, hiding somewhere to be found and picked off with time. There are lots here who would look out for you, watch for your wellbeing, and you will have nothing of that on your own. There are herbs here that you will not have tried that Eerol imports from other parts of the continent or country. All that we have will be at your disposal, for your work and comfort. The men have all been under orders since the woods not to speak of this, not even to their wives, which is something that we ask of them rarely. They will not break that trust." He relaxes his stance. "I will not compel you to stay, nor will you be forced, but it would be my advice to you. There is some safety in numbers. If you do not choose to do so, we will find you a place to work beyond these walls. If that is still your desire, we will see it to completion."

Fitz nods, standing. "We have a plan in place for an exiting party in case of trouble at hand, for the safety of those here and those included in that exit. For your own safety and that of others, you will be added to that party."

The torch on the shelf stutters. *I am too tired to make this choice tonight.* I lift my eyes. "I will beg your pardon for tonight, on this, if the offer of delay stands. It is late, and I am tired." My throat is thick, tightening, my head pulsing. *I am going to weep if I stay here, stay and speak of this now. I cannot speak of this now.* I lift my eyes, raise them to Fitzclaste. "You will forgive me if I ask to give an answer at another time, when I have thought on this more?" I flick my gaze toward Ciaran. He is still watching, face completely unreadable once more. *Like a mask, over all but his eyes.*

He nods, straightening from the table. "Of course. We have kept you too long tonight. This will wait for another day." He inclines his head toward me, honor. "Thank you, Eness Finch, for what you did for those men in the woods. You saved their lives at the risk of your own, and words cannot repay you for that, nor can all our thanks in the days to come. But you carry with you the gratitude of all of us and the aid of any in this room, should you need it. Thank you, for what you have done." He bows lower, adding respect in the tilt of his head.

I swallow, stand slowly, and my legs feel unsteady, like water and tallow. "If I chose to leave tomorrow, would you permit me?"

He inclines his head. "If you choose to leave, we will find you a place to stay and see to it that you are settled as safely and well as is within our means. You will be seen to safety in whatever you choose."

"And if I stay, I can utilize the books here for my attempts to block this?" I gesture toward my eyes. He nods. I incline my head toward him, my heart lighter. "Then I will continue my request for time to consider it, to speak with you another time. Thank you, for your hospitality this last fortnight, and then some…" my eyes flicker to Fitzclaste, "… and for all that you have done. It was not looked for, and more appreciated for that. Thank you for your generosity to a stranger."

Ciaran half-smiles, and it is bright, brushing his eyes. Fitz inclines his head. "Goodeven, Eness Finch. Rest well." He bows, a slight bow. I turn toward the door. Fitz nods at the edge of my vision, toward someone.

I pull the door open, step through, and something is moving through behind me, looming. My eyes snap upward. *Sradfaang.*

I sway, and press my hand sharply against the wall. He speaks. "I have been asked to see you to your room." His eyes are above my head, his hand hardly touching my sleeve. "You will permit me." *It is not a question.*

I press my hand against my side, step away. "I appreciate their concern, but I will be well on my own. Thank you."

He looks down at me, expression barely readable. "You will be, but you are also spent and can scarcely walk without weaving your steps. I have orders from Fitz to see you to your rooms. You will not speak against the lord of this place and I will not leave without completing my task."

I incline my head. "I will not speak against him, but it is not needed." My limbs are heavy, head pounding harder. I steady my hand against the wall, step forward and he moves with me, his steps quiet. Everywhere is silent, ringing with the stillness of night. I grimace, step forward, and he glances down at me.

"You used the song on Tulé, didn't you."

I glance up at him sharply, and my head pulses. My eyes burn. "Aye. He was dying." I glance up the hall. There is no sound of steps beyond ours.

He looks up the hall, his eyes scanning it. "No one is awake near here to hear us. Does he know of it?"

I shake my head. "Gót. Only Eerol knew before tonight. He was unconscious."

A smile tugs at the edge of his mouth, almost self-satisfied. "I thought the healer did not look as surprised as he should have when he was informed. As far as you know, there are no others beyond these walls that know of this gift?"

I press my hand against the wall, slow my steps. *The world is swimming at the edges.* "Gót. No one. Why are you questioning me of this now?"

He looks down at me. "I cannot guard well if I do not know the dangers presented. This gift adds a new one, to your watch, and to the watch of this place. I would have the men here responsible for you informed if there is to be greater danger. I trust there is not."

My brow furrows. I press my hand against the wall. *The world is fully swirling at the edges.* "Is not your guard of me ended now? Have you not been reassigned? Forgive me if I presume."

He looks forward again, up the hall. "It did not. Currently, it is part of my task to work for the extended security of this place, with the guard here. Your safety remains my charge until that is ended. Fitzclaste would see you safe, until your choice is made, and beyond that, with the extra risk to your life, so he has not reassigned me."

I lift my head. "And if I leave, will you have freedom then?"

He lifts a brow, expression dry. "Is this not freedom? I tend what I wish to tend here, in service to my country. That is freedom."

I look down, shift my grip on the wall. "Will your superiors not miss you, in the near future if you stay away?"

He shakes his head, eyes up the hall again, passive. "I tend the work I choose, as I have said. It is a privilege granted the Tyrńâk Knoc'gnori, and one that I exercise when it is fitting. My next task beyond these walls will be reassigned. The safety of this place is more important than it for the time being. It was a menial thing."

I look up at him, and start forward again. The rugs are soft beneath my feet. "Do the Knoc'gnori not serve at the word of the queen's generals, as any other soldier?"

He smiles, a wry thing. "Gót. They serve at her bidding and answer to only her. We have our own freedom among our ranks. We go through the training to gain that freedom."

He pauses, and we are before my door. I press my hand against the wall beside it, step away from him. "Thank you. May you rest well until the day to come." I incline my head, respect and honor, and he inclines his back with the same. I step through the door, and my head pounds, pulses. *He does not answer to the generals or dukes or lords. He answers only to her. Does he then work at his own will to undermine her, as the captain does?*

How far does he take this freedom? How far can he, while still in her military ranks?

My head is aching, the world too heavy. I step forward, and there is a murmur across the room, a voice for a moment, garbled with sleep. I pull the door shut, and there is darkness. *It does not matter, for tonight. The Knoc'gnori are not my concern, not here.*

XXVI

Wounds Tended

I groan, and the world is pressing in on all sides, dragging downward toward something.

A voice speaks softly—a woman's voice. Another responds, quiet, sharp. The wraps are heavy around me, sleep slipping off too quickly. Everything is warm, close around my shoulders.

Shapes shuffle around the room, candlelight flickering behind a moving shape. *A hand. Iris and Tollah will be rising for the day.* I drag my head up. The air feels hard and heavy, sweat clinging to my skin. Tollah's eyes flicker to me from beside the hand-cradled light, her face half caught in it. "Eness." Her voice is a breath, low with night. "You need not rise yet. Dawn has not come and you were weary from the day."

I shake my head, her voice strange in the departing sleep. *I do not know that I could rise now, if I chose to.* "I am not rising, only awake." I swallow, my throat dry with the night watches. "I apologize for disturbing your rise."

She half smiles, all shadows but the light of her eyes in the golden glow of the candle. "You are apologizing?" She laughs, soft and breathy. "You are sorry that we woke you from sleep?"

My eyes prick, burn. I half smile, adjust my feet beneath the blankets. Iris steps up beside her, twisting her hair up onto her head, the movement casting dancing shadows across the room. She inclines her head. "You should stay and rest a while longer. We are going to go help Nellie in the kitchens, but no one else will be up for a while yet but the guards. You could sleep nearly another watch." She turns, slipping past Tollah.

I drop my head backward against the wall, braid pressing against my neck. The door opens and shuts softly, no light pouring in from beyond. *The torches have not been lit yet.*

Tollah is standing beside the shelf, the candle on it now, her hands brushing through her coiled hair, her eyes on me. "Were the wounds severe?" I look up at her and the light flickers across her face. She continues. "I heard there was much blood, though perhaps you are used to that. I am not. My brother was out there, and I have heard little news of him, other than that he still lives. And Mirah's husband was there. We heard so little before we turned in. Are they truly well? Was there so much bleeding?"

I wrap my hands into the blankets, push them away from my arms. *The room is warm.* "The wounds were severe, but they were tended and should heal cleanly, beyond lasting scars on most of them." I shake my head, and the world clears a little, sharp in the dark. "You may go down and see your brother this morning, if you choose, after dawn has come. It would do good to the men to see their family down there, I trust. I will speak with Eerol about is when I rise."

She smiles, her hands twisting a tie into her hair. "I will tell Maylah then, once she is up. Are you well? You seemed weak last night, more tired than the rest of them when you came in. Tejan worried for you. She kept asking lord Fitz to see if you had turned in."

My eyes burn. I look down, shielding them with the darkness. *Did Fitz send for me to send me to bed, when he called me? I would not have come up, if they had not asked me to that meeting room.* "There were many men to tend, and I am not used to so many at one time, nor to riding. It was a long day."

She nods, lifting the candle from its shelf. "I am sorry. I will leave you be. You ought to be resting, not answering my thousands of questions so early in the morning watches. You will have enough of those without me. I am sorry." She inclines her head and slips out through the door.

It taps shut behind her, soft against the wood of the frame.

I purse my lips, press the side of my head against the wall. It is cool, solid, wood grain even with age and workmanship. Shadows press in, night watches heavy. *'My thousand questions.'* There will be more, when dawn comes. More with those who love the men below. More with what is to be done. More with my wellbeing if I cannot walk. I press my eyes shut. *Would it be safer to stay, and where questions are asked but there are others to aid, or to fight alone, where there is no one to caution, no one to fight for, no one to warn? There are no secrets to be held where there is no one to pry into them. No one's safety but my own to worry for in my actions and with my life. Blått would be fine, in the event of a soldier raid, but these people? If they were found, what other secrets of theirs would be dug up and brought into the light?*

I press my eyes shut against the darkness. *Lord Ciaran was certain, his words firm, polished, and thought through. He was sure of what he said to me, that there would be wisdom in staying here, in company.*

But can I be certain, with so little known of him, of any of them but the kindness they have offered? A board creaks in the hall—a step, somewhere down it. *If I stay, I will at last have help. My task will no longer be alone.*

But if their trust is misplaced in those here, there will be no more chances to save my people. My work will be ended. If no others are trying, if few others are working to aid them, to save them on the other fronts of the kingdom, there will be few left by the time the warm months come again. There can be few left now, stretched throughout this kingdom. The darkness presses in, warm with Stråle, warm with the season when all should be green and heavy with life. *She can have few more of us to eradicate. It has been many seasons. But she will turn her work to others, to keep her grasp on fear, if we are gone. It will not end with us.*

I fold my hands in my lap, lean my head backward against the thick grain of the wall. *Five turnings I have failed, alone. Creator, is it worth it, to pick it up again, so late in this fight? How many are left in this country?*

Darkness settles in, full and heavy.

·▶|◀▶|◀▶|◀▶|◀▶|◀▶|◀·

The floor of the healing rooms is cool beneath my feet. My neck aches. Two of the three beds visible through the archway are full, soldiers in dark uniforms still in them, but the third is empty, the man gone. My eyes burn. I glance around the room sharply. One of them looks up and his gaze is aware, sharply aware. I look away, step forward into the room.

Eerol brushes past the archway, his movements ever-quick, something flapping in his hands. There are heavy circles beneath his eyes, lines around his mouth that were not so deep last evening. Dark marks stain his clothes, stains on the thick cloth in his hand. *He has stayed up through the night watches. Who helped him, after I was called away? Did the other men stay to aid?*

I move to the side, take my apron from the chair where it was left before we took to the woods. Eerol glances at me, and his eyes snap away and back, scanning over my face, over my form. He wipes his hands on the stained cloth. "You can tend the men there." He points almost idly toward the men that I tended last evening, the men of Sikkerhet by the door.

I incline my head. "Where is the man from the third bed?" He glances at me again, and back across the room. There is a man sitting on the edge of the bed now, his expression dazed, Tren beside him helping him back into the cot. I shake my head, look away. "I did not see him. I apologize." Eerol turns away, his brows drawn low, mouth muttering through words, a finger lifting for each on, like a list. I glance around the room once more. *Blåthjortt is not here this morning.* I turn toward the healer. He is still muttering. "Eerol," I twist the strands of my apron on. "I can take care of this for a time. You may go rest. Please go rest." He lifts a brow, looking back at me over his shoulder. His eyes are sallow with sleeplessness. He shoves the sleeve of his shirt up and there is blood on his skin beneath his shirt. *How many wounds, did my voice not close?*

His eyes are darting around the room, taking it in. He nods, absently and his shoulders sag. "All should be quiet for at least half a watch." He brushes a hand across his face, over his grayed hair, eyes still shifting around the room. "Ask anyone here for help. There have been others tending to food and drink and helping the men to the chamber pot as you saw. Send someone to do those things, and do not attempt them yourself. You will have enough to do with wound care and fever watch without those. The bandages have not been changed this morning and many of them have new stitches." He nods again, his eyes snapping back to me. "Send someone if you need anything and wake me. I will be back inside of a full watch but send someone if I am not. I will not sleep over long. Fetch me when a watch is done." *A single watch will not be long enough to give him back the watches of sleep he missed.*

I incline my head. "When I need you, I will send someone." He nods again, shoulders sagging further and turns away. I turn toward the men he gestured to. Severin is in the first bed, the bandage I placed last night barely shifted from where it sat around his head. *The knot was good.* I step up beside him. "Gooddawn."

He looks up at me, and nods. "Gooddawn. You can walk a sight better this morning than last night. Was that your first ride, healer?"

I smile, my face warming. "Gót. But I am new to it yet." *He is far more alert, this morning that he was last night.* I gesture toward his side. "Has your wife been down to see you?" I lift the edge of the bandage at his waist, pull it free beneath his half-open tunic.

He nods above my head. "Aye. She came by last night, and about had a fight with Eerol, so it was not long." He half smiles. "He was not pleased about someone unneeded being down here, but I was glad to see her. She took the dirty bandages when she left so that he was not so ill impressed." I half laugh. The wound is dark this morning, a faint red rim around it. But it is still closed beneath the stitches, crusted now with blood and herbs.

I turn, grab a jar of salve from the shelf behind me. "You ought to be able to leave this room today and return to the upstairs if you are steady on your feet. There is nothing keeping you here. But you will need to be gentle on your side for the next few days and lift nothing heavy, or you will reopen the wound. You will not want me to redo those stitches when you are fully lucid." I half smile again and swipe salve across the wound.

He grimaces, inclining his head, just barely. "I would not. And that would be welcome. I do not care much for these cots, though they are a sight more comfortable than they might be."

I smile, swipe the salve across the lip of the jar. "Then I will check your wound, and if you can stand and walk across the room in an even line, you may leave." He nods, adjusting his head against the wall. The bandage is twisted, tucked away in a method that I have not used in turnings. *I must have been tired last night, to have used that knot. Aílé would have laughed to have seen it. It was not her way.* The wound is sealed beneath it—a dark, bloody line, rimmed by a circle of red above his brow. But it is sealed, like his side, salve still thick across the inside of the bandage. I twist it back into place.

His eyes lift to mine. "Is it so bad?"

I shake my head, step away from the cot. I fold my hands. "Gót. It looks very well. If you do not pull too much, it will heal cleanly. You are fortunate, it was not worse." *Is it deceitful, to not give credit where credit is due? They cannot praise Elnial for a thing they do not know that He has done.* I nod my head, toward the room. "The Creator was gracious to you all, I think. Your wounds are healing well, all of you." He stands slowly, height towering above mine. I gesture for him to start forward. His steps are even, hand clasped over the wound on his side. *Protective. But if he does nothing strenuous for half a moon, he will be well.*

He inclines his head back toward me. "He was indeed gracious. I am thankful that you all were there when you were." He starts back toward me, his voice lowering. "We had given up hope of being found." His eyes meet mine, gratefulness deep and full. I incline my head, look away. He shakes his head. "I did not think I would get to see my wife again, nor meet my child."

I look up sharply, set the crock in my apron pocket. "Is your wife with child?"

He grins, placing a steadying hand against the wall, his steps stopping. "Aye. We look forward to getting to meet the little one. Thanks to Elnial's grace in your arrival, I will get to." He inclines his head again. I smile, lift a rolled bandage from the basket beside me and slip it into my pocket. "Be well then, on your way, Severin. May you welcome your little one in peace." He inclines his head, turning for the archway, his hands already working to do the loose buttons of his tunic. I turn away. *I did not take the time to see who was conscious and who was not during the song, but he knows nothing of it. There was no time. Many of them could have been awake, in the dark of the woods. Including the soldiers. Will the goblin have spoken with them all, to tell them to keep silent? To hold back knowledge of healing from even their own wives?* My eyes flicker up.

The soldier in the center across the room is watching me, his beard dark, his eyes pale, and his expression steady. He lifts a brow, still watching me. I look away—a shudder runs up my spine. My eyes flicker back to the soldier next to him. He is young, his hair pale, curled and rustled. He is looking down, at the lump of his feet beneath the covers. *Their hands are still bound to the bed, all three of them. But if they look to make trouble, they will.* I glance around the room. Tren is across it, helping another man up and toward the chamber pot beside his bed. Beyond him, the room is silent but for a conversation between two of the wounded near him.

In case of an altercation, whom among the wounded will be able to aid? Many of them can hardly stand. I turn away, step up to the next wounded man, my back to the soldiers. He is laying back against the wall, like Severin, his leg propped up high on a pillow. His eyes meet mine. He is big, a broad man, features firm, eyes narrow, like Tollah's, features hard. He lifts a brow, shifting a bandaged shoulder and grins. "You are back." *I do not remember speaking with him last night.* I blink. *He was not conscious. I did not speak with him.*

I half smile. "I am. But you were not awake when I last was here." I pull the crock of salve from my pocket, set it on the bed. I lift my eyes to his, reach for the bandage over his leg.

He grunts. "No I weren't. But my wife told me that you were down here late into the night last even."

I glance at him. "Has she come down then? Are you well this morning?"

He grins, an easy, kindly thing, strange on a man so large. "Aye she did. And as well as a man with a trussed-up leg can be, I'd have to guess. Eerol says it is a miracle that the bone was not shattered, with where the blade hit me. Should have smashed right through." He lifts a brow at me, only halfway, glancing toward Severin. "There seem to be a lot of those going around. Elnial was kind."

I look down at his wound, and my eyes burn. *Many miracles, aye.* I lift the bandage from the wound. *Eerol was right. The wound is deep. If this was done by a broadsword, even with a glancing blow, it should have shattered his thigh. It may have shattered it, last evening before healing came.* I prod at the wound with the tips of my fingers. It feels clean, the skin swollen, but no sign of bone shards or fragments of the woodlands in it. I draw my hands back, reach for the crock in my pocket. "Elnial was indeed gracious to all of you." I lift the crock, swipe the salve across the wound. "Do you have family here, beside your woman?"

He nods, grinning softly. "Aye. A sister and a proud boy. The little sod looks a sight more like me than his mother, though. Poor lot."

I laugh, pull the wrap tight beneath the wound. "That will not likely be a trial to him. Most boys that I know enjoy the little bit of fierce looks they have while they are young."

He shakes his head, grinning sideways at me. He looks down at the wound idly, his smile softening. "Well, Jørn certainly does enjoy that. He is a sight taller than the boys more than a turning older than him though. A strong boy. He has his grandmere's eyes." *Jørn.*

I pull the wrap tight, tuck it into its place. "Norla is your wife then?" There is another bandage across his shoulder, wrapped securely, lifting his arm slightly from his side.

He nods. "Aye. You met here then? And my boy?" I pull the bandage free, and it slides, curling down his arm. *His arm is bigger than both of mine put together.*

I swallow. "Aye. I have met them both. Your wife is a kind woman. What is your name, sónya?" The wound beneath the bandage is a slight thing, though it would have been deep, before the song put the red rim there. A stab wound, cratering the skin where it has healed. *It may have cut through to bone.*

He glances down at it. "It's Tollak. We appreciate your work these last few days, healer." His voice is solid, gruff, nothing more to it, not like Severin's, which hints at things unspoken. I nod, lifting his arm, and wrap the bandage back over it. *It will need no more care, only time to heal.*

I tuck the bandage back under. "It is an honor to be of assistance. You all are a gracious bunch."

He nods, eyes lifting to mine again. "Aye, many of them are. How long till you think I can be back on my feet?"

I laugh tuck it back. "I am afraid you may have to be content with hand work for now. That is no slight wound, Tollak. You will have to let it heal, though Eerol will have the final voice for how long. I am only help, but I think it will be a spell."

He sinks back against the cot, shifting his massive shoulders. "Aye. I thought as much. But with Severin leaving, I was hopeful." He looks down at his leg. "It was worth it though. The man who did this is not still standing to tell the tale."

I glance across the room at the soldiers, and back towards him. "Rest then. If you have need of anything, you need only ask and I will tend to it as I can." He grins, appreciation in the nod of his head.

I turn away. *I would that I could have sung for longer. They would have both benefitted from it.* My eyes flicker across the room, toward the soldiers. The one in the middle is no longer staring at me. *Three of them healed, with five of our men. If I had not healed the soldiers, had known and let them pass, could I have held out long enough to heal these men completely? Could I have let the soldiers die, when I was able to save them? Could I have ignored their lives, their life blood leaking from their veins, and let them pass on so simply if I had known they were there? There would have been more questions, from all involved, if the men had come back, blood covered and healed, their wounds ringed with red.*

The soldier with the golden ringlets is still staring at his feet, his eyes vacant, his hands idle in their restraints beside him. *His mind is not here. Could I have let him die in the woodlands, far from any who loved him, far from any who know his name? Could I have let him die, knowing that I might have spared him?*

I turn away, swipe my hands through my apron. *I could not have. Not like that. They will await their trial, at the court of Fitzclaste. What becomes of them now is not mine to decide, but I have healed them enough, and they will live to see it a trial, however it is done. That decision will be made by others. I will not have their blood on my hands, Creator help me. Their blood is not mine to spend.*

XXVII

Gold Trim Soldiers

I press my hand against Blått's head, step down the staircase, voices soft and strange on the stone below, several voices muffled together. *Stay or leave. I could continue my work here—there might be aid for it at last. But I do not like the risk in staying.*

My feet brush the stone at the bottom of the stairs. The voices are louder, gruff, not like they should be, with a man speaking to a friend. I slow my steps, glance around the corner. The beds are empty across the second room, steps shuffling somewhere in it. My heart slows, eyes burn. I press it back. *Soldiers. Have they gotten free so soon?* My eyes dart around the archway.

There are men standing to the side of the empty cots, only half-visible through the archway. The goblin is among them. My chest lightens. *They will do little damage, wounded as they are if he arrived early enough.*

There is another man beside him, a man whom I have seen before, his stance familiar. He is speaking, his voice clipped and even—not yet raised, but precise. "...This is not the time or place. You will have your opportunity before the court to speak and to make your case. For now, you will come along willingly, or you will be bound, gagged, and carried. Those are the only options presented to you, soldier. Choose one and do not make me degrade you to that." He tilts his head to the side, just barely.

Captain Flint. He was not here before.

There is silence for a long moment. Someone speaks, and the voice is rougher, though not harsh, like I thought before. *Rough like a dry throat, like lack of water after a man has slept long.* "I do not understand this. I have asked to speak with the lord of this place. I would have words with him before we are banished to whatever deep hole you have us bound for. If you are speaking of reason, let me speak with him, please. I ask nothing more than this. Unless you are part of the Movement, you will allow me this. Let me speak with him."

Sradfaang's head tilts, just barely, a threat in it. "You will not be banished to a hole today. And you will have time to speak with those that it is appropriate to speak with at a later time. Now you will come quietly. I do not wish to haul your body up the stairs today, nor do I wish to carry it out back."

Captain Flint shifts, and I can see the soldier's face for just a moment, his eyes alight, jaw tight beneath his beard. *The soldier who watched me this morning.* His eyes catch mine, and Captain Flint half-turns, glancing at me. His gaze is passive. "Eness. You will return upstairs and find me the healer."

I slow, straighten. *He knows I am a healer. Does he need Eerol, or is he working at something?* I incline my head, step forward. "I will. But there is something I must stir first, or it will burn while I am gone."

He inclines his head, turning away. "Be quick. Both healers. I would like Eerol to tend these men once they are in their new quarters and see to it all is well with them. We do not treat our guests like the Movement treats theirs." *The Movement? What Movement do they speak of?*

I nod, turn away. *These men have seen me tend to the others. They will know that I am one of the healers already, or at least have guessed at it. Sradfaang must know that, know that this will do little if they are pretending I am not among them. They are already aware of what I am here, unless they assumed me to be just a helper while Eerol rested.*

I grip a cloth and lift the pot from the stove and set it against the table. It thuds hard, heavy, filled brimful. The salve inside is thick, nearly done, and it scarcely moves, steam thin on its surface. I set the cloth down beside it and turn for the stairs. I keep my head down. *Are the soldiers still so much of a threat that they cannot acknowledge who I am before them? What have they said, that would draw concern from the captain?* I glance down at the hound beside me, click my tongue twice. He moves toward the fireplace, his steps even, eyes reproachful. *But he will stay out of the way, if they do not dally long here.*

I bolt up the stairs, stone cold beneath my skin. *Eerol is speaking with someone, checking something, but I do not recall where, or what he said before he went.* I turn, my eyes flickering around the hallway, and there are footfalls in it, someone coming around the corner. *Tejan.* She smiles, softly, a tray in her hands. "Eness? Are you lost, Iai, or looking for someone?"

I half-smile, shake my head. "I am looking for Eerol. Do you know where he has gone to?"

She shifts the tray in her hands. "Last I saw him, he was in the kitchens. You may check there. Tollah may know if he has left them. Are you well?"

The kitchens? That was not where he had spoken of going. I incline my head, half-bow. "I am. Thank you, Tejan."

A smile pulls at the edges of her mouth. "La. I hope that you find him swiftly. Anything I should know of happening?" She balances the tray on her hip, eyes even on mine. There is the sound of footfalls, behind me, men moving toward the stairs. *I should be gone before they crest them.*

I dip my head, step past her. "They are moving the soldiers and want Eerol to check on them after they are moved." She inclines her head and I move up the hall. There are lots, walking and talking in the halls, their heads thrown back in laughter and their eyes on their hands, on their work. I move around them, step past the doors into the great hall. It is empty, but for a woman on the far side, scrubbing at a table, humming, the sound hollow in the empty space. *Iris.* I move around her, around another table, and step through the open doorway.

There are people everywhere, moving, lifting, carrying, slicing, their hands all busy, mouths all talking. I look around the woman in front of me, the noise heavy in the room, tilting my head with their movements. There is a grayed head on the far side of the moving women, down below the height of the counters. He is speaking, head low, tones that cannot be heard over the clanging pots and chatter of voices.

I step around the woman, skirt around another and he glances up, heavy brow quirking at me. "Eness. What do you need? Has something happened?"

Do I look so harried? I fold my hands, incline my head toward him. "Captain Flint has asked for you, for your help with the men they are moving to new quarters."

He lifts a brow, knowledge flashing through his eyes. His hand shifts on the arm of the person next to him. *Of the child next to him. He is tending a wound on a child. I should have noted that, when I walked into the room.* A woman's laugh rings out sharply behind me, followed by a light cough. He glances behind me, muttering something and inclines his head, to me. "I will come. I did not realize he had arrived."

He looks down at the girl next to him, and her eyes are wide, watching. She licks her lip, and he half-smiles. "Lila, this healer is going to finish with your arm. I have to go, but she will be gentle with you. She is kind. Kinder than me, mayhaps, and she doesn't scowl so much, which may make it easier." He wiggles his brows at her, and she giggles, pressing a hand against her lips. Humor dances in her eyes.

I smile, kneel beside her, and Eerol is standing, his hands pressed against his knee, stretching. He points at her arm, a vague gesture. "It is a burn, not a bad one, but I have put salve with egg white on it, and it should be wrapped up as well as you can. The bandages are there." He nods toward his bag, leaning against the wall by the girl.

I lift it, glance up at him. "They will have left the healing rooms by now and be up the halls somewhere. Captain Flint did not tell me where they are taking them, but you will know?"

He nods, waving me off, and is gone, moving through the noise and the chaos of the women across the room. One of them is singing now, her voice high and even, clear, another woman laughing beside her.

I turn back to the child. She is watching me, her lip trembling, just barely. "Ist it gonna hurt?"

I smile, lift a small bandage roll from the bag. "Gót. I am only going to wrap it. Eerol has already done the only parts that will have any hurt to them." I pull the end of the bandage out, unwind a length of it. "It will not feel good for a few days though, while it heals. It may be hot sometimes, and ache, but this part will not hurt at all. How did you wound it?" I lift her arm, set the bandage against the side of it. The burn is only blistered in a few places, the few that there are jut out from beneath the thick, reddish salve with the pale sheen of egg white in it. *It will heal cleanly enough.*

She looks at me, staring at my face, at my eyes. "Jørn says your eyes is purple, but I thinks him was wrong."

I pull the wrap around again and my jaw tightens. *When could the boy have seen my irises change?* I press the bandage gently to her skin, keep it in place with my thumb. "Sometimes the light makes your eyes seem different colors than they are. I bet yours sometimes look a different shade, too. In full light or with the color of your dress."

She snuffles, wiping her nose across her bare arm, and grins at me. "Na. My eyes is j'st brown. Sometimes Jørn j'st is wrong. I's tells him that no one has purple eyes, but he says that you does, and now I'm gonna tell him hims wrong. I think if you's had purple eyes, you would'a been the prettiest lady I ever seen, but you does not so you isn't." She shrugs a little boney shoulder, her eyes on my hands over the wound.

A smile tugs at my lips. I tuck the wrap into place. "Well, then. I will settle for just a little pretty, since my eyes are only gray. We are done now. You should go find your tá. She will want to know about your arm, to see how it is, if she has not heard. You can show her your bandage." I smile at her. "You were brave, Lila."

She blinks at me. "My tá left. Fár said hers dead now."

My heart sinks, eyes burn, twisting. "Oh." She is just staring, solemn. I press my hand against hers, but she is still just sitting there, watching me, nothing in her eyes but that searching expression they have always had since I knelt here. *There is no grief in them, no understanding, only the childlike knowledge of what has been told them.* My eyes burn harder and I push it back, turn my head away sharply.

She giggles, pulling away from me. "Him wasn't right, healer lai. Your eyes does funny things like I never seen, but they isn't purple. I wish my eyes was blue like that. Then I could brag to Jørn because hims eyes isn't blue like that."

I force a smile, and take her unwounded hand. I pull her to her feet, gently, stand after her. "You ought to go find your family, Lila. You are free to go now. My eyes shall be our secret, aye?"

I let go of her hand, and she looks down, staring at her arm. "Aye." Her voice is absent, eyes still staring. I purse my lips, glance back over my shoulder toward the halls. Lila spins away and is gone, a swirl of skirts through the ever-moving figures of the women. *She will have forgotten in a moment that she ever saw my eyes. The child seems to live somewhere else in her mind. She will have made up a story about it, if she has not forgotten. But people do listen to the half-truths of children.*

I turn toward the kitchens. *I do not know when to return to the healing rooms, what the captain was playing at. He asked for both healers, knowing surely that he was sending one away.* I lift the bag from the floor, fold my hands around it. *He will come tell me what he wants of me, when they are done settling the soldiers where they have placed them.*

Lila cuts out of the crowd again, twirling around another figure on the far side of the stove. I grimace. *It is no wonder she got burned as she did.* She is laughing, the woman beside her saying something, an older woman, one I do not know, ushering her away, scolding. Lila laughs again, a young laugh, and she is gone, through the doorway, something tucked away in her hand. The older woman laughs, shaking her head, exchanging words with Tollah beside her. *Lila will be well, if she gets no fever tonight. It is not a bad burn but for the blisters.* I smile and step away, through the bustling women.

•▶|◀▶|◀▶|◀▶|◀▶|◀▶|◀•

There is a footfall behind me, in the hall. "Healer?" I turn, satchel slung over my shoulder. *Captain Flint.* Sradfaang is behind him, light from behind blocked by their figures. Flint steps forward. "I would speak with you, if you have a moment to be spared."

I glance down the hall, toward the passage to the healing ward and back to him. "Where would you go?"

He inclines his head. "Down the stairs is fine." *It must be a light matter then, if he would speak of it before the men. Words carry in the healing ward.* I incline my head and he steps past me, down toward the stairs. He starts down them and I move after him, the goblin behind me. He slows at the bottom, not even glancing into the room beyond and turns left, away from the healing rooms, behind the staircase into the dark space where I have not been.

My eyes sting faintly. *I was wrong. He does seek quiet.* I step after him, and there is the shadow of the goblin falling across the ground before me, his presence heavy, though his steps are still masked. The captain halts, the air damp around the bend, where the light scarcely reaches. *There is nothing back here but shadows, not even storage.* The cave is a rough-hewn room in the dark, nowhere to go but back in it. I can barely see the captain's face, scarcely see the goblin where he has stopped beside me.

Captain Flint lifts a brow, turning to me. "We have moved the soldiers to another part of Sikkerhet to be watched until it is decided what is to be done with them. For the time being, I would recommend that you are not the one to tend to them, and I have already spoken with Eerol about it. He is in agreement." He shifts his hand, relaxed by his sword hilt in the darkness. "I would suggest that not only because I lied to them a moment ago." His eyes meet mine. "Ciaran and Fitz have told me of the gift that you were carrying when you arrived here, which is no small secret. None of us would like to see that or you fall into the hands these soldiers serve, and I would not like to give them any chances to ask any questions of you. When we know more of their loyalties, I will speak with you again, as is fitting, as well as to Ciaran and Fitzclaste. Is there anything you are concerned with?"

I fold my hands. *What else is there for me to worry about in that, aside from their knowledge of me?* "Gót. I have no wish to get any closer to them than need be. I would be happy to not speak with them again during their stay here. If there is anything I need to know, I trust that I will be told. Where were they taken?"

He inclines his head. "Then I am glad you will not need to go closer than you have already. You may report any concerns to Ciaran or Fitz. Sradfaang will likely already be aware of them." He half-smirks. "If he is doing his task well."

Sradfaang face is expressionless above me, unperturbed. "I *always* do my task well. Perhaps you should look more to yours, captain." There is a flash of white in the darkness, sharp. *His teeth.* "I recall something about a missing boot."

The captain inclines his head, toward the goblin, grinning. "You do yours well. But one of these days perhaps you will go soft. You are growing old, my friend. Old and green. I may misplace a boot but growing old seems worse."

There is the flash of white again—the goblin grinning. He tilts his head, stepping aside to let the captain by. "You are not as young as you once were, and I am not many moons your senior. Losing a boot may be a sign of an addled mind. I would rather be green than pasty, like you will be if you ever leave off the trails you take to and stay in one place for more than a moon. How many turnings is it now? Thirty?"

Captain Flint laughs, his head thrown back. "And you? You've got at least two turnings on me. Neither of us are new earth, and these trails seem to be more my companion than yours. Would you give up your work to stay in one place? I would like to see you turn pasty, rather than that green skin."

Sradfaang grins. "Not until my task is done. And my family never turns pasty. We get darker with age."

The captain inclines his head, folding his arms. "And if I give up my task, yours will become more troublesome. As long as you are stuck, I am." He turns, inclining his head toward me. "I am glad to hear that you are well, and to know that your safety is being looked for here. What you carry is worth more than a hundred men, and I am glad to know there are few who know of it. We intend to keep it that way. They will tell no one else. Keep it quiet. You should have already been asked not to use it again in the time you are here."

I shake my head. "I have not been. But I do not intend to."

He inclines his head. "Good. Is there anything else you would know, while I am here?"

I shake my head. "Gót. Only if where the soldiers are, they are secure? They may have heard what was done in the woods."

He nods, glancing at me. "Aye. We would not do otherwise with them. And I will look into that and see what can be discovered discreetly. If that is all, than gooveven to you, Eness Finch. If you have questions, you will find Ciaran and Fitz. They will be happy to speak with you." He inclines his head, turning, and is gone around the corner, the goblin following after him.

I fold my arms, tighten my grip on the bag. *Ciaran was right, last night. It seems a shame to keep the song quiet after it has been used. The gift has finally served again, only to fall quiet once more.* I step up the hall, and there is a laugh in the rooms beyond, high and strange like a woodpecker's call. *Eerol's. He is back down, then.* I half-smile, and it is brittle on my lips. *I will keep it silent, once again. But it may never be used, if this war stretches on into deadening times and it is to be silent while it stretches. Perhaps the lord is right. That it would be better served, in a place like this, in the times to come and not ferreted away, like so much gold. What use does gold serve in the darkness?*

XXVIII

Of Table Talk

Voices are rumbling together, landlots moving toward seats. All of them are speaking, voices high and scattered, trickling across the room. I press my hands together beneath the bowl. *Perhaps it would be better to eat downstairs, men down there or not. There are many lots up here this evening. I am in no mind for conversation but that of the men below, which will be quiet tonight.* My head pulses duly, shoulders ache.

"Eness, aye?"

My eyes snap up. There is a woman beside me, her eyes sharp and dark, gentle, her figure tall. *Ruidún, Severin's wife. I have not seen her since the night of the woods.* She inclines her head toward me, respect and greeting. "If you have a mind to, we would be glad for you to join us this evening. There is a spot on the benches, near me and my husband, and we would be honored to have you in it. I do not know if you remember me. We met in the halls a few nights back, when my husband was injured?" I glance toward the tables, shift the bowl to my other hand. *It is warm.* Her brow creases. "Of course, if you would prefer not, that is well. I only wished to invite you after the way you tended all the men, the other night. We are grateful for your service. I did not intend to trouble you. I apologize."

I half-smile, shake my head. "Gót. I would be honored. I am only a little tired tonight."

Her eyes light up, and she moves, stepping toward the tables. "It is over here. My husband is already seated." The room is quieter, a tale being spoken somewhere, the words quiet over the rumbling voices. *A tale to the children, perhaps.* She slows by a bench on the far side of the room, working her way down around the backs of those already seated. I follow. She slows, stepping over the bench into a seat and drops onto it. There is more than one beside her, vacant, spaces between her and another woman. *Iris.* I skirt past her back, step into the empty place beside Ruidún.

Severin is across the table, his eyes meeting his wife's first— warmth in them for her—and then mine, softer, but still kind. "Healer." He inclines his head. "It is well to see you here. How are the men still below, tonight? I have been on watch since I got out and have heard little of them."

I half-smile, incline my head. "They are healing. Only two are still down there, and Tollak should be the only one left after tomorrow's dawn. His leg will take more time to heal than the other. But I had thought you were to be healing your ribs, moving slowly until the stitches were removed so that they do not come free on their own?"

He flushes slightly, his hand gripping his wife's. He smiles. "I am taking it slowly, but sitting on a watch tower and looking out over trees is a simple thing. If there is trouble, it will not matter if I am wounded or not, I will go. And if there is not, then it seems to me that sitting up there and sitting in my rooms are nearly the same stress to my wound."

I look away, a smile tugging at the edge of my lips. My eyes flicker to the man beside him, across from me. *Ciaran.* My eyes snap back to Severin, sharply.

Severin is lifting a bite of his stew now, his wife taking up hers. "It is good news, that the others are nearly all out now. I have missed having Tohm on watches with me." *Tohm, one of the men, who should have lost the use of his arm, the last man down there but for Tollak.*

I nod and turn my head toward Ciaran. His eyes meet mine. *Has he been watching quietly?* He inclines his head. "Healer. I trust you are well tonight?"

I glance down at my stew. "Aye, I am. Thank you. I trust that the events of today all went well?"

He nods, slowly, carefully. "They did. As smoothly as can be expected. Captain Flint informed me that he spoke with you this afternoon to fill you in on the outcome of their meeting, as much as need be."

I set my spoon down, incline my head. "Aye, he did." Severin is watching beside him, his eyes steady on Ciaran, but he asks no questions, says nothing, his wife chatting with the woman beside her.

Ciaran's eyes are still on mine, careful and barely readable. *They are never readable, but when he chooses for them to be.* He moves his hand to his mug. "You have been settling in well, this last fortnight, I trust? There has been more on your plate than I would have wanted, for having been so newly here, but I trust that Eerol has not given you anything that did not need to be done. He does not give idle hand work often." He half-smiles, the mug below his lips. "Not to those he trusts."

I half-smile in return, nod. "Aye, though the first few days, most of his tests were the kind of labor that I would not do unless the season was dead and my hands completely idle. As you say, that was work to a healer he did not yet trust." I laugh, and it sounds strange.

A smile catches in his eyes, never reaching his lips, but it is bright and there. "Well, I trust that is no longer the case. He speaks highly of you now and your skill at your work. You could tend a fort like this on your own, if you chose. You have more than the hand for it, from all that I have heard from those who have seen it."

I look down, pick up my spoon once more. I shake my head. "Gót. My skills lie mostly in herbs, for that is what I have tended. I would have more to learn than all of his knowledge together if I were to tend a place of this stature, tend this many lots. My knowledge is rudimentary at best and has not been used much but for seeking out herbal work, as you know."

Severin shakes his head, leaning forward on the table. "That is not what I have heard nor seen and many of the men here are a testament to your skill and knowledge in that area. If you ever chose, to take up a place like this, your skill would like as not be more than sufficient for a place like Sikkerhet. You are gifted."

I half-smile, bite back the grimace rising to my lips. *Gifted. More than he would know.* They are turning back to their food, Ciaran watching the room, his eyes slowly moving from table to table, person to person, the mug held calmly in his hand. *What is he looking for, or is it only his habit?* I set my spoon down, turn fully toward him. "What is your title, sónya? I have noted the way you are spoken to, respected, but I have never heard a word of your title. You must surely have one."

His eyes move slowly to mine, back from the room. He lifts a brow, setting down his mug. "I was a military leader, before I came here. It is for respect of that that I am honored in this way, my council sought. A great honor, given. My title itself is of little matter, here. We are far from the military, far from the forces of Queen Georwyn." He sits back, resting his forearm on the table before him.

I shake my head. "Far, aye, but not so far that titles do not reach, I think, or you would not be so well respected, nor so careful. Would you be known, if you were seen by the soldiers below?"

A smile tugs at the edge of his lips. "It would depend on where they have come from and who they are. Many who knew me during my time would not be so far from the cities. There are few now who knew me that would stray this far, unless they were under discipline to be put in the outer ranks. I have been gone for many turnings."

He shifts his arm on the table. "How has your stay here been to you? I am sorry these last few days have not been kind, and I am hopeful the ones ahead will be a little more gracious, that you may find some rest. We have rarely had trouble of this kind in the time we have been here, and I am sorry that it has come during your first days."

I purse my lips. *Does he wish so little to speak of himself?* "They have been well. I am still learning my way around these halls and the names of those in them. There are many landlots here. How long have you all been in this place? Was this the first time the queen's men have made it so near?"

He lifts a brow, the scar on his cheek shifting just slightly with it. Ruidún leans forward, setting her hand against the table. "Fitzclaste and Tejan have been here for far longer than anyone else, along with their children who came with them, but have left. This is their home and has been for ten turnings I believe. Perhaps longer."

I incline my head. "And the rest of you? How long have lots been hidden here, and how did it begin?"

Ciaran half-smiles, real, full, and it is there for a short moment. "It was begun because it was needed. And the others have all been hiding for eight turnings or less. It has not been long that it has been a safe haven for more than the few that Tejan and Fitzclaste kept with them in their own close family."

Eight turnings or less. What time is long, if that is not? The full fifteen turnings since the queen came to the throne with her husband's death? Is that long? He cannot be many turnings my senior. None of these three can be old enough that they would speak of eight turnings as so few as to be nothing.

I incline my head. "You have not been here long then, Ciaran of the title of no account?"

He inclines his head, that smile flickering on his lips again. "Only a few turnings. My days here have not been many."

I frown, my eyes scanning over his face. Severin is speaking again, to only him, something about hunting, about stags and rabbits and hounds, the thread of conversation gone in a breath. Ciaran's gaze is still half on me, watching. I turn my head away, lift a bite.

Someone drops into the seat beside me, heavy. I look up sharply. *The captain.* He glances across the table, nodding to the golden man. "Ciaran." Something glimmers at the edge of his mouth. *A grin. What amuses him, here?*

The other man inclines his head back, his eyes moving to him, finishing his words to Severin. He turns fully toward the captain, movements smooth and even as they always are. "Einion. Did you and Srad gain what you were searching for?"

The captain nods. "Aye. They knew nothing when they came here. It was a cursory scout, sent further than normal." Ciaran nods, his eyes steady, and Einion sets his spoon down. "I will speak to Fitz again. We will go ahead with what we discussed, if your thoughts are unchanged. Sradfaang believes it would be wise to move forward as quickly as can be managed with them so there is little talk or time for things to shift." *With the soldiers.*

My eyes flicker over the table, Ruidún speaking with her husband. He is laughing, her hand in his over the table. *They are not listening, paying no heed to what is being said between the men.*

What will they do with the soldiers, wherever they have placed them? Will they cast them out? Surely they will not execute without a full trial.

I glance at Ciaran. *There is little choice, if that is the only option. No magistrate will rule in favor of our men, against the queen's soldiers.* Ciaran takes up his spoon again, and Einion's eyes flicker toward me. "Eness. I trust that your stay here has been smooth, but for two nights back. You seem to have recovered quite well."

I glance at him. "Aye. And you, from your travels?"

He nods his head, dismissal in its tilt. "Aye. Always. It was a simple enough journey and not far. You keep yourself busy, in the healing rooms?" He lifts a bite, "I take it Eerol has taken you in, since you were down there earlier. That is a good surprise. I thought he would not, when I sent you. He has never let another down there, not to work with him for more than a fortnight. They always end up working somewhere else in the fort where their gifts are of more use."

I lift a brow. "I am surprised. He did not seem troubled by my coming, not after the initial trials. Only gruff. And he had more than enough labor for two. Was that not one reason why you sent me here, to be of use to him?"

A grin tugs at the edge of his mouth, wry. "Aye. And only gruff and a few trials? I would have thought he would not be over that, yet. He has gone soft. He threatened to extend trials before for more than a full moon, when we offered to bring him help last time I was at Sikkerhet." He half-laughs, twirling the spoon between his fingers.

"But then, I thought he might take to you a little more kindly. You look like his daughter, turnings ago, when I last saw her."

I look down, look away. *Eerol has not mentioned his family. He does not wear the wrist torc, to indicate marriage.* Ciaran is speaking with the captain again, words about birds and hunting grounds mixing in with the voices around us.

·▶|◀▶|◀▶|◀▶|◀▶|◀▶|◀·

I shift the crock in my hand, stare at the shelf. *There was a place for this, but I do not know where it was.* I glance through the crocks. There is no color organization to them, no difference between the tones of the clay to symbolize what is inside. Only row after row of simple crocks, in varied tones of blue and tans and reds scattered across shelves.

Anna's head lifts on the edge of my vision, her eyes turning toward the man seated on the cot across from her. His foot soaks in a bucket of salt water, propped up. "It is not broken, is it?" She asks. Her voice is soft, and I barely catch her words; not the chipper tone of her normal speech, but something gentler now.

The man smiles, strands of hay still caught in his hair—Jakob, of the stables. "Gót. The healing kúráh has tended it, and it is not broken, only bruised rather remarkably, though that steer tried." He shifts his foot, grimacing. "I think he would have liked far more than my foot to be broken if he had had his way."

Anna laughs softly, lifting the grime-stained cloths from the floor. She tosses them into the basket on her hip, swinging it to catch them. "I do not think that he tried very hard then. A steer could do greater damage than that if he chose. And you are strong enough to give him trouble if he tried more than this, I would think." She shifts the basket back into place. "I am glad he did not try harder this time."

Jakob grins, a lopsided smile, just for her.

I turn away sharply. *I have heard nothing of a courtship or anything between these two. But I have heard little of any of them, beyond their names.* I snatch up another crock and spin, set it on the shelf beside the bone salves. *If there is not one, there should be one soon. That smile was not meant for someone you do not like, as a man to a woman.*

Anna turns toward me, her eyes lingering on the stable-hand beside her. She draws her eyes away, and they are still alight. "I heard there were soldiers brought in. Where are they, if not here? We have seen nothing of them above." She glances through the archway, into the dark hall beyond.

I shake my head, push my sleeve back up my arm. "Nothing is kept back there, certainly not men. I do not know where they are gone to. They were not kept here long after they were brought in. Only a day."

"So then, they were here?"

I glance up at her, brush leaves from the table into my cupped hand beside it. "It is not my place to speak of them. You may ask Sradfaang or Fitzclaste about it, if you wish to know more."

She inclines her head, eyes grave, glancing back at Jakob again. She stoops, lifting another rag. "I hear that Eerol may leave?"

My heart stills. I swallow hard, bite back the burning of my eyes. "What reason would draw him from these walls? Is he not in hiding?"

She nods, still speaking toward Jakob. "He is. But I heard he may leave and go back to his village and home. He has grandchildren there, and I heard he will return to them so he can help them with something. I didn't get the full story." Her eyes move back to me, and they widen. Her movements freeze. "You had not heard of this?"

Heard of this? He cannot leave. I will be alone here, with this task and place, and I have not given an answer as to whether or not I will stay. What will this place be, without the healing man? I swallow hard. "When is he rumored to leave?"

She shakes her head sharply, moving the basket higher on her hip. "I am sorry. I should not have spoken. I thought you knew. You will have to ask him about it. I should not have spoken." She turns back toward Jakob, speaking softly to him. He grins, taking her hand in his. *They must be courting.*

I turn away. My heart sinks in my chest. *Did they not say he has been here for turnings? Is my choice gone then, to stay or to go? A place of this size cannot be without a healer, not when there are women and children present. Not with the potential for warbands again so near at hand. These last days have been proof of that.*

There have been few others who have helped with wounds. They have only tended to the ill by helping to chamber pots and helping with food and water. The rest must fall to someone.

I turn, grab a bag of herbs, and it is light. *Half empty.* I grab the one next to it, and it is the same. *We are nearly out of echinacea. We will need that again, to fight infections and wounds. I should have gone for more.*

I set the bags on the table. *This will have been a rumor. He would have told me, if he was to leave. He would not surprise me in this way, by alerting others before I am aware.*

I glance toward Jakob, and Anna is stepping up the stairs, the basket leveled on her swaying hips. I snatch a towel from the table and walk toward him, drop to my knees beside the bucket. I place the towel on the floor, beside the bucket where his foot is beneath the hazy water. "You may pull it out. Set it here."

His leg lifts, and he sucks in a breath sharply. The cut is deep, but no longer bleeding. It is clean now, after the brine. He sets it against the towel, and I shift on my heels. "You are fortunate you did not lose a toe, Jakob of the stables. Cattle hooves are not known to be kind when they injure, as this one has."

He half-grins, a slight thing, and he speaks through clenched teeth. "The steer does not have many days left in this world." He wraps his hand around his knee, his foot wavering above the cloth and hisses through his teeth. "I think he knows it. He has been antsy, the last few dawns. Aggressive when we have come near."

I smile, glance up at him. "So, he tried to take some of you with him when he goes?"

He shakes his head, laughing, his foot shaking where it hovers above the towel. I pat the cloth and he sets his foot against the cloth slowly. "Gót. I did not mean that. But he is restless, and it is a wonder that he did not wound someone sooner. I will not be going in his stall anymore, nor will anyone else. I can clean it well enough over the walls. I am tall enough, if just barely."

There is movement behind him, through the doorway, in the room beyond. *Tollak.* He is hobbling, moving his hulking frame across the floor, movements staggered. His broken leg is jutting out in front of him, an awkward thing, a bandage trailing out behind, free from the wrap.

I twist a cloth over Jakob's foot, my eyes half on the man beyond him. *If he falls, I will not be able to get him up again on my own.* I glance at Jakob. *He will be little help, with a hobbled foot, after so much blood loss. Tollak is a big man, and he is not using the crutch, as he should be.*

I tuck the bandage into place around Jakob's leg, stand. "Your foot will heal, but if the gash opens up again, come find Eerol or I. Do not let it fester. I do not want to stitch it, with where it is, but if it opens again, it will need to be done, or it will not heal cleanly. Bring it back to me if you get it dirty again."

He stands, and he is towering over me. *I did not notice that he is a big man as well, though not as big as the towering man beyond.* He bows toward me. "Dirt in it? That will not happen, in the stables." He grins. "Thank you, kúráh. I am indebted to you."

I smile, step away. "It was no trouble."

He turns toward the stairs and I move by him, into the next room.

Tollak's face is ashen, his skin bright with a sheen of sweat, a hand pressed white against the wall. *His arm is trembling*—I step forward, press my shoulder under it. "What were you doing, sonyá?"

His eyes dart down to me, free hand hesitating above my shoulder. "I thought to take a turn about the room, but the rooms seems to be taking me for a turn instead." He grimaces. Sweat trickles into his shirt collar, his eyes searching, uncertain.

He swears, dropping his hand on my shoulder, and I stagger, his weight pressing hard on me. He grunts, pulling his hand back. "I am sorry, kúráh."

I shake my head sharply, press his hand back against my shoulder. "Gót. Do not worry for me. Use my shoulder." His weight presses on me once more. I grit my teeth, straighten. I lift my eyes to his. There is pain written across his face, something lost in his gaze. *He needs to be up and about. I should have seen to that before. He will lose his aim, sitting on that bed for another day.*

I lift my head. "We may go a little more, and then rest. You can rise again later, if you are feeling up to it and there is someone here to aid you." My voice is tight. I force myself to breathe easily, his weight heavy on my shoulder.

He nods, his eyes still half-aimless, unfocused with pain. "I didn't think it would hurt so blasted much t' stand. It didn't yesterday, or the day before."

I nod my head. "Those days you had a crutch and were still drinking a hearty tea for pain. It does much, for pain, more than you would think." My breaths puff, his hand pressing harder upon my shoulder. *He should have used the crutch. I am a poor substitute for it.*

He grins at the ground ahead, a pale, slight thing. "Aye, that I was." He grimaces, propping his bad foot forward, and I grunt, press my hand against my hip for support, propping my arm up beneath his. I push back the changing of my eyes. His eyes flicker down, and he pauses, breathing heavily, a trail of sweat trickling down his jawline into his scraggly beard. "Are you sure you can handle this? I am too heavy for you, healer." He starts to move his hand.

I shake my head, adjust my palm against my hip bone. "Gót. I am well, and it is only a little further to your cot." He steps forward, and I move with him. He pauses by the cot, stares at it, great brows furrowing. I swallow, glance down. It is low, for him, a long way down for a man with only one good leg. "I can call for aid." I glance over my shoulder. There is no movement in the first room, Eerol still gone, Jakob gone now too. *How did they get him down before?*

He puffs out a breath, shaking his head. "Gót. Give me a moment and I can get down, bad leg or not. It will be well." His breathing is sharp, each heave rasping through his clenched jaws.

I shift my arm again, rolling my shoulder, and his hand moves with it. *He ought to think about something other than his breathing, other than the pain and his limbs. It will help him gain his breath sooner.* I glance up at him. "Have your family been down to see you today?"

He inclines his head, puffing out a long breath. "Aye, my wife and son. And my sister. She says you share a room with her. I hadn't heard that before." He glances at me.

I blink. His eyes are set back in his face, nose precise, straight forward. *Not Iris. There is no resemblance there. Tollah then. I should have seen that before. They have the same life to their skin, their names are nearly identical.* I half-smile. *She is tall too, like him.* "I did not know she was your sister, but I see it now. Are you two close in turnings?"

He grins, shifting his weight. "Aye. The closest you can be. We shared a womb. Twins, she and I."

I blink. "Twins?"

He laughs, breathing easier. "Aye, twins. Have you not met twins before, healer? I'd 'a sworn you'd have seen everything, in your field, being a traveling healer."

I laugh, shift my hand on my hip bone—it is grating, his weight pressing hard. "Gót. I am no traveling healer, but a healing hermit."

He laughs. "I could 'a sworn I heard you were a traveling healer. I cannot place your accent, what little there is of it. I guess I ought not to swear with as much as I got it wrong here." He grunts.

I smile. "My childhood was near Blackwater. There is much variety, in those that live there, to keep accents faint, even in those that stay for many turnings, as I did."

He grins, toward me, a side-eyed glance. "That might explain it then. My wife's family is from Blackwater. She has no accent either. She says we were meant to be that way." He inclines his head. "I am ready to sit now, if you will help. I am sorry for the trouble." I move with him, and he shifts forward, lifting his bad leg up onto the bed. His hand tightening on my shoulder, weight pulling it down. I grimace.

He grunts, adjusting his leg again, awkwardly, between the bed and him. I brace myself, hobble forward a step.

A footfalls behind me, Eerol darting into my line of sight. His brow furrows. "Tollak, what in the hot blaze of Hartwool are you doing?" His voice is sharp. He grips the man's arm, lowering him sharply toward the bed. "That was no simple break, and with only the healer here, you ought to have stayed in bed. Where was your crutch, you big tree ulcer?"

Tollak grins, but it is lazy, exhausted. "'Only the healer.' She is better than three of you, old grunt, and I'd take her help and chat any day."

Eerol narrows his eyes, but they are laughing. "She may be worth more than three of me, but she cannot lift your heavy hide as well as one. Sit down, you big bear-faced oat monger." He is lowering him to the bed, not even straining. I step backward, away. I lift the blanket, stack it beneath Tollak's bad leg. He nods at me.

Eerol dusts his hands off. "There now. Has Norla been down today?"

Tollak nods, grinning again. "Aye. She brought the wee boy with her."

Eerol nods again, dusting his hands against his apron. "Good that. You stay there then, until another day. They'll bring you down supper again tonight, but if you move, I will have words that will not be kind for you, and they will not be sparse. Getting up on your own was a fool's errand."

Tollak laughs, shaking his head, and it echoes in the rock of the halls. "I wasn't alone. I had the healer with me." Tollak winks at me, and Eerol scowls, lifting a cup from the shelf beside him.

"If you think to do it again, I do not idly threaten words. Stay put. I will help you up again later."

Tollak's grin broadens, his head sinking back against the wall. "'Again?' You did not help me up this time."

Eerol glances at him, his expression dry as the dust.

XXIX

Ágë

Eerol shoves his sleeves back, his face red, sweat clinging to his brows. "Well, then. Now that we have that done." He stands, his hands filled with the beams of the cots that are cots no longer. The pegs that fitted them together are scattered across the floor.

I press my hands against my knees, glance at him. "How are the soldiers doing, where they are?" Will they still be here, the men who have no place in a safe haven that hides others from men like them?

Eerol glances down at me, his brow cocked. He shifts a pole to his other palm, holding them together, three in one hand. His hands are large for a man not tall. "They are in a storage room, and they are healed enough. Not caused too much trouble. Yet." He snorts. "Doubt they could if they wanted to, with Faang and Einion both here, even if there weren't the rest of the men."

I look down at the poles of the cots they occupied only days ago. If they are expecting trouble, would it not be wiser to move them somewhere else, where there are not lives at stake? I grab a pole and pull it toward me. I glance up.

Eerol's eyes are on me, his brow still raised. "You might've taken them up on leaving, if you were worried, civ."

I blink, turn away. "I was not thinking of not being here, but of the trouble queen's men could cause if they were to get free. And I have given them no answer. I can still leave."

He grunts. "Soldiers seem to have a habit of turning up where you do not want them, ey? They do that for me too." He shakes his head. "You will not leave, will you? When will you give them an answer?"

I keep my eyes away from him, on the floor. "When I have decided. And soldiers had never shown their hand until lately, with the captain's arrival at my home, and the soldiers in the woods."

Eerol shakes his head, stooping to grab the last set of poles in his free hand. "That is not what Einion said."

I lift a brow, turn back toward him. "What did the captain say of it?"

He tucks the poles into his arm, standing slowly. "That he guessed that you had seen trouble before, from the queen's men, by your reaction to them. He guessed it was not just from the knowledge of what could happen, with your blood. And it will not have been from the Movement, for you have made no mention of them."

I flinch, set the pole down. "I have heard little of any movement."

"What then? Did they kill your family?"

I turn toward him. "Soldiers came to one of my villages, turnings ago, after I served with Aílé, my herb master. They were hunting my bloodline, and killed half the village as punishment for hiding one of them."

His brow lifts. "For hiding you?"

I look away, shake my head. "Gót. It was not me." My voice is soft. "My parents had passed by then, and no one there knew of my bloodline. I had not been there long; I was only working alongside the healer for a matter of seasons. There was another fian there, who stayed. The village harbored him willingly, knowingly. And they died for it."

He inclines his head. "Have you washed those bandages yet?"

I shake my head, hobble forward. The poles are half-hiked up under my arm, awkward. "Not yet. Where were you from, before this?"

He glances back at me, over his shoulder. "Nowhere of interest. A city. A village."

I set the poles upon the cot, with the others, stacked by him. "A city? Were you a healer there? A city healing man?"

His hands have picked up their pace on his work, and I can see nothing of his expression with his head turned away. "Aye, a healer. What else? But gòt. Not a city healer."

I snatch the pot of bandages from the floor, soaked in water, in soap suds from the bar beside them. "You worked then outside the city then, or on your own?"

He straightens, hands still on his work before him. "Gót." His shoulders shift, hands pressed into the table before him. "I worked for a duke. In his palace. In G'Nouran. That is where my family lived."

G'Nouran. A city near the capital, of carnage, small and known even in the mountains. It is centered around the palace of a duke, a duke whose name I have forgotten. A duke known only for his firm hand, for his work for the White Lady. My eyes twist. I swallow hard, turn my head away. Blått stretches in the room beyond, standing, his tail already wagging again. "You left then, because of his work?"

He turns back toward me, weariness in his eyes. "Aye. I left because of his work. I did not control my tongue, so I left, to save my hide, and my family's by association. Duke Pranciskus's wife is a friend of the queen, a dear friend, and he is a harsh man, no gentle ruler of his people. I knew that and I still did not control my tongue." Grief crosses his face, and he turns away, setting a clean knife back on the shelf. "I would have been able to do far more for them if I had stayed and kept silent, but I let my tongue get the better of me, and so Sradfaang brought me here to be of service in the mountains."

I lift my head. "Sradfaang brought you here?"

He grunts. "Aye. Wasn't too happy about it, but he did. He had just finished escorting the duke's uncle, a higher-ranking officer from the queen's military, and heard me say something before it got back around to Pranciskus or the queen. He was leaving the next morning, and took me with him, secretly. I doubt the duke even minded that I was gone. Saved him the trouble of having me court-martialed, if I was not there. The prude." He chuckles, the sound wry. "I should have known better than to work for him. There was trouble in that, and I reaped it, when I left. I have continued to reap it, these last ten turnings while my children grew up without me."

There is a step on the stairs, a voice echoing down them. "Healers! It is time for the evening meal."

Eerol brushes his hands against his clothes and turns toward the staircase. I have missed my opportunity to ask him of his leaving. He sets his apron and the last of the poles aside, clicking to the hound. "You staying here, goodling?" He grins at Blått, and the hound stands, stretching, his tongue lolling and eyes glad. I will have to ask him another time, when the world is slow again. He starts for the stairs, my hound trotting after him.

Norla smiles, her hand tucked into her son's tiny one, in the long halls leading to the great one. "I am glad he is not losing his spirit down there. I cannot tell, not from the short times we are there, how he is doing, other than that he smiles, always smiles. He brightens up for us, I think." She glances at me. "I thought I might send Jørn down to sit with him tomorrow, if you would allow it. He might stay when I cannot. But I do not know. He does not always listen. He is too young for that, and I do not want him to be underfoot. If he will be in your way…"

I shake my head. "That would be well. I will keep an eye on him, while he is there." I half-smile. "Though I expect he will like to spend time with Eerol more than he will with Tollak. The man seems to have a soft spot for children. And a knack for amusing them when they are near him. They crowd around him for humor whenever he is near."

She laughs, clear and light, and Jørn looks up at her. She nods. "And they have a soft spot for him. I do not understand it. The man is gruff, but each child hangs on his every move, every word, more than they do with Caj or Ágë or any of the story weavers. He does have a knack with them." She steps into the great hall, and the noise grows, voices crashing together and laughter rolling out. The evening meal. Blått presses his head against my leg, eyes watching, excited, but they are not alarmed, not by this. I might have brought him to the meeting halls sooner than I have. Eerol was right.

I plant my hand against his head, rustle my fingers through his fur. Norla is gone, into the crowd, Jørn pulling her hand along with him. I step to the side. Captain Flint is ahead, speaking with Fitzclaste and another man. Nevak. The blond man nods, his face tense.

I turn away, step under a waving arm. Ciaran is there, a smile on his face, a woman speaking in front of him. Her hands are animated, eyes alight. Iris. She looks down, a blush playing across her pale face, but her eyes are still bright, gentle. What are they speaking of, the weaver girl and the golden man? I step past them, lift a bowl, and there is a shout, over the crowd.

"Ágë!" The voice is a man's, high, cheerful.

Someone not the length of a horse from me looks up sharply, his face grim, his eyes rimmed with the thick, dark lashes. Ágë.

The voice across the room continues, a hand with a mug raised dangerously high over the crowd. It sloshes. "Give us a tale. It has been an age since we heard your mind, heard a tale from it in anything but from poems. We would have a tale again, if you would share one with the likes of us."

Ágë lifts a brow, his face dry, almost grim. "With a speech like that, Raf, you are already weaving. Why do you not give them a tale tonight and spare them mine?" There is a laugh, rippling across the crowd, a chorus of notes and voices. Ágë smiles, a half-hearted thing, and inclines his head. "If you will sit, then I will weave."

He turns, climbing onto his chair. He perches upon its back, his face toward the room, alone now but for my figure a few steps away. The rest of the room is seated. I move backward, and he speaks, his gaze fixed on the crowd. "What would you have tonight?"

There is a hush over the crowd, the room falling into silence. My eyes flicker toward the tables. Fitz and Teja are at the table in the room's center, Fitz's arm around her shoulders. He lifts his head. "Pick a story you have not told in many turnings, Ágë. A tale you have been perfecting at your work."

Ágë smiles, and it hits his eyes this time, though they are cast down toward his hands between his knees. He clasps his fingers, movements slow, thoughtful. The room is still silent, but for a child's voice attempting to whisper somewhere at the back of it, the words loud in the hush. Lila. She does not seem to ever truly whisper. The Story Weaver lifts his head.

I turn away, eyes flickering over the tables. There is a place, down the one closest to me, near the end of it. I step forward, Blått's feet tapping behind me, and I slip onto the bench. He curls up beside me, head against my knee, and the Story Weaver is beginning. His voice is clear, flowing, and there is not a sound in the room but him and the whispering of the child.

"As many tales begin—," He lifts his head, scanning over the figures, "—this one begins with a birth. Not the birth of a man, or a praor, or a cavene, but of a horse." His eyes land on someone and they flicker away, sharply. "The foal was born by a river, the spawn of a wild steed of the Thànnorag hills in the west. Male it was born, and it grew to run the plains and fields at paces that few horses have ever reached, not in this age, or in any of the ones to come.

"There was a man from the border between our land and theirs, an Avridallen by birth. He saw the stallion as it flew across the fields one day, and a longing was stirred in his heart that had been quiet since he was a child. He had lived all his life on his father's farm, but with the stallion in his sights, he knew one day he would run free, the horse beneath him, to somewhere beyond. The horse had spent a mere two turnings on those plains, but his time there was coming to an end.

"The man set about to get his rope about the proud neck, but he knew, knew from watching day after day as the sun faded and the horse flew home, that it would require a level of strength and cunning that he had never before used, not in all his days on the earth. Twice he tried, and twice he failed, and it was gone again, lost beyond the rolling hills, with a nicker and a whinny thrown back behind him into the wind.

After more than two full moons of planning, the man was in a tree one day, his hands busy releasing a lark that had been trapped by a spider's web, and he cast his gaze down to find his quarry beneath him, grazing peacefully under the branches of the great elm tree. He had prepared—it had been a season since he began carrying a rope at all times, but he had left it on the ground, to prevent it from getting caught upon the branches as he climbed. Laughing at his choice and cursing to himself, the man seized a vine from the tree and fashioned a coil from it, slowly, carefully, and he anchored it to the trunk of the great elm tree beneath him."

Ågë lifts his eyes, watching a child near the front of the room, and the story weaver raises his hands, twisting a rope in the air. The child is motionless, eyes wide. Lila. No longer whispering near the back. Her arm is still bandaged, Jørn and an unknown child beside her.

Ågë continues. "The steed did not sense his presence and stepped closer to the tree, and he was caught with a loop about the neck from the vines that curled up upon the elm tree." Ågë jerks his arms to the side—a rope pulled tight.

"Furious with the loss of his freedom, the stallion raged, trampled and pulled, but he was left to fight with a tree, the man's weight not behind the rope but the trunk of the elm, and therein lay the man's victory. The stallion was caught. He could not escape from the vines. He could not win against the roots of the great old elm tree. The ground was wet from the rains, and his hooves skidded, sliding, the earth no friend to him that day.

"For a full turning of the moon, the steed was left there, tethered to the elm tree with the vine that did not wither though the days passed on. Each day, the man made the walk from his home to visit the horse beneath the branches of the tree, offering him bits of the grain he had stored and the fruits he had labored to dry, until at last, the steed ceased to kick and bite and stamp and allowed the patient man to touch him, to run his hand along his shoulders, along his proud, long neck.

"That day, the man slid a rope around the horse's neck, a real rope this time, and led him back to his father's farm. The horse pranced proudly, his head held high. Though his neck was bound, he did not pull away but honored the man's conquest until they reached the stables and the fields.

"The man knew now, recognized the longing in his heart. He would explore the four corners of the Fresh Isle on the horse's back and to know as many blades of grass in the Creator's world as he could, to see as many stones as he could reach, and watch the sunrise from a thousand hills.

"From that day on, his restlessness began to grow, the force of it swelling each day, growing by night. Each day he would work in the fields with his family and his father's workers, and by moonlight he would work beside the horse, training, learning of it.

"A full moon he waited, working with the horse, gaining the trust of the stallion bit by bit until he could ride on its great back at speeds great and steady, and then he could wait no longer. His horse was caught and saddled and he would go, to betterment and the ends of the world.

"With the new moon fading into morning, the man bid goodbye to his father and mother and six sisters and all that he had known and mounted his steed. He said that he would return someday, come back to them and tell them of the world, tell them of all that he had seen and heard and share the wonder of it all, in the times to come, all that he had seen of all the Creator had made.

"The steed accepted the weight of his bags willingly, his sides trembling with excitement. He knew that the time was upon him that he would get to run free again, this time with a welcomed burden on his back. The man turned him from the rising sun, and they set out to face the world beyond, and the wonders held within it.

"And with this, the journeys of Gilliad and Eusebus were begun, in the Lands of the Setting Sun. Many and strange are their tales, from over the Fresh Isle. Many tales have been spun in all the turnings that followed, all over the land and over the seas to the furthest reaches of land, and even to this day."

• ▶ | ◀ ▶ | ◀ ▶ | ◀ ▶ | ◀ ▶ | ◀ •

I lift my hand to the door, knock once, softly. The voices inside the room beyond slow.

The door creaks open, and there is Jons, his face unimpressed. I meet his gaze. "I would speak with Ciaran or Fitzclaste, if either are here."

He frowns, dark brows heavy. "They are both here, but what reason do you have to seek them? They are meeting."

I fold my hands. "I have given no answer to a question that was asked. I would speak with them, if my timing it not poor."

He turns back, looking into the room, and speaks in a low voice. "It's the healer woman."

"Let her in." Fitzclaste's voice. Jons pulls the door open, stepping away. I move inside, past him.

Ciaran is standing by the table at the middle of the room, on the far side of it this time. His tunic sleeves are rolled up, a half-unfolded paper in his hand. Fitzclaste is beside him, his arms folded. Ciaran flicks his eyes to me, inclining his head, slowly. He straightens. "Healer. Is something troubling you?"

I shake my head. "You have asked a question, and I have given you no answer."

Ciaran nods again, just barely. "What choice have you made, Eness Finch?"

I meet his gaze. "I will stay, so long as I am given permission to use the herbs I find in the healing rooms for my task, and the freedom and permission to travel beyond these walls to collect my own for my work and for the healing ward. I have heard no rumors of me in the days since we last spoke, and with that, I will stay. You all will not last the dark moons with the herbs that are in the healing rooms now. If you will allow me these two things, I will gladly stay and serve, for as long as I am able to, for as long as I am needed and it is wise to stay."

Fitzclaste smiles, his arms settling beside him, but Ciaran merely inclines his head, eyes steady on mine. "I will speak with Sradfaang. You will have full freedom to travel beyond the walls. Nothing keeps you in." He turns the paper away from me. "However, with the recent danger, that you will be aware of after going out to find the scouting party, we ask that you not stray far without a guard. We are taking extra precautions to ensure everyone here is kept safe. For that reason, no one will be going out alone beyond the perimeter, at least until the danger settles once more. Is that acceptable to you?"

I incline my head. "I am more than willing to take a guard if need be." I press my hands against each other, meet his eyes again. "Will you answer a question of mine, if you have a moment now?"

He inclines his head, slow, careful, but there is a smile, brushing at his lips. "As I am able, I will answer."

I incline my head. "Who here stands the most to lose, if Sikkerhet were found out by the queen's men? I know there is danger. I do not understand how the risk is spread on those that are here."

He watches me for a moment, his eyes quiet. "That is a question I do not know that I can answer to your satisfaction. It is a long answer and not one that I can give without endangering the safety of many. I am sorry. If it were in my power to answer, it would be given."

I nod, turn toward the door. "Do not worry for it. I thank you for your time and I will return to the healing rooms and leave you to your tasks."

Ciaran bows.

Fitz mirrors his movements beside him, a smile still on his lips. He moves to the door, pulling it open before me. "Thank you, Eness. It gladdens my heart to know that you are staying for at least the time being. I was not looking forward to sending you out into the wildlands on your own, should you have chosen that. There will be many more than me that shall be glad of your staying."

I half-smile and turn toward the door. "Thank you. I am glad not to be leaving again. There is fair company here, in those you and your wife have sheltered."

His smile widens, crinkling the corners of his eyes. "Aye. Aye there is. Elnial has been gracious in those He has brought to our doorstep, and you blend with them well. Thank you, Eness. If you have need of anything, you know you may ask of us."

I bow—thanks—and turn toward the door. Jons is on the other side of it, watching. I nod toward him and into the halls beyond. The door clicks shut behind me.

XXX

Eusebus

Erol shifts, his eyes flickering toward me at the edges of my peripheral. I force my eyes to stay down, smoothing tallow into the leaves of the salve. It clings to my fingers, slipping and blending coarsely, unpleasant and greasy on my skin. He shifts again, grunting under his breath. I glance at him, keep my head down. *The man seems off.* He moves his feet, setting down the pot. I watch, my hands deep in the half-blended tallow.

He leans backward, just slightly, hands pressed against the table. "What will you do, Eness Finch, if you stay here? How will you spend your time?"

I look up at him, my movements slow, hands in the tallow. He does not turn, does not look at me. I press my wrists down. "Have you spoken with Fitzclaste or Ciaran?"

He shakes his head. "Not of late. Will you stay?"

My jaw tightens. I look down. "I will, but only so long as it is safe, within reason and wise council." I lift my eyes. "Will you?"

He looks up sharply, his face softening, hand setting a spoon to the side. "So, you have heard." He takes a step toward me. "I am sorry, Eness. I cannot stay." He reaches up to the shelf, lifts a paper from it—folded, small. "I have received a letter. My son-in-law is in trouble. I have been here ten turnings, perhaps eleven. I have been here, and my family has been toiling too near the capital and too near trouble. I can wait no longer to go back to them. This is my time and I will face it, I will go back to them and see what can be done. They have been sorely oppressed of late, homes burned, lives taken, and I cannot stay any longer away while they die. That is my place, with my children and grandchildren. I have served my prince as long as I can in silence, but now I must go. I have caught my horse and he is saddled. The time is come, 'to betterment and the ends of the world.'"

I shift my hands in the thick tallow. "So, you should go. When will you leave?"

He half-smiles, his head shaking. "You are too kind to be so gentle with this old man, Eness. I have thrust this upon you in the wrong way for you to be this kind." His expression hardens. "Within the next half-fortnight."

My throat burns, tight, fingers cold beneath the slime along my fingers. *What will become of this place, if I must leave, after he is gone? That is not a trail that can be tread today. Now I will stay and he will leave.*

"Well, then." He lifts his eyes, relief in them, and lifts a cloth idly from the table, twisting it between his hands. "My task truly is before me." He looks at me. "Seek council, as you stay. Ciaran is a wise man, as is Fitz. Ciaran will not keep anyone in a place that he does not trust and look for their own safety and well-being in, and he is far-seeing. He has looked out for his men for many turnings, though he is young. I do not know all you are seeking in this world, but there is a chance you will find it here, if you stay long enough to find out."

I nod my head. "I will ask as it is fitting. But they will not know much about what I am seeking. My task is not in their knowledge, for it lies with herbs and the nature of my race."

He twists the towel through his hands again. "I am sorry to be leaving now when I might have been of some help to you. But my children have no healer there, not anymore. I can wait no longer to meet my grandchildren, to see their faces, to know all their names." He looks up. "Thank you, Eness Finch. You are welcomed here, wished for. I do not know if Einion knew how much he was doing, when he sent you to us when he did."

I nod. *He did, in some way.* "The Creator be with you. I will stay as long as I am able and do what I can. It may be well matched, that we are here. I was losing my ability to continue my own work there. And it seems that you were losing yours now." My throat feels tight.

His hand slows on the cloth. "Then the Creator give you success on your ventures." He glances at me. "Fitz told me what you are aiming for. It is a good aim. There will be herbs here that you may not have tried, herbs imported from Menant or Grior here. You may try those, and can ask Aorla to obtain more for you, when next she is back. She travels the most of any of the messengers, and will get you what you ask, if you speak with Fitz first for it. Perhaps you will have success in staying, where you have not yet in the wilds. Perhaps it was for this reason you came." He bows, gratitude raw in his aged eyes. "Thank you, Eness."

He turns, moving into the room beyond where Tollak sits, red rims around a sword wound and leg no longer shattered.

XXXI

New Stones

I twist the bandage in my hand, pulling it tight, back into a roll. The basket shifts beside me, Blått dipping his head into it. I swat at him, press his shoulder with the side of my arm. "Gót. Those are not for you." He jerks his head out, glancing sideways toward me, his eyes reproachful.

I shake my head. "Those are newly cleaned. You will not get them full of hair before they can even be used. Leave." He turns to place his head back in the basket, and I lean forward, shove his shoulder hard. "Go, Goodling. Gót. You may not sniff them. Go." He stares at me for a moment and turns, starting away slowly. His tail is between his legs, head down.

I shake my head, pick up the end of the bandage again. The rooms are quiet but for the tapping of Blått's nails on stone. Someone whispers something in the other room, a small voice, too loud to be quiet. *Jørn.* He giggles, and there is a rumble of laughter, Tollak's, and a grunt. "Whoa there, lad. Watch the leg. It is only mostly healed."

I shake my head, turn back to my work. My eyes flicker to the shelves lining the free wall in the room beyond, where the cots do not sit. Herbs, new and old. Herbs that need to be replenished. *How many herbs will have come and gone back at the cottage? How many will have begun to rot before those from the villagers come to collect them and realize I am no longer there, have been gone for seasons? There will be leaves strewn across the floor, dust settled on the fireplace and pots, evidence of time gone, and they will not have the herbs and salves they need in the dark moons to come.* My lips tighten.

The hound snorts, his head against his paws by the fire.

I glance at him. His eyes are on me, pitiful, tail motionless by his great shaggy body. I lift a brow. "If you were going to be discontent in here, you might have stayed in the stables today." He whines, the sound high and soft, and shifts his head. I shake my head, turn my eyes away. The bandage is done. I tuck the end of it in, set it in the other basket, nearly empty beside me.

A foot falls in the room behind me, steps steady and sure. *Eerol's.* I turn toward him. He is reading over something in his hands, a small book, the leather of its cover worn. I grab a new strip of cloth, twist it into the beginning of a roll. He glances down at Blått. Blått blinks at him, his head still between his paws, piteous. Eerol stoops, folding the book beneath his arm. "What did you do to the hound that he would mope by the fire?" He runs his hands over Blått's ears, rustling his fur. "Has he been down here all day? Did you let him out?"

I shake my head, twist the bandage quicker. "He is only moping because I would not let him put his head in the bandages. I do not want his hair all over them. He has been out many times."

Eerol looks down at the hound, straightening. "You might have been more pitiable, if you had chosen another thing to be down about. As it is, you will just either have to mope on your own, or come with me to my worktable and I will give you sympathy there, for I am not staying here. My back is too old to stay bent like that." He moves and the hound leaps up after him, his tail wagging, tongue out.

A smile pulls at my lips. I shake my head, set the roll of bandage aside. "Eerol." He glances back at me, his hand stroking the hound's head. I lift another strip of cloth. "Where do you keep the uncommon herbs, and what have they been used for? I may have heard of some, but I would know how you use them before you go."

He sets the book against the table, turning. There is a laugh from the room beyond, high and sweet—Jørn's again. Eerol looks toward the shelves, moving toward them. He steps onto the stool, reaching for the high shelves, for the crocks tucked away there, nearly out of sight. Turning, he steps down again, two of them in his hands. "Here. We'll start with these. You may do what you wish with the rest of them as well, when I have gone. The crocks of the special ones are labeled, since they were purchased from a merchant out near the border."

He sets the crocks down. I stand, set the cloth aside. He draws the lid off one of them. "This is calluna, or heather. It is from the coast of Thànnorag. It does well to fight infections that live inside you, though I have not used it often, as it is hard to get your hands on." He lifts the lid off it, and I sniff the plant inside. It is a light smell, a smell almost like a musk, but only barely there.

I look up at him. "It is a mild herb."

He inclines his head, already lifting the top off the second one. "La. But it has worked well the times I have tried it. It was offered to me by another healer, turnings ago, and I was glad when a messenger brought it to me some seasons back. Here," He inclines his head toward the pot. "This one may have some property that is useful to you in your hunt. It is called valerian."

The substance inside is a powder, brown, with the marking of roots within it. The air is scented with something foul, like unwashed bodies. I grimace, press a hand over my nose.

He grins. "Aye, it does smell foul. I enjoy showing that one off when I think of it. You should have seen the goblin's face when it was brought in." He snorts in laughter, tucking the lid back on. "I thought he would have a conniption. But, it serves well to quiet emotions, if you can disguise it in tea or stew. I have used it, in extreme cases of anxiety, and it has helped to calm the nerves. Works best mixed with lamb broth, to cover the taste."

I look sharply at the side of the pot, the name carved into the pottery before it was baked. *Valerian*. "Thank you, Eerol."

He nods to the shelf. "The others I have kept up there for a reason. There is nightshade, which does grow here, but sparingly. It can kill, but you will know that and how to use it. There is periwinkle, which helps with swelling in the very old, and has finally begun to grow around here, so I should move it to the lower shelves. It will be prolific, in a few turnings, if let go unchecked. I do not know how the seeds are spread."

A figure steps through the archway, Norla. She smiles, stepping up beside me, nodding a greeting toward the healer. Her face twists sharply, and she grimaces, turning away, a hand pressed over her face. "What is that?" She coughs. "It smells like the worst of the old cheeses Nellie tried to serve us."

Eerol cackles, lifting the pot from the table, his eyes twinkling brighter. "Nothing to be worried about, but it does smell a bit like old cheese." He chortles again. "Is it time for dinner?"

She nods, turning toward the room beyond. "Aye. I thought to retrieve my son, to see what trouble he has gotten into, and if my husband still has his ears attached." She smiles softly. "Jørn has been in a talking form of late."

Eerol chuckles once more, this time softer, like her smile. "Oh, aye. That child will be a wordsmith when he is grown. Or at least, a very word-filled farmer."

Norla laughs. "Like his grandfár? You would have liked him, Eerol. He spoke like you." Her smile softens, something like grief crossing her eyes. She turns, stepping through the archway.

A voice chirps up. "Tá! It's time to go outdoors?"

Norla laughs, and it is echoed by Tollak's, deep and low. "Gót. But it is time for dinner, and I will bring your fár his shortly."

There is the patter of small feet on the floor, and Blått stands, stretching from beside the table. I glance at Eerol. "Has there been any news from the lands beyond?"

He glances at me, lifting his book from the table, setting it upon the shelf. "None that I've heard, but what is normal. That I will spare you."

My eyes burn. "Have there been more massacres?"

He smiles, and there is bitterness in it. "The warm months have come. She has sent her men out. There will be massacres in all corners until the cold comes again, or she is no longer on the throne. There has been no news, other than that. And I do not expect there to be."

I shake my head. "Is that all the news that comes this far into the hills?"

He glances at me, his eyes shrewd for a moment. "That depends on who you are. Not all news gathered is spread. We have messengers for a reason, Eness." He turns away. "If you want news here, you have to ask questions of those who get those messages. They try not to spread it." He pulls his apron over his head and ducks around the archway, speaking shortly to the man beyond.

•▶|◀▶|◀▶|◀▶|◀▶|◀▶|◀•

A woman is bustling up the far hall, her eyes scanning the rooms around her. I pause, Blått's head pressing against my side. *Tejan.* She glances up, a smile crossing her features. She steps toward me, glancing at Blått. Her smile broadens, finger brushing under his chin. "Eness. I was searching for you." She brushes her hand across Blått's head and straightens. "Do you have a moment? Fitz asked me to speak with you about something this morning." She gestures to the open door beside her.

I step forward, through the doorway, Blått following close behind.

She steps in, pulling the door closed. There is a window open on the far side of the room, large, with clouded glass covering it. Only faint strands of sunlight come through it, scattering across the floor. She turns toward me, her hands folded, neat and graceful. "We have had a message, from an emissary from Menantia, known to my husband. They speak of possibly visiting, and my husband and Lord Ciaran both think that it would be wisest to make you aware, before they arrive. We would like to keep you safe, as best we can, and avoiding contact with those outside would be a simple way to attain that and keep there from being a possibility of a situation developing, in the case that you are known beyond these walls. It is an extra precaution, if you would take it."

I meet her gaze. "You mean that they are not trustworthy or that they imagine I would be recognized if mentioned anywhere beyond here?"

She half-smiles, her eyes calm, quiet. "Gót. Only that Fitz does not know where their allegiances lie, nor does he fully know your past. We would wish for your safety in all circumstances where possible, as you gave us your trust and time. You need not hide fully, but it may be best for you to stay away from direct conversation. Are there those who would know you beyond these walls, if their paths were crossed?"

I shake my head. "I stayed in a small village these last many turnings. Before that, I was hardly more than a child, and known for nothing but my work with my herb master. I would not be known by anyone they would cross paths with. And it should not be hard to keep from speaking with them. I am mostly in the healing ward, and I imagine they will be with you and the lords. I will be below more when Eerol is gone. When do you expect their arrival?"

She inclines her head, her expression thoughtful. "We do not know yet. They are taking a slow path here from Langfort. A guide will be sent for them when they are closer to ensure they do not know the way, but it could be as long as a full moon cycle, largely dependent upon the way he takes them. We thought it best to let you know as soon as may be, so that you can be prepared in case they arrive early. We would like there to be no surprises that we cannot handle when they do arrive. We do not like surprises here, unless they are new guests brought in." She smiles.

I smile back, my lips tight. *Do they trust them so little, or are all within the courts so unworthy of being trusted across the other countries too?* I incline my head. "I will do my utmost to stay out of their path. To what end are they being allowed within our walls?"

She nods her head again. "You will have to speak with my husband and Ciaran about that. I have my reasons, but I would have you weigh theirs if you wish to know more. If not, I would bid you not trouble them now. The choice is being weighed diligently."

She fully smiles, her eyes gentling, and takes my hand, squeezing it lightly. "I am glad that it is you taking over in Eerol's stead. We do not like to see him go, but I am glad he is finally going back to his family, where he should be. I have long thought it was time for him to return to them. But he has been waiting." Her jaw tightens. "I pray the Creator goes with him there, to guard him on his way."

I half-smile. "He has gone with him so far, all the turnings that he has been here, has He not?"

Her eyes glance over to me, as if taking me in full. Warmth lightens her eyes. "Aye. He has that. And He will go with him there, even to that city." She folds her hands again, her jaw tightening once more. "How are you settling? This is quite a change for a hermit in the woods, this place with all its bustle and noise, and I wish to have spoken to you sooner about your time here. I am sorry for the strife that it has been to you, with your gift and heritage both, coming here and trying to keep them closed off from us. This must have been trying on all fronts for you, when you arrived. I wonder that the captain ever got you to us, with all the reasons you had to flee."

I smile. "I had lived alone far too long. There was not much left for me there, after so many turnings. I would not have chosen this place, but it is well enough that it was chosen for me, in the council of the captain and goblin, and you and your husband welcomed me. Your home is far more beautiful than any I have ever been in before. It is an honor to be within its walls. It will be a beautiful place to spend seasons in the times to come."

She smiles, reaching out her hand again. She grips my arm, squeezing it gently, her hand thick-veined with use and time, a grandmere's hand. "I hope that there will be something here for you, a joy of a kind, and that we have not been the only lots kind to you. Many of these people are accustomed to their own company, but I hope that they are all welcomed you. We are thankful and honored to have you with us."

I smile, slipping my hand over hers, and incline my head. "They all have been gracious and kind both. Thank you, Tejan."

She laughs, throwing her head back, her hand lifting from my arm. "I believe that you have done far more for us in the near moon that you have been here than we have for you." She grins. "Thank you, for speaking with me. You may return to your work now, with your hound." She half-laughs. "The children will be glad that he is here, if they ever see him. I have not heard any squealing at mealtimes to give me reason to believe that they have caught a glimpse yet. Have you brought him up to mealtimes yet?"

I shake my head, running my hand across Blått's neck. "I do not often take him with me, and only have tried these last few days. A hound at a feast sounds far more like a Thannon thing of old than one of ours." A smile pulls at my lips.

She laughs, the sound easy and clear. "Aye. That it does. Thank you, Eness. The grace of Elnial go with you." She nods, bowing through the door.

XXXII

Out of the Mouths of Infants

I tilt my head, listening to the sounds of evening. There are voices, faint through the wood, steps in the hall fading away. Blåthjortt's nails tap against the ground beside me, his steps smooth. I shift the basket on my hip, half-smile. *There is no sign of visitors today.* I step forward, press the door open at the end of the hall. The voices are growing louder with each step, mixing from the ones from up the hall—children's voices, laughing and chattering like the birds in the woodlands.

I step up to the open door, pause, glance in, the noises louder. Ruidún is leaning against a chair, knitting in her hands which are moving quickly, a smile set on her lips, contented. Her hair catches in the light of the window. She glances up at me, a smile pulling at her lips. "Eness, Come in. Would you sit with me a moment?" The children do not look up, chatter continuing. I step forward, incline my head.

There is a shriek, high and piercing. "Hound dog!"

Something bowls into Blått's side, knocking the hound against my hip. A little dark head is cradled against his side, barely reaching over his back, arms clasped around him. "Ruidún! Her has a hound! Ruidún!" The child looks up. Jørn, with his big eyes, blue like his father's, round like his mothers. He is grinning, arms tightening around the hound.

I drop to the floor beside him, search Blått's face. He looks calm, tilting his head back to nuzzle the child gently, his mouth closed, tongue gone. *He has not been so close to children before.* I drop back onto my heels. *He is calm.* I keep my eyes on his face.

There is a foot beside me, shoed. "Is the hound safe with children?" Ruidun's voice is quiet, barely above the sounds of the two children.

I purse my lips, place my hand on the Blått's head. "He is not a violent hound. I think he will be alright with them, but I will stay close." I glance up and back to the hound and the boy.

Ruidun's eyes are tense. She nods, but she does not move back toward the chair, does not take back up her knitting needles.

Jørn looks up at her, his eyes bright behind a tuft of Blått's fur. "I hears she has a hound, but I never seen him. Does him has a name?"

I half-smile, plant my hand on Blått's head. "Blåthjortt." He stares at the hound, his little nose wrinkling. I laugh. "It means 'blue deer', because I found him in the woods running like a lost stag when he was a small pup. He still likes to run, when he is outside, and is fast, like a hart."

Jørn grins. "'Blue deer.' That's a funny name for a hound. Does hims take down deers? Can him hunt them?"

I nod, and Ruidún is smiling, her arm cradling her stomach now. I scratch behind Blått's ears, ruffle them. "Aye. He is a good hunter. Fastest rabbit catcher I have ever yet seen."

Jørn grins at me. "Prince Ciaran said that he once had a hound that was a better hunter than that was. But I never seen it, so I think this one may be a better un at it."

My heart slows in my chest, eyes burn. *Prince Ciaran?* I snap my eyes up to Ruidún.

Her face is ashen, eyes large, alarmed. *Prince Ciaran.* They flicker to me. She drops to her knees beside the boy. "Jørn. Do not say that. Where did you hear such a thing?"

He blinks at her. "From Prince Ciaran. He says that when he was back at hims home, he had a whole pack of hounds, but one of them was the faster one. He liked to take them hunting, and they could take down deers all the day long."

She shakes her head hard, a tremulous smile brushing her lips. "Not that, love. Do not call him a prince. That is foolishness."

He looks up at her. "But he is. I hears my fár say so to tâ when I was sleeping. He says that he does not know when Prince—"

She lifts her hand sharply. "Jørn, that is *Lord* Ciaran. Do not call him prince. We will go speak to your tâ about this."

My heart thuds harder in my chest. *Prince Ciaran. Prince Harvalach, the son of the White Lady and the late king? She is said to be tall, blonde, regal. He would not tell me his title. No one has said it. He said he commanded armies, before he came here.*

A shudder crawls up my spine. *The Heir of Auvridal. His mother has killed thousands of my bloodline. He was said to be dead these last five turnings at least. Were not the latest hunts said to be on his account?*

My eyes burn, heart thuds harder. I look away, stand slowly. *Prince Ciaran. Has he stood by while our people are butchered, hiding away in this haven? He has been here while the death toll has climbed higher. What can they do to stop it, in those rooms? Have not these last five turnings of slaughters been worse, because of his death in the south?*

Jørn is still talking, his voice high and clear, Lila's cutting in every few words. I swallow. *Has he been hiding, or helping her mission by staying out of her way, here, where no one can find him? By infiltrating the safety of this haven?*

I stand, Ruidún moving with me, her eyes on mine. "Jørn." Her voice is calm. "It is time to go find your tâ. Come with me." He nods, stepping slowly away from Blått, his eyes still on him, fingertips brushing through his fur. Lila is with the other child, across the room once more.

I nod toward Ruidún, move for the door. The basket is light on my hip, empty still where it should be full. My heart pounds in my head. *I ought not to have strayed from my trail.* I turn down the hall, and there are footsteps behind me, many of them tapping against the floor, and the chatter of children, laughing.

Ruidún's voice does not mix with them, but her steps are firm and loud with theirs. *If it is true what he said, then she will be going to make someone know what I have heard, what Jørn said.*

I push the door open, and the stable yard is ahead. A cow is walking across it toward the woodlands, a man hobbling behind it on an unstable leg. *Jakob, of the broken foot. He is out with the cows again, though it is not fully mended.* My lips twist. *He will have gotten much dirt in it by now, if he is not wearing a thick boot.*

I turn sharply, move into the woods out of his sight. Branches knock together ahead—there is the taste of storm in the wind—like the unshed clouds and leaves blown before it. I duck under a branch, my hair catching and it is gone. *I should have trusted the dread in my stomach when I arrived at the door. Sradfaang will have known, must have known, when he brought me here, who that man was. He spoke often of the safety of this place, of the risk to someone here. He said there was a risk here greater than mine.* I press another branch out of the way, the hound's step crunching against the ground behind me.

I pick up my pace. *He was earnest, when we spoke, earnest about the safety, safety of more than just me.* I pause, my eyes flickering toward the ground, a glint of yellow caught over the leaves. *Saint John's wort.* The yellow flowers bob in the coming wind, their heads moving around each other, just missing each time, dancing. *Have they been hiding him out here all this time, hiding him away from the world that was broken by his mother's hands, is still being broken by her actions day by day on his behalf and the behalf of his dead father? How many thousands have died, of my blood and others, while he was hidden away from trouble and danger? How many of them have died because of his death?*

Could he not have protected them by now, a man of his standing, if he had not been here? The prince who was to have been crowned turnings ago, who disappeared?

There is a step behind me, heavy on the earth. "Healer?" The voice is tentative, careful. *Not Jakob's.* I turn, eyes flickering back to the man. *The man who cut himself in the armory. Tulé. I have not seen him since then.* His eyes are wider than they should be, his features delicate. *Nervous.*

He shifts his feet, leaves crunching beneath them. "I am sorry to ask this of you, but if you are going beyond these trees I cannot let you go alone. I was told everyone is to come out in pairs, for the foreseeable future?" His voice is uncertain like the baiting winds. *Told by Sradfaang, by Fitz. They knew whom they were hiding here, within these walls. They knew whom they hid.*

He has not moved. *He is waiting for me.*

I incline my head toward him. "I was not going far, and as you see, I have my hound. Will that not be enough for a few moments?"

The door opens beyond his shoulder. My eyes flicker to it. A figure steps through it, tall and darkly garbed. *The goblin.* I nod to the man again—he is speaking, but I cannot recall what he is saying, nor what he has said. Guilt pangs in my chest. I wave my hand, force a nod toward him. "Do not trouble yourself. I will return." *They have found me. There will be no more time to think, time beyond the walls of the building now. My time out here is lost before it began.*

Tulé nods, relief etched in his face, and I do not hear what he says next, a word of thanks, mumbled faintly, or something else. I cast my eyes down, move up the slope toward the goblin. *She went for him, then. So it is true, what Jørn said.*

Sradfaang has not moved from the doorway of the yard, his head higher than the frame of the door. I keep my eyes on my feet, Blått's head up and his eyes alert beside me. *Will they acknowledge what was said, or pretend the child said nothing?*

I step by the goblin, through the doorway. The door clicks shut. A shudder creeps up my spine. I slow, and he is moving past me, up the hall the way I came only moments ago.

"Come along, healer." *An order.* He turns at the end of the hall, moving through a door that I have never been on the far side of before. There is a hall beyond it, narrower than the others, only two doors down its walls. He stops by the second one, on the right, and pushes it open before him. He stops beside it, waiting. "Go in."

I swallow hard, step through the doorway. The room is furnished, comfortable with rugs and a long chair-like structure. The space is lit only by the light of a lantern hanging from the far wall, not a single window in it. *We must be near the heart of Sikkerhet.*

Ciaran is sitting in a high-backed chair before the glow of the lantern. He stands, inclining his head to me. *Respect.* I incline mine back, just barely, and he gestures toward a seat beside me.

There is another man, standing at the back corner of the room that I did not see before, half in the shadows. *Havard.* His dark brows are drawn low, eyes on me. *But this time, there is no Fitzclaste. Only the goblin, the prince and Havard, in the room.* I drop onto the edge of the chair.

Ciaran moves back into his seat, his motions careful. *Courtly. I should have noticed it more before.* His eyes move to mine. "You need not be afraid, if that is fear I see in your eyes, healer."

Fear? I look down, look away, toward the hound by my knees. *Did my eyes shift, give away something that I have not recognized?* Ciaran is still speaking, slowly, measuring each word with care, like a man of politics would measure them. "Ruidún told me of what you heard, what Jørn said in the sewing rooms. The boy was not intended to have known, and I am sorry that you found out through his words and not our own. It has been a secret well-guarded, for reasons that I am afraid you have not been made aware of since you did not need to know."

I press my hand against my knee. "Keep secret, lure people like me in? Or do you hide from the death that rides our nation?"

His eyes are settled on mine, emotionless. "To neither end. My mother has been hunting for my head for the last five turnings along with theirs."

I clasp my hands together. *Does she then hunt for him, too?* My eyes burn further, ache. *Could he not have fought back, rather than run to the forests, rather than hide away in the wastelands of the woods?*

"Let him speak, Eness." Havard's voice is low, dry from behind the prince. I tighten my hand, force my eyes to calm.

Ciaran—Prince Ciaran Har'valach of Auvridal—inclines his head. "Thank you, Havard. But I would hear her thoughts, if she share them."

My eyes burn. *What would he do, with my thoughts?* My chest is hot, jaw clenched. "I have nothing worth sharing, my lord. I would take my leave, if there is nothing else. I will not share your secret, will not share who you are. It will remain hidden, as you intended."

Ciaran looks down, shaking his head, just slightly. "I am sorry, but I cannot permit you to do that until we have spoken further. If you do not have a wish to share your mind, I will share mine, if you will permit it."

My hand grips the edge of the chair—I force my eyes to move to his gaze.

He inclines his head, speaking again. "As you wish, then." He shifts forward in his chair, the silence in the room deafening. "My mother did not handle my father's death with any grace, as all the world knows. Murder in the night is not a thing handled with grace. I was not at the castle when he was killed, gone for tutorage, still a child.

"When I was old enough to return and started hearing what she had done and was doing," His jaw tightens, but his eyes do not leave mine, "I spoke with her. She gave me reason to believe that I was heard, and that she would change her course, but as you know, she did not. I was naïve enough to believe that she had, too sheltered to see anything beyond the words she told me. I knew little of the world and saw little within the castle to give me reason to mistrust her given word. Her councilors all agreed with her and backed up her story when I spoke with them."

He nods his head at me. "I am sorry for the length of this tale, but for the sake of the lives in our country, I have to ask that you bear with me until it is said." I incline my head.

He continues. "I was sent away, for the next five gråsvings, and I heard little until their end when I returned to the palace. I was to gain the throne, in the next turning, if my mother deemed me fit, and I did not tread as carefully as I ought to have. When I returned and began to hear rumors, I tried to confront her, face to face, to speak with her about what was being done within the kingdom. But she dodged me with some skill. She was dealing with the events of my brother then, and I was sent to learn new arts in another place, where I again heard little, a little more of our country this time, through the contacts I had built up over the seasons prior.

"When I came back to the palace, more than two turnings later, I cornered her in the hall where she could not escape my questions. I will not air all my mother's sins before you, but she gave me more leave to believe her then, and like a fool, I did yet again. That night, she tried to have me assassinated in my sleep."

My heart sinks into my chest.

He continues, his voice slow, more careful now, eyes still on mine. "I escaped, through an honest guard, and took to the woods. From there I was found and eventually given a place to work, here, in this haven. I do not pretend to be innocent of the death toll that followed in my wake when I left, nor am I ignorant of the story that was spun of my death. You are aware of the destruction that would come to this place if it was found out that I was still alive, the death that would come if it was found out where I have been hidden here. You know my mother's wrath well from your own timestring, I will imagine." He straightens. "There is no idleness in my men and I am doing what I can to combat her during my time here."

I tighten my lips. *How do they combat here, from a fortress, far from her cities, far from towns and roads and outposts? Did Eerol not hope his prince would do something, would end this war? Did he know that the prince was before his feet, hiding away, doing nothing in the shadows of the trees?* I shake my head, stand. *The healer was too suspicious not to know.* I shift my hand. "Thank you. I would ask your leave. I will not share your secret but I would return to my task, if the tale is done."

He leans back, his brow lifting, just slightly. "You have no questions?"

I lift my head. "There are few questions I could ask that would give me any clarity as to why the queen's son is hidden in the woods while the death toll rolls out."

He nods, slowly. I stand and he follows my movement, inclining his head toward the goblin by the door. I turn. My eyes burn, shift, and I look down, away from the goblin, move by him through the door.

I did not bow. I should not give them a reason to doubt that I will keep this secret. Not them. I look back, incline my head, and the prince nods, his held high, that careful look across his features once more. *Guarded.* I duck through the door the goblin opened, and it shuts again behind me, soft in the empty hall.

What is this place, then? My eyes burn. *Creator, there is a man here, whose death has brought on the ending of the lives of hundreds, and yet he lives. What can I do here, where his shadow dwells? He is safe here, while death runs rampant in his name. Was that not what he said?*

Creator, please help them. Please save them from her hand. He is the prince, their prince. Does he not seek to save them? How can he, so far from all that is happening?

I start up the hall, steps falling fast, Blått's even on the ground beside me. *Her cruelty did not fail to reach him, nor his brother. He was not left out of it, through all of that.* I glance back up the hall, my steps slow.

There are the faint murmurs of voices, from the room I left moments ago. *What are those in power doing, to help or to hinder, here? Do they plan to wait for the lives of those hunted to wither out while they work?*

It will not end with the death of the last of my blood. It will not end with them. It will continue and grow until the whole of Auvridal is awash with it, all of our lands awash with growing death, if they do nothing.

My work and hands will mean little, if they are standing idly by. It has meant little, if there is not work done, around me, in the larger parts of the country. I can do little to stop this alone. I turn again, and my heart thunders hard in my chest.

XXXIII

Only Hearsay

There is a step beside me, echoing in the silence of the room. I glance up, the cup half-lifted in my hand. *Lord Fitzclaste.* I set the mug down.

His face is drawn, eyes watchful. "Healer. Is anyone here with you?"

I shake my head, move the steaming mug of tea to the side. "Gót. Are you in need of something, Lord Fitzclaste?" I turn back toward him.

He has folded his arms, his face intent, listening. He nods, slowly, the movement measured. "I need nothing. But I wished to speak with you after I was informed of what occurred yesterday." I look down and my jaw tightens. *I have not had enough time to think of it, with everyone coming in and out since dawn. It is too soon to speak with him.* He is watching me carefully, like the prince did yesterday, only his eyes are kinder. "Is your trouble with him, or with Tejan and I for what we have done?" His voice is measured.

I pull the mug back into my hand. "I do not wish to speak words that may be taken in a light that they are not intended. I have not had time to consider. It has only been a few watches since I learned of it, and as you know, your home has been busy this morn." I half-stand. "Would you take tea?"

He nods beside me. "Aye. That would be well. I know that what trust is still given is not likely to me that you would consider my word after we have sheltered the crown prince in our home. But I would keep peace, to guard Ciaran, and all those who have taken refuge under my roof, for as long as I may. Teja and I both seek to have this settled before the Menantians arrive, whenever that may be. Since we cannot be certain of when they will arrive, I would speak now, if you will humor me. If not, I will come back at another time."

I slow by the pot, steam curling off it and glance back toward him. *The man is always moving, always has a task on hand to be done or a word to be seen to. He has made time now. I cannot ask him to come back later.* I lift the pot, set a mug on the table with my free hand. "I hold my quarrel with everyone who was sworn to protect our people but has wrought their blood as one brings sap from a tree. You and Tejan are not among them. I have seen your care for others in your work and speech this last moon."

I slow the stream of water, set the pot aside, and reach for the tea crock. I turn back to him. "Prince Ciaran has hidden away while his country suffers. The country his family was sworn to protect. I do not pretend to understand the business of kings and dukes, but was his vow not to be to protect our people? If so, then why does he stay at arm's length, and why did he run, and cause the deaths of hundreds more." I pull the bag shut, shove it back into the crock. "She used his death as an excuse to extend her death toll."

He nods, accepting the mug. "Aye. She did, in blaming the death cult. I recall." His expression does not change, *Cautious. They are all cautious, as they should be.* "And she continues to use it, a reminder day by day that if our prince could be turned, to the side of the very people who murdered his father, then who is free from their reach? I know her politics, healer. But he could not have known what she would do, what the Soaré Gâr would ask her to do, in the wake of his disappearance."

He shifts his stance. "His vow had not been made. But he has done, and continues to do, his best for this country and all who are in it, while here, better than I imagine he could from the palace or anywhere closer at hand. He has not been idle for any of the time I have known him, not even before he was thrown from the palace. I have never known him to be frivolous with his time. He did not speak to defend himself yesterday, but I will, if you will hear me, and I would ask a question. Are you imagining that it costs him nothing to be here? To work in quiet places while his country is at war, his people being killed by his own flesh and blood? That, I think, would cost any man, Eness."

I look down, grab my own mug. "How can he be immune to the teachings of the woman that bore him? And what does the Soaré Gâr have to do with the queen, sonyá? I have heard nothing of the sun god people in turnings."

He cradles the mug in his hand, shifting his stance. "I apologize. I thought that you would know of the Soaré Gâr's involvement, not be gathering new information through this. I apologize. The Soaré Gâr had a hand since the second or third turning after Georwyn came to the throne, I am not sure the date, for they were quiet about it for a time, and my informants did not pick up on them until they had nearly made a play for the queen's ear. As much as the Movement is involved through fire and bloodshed of innocents, the Soaré Gâr is involved through whispers and words placed carefully at a fitting time, bending ears to their will. My information at the time informed me that it was their encouragement that placed the statements about Ciaran's death across the country, that he had turned to the Movement and tried to slay her in her sleep."

My heart slows in my chest. "They accused him of treason?"

He inclines his head. "Aye. That and more. We have spent much of the last five turnings undoing what she did in a breath that night, to turn hearts back to him. Wars cannot be won, silently or on battlefields, without the hearts of men."

He studies me, steam curling into the torch light from the mug beside him. "Ciaran would have told you much more, I think, had you questioned him, last night, as you have me." His face softens, the smallest amount. "Why did you ask nothing of him? You should question him while he is near, while he has offered to be asked. He would have told you much and still will, if you will speak with him. You will find him an honest man, if you choose to look, and an answer to many questions you have not had the access to while in the forest. Your place in this war may grow in importance in the days to come, and I would know fully what side you are on. There are many."

I wrap my hands harder around the teacup. "I do not know him enough yet to question and trust his answers. That is why I asked none. Any man can say things to win hearts. Your trust in him does you credit, but I would tend my own tasks."

He lifts a brow. "If ever desire, I would tell you questions to ask, or Tejan can do the same, questions we had for him over the turnings since he arrived, but I do not imagine that will help you now. I will not press you on this, Eness, only ask that you consider him, before you choose where you stand for the days to come. Use the time you have here. Seek to learn of him through those here. Men cannot keep masks up at all times, and he has been here far too long for us to not know something of who he truly is. There is a lot to be known about a man by the men that follow him."

The mug in my hand is hot, searing slowly into my skin. I set it down, grip my hand with my other. *And much to be known about a man by the way he treats those beneath him.* I incline my head. "I will look. But I will give no promise for my answer. Thank you for your time in coming down here, Lord Fitzclaste. I will speak to no one of his title. You have my word, given freely. His title is yours to keep, as you will."

He inclines his head, taking a long sip of the tea. *The heat did not trouble him.* "Thank you, Eness." He begins to turn, his movements slowing. He turns back over his shoulder. "I know my wife has mentioned it to you before, but you are always welcome to take your work to the sewing rooms in the afternoon. Many of the civs gather there on days that are slow, and you would be welcome. Much can be learned, by going where the women talk." He smiles and turns, stepping from the room.

My hands are clammy and clasped together over nothing.

• ▶ | ◀ ▶ | ◀ ▶ | ◀ ▶ | ◀ ▶ | ◀ ▶ | ◀ •

The light of the sewing rooms is soft, Blått's head gentle against my side. Anna looks up sharply, her mouth midway to forming a word. "Eness!" She grins, hands still working fast at the needles in them. Knitting needles, something half made below them.

Norla inclines her head beside her, the women of the room each looking up toward me. Several of them are still speaking near the back, Amalie and Tollah among them, something small cradled in Norla's arms. Norla nods to the seat across from her, a bench with a low back, where Nieave is. I incline my head, drop into the empty seat.

Anna is still grinning at me. "I was wondering when you might make it up here. It has been a long while since you came to the fort and I have never once seen you come for the afternoon to work with us."

I half-smile, Blått stepping off toward Tollah. She is clicking her tongue at him, her hand out to pet him. *I would not have come yet, if not for Fitz.* "My work is not practical for rooms of hand work, so I am late in coming. I apologize."

Norla lifts a brow. "But you have brought some with you, I see." She nods toward the bag beside me.

I incline my head, pull out a small sack from the bag. "Aye."

Iris raises a brow, pushing a needle through the stitchwork in her hand. "What are those?"

I set the sack down, draw out a needle. It is long and hooked and tarnished. "Needles for stitching."

Her face blanches. "For stitching skin?"

Norla pats her leg. "Aye. Don't stare too long at them, love."

Anna shifts her legs, folding them beside her on the bench. She glances at Norla. "How long ago was that confirmed?"

A quiet settles over the room, the tenor of the space changing with the conversation of before. The women behind me are still chattering, their voices eager and strange in the hush of the place.

Norla speaks. "A few dawns back. And it has not been confirmed, only hinted at in a message Tollak received. The Movement has not been quiet this last season, it seems."

Anna's eyes are soft. "Will that not be adding stress to Fitz and Tejan? Their children are near there, aren't they?"

Nieave inclines her head. "Their son and his family are not two cities from the attacks, but they were not harmed. Tejan and Fitz are wise. They will not stew in worry over things like this, but they will be on their knees more, I think."

Norla nods. "I do not know how much longer the Movement will stay sporadic like this. Twenty turnings is a long time to see little fruit for your efforts, unless they are doing more than we have seen, seeing more than we know." Her jaw tightens. "They may be, from the reports."

I rub a cloth across the needle in my hand, scrub at the tarnishing along it. "Which movement is this?"

Iris looks at me, startled. "Do you not know of the Movement?"

I shake my head. "I know of many movements."

Norla bobs her head, speaking. "The Maa'eulé. They serve the mountain god. They seek to tear down countries." *The Movement they have spoken of many times. There is information to be gathered where the women speak.*

Anna inclines her head. "I do not mean to sound harsh, but I thought you would have heard of them. They are the ones credited with the death of the king." She gives me a sharp look.

My eyes burn. I push it back, incline my head, my hand working at the tip of the needle, the metal tarnished there. "My village was quiet. I always thought it was a small group of assorted men who killed him, not any organized group."

Norla nods. "Assorted, aye. But they are not small, nor are they unorganized. The Maa'eulé are a group of extremists. Tollak says that they may be scattered across the entire world beyond our shores. I know little about them, other than hearing of their work and their claims to the acts done in the last many, many turnings. They have burnt many cities to the ground."

Iris makes a strange noise. "That is why I think it is not wise for so many of us to be settling down and marrying, pretending it is not happening around us. This is no place to be starting families, with the queen's work and theirs crossing each other. We can surely do more without each other to care for."

Nieave looks at her sharply. "We cannot do more without each other, Iris. Do not let your frustration cloud your words."

Iris looks out toward the window, shaking her head. "I am not. I just do not think that it is wise for everyone to be settling down, to bring children into this, while the world is so violent around us. What if it does not quiet, not for turnings? What if these people never leave?"

Norla smiles, and it is tight lipped. "Do you think we are wrong then, who have brought our children into this world, to raise them?"

Iris shakes her head slowly, dragging her eyes from the window. "Gót. But you and Tollak have been married for many turnings, were married before the first of the major attacks happened after the prince was killed. Those of us who are not married, might we be wiser to stay here and unmarried?" There is a searching in her eyes. *A need for hope.*

Nieave's hand takes Iris', gentle and careful. "Ágë will wait for you. He will not force you into something that you do not wish to do. You know that, Iris."

Iris shakes her head sharply, her eyes flickering toward her. "He wouldn't. But I stand by my convictions. And am I not right, too? It is foolish to be trying to pretend that our country isn't falling to pieces when it is. He doesn't see that."

Norla's jaw tightens across from her. "He does see that, Iris. He sees it and he knows as much as you do. If you spoke to him of your concerns, he would heed them."

Iris looks away again, her hands folded beneath Nieave's. She shakes her head. "I know that. But is it not better for us to give of ourselves, than to try to build homes and community and settle at a time when our world is crumbling?"

Norla lifts a brow. "Is it not better to give ourselves something to fight for, something worth building, at times like this? We cannot all fight on the front lines, Iris. And the front lines have nothing to fight for, if there is no next generation. Speak with him. He will gladly listen if you will give him an opportunity to."

Iris looks away again, quiet falling on the room but for the voices behind me.

A laugh rings out, high and girlish. Nieave shakes her head, turning her eyes toward the woman on the end, beside Anna, a woman I do not know. "Gwynn, how do the sewing rooms fair?"

The girl at the end—Gwynn—smiles, straightening. "Oh! They are well. Iris and I were just finishing up a new dress for Lila. She tore a massive hole in the last one, and her fár finally asked us to make another, so we have. I am starting a new tunic now, to have on hand. Our spares are in use." She half-starts, looking down. *Was she not to say anything, about the use of the tunics?*

Norla looks at her, shaking her head, her needlework lifted into her hands again. "We know of the soldiers, Gwynn. Do not fret yourself. But I would keep hushed about them beyond this circle." She smiles, a comforting thing, and the girl nods her head. *She cannot be more than fifteen turnings. How did she come to be here?*

Anna leans in, grinning, mischief in her eyes. "Well, as a new subject you might not have heard yet, I have heard it said that the Menantian emissaries who are coming are to be those at the height of fashion in their country. We shall get to see their colors and styles from our own home. That is something that few can say. I have heard the emissary proper is a woman. I shall look forward to seeing her skirts and sleeves. I haven't seen royal fashion in an age, and hers will likely be something to see, given that she is visiting a lord."

Gwynn grins beside her, leaning in, her hands still moving on the garment in her hands as though she were looking. "Do you think they will wear traditional garb here, or only travelin' clothes? I should like to see either of them. A travel garment from another country will be somethin' to see."

Iris hums idly, coming back to herself. "Either way, we may learn something from them, something new to try, whenever we get new fabrics again."

Norla smiles softly, looking across the room. The conversation lifts, voices chatting, returned to their normal course. I press my hand against Blått's head, and Norla's eyes meet mine, tight around their edges. She smiles, nodding her head at me.

I lift my head. "How long have you been here, kúráh?"

Norla smiles, something like relief in her eyes.

XXXIV

Claw

I step down the slope, mud sinking between my toes from the stream. Flowers dot the hillside: the last of the larkspur and a few bluebells, oddly late, where these waters flow. *I have never seen any so late in the season.* I step around a cluster of them, buttercups bright in the patches where the sunlight cuts through the trees. *These flowers will all be done now, gone for the season back home. All but the buttercups, which bloom for a season yet, nearly until harvest time.*

I stoop, clutch my skirts in my hands, and someone moves up on the slope—a voice cuts through the trees. "Do not go too far. Sradfaang will have my throat if something happens to you." *Jons. My guard for this outing. The goblin was out with the prince somewhere, gone. He and the prince have been often conversing.*

I glance up at Jons, incline my head, strands of hair falling over my cheeks. "I will go no further than need be." I flick my eyes back down, lift the tiny flower from the edge of the stalk. There are no leaves on the stem, only the small pale blooms, shaped like breeches, wide and white with yellow at the very end, down where my finger touches. I smile. *Little Blue Staggers. Old Man Britches. They are said to make cattle that feed on them stagger and sway and lay down to sleep the day away early. But not the men that have tried, or so Aílé said.*

I drop the edge of the flower and turn my hand toward another, beside it. It is a small pale-pink flower, close to the water. There are many petals on its little dancing head, bobbing though the wind is faint. A spider web caught on the edge of it dances with each pull, move for move. I slip my knife out of its sheath and slide the tip beneath the ground where the roots grow. *Rue anemone.* I lift the plant from the ground, set it in the basket on my arm. Mud clings heavy to my fingertips.

There is no sound of rustling now, only the brush of the leaves in the wind. I lift my head, glance back behind me. *Where did Blåthjortt go?* The brush around me is empty, blue and gold and white blooms curling in the deep greens, up the slope into the forest beyond. A few more rue anemone add dots of palest pink to the slopes, bringing a tiny taste of the colors of late stråle. I drop my knife onto the plants in the basket, stand. *He has not strayed far before, when we have been out here.* I glance over my shoulder.

Jons is leaning against a tree, up the slope. His hand is moving on a small knife, whittling it against a chunk of cut wood. He gestures up the slope with the wood block. "The hound ran off up into the forest a time ago. I thought you would have heard. Or noticed by now. He has been gone a good long spell."

I flick my eyes up the slope. "I did notice, but I thought he would have come back before now. He does not usually stray so far." *But he has been indoors much of late. Perhaps he is just running, chasing squirrels and rabbits and the like. How soon will another band of soldiers be near, after the last?* The trees around are tall, the brush thick beside me with silver green leaves climbing up toward the sky.

I drag my eyes back to the steam, step forward in the water. I slip my blade beneath the roots of another rue anemone, whittle the plant from the earth. Something rustles in the brush ahead, high in the branches. I glance upward, slip the plant into the basket. The knife in my fingers slips, wet with the stream. A branch dances, far in the brush, leaves jostling sharply. *It could be a hare or hound, that high in the brush.*

Or a squirrel, darting across branches. They often make movements bigger than their size. The wind shifts again, and something feels strange in the forest, too still. *It does not sound like Blåthjortt. There are no birds calling. That is not the way it should be, on a bright day like this. Could men have come close, without being seen?*

There is a sharp intake of breath, up the hill, Jons. "Healer, step back." His voice is sharp, even.

Something moves in the bush, huge, and the branches swirl aside for the hulking mass of a bear. A roar blasts the air, the massive bear stepping forward, once, twice. I skirt backward, stalks of plants catching on my feet. The creature's teeth are white, large, in its great mouth, high over my head, staggeringly high. Its size is wrong, wrong below the trees. *No, no, no, no.*

I stumble backward and it moves again, a sound rumbling through the air from deep within its chest, head still high above though it is down on all fours like a hound.

It lunges, swiping out a great paw. I jump backward, stumble, knife clutched useless in my hand. Air brushes across my chest. My ears ring, feet stumble in the mud. *There is nowhere to go.*

Someone is shouting something, shouting above the sounds of the massive creature, above its great and terrible head. "Run! Healer, run!"

I cannot outrun it, it is too close already. I stumble backward, move slowly, and it darts forward, one of its steps equaling many of mine. My foot sinks, water crawling up my skin, pulling me down toward the earth. *The bog, the stream.* I scramble back, each step sinking, and there is no more shouting. The bear's head snaps toward me, teeth bared. I jerk backward, scream.

Pain bursts from my arm, I am falling backward, teeth ripping through my skin. The creature roars, and the ground shakes with it. My arms splash in the water, my hands sinking down, down into the bed of the creek where rocks and stones grind against my skin. I scramble backward, my hands caught in the mud, sinking, sinking, vines trailing around and pulling me down.

There is a shout from somewhere, and the creature is moving toward me, its mouth wide open, spittle flinging toward the creek bed. I pull my feet under me, stumble. The stream is pulling, dragging my skirts downward.

The bear swipes outward, a massive paw toward my skull.

I jerk backward, and there is no ground beneath me, only water, crashing above my head, swirling above me. I pull toward the surface, lungs burning, coughing. Something collides with my chest, shoving downward. My lungs burn, water crowding into my chest, pain everywhere, pressing, crushing. My shoulder press into the creek bed, roots snapping beneath my back in the soft mud. My lungs scream, the water a thousand shades of gray around me, and there is the bear's snout, cutting through the water toward my face, dark and huge.

I scream, bubbles white and everywhere, and the mouth is gone—water crowds into my lungs, burning, and the bear's paw presses down, my back grinding into the silt beneath me. My body screams, coughing against water, pressing downward, down. *This is death.* Pain bites into my neck. *I am going to be crushed on the floor of the creek.* The edges of the world darken, fading, the light no longer dancing above.

The weight lifts.

I jerk my head above the water, scramble back, and my arm strikes something hard—pain burns up my arm. I cough, hacking, my throat grating, arms weak and there is a blur of fur, deep brown in the light of the sun. The bear-like creature roars, his head away from me. The world is fuzzy, water everywhere closing in around me, pulling, shoving. I cough, and my lungs burn, skin burns, arms burns, and I cannot get air to obey in my chest.

Something strikes my arm behind me and I jump. It does not move, blurred, water in my eyes, hair down my face, clinging to my skin. I swipe my hand across my face. *A boulder in the stream.* I wrap my arm around it, pull my body above the water, and there is a roar again, the water rippling out from shore.

My hand swipes across my face, forcing back the hair clinging there once more. The bear's back is to me, massive and thick-coated, shaking with each lunging step, roaring, snarling, its tail motionless.

Someone shouts again, a battle cry. *Men. It is attacking me. Elnial be with them.* There are two of them on horseback, the horses not rearing back from the enormous beast or attempting to run. The creature is larger than both of them combined. It swipes forward, and one horse screams, falling—I scream.

Everything burns white, blinding. I am screaming again, gasping, and I cannot get air, pain caught everywhere. I cannot breathe. I press my head hard against the stone, wait, and the creature does not turn. Another man shouts, and the beast snarls. I bite back bile. *I cannot run. If I do not, they will push it back onto me in the stream.* I grip the rock tighter, water swirling, and the bear roars, roaring again, the sound crashing like a ancient tree in the forest. Something barks.

My head snaps up, heart pounds. Something blue flashes by in front of the bear, filling the air with the sound of barking, and the creature is shifting its weight, moving to strike. *No, no, no.*

Something snaps into the side of the bear, a stick. It sways with each movement as the beast swipes toward the hound. *A spear shaft.* The bear slashes toward the side, and there is a man before it, a sword in his hand, gleaming in the sunlight. *Jons.* He swings forward and the bear's paw moves toward his head, fast, so fast. He ducks easily, moving around it. He steps forward, toward the bear, and drives his blade upward toward the chest of the creature, the dog darting around his legs, barking, barking.

The bear bellows, waters rippling, paws swiping madly, wildly, and someone pulls Jons backward, jerking him away—a paw swings over his head.

Sradfaang. He shoves Jons behind him, knocking the bear's massive paw back with his great sword. Another man moves forward, his hair glinting gold in the light of the sun, and he steps into the reach of the bear. I turn my eyes away.

The water is pulling at me, dragging me down into the creek bed. I jerk my legs and a gasp tears through me—black spots dance across my vision. The air is gone from my lungs.

I pull my legs harder, but they barely budge, still below the rock, in the current of the stream where silt is flowing down, swirling. A sob catches in my chest. *I am trapped.* I swallow hard, scramble, and my lungs scream. *If the bear comes back, falls back?*

There is another shout, Ciaran's voice.

Something crashes against the earth, the water pooling outward. The bear is against the ground, its massive foot twitching in the stream beside me, sunk into the churning waters. Its sides heave, then they are still, the fur slowing, stilling, foot no longer twitching. *It cannot be dead, not that simply. Cannot have gone down that quickly.*

The goblin swipes his blade against the grasses beside him, speaking to someone I cannot see behind the bulk of the creature. He glances over at me, sharply dropping his blade against a tree. "Carry that." He nods toward the blade, his voice faint in the ringing silence.

He moves into the stream, wading toward me, and there is a man beside him, blood sprayed across his face, dripping down into his beard. *Prince Ciaran. He charged the creature and survived.* I swallow, press my arms under me, and pain sears up my side—I gasp. *Do not move. Do not move. Do not move.*

I cannot get air. My breaths hiss through my teeth.

"Healer." The words sound far away and too close, rough like gravel and high like the wind. "How bad are you wounded?" A hand touches my shoulder and I pull away. Pain sears through my side.

I suck in a breath, pull to the side of the stone. "The bear…"

The prince shakes his head, his feet lost in the churning dark of the stream. "He was dispatched. Where are you wounded?" His eyes are sharp, concerned. He crouches in the water.

The goblin swears, words in a tongue I do not understand, and it sounds wrong. A hand brushes my arm, where the pain is not, the blood is not. "That will not kill you. Where else are you wounded?"

I shake my head, heart still thundering in my chest. It hurts, aches. "I am well, if I can…" I draw a breath and white bursts again, stealing my vision. I gasp, press my head hard against the stone. It is cool on my skin, cool beneath the pulsing of my skull.

The prince shakes his head, and I can barely see him through the slits in my vision. "She should be moved from the water, if she can be, before her injuries are assessed any further." His eyes meet mine, light catching dully on the water swirling around his boots. "Can you rise, Eness, if you have assistance? I will take your arm, but I do not want to harm you more by moving you."

I purse my lips, eyes burning and damp. "My skirts…" I grit my teeth, "…they are caught. I cannot move my legs enough to rise." My voice is hoarse, cutting out.

Sradfaang is already moving. His hands grips my legs, pulling them from the rocks and mud below. I press my hands under me and pain sears across my side, the world going dark. My hand collides with the rock, water pulling me back toward the stream and my skirts are heavy, tugging, tugging downward.

A hand wraps around my arm tightly, steadying. "Eness. Do not rush yourself." The prince's voice trails off. "There must be a better way than this." I look up, and his eyes meet mine, faint behind the haze, behind the swirling darkness.

Sradfaang speaks. "I can lift her out of the stream."

I shake my head sharply. "I will walk. Let me walk. I am up now." I step forward, and the hand does not move from my skin. *It is gloved.* The stream swirls around my legs, current pushing against me, and my skirts twist in it, jerking down toward the rocks. The prince moves, his hand shifting to my other arm, and the current breaks, its press gentler. I glance down. Water swirls about his legs, breaking around mine. *He is breaking the current.*

I grit my teeth, step up onto the marsh bed beside the bear, and my foot sinks deep, jarring in the mud. The bear's fur is motionless, blood coating it where the water and grime does not. Wind ripples across it, like a breath.

I stumble backward—a shudder crawls up my spine. My eyes flicker to the goblin, steps away from me. *He is small beside this creature from the forests.* I press my hand against my side. *I should be dead, should have died when it shoved me under the water into the creek bed.* The goblin is speaking, somewhere above me.

I shiver, cough—the world screams, white flashing across my vision. Air is gone, pain searing through my chest.

"Eness?" The voice sounds too close. I press my hand against the prince's side, shove him, but the voice is not coming from him. He does not let go, only loosens his grasp about my good arm, still steadying me. I suck in a breath. It shakes in my chest, biting, shallow.

"...her side is cut and she is struggling to breathe. We need a healer...a good healer..." *The prince's voice.*

Sradfaang's voice cuts out. "There is one in the village, a half-day's walk from here." The prince nods, stepping away from me, and another hand wraps around my arm. There are other voices, speaking, near and far in the forests. Sradfaang looks down at me. "Where else have you been wounded?"

I press my hand against my side. My arm is warm, damp; everything else is cold despite the sunlight flickering across my skin. I shiver, press my arms tighter against my side. My lungs feel filled with liquid, the air heavy and thick and still but for the voices in the air. "It is only the side."

There is a man helping a horse up from the ground beside the massive dead beast. Blood is smeared against the side of the horse, dark and thick. *But it is rising, standing on its own feet.*

My eyes burn, hand clenching against my side. Something presses against my hand, warm, moving at the edges of my vision.

Blått is beside me, his head pressed against my hand, eyes looking up at mine, wide, pleading. There is blood on his muzzle, hair caked against it—not his. My heart lightens. *Praise be.* I press my hand against his head, eyes flickering over him. *He is unharmed. He was not wounded.*

I sway, and the hand latches onto my arm once more. "You should not still be standing." Sradfaang's voice is faint.

A man steps down the slope before us, dirt smeared across his clothes and his face, his dark hair clinging to his forehead. *Jons.* He nods, eyes scanning over me, and swipes a hand over his eyes. "She is alive. Praise be the Creator." He nods at me, his hands gripping at the hilt of his sword. "I thought you were a grass-breath, when you did not run. That was no small beast and you did not even move. Curse it. I thought you were dead. Did it miss, in the stream?"

I grimace, shifting my hands. "Aye. I could not have outrun it."

Jons swears again. "They are not supposed to be near here."

The goblin shakes his head. "Get the horses. She cannot walk back." Jons nods, stepping away, his movements fast in the marsh of the war-torn ground. The goblin is looking up the hill, his face grim.

Ciaran glances at him, turning back toward us. "You cannot lift her onto horseback if you cannot grip her sides." He turns toward me. "Can you mount, if we find you a step? You will not have to mount on your own."

I shake my head, and my eyes are burning again, swirling. *Swirling with tears.* I bite them back, press my hand harder against my side, above the pain. "I cannot. I can walk back. It will be simpler."

Sradfaang shakes his head, his eyes narrowing to slits. "You will not make it up the slope."

Someone is stepping up before us, his face familiar, form tall. *Einion. Captain Flint.* His sword is dripping, water and blood and hair coating the blade, slipping down it to the footmarks in the mud that cakes up his form.

I step back, and his eyes flicker to mine. His blade lowers, pressing against his leg, smearing the carnage there, against his breeches. He looks up at the prince, his eyes flickering back to me. "The horse will live. Will you be able to walk, healer?"

I shift my feet, skirts heavy, water dripping against my legs. "Was there anyone else wounded?"

He shakes his head, the movement sharp. "Gót. It was only you and the one horse."

I swallow hard, force my lungs to work, to breathe. "What of the rider?"

He glances at me, a brow lifting. "I was the rider. I was riding out to meet Ciaran and Srad." I glance up, flick my eyes over him, and my vision is blurred. He lifts a brow again, his gaze patient. "I am well." I nod, look away, and the goblin's hand moves on my elbow.

"She is still bleeding. I am taking her and the prince back to Sikkerhet before anything else can happen. You can handle the rest of this." The goblin's voice is dry, unimpressed. He turns, clicking his tongue, and Blått's head shoots up from my hand, his ears alert, slightly lifted. The goblin nods, back toward the fort, and the hound bolts away up the slope. *He commanded my hound. I do not know when he began to do that. He might have known how since the trails.*

Water trickles against my ankles, falling in thick streams.

"Can you walk to a horse, healer?" The goblin's voice sounds far away, and I nod, force my leg forward beneath the heavy fabric and the mud clinging to the soles of my feet.

Einion shakes his head. "She is gray with shock..." The world feels hazy about me, blurring over, and another voice replies.

XXXV

Bones

Voices are everywhere, questions I cannot hear to calculate. My hand is pressed against my side, warm in the creeping cold. My breaths are not deep enough, each shallow in the thick air.

"Where am I taking her?" *Sradfaang's voice, above me, sharp, irritated.*

"Take her to my quarters. She will not be disturbed there." There is a protest somewhere, a woman's voice, hazy, and I cannot focus on her words. The woman's voice is gone and the man's voice is speaking again. "She cannot go there and she cannot go back to the healing rooms where her work is. We have no empty rooms. Take her to my quarters. That is not a request, Tejan. I will sleep somewhere else and there is nowhere else quiet for her to go. She needs aid immediately if she is to be well."

Something is lowering me back to my feet. *Or perhaps I was already on them.* I stumble, the floor strange, and a hand on my arm angles, pulling me upright. Figures move ahead all turning down a hallway. We turn, away from them. *We aren't following?* The hand pulls me to the side, barely touching my skin. I stumble, step slowly and quickly, and it's too fast and sluggish like the world around me. *Something is wrong. My arm is numb.*

The goblin pauses beside me, a door open before us. It is open to a staircase winding upward, not downward into the earth. *There are stairs here leading up? Should we not be going to the healing rooms, to the salves and cots?* He steps forward, drawing me with him. "Choose your pace. I will keep you upright in the event that you falter. I would carry you, but it cannot be done in these halls. They are too narrow for me."

I step onto the first stair, draw a breath—it stabs in my side, sharp. A grimace pulls at my lips. I press my hand tighter above my ribs, step up once more. A stair follows the stairs before, wooden and wobbling beneath my feet, and my skin slaps against each one. My skirts coil around my calves, wet and clinging, branches pricking my skin from within them. I stumble, suck in a breath. Pain sears my side again—my lungs are empty, aching, shallow.

The goblin is motionless beside me. *When did we stop moving?* I force my eyes upward. He is looking forward, up the stairs. "This is not what Ciaran intended." He glances down at me, his expression tight. "Do you wish to be carried, healer?"

I shake my head, sharply, and everything burns. "Gót. You have said it cannot be done. I have made it here, I will make it up." My voice is thin.

He steps forward again, his hand taking my arm with him. My breaths are needles in my chest, sloshing.

He pulls toward the side, the pressure strange on my prickling skin. *We are at the top.* I stumble forward, and we are moving through a doorway, somewhere I do not know. His hand releases my arm. "The women will be here in a moment to clean the wound. Sit down." He inclines his head toward something close by me. *A bed. We are in a room?*

I glance up, half-sit. The room is large, the wood panels each carved with a careful pattern. "Why are we here?" *Why have we not gone to the healing rooms, where my pots and salves are? I could have tended the gashes then, mine and any others. Were there others wounded? Was there not a scream on the field, something falling? Was someone wounded that I did not see?*

My hand presses against the bed, and the world swirls. I grit my teeth and the goblin is speaking somewhere beyond my vision. "You needed to be somewhere beyond the normal movement of the fort…"

Someone screamed somewhere. The beast hit someone, other than me. There was someone else wounded.

• ▶ | ◀ ▶ | ◀ ▶ | ◀ ▶ | ◀ ▶ | ◀ ▶ | ◀ •

My hand is working at my arm, pulling a short hair from the middle gash on my arm. Each strand of fur the length of my finger, waved and thick, fine. Blood is coating my skin, rolling into my night dress in a small streams from the gash. I blink, stare at my skin. *I do not remember changing into a night dress. Have I cleaned this?* My eyes flicker upward, hand dropping against my arm, and my lungs hitch.

Someone is standing a few breaths from me, speaking. "…you need something, healer?"

I blink, lift my hand again. *Fitzclaste.* His face is drawn, eyes watching. I shake my head. *My mind is foggy.* My back aches. I flick my eyes back to the gashes. Blood trickles from the four huge marks, cleaving into my skin and pulling it open. *They will need to be stitched closed, pulled back together, or they will heal open, flayed like this, and that scar will always be on their skin, whoever has this gash.* I purse my lips. *I cannot stitch it closed, not with one hand. It is my skin. My gash. I cannot stitch it closed.*

My eyes dart upward. Someone is speaking. A woman bows and ducks out of the room, and the voice is speaking to me, asking something. "…you have need of?"

I purse my lips. "Is there someone—" my voice is thin, and there is not enough force in my lungs to make my words come out, "—who is good with a thread, who will not get sick at the sight of skin beneath a needle?"

Fitzclaste shifts his hands on his arms, and I grimace, angle my weight off my ribcage. It screams. They are speaking again, words low, and I cannot catch what they are saying in full. "…Iris does not do wounds well, neither does Anna or Gwynn. It will have to be someone else, if Einion does not return with that healer soon…" Fitzclaste nods, and the woman is leaving the room, turning from it. *Tollah?*

I look back toward my arm, my head heavy, arm limp. *There are still hairs in it to be pulled from the gashes.* They are long, all the way from my shoulder to below the crook of my arm. *Fur. I will not be able to get it all out on my own. If it is left long, it will fester.* I cough, and my chest burns.

XXXVI

Ragnar H'olbrenkir

Someone is mumbling over my head, words a chaos of paste and sounds. Someone is mumbling over my head, words a chaos of paste and sounds. My head is hot, arms cold, chest heavy.

"...this is normal, though she ought to be dead. That would be a better kind of normal. Odds, what. How big was that bear thing, ey? Once we get this paste on and get some on her chest, it should help keep the coughing from getting too close, keep her living for a while yet. I have paste for her ribs too. You say she was the healer here? A shame. But she made some good pastes... A pity. I might have bought some from her." *Pastes?* "A pity the more. What kind of paste did you say you are holding, civ? Oh, ey. That will likely do the trick. Bring that over and let's put it on the wound. Did you let her clean it? Good fortune to you that I was not out...She seems to have been a good healer once. Pity, that..." Words swirl together again. "...she might have slipped, sitting on the edge of the bed. It is a good thing I arrived when I did. Good, what. Shame... shame about her lungs... ribs... they don't often recover from this. Pity..."

I grimace, darkness pressing in. I do not push it back, do not force it away again.

A groan tears at my throat. I lift my head, the world dark. I cannot get warmth through my skin, cannot get my lungs to stop aching, aching down in my chest. *Were they crushed?* Someone has forced something pressed against my lips, the pressure of it heavy on my mouth. Liquid trickles between my lips, warm. I swallow hard, and it catches in my throat, caught on air. I cough, pull my head away, but there are fingers clamped against my jaw, pulling.

They drag my head back, liquid pouring between my lips again. "Not yet. Not just yet. A little more marshmallow root and your lungs will—" I gag, and my ribs explode with fire. Stars flicker across the darkness beneath my eyes. "Come on now, little civ. Just a little more…you got the little more…"

I cannot breathe.

My pain burns through all of my chest, and the man is still speaking, speaking about pastes, his fingers clamped on my jaw, cup pressed against my lips. I shiver, curl my arm around my side and it burns, everything burns, the man speaking on. The cup moves, liquid against the side of my cheek now, as though forgotten.

I force my lips to open, force my mouth to speak. "It's… not paste..." *Fever. I have a fever. The world is sharp. What sets in after fever?* "…Willow bark…a tisane… the shelf..."

There is a laugh, high like an old wagon wheel in the village square. "I didn't put willow bark in that. It's a *paste* for keeping wounds clean, for keeping out infections, not a tisane. I made it myself. Her fever must be spiking… Willow bark. Bah." He laughs, the sound less like a squeaky wagon, more like a hen at the butcher block. "I never heard of willow bark tisanes…"

I cannot keep my eyes open. Everything feels wet, soaked, and my lungs are aching.

•▶|◀▶|◀▶|◀▶|◀▶|◀▶|◀•

Something brushes against my arm, cool, soothing. The pain there is faded now, dull. My eyes feel heavy, the room too bright. I lift my arm, grimace, ribs aching. Pain crashes against my skull, lungs screaming. I suck in a breath, and it does not come.

"Breathe, healer, breathe gently. Those ribs are solidly broken." *That voice is foreign, the tones even and grated around the edges.* I drag my eyes open, turn them toward the voice.

My heart slows.

There is a man kneeling beside the bed, only a hand's breadth from me. His hands are working something over the stitches on my exposed arm, his hair dark, beard dark, shoulders clad with black cloth, gold etched into the cloth there. *A soldier.* My eyes widen, burn. I jerk backward and snap my eyes shut. Everything screams. *A soldier. Elnial, no.* I grip my side, and everything is white for a moment, fading out, ringing.

Someone swears. "Healer, I mean you no harm. Lay still for a moment." The sound is faint in the ringing of the room. *Healer?*

I force my eyes to open, to meet his, and my sides are still screaming, heaving. I cannot get enough air, cannot push the whiteness back from the edges of my vision. His hand is out in front of him, a warning or caution. Someone moves behind him, steps pounding quickly, sharp.

"Healer. He means you no harm." Captain Flint's eyes swirl into focus. His eyes are calm but there is concern in them. "He has some skill with a needle and with herbs, and we have had need of both in these last two days." He nods toward my arm. "Let him finish tending that, or you may lose it in the next fortnight. Those wounds have not been properly cleaned."

I drop back against the bed, force my breaths to slow, to calm beneath the pinpricks in my sides.

The soldier is watching me, his hands close to himself, fingertips of his left dominate finger still green-brown with salve. He is watching, leaning back on his heels. *He is waiting on me.* My eyes flicker to the side of the bed. There is a crock on it, nearly lavender in hue, a small one. *One of mine. One from home. He chose the right one to fight off infection in deep cuts.*

I swallow hard, set my hands against my ribcage, where my breaths are kept small. "How did you know which crock to get?" I swallow again, and my throat is still dry, voice shallow. "And where is the man who spoke of pastes?"

Captain Flint tucks back a smile, his expression almost wry. "He was right. You did not care for the healing man. And I told him which crock to use."

I suck in a breath. "Healing man? No man worth his seasons in healing refers to salves as—" My sides tighten, and I grimace, readjust my hands, "—paste. Paste is for cooking and binding things. Paste does not go on the wounded. Not on wounds and cuts."

Captain Flint smiles faintly. "Then I am glad Ciaran sent him back to the village." He lifts a brow, eying me. "It was a strange thing, that you survived that attack. That was no small creature that you disturbed."

I shake my head, slide my arm back toward the soldier. "I do not know how you are not burying my body. Elnial was gracious."

"He was." He inclines his head toward the soldier. "Ragnar will finish rebandaging that arm if you will let him, and then you ought to take your rest. The fever almost took you last night."

I purse my lips, my eyes burning. "It cannot have been too close. I still have my mind." *Fever. That will be why my body is so weak. Even with the ribs, it should not be so weak without it.*

I flick my eyes around the room, strain to see the floor beside him. The room is vast, rugs spread about it in places, but there is not much else in it beside the cot I am on and a chair behind the captain, across the room, and a table. I lick my lips—they are dry. "Where is Blåthjortt?"

Ragnar stoops, frowning sharply. He glances up again, the crock in his hands. He lifts the wax from it. "What is Blåthjortt?"

Captain Flint glances at him. "Her hound."

Ragnar nods, adjusting his hand under the crock, setting the wax to the side. "He was kept downstairs. I believe I heard something about the stables." He looks up at me. "Will you let me tend your arm? I will go carefully, and you may correct my form as you please."

I scan his eyes. His face is one I have seen before. There is a red mark on the side of his neck, faint in the light of the room, a red ring around a thin white scar. It will have bled much, when it was given. *A soldier I healed, in the woods. The ones that were locked up.* I draw in a sharp breath. *Is there is no one else to tend it? I cannot, not if there are stitches to be fixed. And I am weak. The captain has given his word of trust for him. But was this man not taken in for attacking our men, here?*

I nod, and he stoops forward, brushing his hand across my arm, his fingers working at the lowest of the four stripes of the bear claw, threads moving with each brush of his fingers. I swallow, his fingers cool with the salve across my skin. "How did you come to be here?"

He looks up, then back to his work. "To be up here?" I nod. A smile flashes across his face, quick like lightning, like every expression of his face since I awoke. "I asked."

"You asked?" I force my arm to stay still, to stay beneath his hand. *They chose to trust this man, that simply, after he nearly killed our scouts, our people? He put their lives at risk, put this haven at risk by their presence in the woods. They are still a risk, if they were to escape, and they would let one free on a word? Ciaran and Fitz surely would not be so foolhardy. Sradfaang surely would not.*

I swallow hard, pull my arm backward, and my side throbs, pin pricks of pain cutting through it. I swallow hard. "You asked and they let you out? There must be something more to it, more than a mere asking for an unknown soldier to be let out of a captive room to wander these halls after he nearly cost the lives of many of the men here."

His eyes meet mine, earnest and bright blue like I have never seen. "I heard them say that someone with knowledge in the healing arts was needed, through the door of the room where they have kept us." His voice is steady. "And I heard you sing, in the forest a fortnight ago. I was awake when you sang in the forests."

My heart slows in my chest. I swallow hard, tighten my arm on my waist, and my ribs scream. *Curse it.* I force my breaths to calm, but they are still shallow, still too short. *My eyes are burning. They will be a hundred colors.* I force them to stay shut, draw in a breath slowly. "You heard, and so—" my voice is tight, the world narrowing. "—they just let you out, to tend me? An arm for an arm? Would you take my life for the wounds on you, wounds given by these men?" I open my eyes, meet his.

He straightens, his gaze grim. "I heard your song, and I know who it is that is hidden here, though you may not. If you do, then you will be on his side, and if you are, then healing is. I will not fight against that which Elnial has blessed. It is only a fool who does so."

My eyes shift, burn again, and I cannot force it back. "So now you would fight alongside him? A man you do not know, do not trust?"

He smiles, a smile of self-deprecation. "I would fight to my dying breath. I did not know for certain he was alive before we were ambushed and left dying in your forest. One of your men spoke of him, as his life-blood drained away, his mind half-gone. If I had known who the men were..." His jaw tightens. "Perhaps my men would not be dead now. But there is no time for what is not. I am grateful for my life and the lives of my men that were spared. My timestring is at your disposal, Song Weaver, to do with as you will."

My hand grips my side. "You would defend them with your life, though they tried to take it from you, not a full moon ago? I did not see how deep your wounds were, but from your scars, I would guess that you would have died in that forest if I had not sung. You would switch in a moment to the side of the men that tried to kill you?"

He inclines his head, hands clasped around the lavender colored crock on his knee. "Their life blood I spilt. My life blood they spilt. But I mean what I have said. I owe you both, you and the man who spared my life when he could have taken it. I would give my life, if called for, for either of you, the Swan or you. I have waited ten turnings for there to be a change. I would not wait ten more, not now that I know what is within these walls, at my reach: Healing and a Song of a new hope for our people. Someone who can lead them out. I will fight for what Elnial has blessed. I will not walk away from this, not willingly when I could be part of the good coming at last to our country."

I swallow, my eyes flickering between his. *'Good coming at last to our country.' Is that what the prince in the shadows is?* There is earnestness in his eyes, sincerity bright within them. "Is your loyalty then to the queen? That is what the lines on your shoulders say, will say to all within this country that you claim to love."

His head tilts forward. "My uniform tells of my loyalty to my kingdom. I desired to serve it, not her, and I will continue to serve it, wherever I am placed. My heart is with Auvridal and its people. I did not take on these marks to serve a queen." His jaw ticks beneath his beard. "My loyalty has been to the people alone since she betrayed her loyalty to us with her edicts."

I swallow again, the sincerity of his eyes not slacking, not cracking. *He is in earnest. There is no lie in his eyes, in his manners. Can I trust Sradfaang and Fitzclaste, and not the men they offer trust to?* I tilt my chin toward the slashes on my arm. "I am sorry. I have not been a friend to soldiers, not in my timestring. I am sorry to give you trouble, but I would understand before I decide to allow a man near me who was recently bent on destroying the men I have taken up my work to tend. Thank you for your assistance, sonyá. Sradfaang and Fitz have spoken with you?" *The soldier would not be able to lie to him.*

He grimaces, a rueful thing. "They have, extensively." His hand extends toward my arm, and there are yellowed callouses across his palm, his skin rough and worn, scars around his fingers. *A soldier's hands, not a healer's.* He lifts a brow. "May I finish this?"

I shift my arm toward him, and the skin pulls tight around the stitches, aching. He swipes the last of the salve from his fingers over them, speaking again. "I am sorry, for the strife I have caused you today. And for the trouble we all caused in the woods. I do not know if you knew we were there or not when you healed us, but I am grateful, for my men."

He lifts a new finger of salve and brushes it across the lowest gash. It is cold against my skin. I push back a grimace. "Do not apologize. It was little enough of your doing."

His eyes flicker over my face, and he smiles again, a sharp and rueful thing. "'Not our doing?'" He shakes his head. "What kind of tea would you take?"

I place my hand across my stomach. *Where are the teas, the ones for wound*s? "There is one, in a bag that is nearly red, like a beebalm flower, high on a shelf. It is a bone healing remedy. And you said you were ambushed?"

He frowns, lifting a roll of bandages. "Aye. We were. Are there herbs that help much with bone setting? I have never heard of them. Our surgeon should have known that."

I swallow. *My throat is dry.* "With bone healing, not with setting. There are many of them. I do not care for most of them." I grimace, shift my back against the cot. "Most of them are bitter, like dandelion root. The wounded will rarely drink something so bitter, so they are little use unless the invalid is unconscious. You were ambushed following orders in a forest. That is not your doing, except that you placed yourself under the command of the officers who sent you there."

He dips his head, lifting the end of the bandage roll. "Thank you. I have let you talk too much, but I will ask you one more question, and then you should rest, or Tejan will have my hide." I glance up at him, and his eyes flicker from my eyes to my arm. "How are your lungs fairing? The paste man swore that the mallow root he was making you ingest would help remove the water from them, but I know nothing of it, and it sounded far-fetched. Drowning someone to aid them after nearly drowning seems foolhardy."

My lips twist. I shift my hand on my side. *The near drowning. I had forgotten that. That does many things, to your strength.* "Did I cough, after I drank it?"

Captain Flint nods. "Teja and Tollah were worried for you. You would not stop coughing, though you were blanched like a sheet. Which was better than the blue you were before."

I incline my head. "Then it worked. Mallow is only good with sparkroot, to encourage the cough." I half-cough, press my arm harder against my stomach. "He knew what he was about, there. Even if he did not with salves."

Ragnar tucks the edges of the bandage in. He straightens, inclining his head, and Einion mirrors the movement, speaking. "Rest well. Someone will be near if you have need of anything." He turns, moving toward the door, the soldier close beside him.

XXXVII

Máthanmôrs

There are voices in the room, rumbling, low. "...I am leaving at dawn, or a little after. There is a report of a missing duchess and I have been given orders to find her, before it becomes an issue. The queen is somewhat concerned about it given the status, and that is likely not all there is to it. The duchess is Pranciskus' daughter." *Captain Flint's voice.* "I will send word when I get to the palace, if I cannot along the way."

I drag my eyelids open. There are figures across the room, speaking in low voices. Captain Flint is straight ahead, his shoulders back, head up. There are four men, one beside Flint, his golden hair drawn at the base of his neck. *The prince.* He nods, his hair shifting with the movement. "Go. I will send you a report if it is safe, about the meeting with the Menantians once it is completed. And about the word from Giedrus when it arrives."

The captain cocks a brow. "When is Aorla due back with the news, and who did you send to fetch the emissary?"

"The healer is awake." Sradfaang is beside the prince, his back against the wall, arms folded over his chest. He lifts a brow, toward me, not looking my way.

Ciaran does not turn, still facing the captain. "She is due back in the next fortnight. Beyond that, I cannot tell. And we sent Asten."

Captain Flint bows, and Fitz inclines his head, turning toward me. "Eness. It is good to see you are awake. How are you healing? Tejan will be sad; she only just missed you by a few counts." He smiles, gently.

I shift to the side, force a smile to my lips. "Well. Thank you. And I thank you for your kindness while I have been healing. I am sorry for the trouble of it." I glance at the men, shift my hands. "It seems I have taken a meeting room?"

The prince steps up beside Fitz. "You have not. We are grateful for the service that you have done since you arrived, and that work cannot be repaid. Do not trouble yourself about it. I know I speak for everyone here who knows, and those who do not, when I say that we are honored to be of service to you, after all that you have rendered toward us."

I nod. *I should not be laying down, in front of lords.* I paste my hand against my side, drag my body upward. My breaths catch in my chest, but they are easier now, ribs stabbing less than at dawn when I attempted to rise. I fold my legs beneath me on the bed, press my hand against the cot behind me. "Thank you, just the same, lord." My voice is low, hand pressed against my side. "I will get back to my task as soon as I am able and leave these rooms back to your uses. But I thank you for your patience and care."

Fitz shakes his head. "Gót. Do not trouble yourself. The healing rooms can and will wait. Ragnar will do what he can down there until you are well. He can ask you about what he does not know in the meantime, if you are willing. That will be good enough. More than good enough." Ciaran nods and Fitz glances at him and back to me. "We would speak to you of your healing though." He nods toward the prince, stepping backward.

Ciaran turns his gaze back toward me. "These wounds will take time to heal. While you are healing, I would like to ensure that you are not worried for your work below. For that to be the case, if you choose, I will send for another healer to tend them." His eyes meet mine. "Ragnar has some skill, but it is limited. I would not have you pushing yourself to keep up with the work."

I shift my hand on the cot. "Another healer? Would that not endanger us, to bring an unknown in for only a time?"

His jaw twitches. "It would not if it is done with precision and care. You have given up much to help those here. We will not slack on your care, nor burden you while you heal from this."

I look away. My throat feels tight. "Most of the basic tasks can be tended by an invalid. Broken ribs take only time to heal." I turn my eyes back to his." I thank you for your offer, but I will return to my task as soon as I can walk enough to manage the stairs down."

Fitz inclines his head. "As you wish. We will see what can be done about your ribs. I have heard of herbal remedies that serve for helping mend bones at a smoother pace. But you will not be leaving this room within the half-fortnight, or my wife will be put out. She has ordered for you to stay here for a few more days yet."

I half-smile, press a hand against my side. *I would not like to see Tejan put out.* "I will stay here then, or in my own rooms. And aye. There are herbs that make bone healing smoother, but hardly faster. I have had a few of them in tea this last day. Herbs can only do so much to mend what is broken. But I thank you."

The goblin's eyes meet mine across the room. "You use your voice to heal others, can you not heal yourself? I assume it is not possible, if you have not."

I shake my head. "It does not heal me, and I am content with it that way. It would be a temptation if I could use it to my own ends, if it could heal me. I do not imagine that someone who could wield a gift like this should be able to use it on their own wounds. The Creator is wise."

Ciaran inclines his head, his eyes cast toward the floor. "Well then, we will continue to do all we can to see to it that you have the time and place to heal." He steps backward, eyes meeting mine. "Thank you, Eness Finch. Rest well." He nods, turning away. Fitz inclines his head and steps from the room, following the steps of the captain.

I glance across the room, to where the prince stands near Sradfaang. "What was the creature in the woods? I have not known bear to grow that large."

Sradfaang does not look at me, his eyes on something in his hand, half-hidden by his cloak. "It was not, strictly speaking, a bear. It was a máthanmôr, a great beast from the southlands. They are known to be fiercer than the common bear, larger, with spines along their backs."

"Are they not a thing of rumor? A thing of myth?"

He half-smiles, his teeth a flash of white. "If they were, you would not be on that bed."

I swallow. "If they were not, I would be dead, or else the stories exaggerate their strength. I should not have survived an attack by the thing of myth. Nor one by a common bear. But certainly not the thing of old tales. They take down armies."

He grins again, that faint flashing of teeth. "The stories are exaggerated. But I have seen a máthanmôr fight, and your body should be in the grave now, not on that bed. It is a blessing, and one that you should cherish, not question. There are few ever who have faced down one and lived to tell of it. Especially not unarmed as you were."

The prince turns from the window. "I am surprised we have not seen sign of them before now. It was rumored that there was one in the area, but many villagers are of your mind, healer. That they are a myth. When you see the hide, I do not think you will question if it was one, but only be grateful. Its paw alone should have ended you in a moment. We are, all of us, thankful that it did not." He turns, moving toward the door. "Rest well. If you have want of anything, you need only ask. Sradfaang will be staying with you, as long as you are up here. He will help or get someone if you need anything." He flashes a smile toward Sradfaang, a quick expression with triumph in it.

The goblin gives him a dry look. "I am not a messenger boy."

The prince grins and inclines his head. "But we also do not have people here to stand around. Nor would you want them here if they could be spared, I think."

The goblin's expression withers further. "You are correct. I would not wish to have any lollygaggers around. I will become an errand boy only for the time I am assigned to this room with the healer." He inclines his head, respect. "But I am not making this a habit. If you need anything, you may fetch it yourself."

Ciaran laughs, stepping through the door.

I press my hand against my side, over the ribs that are black and blue beneath my shift. The door taps shut behind the prince. Sradfaang lifts himself from the wall, moving across the room, toward the table, and the maps scattered across it. *He can work while he is here. But I cannot.* He glances at me. "If you have need of anything, I will find someone. But I am here to guard, not to run errands, despite what the prince has said. I will go in case of actual needs." He snorts, turning back toward the table. "I doubt you would have errands anyway. All you seem to need is handwork to survive well enough." He shifts something on the table and there is silence in the room, silence like that of night, deep and full. *But the sun is shining.*

I half-smile, and it is tight on my lips. *I am awake now. There is nothing to be done here, nothing I can call for unless I ask the goblin. I will not send a warrior for my hand work below. Tejan would likely not let me have it, if she knew I asked. I would not let a newly wakened invalid tend anything, if they were under my care.* I tighten my lips, turn my eyes toward the window. Nothing can be seen beyond it but the faint shapes of swaying trees. I grimace.

Sradfaang's back is to me, his hands motionless. *The way he has sat for a quarter watch already.* I press myself up from the bed, glance at him again. I can see nothing of his expression, nothing of his face. *Has he fallen asleep?*

The door creaks, opening, and a figure steps into the room. Srad looks up calmly, her form barely moving with the glance. Iris flicks her gaze toward him, nodding her head, a tray in her hands. She bows toward him. "I brought you both dinner." She inclines her head again, a third time.

Sradfaang inclines his head back, not standing. Iris turns, offering a bowl to me. I draw myself up higher, smile, take it. "Thank you."

"Of course!" She nods again, and she sets the other on the table, bowing once more, and she is gone from the room, the door clattering shut behind her. I lift a brow. *Does she fear him, or me?*

I glance at the goblin. He stands, taking the bowl in his hands. I set the spoon down. "Iris was quiet this evening."

He lifts a bite. "It will be your hair. It frightens younglings."

I glance at him. *Is that a jest?* "And not your scowl?" I ask.

He turns toward me, flashing a smile that is all teeth. "I am not frowning. You survived an encounter with a máthanmôr. That is the way they will look at you now."

I tighten my lips. "They will not fear me for that. It was not of me."

"Like your voice?" His tone is sharp.

My hand stills on the bowl. "No one has ever feared me for the song."

He lifts a brow, his eyes moving to mine. "Why then, did your family keep it silent all those turnings? I would say that is a constant fear, not a lack of it."

I wrap an arm around my ribs, the bowl heavy in my hands. "My family did not fear the awe, they feared what would become of me with it. I was a child when it was discovered. If it was discovered, I would have spent my days running from those who would use it or idolize me for wielding it." I set the bowl down, my skin hot where it touched. "Why do you question now? You have not asked me anything about it before and you could have, many times over."

He turns away. "Because I did not wonder."

I shake my head. "The fear that she showed was not to me. I have spoken with her many times. Unless there has been a change, then that was deference for you. Not for me."

He lifts a brow, turning back to me again, sharp humor in his eyes. "And when the tales begin circulating about the civ who faced a creature of myth and lore with her bare hands and defeated it?"

I turn back to the stew in my hand. "Defeated it by lying in the stream, by hiding while it was killed?"

He grins. "Tales grow with the telling. In a fortnight's time, there will be stories about you, stories of what you have done, and they will not tell of broken bones in streams. They will increase with each telling. Are you prepared for that?"

I straighten. "No one should be telling stories of anything I have done. There was no valor or story in running from the creature or falling in the stream." My heart sinks into my chest. "If they are spinning stories of other things I have done, then there will be trouble for many here other than me, for those tales are not safe to tell."

Srad's brow lifts again, this time dryly. "They do not need to tell stories of your song to tell strange tales, Eness Finch. There is little that could be done to keep the rest silent. And secrets will only be kept for a time. None stay silent forever. Yours will come out, one day, whether you choose it or not. Running from it will not save you." He lifts a bite of the stew, the bowl tiny in his hands. "I am not speaking of secrets though, but of stories. Our people are scattered. They tell stories. It is what unites us, or tears us apart. That is how the Maa'eulé have gotten their hold, on this country, with stories and tales. That is how the pathetic sun god cult seeks to regain their hold from ancient times."

I take a bite, swallow hard. "Are the sun god beliefs not dead?"

His brow lifts again—always that brow—and it is derisive. "If they were dead, they would not have the ear of the queen, not be bending the ear of the entire country."

I stare. My mind is slow, the world sluggish. "Are you implying," I set the bowl down, clasp my arms around my waist, "that the queen's actions were purely at the bidding of that cult?"

"I am implying nothing. If you have not heard that, I am surprised that you have any mind to be in the war at all. They have been at the forefront of this since nearly the beginning. Her actions are her own, but they will not stand innocent in the day of retribution."

I shake my head. "What do you mean? I do not understand. Has not the Maa'eulé, the Movement caused these attacks?"

He nods. "Yes. They have. And the Soaré Gâr was behind the prophecy. The one that claims that death will come to the kingdom, if they do not return to Zeul Soáre, the sun god. But it does not make the queen any less culpable. She acted before they climbed to her ear."

I swallow. "Why is this not more known?"

He glances at me, and I do not look to see his brow raise again. "It is. But you have hidden yourself away, where it would not reach you. You should not be surprised when all the world is not as you thought, if you have hidden yourself in a corner so small that the queen's maid servants could not fit in it."

XXXVIII

The Healing Ward

I step down, suck in air slowly, and Norla's hand is steady on my arm, gentle. She looks down at me, moving her foot down the last step. Her eyes meet mine. "Are you alright?"

I shuffle the last step forward. "Aye."

She turns her eyes to the healing rooms. They are empty, not a landlot in sight within them. I glance around. *It feels strange, to be down here without Eerol. He has been gone more than a fortnight, but it does not seem right here without his bustle and movement. Without his talk. These rooms are his more than they can be anyone else's.*

She turns, glancing at me. "Do you need anything? Water? Bread?"

My eyes flicker over to the far side of the room. There is a bucket, full to the brim with water beside the ash-cold hearth. I shake my head, hobble forward. "Gót. There is water. And I am well. Thank you, Norla."

She steps away from me, her freed hands adjusting her skirts, smoothing them out. "I am glad you are here, Eness." My eyes snap to hers. She half-smiles. "I mean that you bring peace to this ward. That is a good thing and will be a blessing in the times to come, I trust. I have wondered what would happen when Eerol left. I have wondered what would happen when things darkened. We have never had soldiers so close before your time. But I should not have worried of it. The Creator has never failed us, and I am glad that it was you that came. We needed someone calm, here."

I look away, across the rooms, across the shelves and crocks, and half-smile. "I do not know what peacefulness I could have brought with me. But I am grateful to have been a help, even for just a season or a time."

She looks back at me, eyes bright, colored dark. "Do you not plan to stay?"

I shake my head. "I will stay for as long as I am able, but it will depend on many things. We are at war."

She smooths her hands against her skirts again, ironing out wrinkles that are not there. "Tollak and I did not intend to stay long either." She steps toward the shelves, lifts a dirtied knife blade, one I left the day I went out and met the máthanmôr. "The danger for us did not seem to be much, so we came but planned to leave again within half a turning at the most and go back home."

I press my hand against my side, above my bandaged ribs. "What changed?"

She glances at me, over her shoulder, strands of brown hair across her eyes. "Tollak's brother turned him in for speaking with a criminal who had spoken out against one of the queen's generals—Scrogfield, I think. We had harbored many landlots fleeing from the crown in our home and if he had known of that, I do not think we would still be here. But Tollah's husband was caught before we heard of what had happened. She, Tollak and I took to the road then."

She looks back toward the knife, runs a cloth along it, leaf fractures falling to the floor. "I have not seen the rest of my family in four turnings." She smiles, and it is bittersweet, tainted at the edges. "My sister has a new child now that I have never met. Perhaps two. It has been more than a season since I have heard from her. Her husband is a fian. I worry for them, worry for the children, who have that blood. The older two both have the gift of that race, the ever-changing eyes. It was beautiful in them, even from the day it began to show, but it worries me, not to have heard from them in so long." She smiles, a tired smile and turns away. "I miss them."

I tighten my hand against my side. "I am sorry." My heart sinks. *Should I ask?* "What became of Tollah's husband?"

She looks back at me, moving toward the cold fireplace. "Fitzclaste arranged for him to be freed. I do not know what it cost him, or what he did, but he is in Grior now, last we knew, settling there. We have not heard from him in more than a turning, but he was there when it was last safe for him to write her. It is not anymore. Letters can only be carried by direct carrier, no longer transported over such great distances, unless you find someone willing to go. It will not be long before she will give up waiting to hear and go to him."

She smiles toward the ground, her hands idling on the fireplace broom. She shakes her head. "I am sorry. That was far more than you needed to know." She half-smiles. "I am afraid this child makes me forget my tongue sometimes. You will stop me next time I ramble?" She cradles an arm around her stomach, barely swollen with child.

I lift my head. "You are with child? Congratulations, Norla. May Elnial establish your little one and make them strong." I smile, nod my head. "I am sorry, for what you have lost. I do not know the strife of not being able to speak with loved ones far away, but I can imagine the strife you must carry with you."

She shakes her head, straightening. "Thank you. But I was complaining, and I have said too much. Our country is still at war. There will be pain, to all of us. I am only thankful that to this day, as far as I know, my family is safe and still well, where they are. I should not be complaining of a split when it is not to the end of this life. We have had no casualties." She turns, lifting a half-used bowl, herbs crusted to the side of it. "Do you still want this?"

I incline my head. "I can still use them for a minor salve." *Though they will no longer be useful for the fever salve they were intended for. I will have to regather the leaves, if there are any left. The juices left in these will have soured.* "Is it a complaint, to speak of what troubles you? Is that not what friendship is, when done rightly? To share one another's troubles and to speak of them when it is fitting?"

She glances at me and smiles softly. "It is. But the heart of the speaker matters, and I was complaining. Thank you, Eness."

She moves back toward the fireplace. I turn, settle myself into a chair. Her face is tense, free hand over her stomach. I lift my chin. *I should draw her mind away from this. She does not need to dwell on what we have said.* "What do you do, when the days are quiet here?"

She glances up. A laugh splits her lips, and she stoops, lifting an apron from the floor beside the hearth. "It is rarely quiet." She shakes out the apron, setting it on the hook set in the stone wall. "But when it is, Tollak and I will go for walks, or I will join the women in the sewing rooms, as you did, the day before the bear attack. There is usually good conversation there, and much chatter, as you found, though there was some news the day you came. There is always some place to go here, where something is happening on the rare occasion I do not have Jørn or work to tend. He keeps me on my feet." She lifts the second apron, sitting on the table. It is stained green, down the front, from pouring the liquid salves. "I have our own quarters to look after, as well. There is always something to be done in our room, if nothing else needs aid."

I glance at her, drop into the chair. "You have your own rooms, you three?"

She nods. "Each family does. It is one of the things Fitz and Tejan fight for, to make sure that we can have our own homes here, so that we can live as families, even while we are away from our homes." She laughs. "It is funny to think of this as anything but our home. We've been here for so long, and Tollak has worked so hard to make our rooms feel like home."

I smile. "What are they like?"

She lifts the broom, swiping at the corner beside the shelf. "It is about the same size as the room you share with Tollah and Iris. Tollak is getting Severin to show him how to make a crib for the baby. There is not much else to it, but our bed and Jørn's cot. But it is the place we get to go home to, in the evenings when all is done. The place I know he comes back to when his shift is over. It will be the place that, Elnial willing, we will welcome our second child into. That is a blessing I cannot speak enough to."

I smile, turn my eyes away, toward the floors, toward the rooms. *Homes in the midst of war? I scarcely took as much pride in my cottage as she takes in a single room, used only for evenings and rest with her husband and child.* She is sweeping quickly, a hum brushing through the room, gentle and soft. *She takes more pride in her work than I have in the past years of mine, years of attempting to save a dying people.*

XXXIX

Arrivals

There are steps on the stairs and the tapping of nails—hound steps, sharp over the others. I turn. Blått is in front of the stairs, walking toward me, his tail high, his mouth open, tongue lolling. I grin and press a hand against my side, above the bandages. "Blåthjortt."

His pace picks up, and he is beside me, placing his muzzle in my hand, tail wagging furiously. I cup his chin, tighten my grip around my waist, and stoop. Something earthy wafts up from him. My sides sting. I straighten. There is dirt, clinging to the fur on his back, hay on the top of his head, caught up beneath his ears, across his tail and snout. I grin, run my hand along his head and lower myself to the chair. "Where have you been? In a sheep's bin, that you would be so covered in dirt?" Someone moves by the stairs. My eyes flicker upward.

Ragnar is the length of a man from me, his eyes watching the hound, not me. I stand slowly. "What has brought you down?" *I do not know his rank, nor how to address him beyond the title given all men.*

He looks at me and something moves in the shadows behind him—Sradfaang. He steps forward and leans against the wall. Ragnar speaks. "I came to bring the hound. It was thought that he should be down here with you, rather than moping around and mopping up the stables. It has been said that he enjoys running through hay piles far too much for him to stay on passing terms with those who tend the cattle."

He nods toward me, posture matching that of the soldiers who invaded my home, sharp and precise like a poplar tree. He lifts his head.

"I also came to check on your wounds, if you do not protest. It has been a day or two since they were checked, I believe. Unless you tended them yourself."

I turn, incline my head "Aye. It has. The salves are over here." I move slowly toward the shelves lined with crocks. My eyes flicker upward, to where the salve for bone healing should be. I grimace, lift onto my toes, my fingers barely gripping it. I pull it down, press my hand tightly against my side. My ribs scream.

Sradfaang glances up from the wall. He snorts, turning away.

I lower myself into the chair beside me, glance up at the soldier. My breaths are harder than before, my sides stiff. "This will take a moment. You may tend something else if you like." I grip the top button on the side of my dress, and slip it free, the wood of it smooth beneath my fingers. I nod toward the table a few steps from me.

He nods, moving toward it. "Do not trouble yourself. I have all the time needed." He smiles, that flashing smile, quick like every expression of his and turns toward the table, lifting a crock from it. "What is this to be? I have little knowledge of herbs."

I turn my gaze back down, slip the next button free, my shift plain beneath it. Blått's nails tap the floor, moving toward Ragnar. He stops beside him, looking up, his tongue lolling out, eyes wide, tail still wagging, though it is slower now. Ragnar half-smiles, his hand still on the bowl.

I incline my head. "That is a scrap bowl. I have not decided what to do with it yet. You may wash dishes if you like, or grab wraps. I am nearly done." He sets the bowl down and turns toward the far shelf. His hand runs across Blått's head, ruffling the hound's ears as he passes. "Where did you come by your hound? He looks to have wolf in his blood. Is he from a farmer's hound and a wolf, perhaps?"

I pull my arm free of my dress, draw back my shift's sleeve. "Perhaps. I came upon him in the woods when he was young. I know nothing of his heritage." My voice is tight, ribs pressing. The bandage around my arm catches on my shift sleeve, keeping it in place. I tug it free, my ribs pulsing more. *This is not a wise thing to be done by someone with wounded ribs alone.* I pull the sleeve back, and there is a stain through the long bandage there, twisting up my arm, red-brown with blood and salve oils. The end of the bandage is tucked in a twist, thick and complicated, with no sign of where the end should be tucked away. *A twist designed to keep the injured from removing their own bandages. One I do not recognize.* I glance up at the soldier. "You will have to undo it. I cannot get the bandage free on my own."

He inclines his head, moving across the room toward me, Blått following in his wake. "That is why I came down. Fitz did not imagine you should be tending your own wounds when you cannot see to clean them. I will do the bandage so that you can do it on your own in the future. I am sorry for the precaution now."

I nod my head, my jaw tight. "That would be well." *He knew I could not have tended them on my own, before he came.*

He drops to his knees beside my chair, flicking his eyes up to mine. "How did you learn your skill in healing, your common skills?"

I glance at Sradfaang. He is still leaning against the wall, a blade in his hand, a stone in the other. He runs the stone along the blade and there is a sharp sound in the air and it is gone. *A sharpening stone.* I swallow, glance back at Ragnar.

He lifts the bandage from my arm and it clings to my skin, dried herbs pasted to the hairs there, pulling them. His gaze moves back toward the goblin, and a smile pulls at the edges of his lips beneath his beard. I settle my free hand against Blåthjortt's head. *There can be no harm in telling him of Aílé. But they must not trust him, not fully, or the goblin would not be here, sharpening blades by that wall. At least Sradfaang must not fully trust him.* I lift my head. "I was taught by a healing woman, Aílé. She was the herbalist and healer in the village that my family moved to after the queen's decree came."

He lifts a brow. "The one fifteen turnings ago?"

I incline my head, brush my hand through Blått's fur along his side. "Aye." Dust spatters to the floor, crumbling from the hound's fur. There are strands of hay woven down in it.

Ragnar glances at me, setting the bandage aside, on the shelf beside him. He turns back to me, lifting a stray thread from the blood caked to my arm. It stings sharply, catching. *Curse it.* I bite back a grimace, keep my eyes calm. He glances at me. "Tell me about her. She sounds more pleasant than our surgeon."

I flick my eyes toward the wounds along my arm at the edge of my vision. They are dark, pale threads licking out of them, stained faintly pink with blood. The stitches are neatly done. I had not seen them before. "If you are trying to distract me from the wound, do not worry yourself. I am not troubled by it."

He lifts a brow, his mouth pulling downward. "I do not try to distract. I merely do not aim to draw this out by strained silence. And I have wondered about where you came from, before you became the healer here. No one speaks of each other's past here."

I shift my arm. *I am being rude. It was a simple question, one I can easily answer.* I incline my head. "She was a strict woman, hard in her manner. Fierce in her disfavor and gentle in her favor. She was wise in herb lore and myth, but not in the way of Elnial. I was glad to train under her, those turnings. I do not know another village healer who knew as much as she held in the forefront of her mind."

His eyes flicker to mine and back toward the wound, hands lifting the bees wax from the top of the crock balanced on his propped-up knee. "Is she still there? In that village that you left to come here?"

I shake my head, comb my fingers through Blått's coat. "She passed into the world beyond more than six turnings ago, in the pale fever."

His jaw tightens, and he glances at me, his fingers coated with the red-green salves. "I am sorry. Did you take her place, in that village?"

I half-smile. "I did not. There was another healer, from Blackwater, who was set to replace her, one she had trained before me. I was eager enough to leave. The town was too large, central to the main roads."

I shake my head, and he is brushing salve against my arm, cool and strange on the inflamed skin around the wounds. "Perhaps if you wish to speak of something as you work, you might speak of your own tale. There is not much more to tell of mine, but there must be some of your own that is more worth sharing."

He brushes his fingers against the edge of the crock. "There is not much to tell of it. I was a low standing noble, and then I was a soldier in the ranks. Now I am a deserter, waiting for orders from the king I thought to be dead, in a hidden fortress."

My head snaps up. "Do not speak of him that way. There is treachery in it and she is still queen. It is foolhardy to speak of him as though he were king now. You do not know what ears may be listening. And you ought to know the cost of speaking freely."

He looks up at me sharply, leaning backward on his ankles. "Georwyn was sworn to protect and serve her people the day she married. She broke that oath fifteen turnings ago and has been breaking it each day since then. Is that the woman you call queen? A queen awash in blood and treacherous to her own people?"

My eyes burn. I shake my head, pull my arm away from him. "You speak strongly for a soldier who served her up until a few sunrises ago, coming and going at her bidding, at her word. The man you proclaim king has not taken up his throne, and it is not safe to speak of it that way when you do not know who may be listening, where your words may carry. You do not know where my allegiances lie, nor that of anyone else in this place. I see your zeal, but it does not do to speak so boldly, not in this land. Many have been killed for less than you just said. You will know that."

His eyes sharpen. "I have seen where your allegiances lie, Eness Finch. You have shown them in risking your life and word to protect the man whom I called king. You have worked for him, served him in this place, and risked your wellbeing to save this people, whom you owed no allegiance or debt to. That I have seen. If there was another soul in this room, Sradfaang would not be resting, but would have spoken warning. I have not spoken without caution. I have seen where your allegiances lie."

I push back the stinging of my eyes. He leans forward again, brushing salve across the highest gash on my arm. His hands are moving awkwardly but they are gentle, dabbing salve around the stitches that pull my skin. I incline my head. "I will follow the prince, so long as he is striving toward the healing of this nation. If he is following in the steps of his mother, or in any steps that do not lead toward unity and life, then I will not follow after him, not for all the ages of the world. I will not serve a destructive king."

The goblin is watching closely, his blade glinting in the firelight. Ragnar inclines his head, slowly, his face no less hard, no less calculating. "You have known of the blood of your people being spilt for many turnings, perhaps have even witnessed it. I do not judge you for your caution."

Sradfaang steps from the shadows, the knife still in his hand, but the stone is gone. "I do not judge you your caution, but you will play too large a role in this, healer, to stand to the side and follow no one. This is a war. You will have to make a choice, to decide whom you will follow and where you will go when the fights come." His eyes narrow on mine, glinting green. "You carry far too powerful a gift to hide on the edges of the fray and pretend to be unknown. You will have to make a decision or that decision will be taken from you by force and time. There will be no middle ground, no canyon side for you to climb up and cower in, no hillside for you to cling to. Your time of hiding is over. Unless you choose cowardice." He glances at Ragnar. "Are you finished?"

I swallow hard, turn my eyes away from him. Ragnar leans forward, his expression dry, fingers prodding the middle gash of the máthanmôr claw. "Nearly. This stitch may have pulled free and I would check it." I turn my head away. *Do they plan something big enough to search out the farthest places of the country? Or does he only mean that I will not be forgotten, not any longer, were I to leave and head to the darkest places where no one would look?*

My eyes burn. I turn them further away from the soldier beside me. *I could not leave. Not any more. I could not run from this, from where the choices will be made.*

• ▶ | ◀ ▶ | ◀ ▶ | ◀ ▶ | ◀ ▶ | ◀ ▶ | ◀ •

I pull the door shut, my hand pulling at the laces on my bodice. The morning air stifled in the hall, first breaths of laughter trickling up from the rooms beyond. Steps sound down the hall, hurried. Someone darts around the corner, brushing hair back from her face. *Iris.* Her eyes flicker to mine, hands still working at her hair, flour down the front of her apron. "Eness!" She inclines her head toward me, twisting the cord for her hair into place. "Lady Tejan sent me. The Menantian party has arrived, just after dawn, and she wanted you to be made aware of it." She drops her hands from her hair. "I assume you know why. I do not. Do you know them? Are they friends of yours?"

I shake my head. "I do not, but I do know why she wanted me informed. Thank you, Iris. I will be down in the healing rooms, if there is any other call for me."

She bobs her head. "I will get back to the kitchens then. We are swamped with preparations. Nellie is all in a flurry, getting things done. We've never cooked for nobility before." *She does not know who Ciaran is.* She glances at me. "Has she been to see you?"

"Gót."

Her lips purse, her eyes flashing with faint frustration. "That civ." She shakes her head, glancing back up the hall. "I will send her to you again, or ask Tejan to. Her cough is acting up again, like it always does when it has been wet outdoors, and she has been sleeping little because of it. I thought she would have gone to you for tea again to soothe it by now. She does this every few moons." She shakes her head again, hair slipping from the haphazard band she put it in. "I am sorry. I should go." She bows, respect and honor, and is gone again, up the hall, her steps fast and small.

He asked me to keep an eye on her. I should have checked in on her by now, if I had not been trapped upstairs for most of the last days. I smooth my bodice. *And now I will spend the next many days in the healing rooms, beneath the earth, until the visitors are gone or this is settled. Time will tell what will be with their coming, for good or for ill.*

Why do those here think they are coming, if they do not know of Ciaran's title? Do they think they come to see Tejan and Fitzclaste?

XL

Tejan

Tejan sets the platter on the table beside me, another one in her far hand. She dusts her palm across her bodice, and glances at the hound. Blått lifts his head beside Tejan's skirts, his eyes wide, eager. She smiles. "Gót, you big goodling. This is not for you. You may go to the stables for yours when I leave, or wait for another to come get you."

I half-smile, set the booklet aside. "Thank you, Tejan. I am grateful to you for bringing it down, but you needn't have. I might have gone for it."

She smiles. "And robbed me of the moment of quiet? I am glad enough to sit with good company in the evenings, where it is quiet and voices are softer. Fitz and Ciaran can mind our guests for the evening." She sits in the chair beside me. "Ruidún and Norla say that you are mending well? How is your mind mending?"

I settle my skirts around my legs. "In what way?"

"However you like." Her voice is steady, calm. She lifts her spoon.

I run my hand along Blått's head. "It is mending. There is time to mend, with the days down here. It has been quiet since I have made it down the stairs again."

She smiles faintly. There is meat on the plate before me, a rare thing, venison by the sight of it. She lifts a piece from hers, tearing a strip from it with her fingers. "It is quiet down here, but there is little healing in that, if you are sitting in darkness. I hope that it is not too dark here. I would that we could have kept you out of harm's way somewhere with more movement. Healing rarely comes by sitting alone for long."

The edge of my lips twists up. "It is bright enough, for today. And I am not unused to sitting alone, though I am thankful for company when hands can be spared. These rooms are not so dark."

She sets her fork down, her eyes searching mine. "You are down here alone too much, I think. I will speak to Ciaran and Fitz about you coming up soon, if it is safe enough. At least for an afternoon. You cannot be kept below ground forever. Does Ragnar not come down?"

I shake my head. "I thank you, but I do not mind. I can barely take the stairs as it is, so it does not trouble me to stay down here and not have to manage them frequently." She smiles again, but her eyes are tight. I lift a bite. "Ragnar comes down when he is needed, which is rare. I think you know the soldiers go nowhere alone yet. They have a man with them where they are taken, so he stays where he is put." She inclines her head, the tension not leaving her eyes. I turn the subject. "How have the emissaries been, since they arrived yestermorn?"

She lifts her fork once more. "Courteous. It has been many turnings since my husband and I were in Menantian society, so it has been pleasant to get to enjoy it once again, from our own home. My father was an ambassador there, for many seasons when I was young." She smiles again. "Fitz and I met after I came back, one of the last times we traveled there for King Hylethlan."

I spear a potato. "You served the king?" She inclines her head. I continue. "The Menantians have been easy, then?"

She glances at me, swallowing a bite. "I am not the one to answer that. I do not know the whole of everything, so I will keep silent, but you may speak with my husband if you can catch him." She smiles. "Norla said she has been down to speak with you a few times?"

I swallow, smile. "She has. I am grateful for her companionship. She and Tollak seem well matched."

She laughs. "They are. She has been a blessing these last turnings. It is strange, to have homes within your home, but she has gone above and beyond to make their room feel like their own, and it has been a joy to see. It must be a welcome thing to them both, to return there, when night comes, a haven within this haven. It will be a good thing, for Jørn, to have a place to call home until they can settle again."

My lips tug upward again. *They praise each other, in this.* I lift another potato. "Norla told me that she is to begin working in the gardens, beyond the walls?"

She nods. "Aye. They are safely tucked up in a rock-cropping. One day, when you are well, we shall take a walk up there. I have not been up there in the last turning or more, but they are beautiful to see, from what my husband has said." She laughs. "My days have been wrapped up here much of late. I doubt either of us would have made it up there by now if he hadn't needed to."

I grin. "You spend your time well, Tejan, the keeper of the safe haven."

She shakes her head, swiping a hand across the air in dismissal. "Gót. I only see to it that it is comfortable here. I do little else to keep it. That is done by all those here and I am more than thankful. I would not have my home be empty. Elnial is good. We did not imagine this, when we built Sikkerhet all those turnings ago."

I tilt my eyes to hers. "Why did you build it, this home far from civilization?"

She glances at me, fork half-stabbed in a piece of meat. "Fitz had a premonition, years ago, that we should build it. We wanted a way to serve our people faithfully, as the roads darkened or lightened. These lands have been in my family for turnings. We could not build on his, they are too close to the capital, but here there was no one but in the village. I wanted it to be a place that could be a home away from home. He wanted it to be a steady refuge. It was large, when we started. Now, like our home, it has shrunk with each turning, with each life that has come to stay." She smiles again. "I would not trade it." Her face is calm, joyful, as it always has been in every situation since I came. *There is always peace around Tejan. Peace and control.*

I set my fork down. "How do you weigh all the lives in the hands of you and your husband? You have many that you care for and carry day by day. You both bear that responsibility evenly, with calm about you. That is not a skill I have seen before."

She folds her hands. "I do not know about that. But I do know that we take it a day at a time. There is a risk, every day. But there is also grace. Elnial has been gracious and will continue to be, whether we are found out or go on living this way until the throne is retaken and Auvridal is given peace once more—though that will be many turnings in the making. We take it a day at a time, with the threads we are given and the peace given by His hand. My task is a quieter one than my husband's. He is responsible for the safety of all those here. I am only responsible with him, to see that they are fed and clothed. A task I am thankful for. I get to see more of those who live here, get to know more of those that we strive for than he does, though he works hard to learn of each one. I am always proud of him, for that, for the care that he takes to know all who cross our doorframe and to carry some of their burdens and worries."

She smiles, eyes softening. "I am thankful for the homes that have been made here in the mountains, even though it is only for a season. These homes within ours will leave, they will branch out into the world and be their own again, one day, Bright King willing and peace comes. Ours will become something new again."

I turn my eyes away. "That is a good hope, Tejan. I pray you all will live in safety until that day comes." My heart aches, heavy in my chest.

She inclines her head to me, turning back to the bite upon her fork. "Elnial is good. We hope and wait upon Him. That hope has never yet put us to shame and I will not see the day that it does." She smiles, glancing down at the hound beside her feet, staring up at her with his great, brown eyes. "Elnial does not abandon, but neither are His plans ours. I will gladly serve where I can, and wait to see what He does with this land. It is His, as they all are."

• ▶ | ◀ ▶ | ◀ ▶ | ◀ ▶ | ◀ ▶ | ◀ ▶ | ◀ •

I press my hand against my back. My side aches, arms stiff. I grimace. Blått's head presses against my hip, his eyes soft, staring up at mine. I half-smile. "It is alright, Blått. I am only sore."

I swipe my hand across his head, turning. The pot is on the table, plants and lard lumped in it, dry, cold. My eyes flicker toward the bucket of water. *It would not be wise to try to lift it on my own, not today. But I cannot work without using the herbs in the way they are intended, in their time. There is no one here.* My lips tighten. I press my hand against the table, and Blått's head leans against my side once more.

Something moves across the room, a figure off the stairs. My chest lightens. Anna steps in, her figure small, a basket on her hip. She looks up, a smile lighting her lips. "Eness." She bobs her head, down and up again to the right—respect and friendship.

"Anna." My eyes flicker to the basket. There are strips of cloth in it, scattered. "You have brought the cleaned bandages. Thank you." I bob my head back.

"I have brought that." She smiles, moving forward, and sets the basket on the floor on the far side of the room. "And I have brought word from Ciaran." She straightens, pressing her hands against her skirts, her voice cheerful. "If you are feeling up to it, then he thinks it would be well for you to come up to the eating hall for dinner." *Ciaran. Tejan must have spoken with him.*

I incline my head. "Thank you, Anna. I will see about it, in half a watch then." *The stairs are still long. I will not be able to do them another time today. Once I am up, I will have to stay up there until after rest.*

She smiles, moving toward the stairs, her hands dusting her skirts. "It is dinner time now. Everyone was already gathering up when I came to deliver these to you. You should come now if you aim to not be a reasonably late comer."

My lips tighten. Anna glances back at me from beside the stairs, her hand on Blått's back now. He is staring up at her, his eyes hopeful, waiting for her attention. *He is growing soft, in the time here, too much attention from too many lots.*

I incline my head toward her, slip my apron from my waist. "Thank you. I will come."

She steps toward the stairs, her hand absently petting Blått's head. "I hear there are to be rolls tonight, with the stew." She grins. "And I have heard that Iris made a new batch of butter, so dinner should be delightful this evening. A good time for you to join us again. How long have you been absent?" She glances back at me, waiting. My steps are slow, almost shuffling on the first step of the stairs, like an aged woman.

I glance down at her. "You are welcome to go on. I am still slow today." I smile.

She shakes her head, gripping her skirts. "It is no trouble. I do not like getting there early for meals, so you have saved me from that. There will be less waiting, and I will get to speak with you, if I wait." She grins. "I have not gotten to do that as much as the others have."

I half-smile, set my hand against the wall. "I am afraid I will not be very interesting company." I shuffle to the next step. "Until my ribs are healed, speaking and walking up stairs are difficult to do together."

A smile pulls at her lips. "Then we can walk in silence. I do not mind, if you do not. Though the news we get here is not often of plants and flowers and homes."

I laugh. "I do not mind silence, but you are welcome to speak. You do not have to keep quiet because my answers are short. I will tell you anything of plants you like, though I have known little of homes and flowers that are not for a purpose."

She smiles softly, turning at the top of the stairs. "Well then." She glances back at me at the edge of my vision, moving into the hall beyond. I step after her. "You have been here long enough. What do you think of this place? I know that is not a question of plants, but we do not often get newcomers here that aren't men."

I glance at her, my breaths shallow in my chest. I press my hand against the wall again. "The people here are kind, and they have been gracious on my weak days and generous on the others."

She lifts a brow walking forward, her head held high. "If, by your weak days, you mean when you have been healing from wounds given by the largest bear anyone has seen in ages that you fought off, then aye. They are good at that, every one of them. Especially Nellie and Teja and Fitz. I do not know the men as well, but those three would give the skin off their back to see someone well. Eerol was like that too." *Nellie. She never came down to see about tea. Perhaps she spoke with Ragnar about it, when I was gone and he was not? That is not likely.*

I half-smile, shake my head. *Sradfaang was right. The story has already shifted.* "I did not fight off the máthanmôr. The men did that. I am grateful they arrived when they did or I would not still be here." The sounds of the hall are increasing, voices like a blanket wrapping up the hall. "The others that I have seen I would guess to be more like Tejan and Fitz. They are all kind." I shift my hand against my ribs. "Havard and Sradfaang are, as well as Norla and Einion and many others that I have met."

She nods her head. "Havard is, aye. He was known for that in our town too—that is where he came from, a leader there, up until a few turnings ago. Sradfaang keeps to himself and the library councils so I know little of him other than his glower, and I do not know who Einion is." I blink. *Does everyone here not know him? They seemed to, those that I have spoken of him to before.* She grins again, mischief in her eyes now. "As for Ciaran," She glances at me, the mischief growing. "I know what the women say about him. That he is fine. Fine like spun silver." Someone laughs up the hall, the sound loud.

I start, my head lightening. *She must not know who he is. I cannot imagine a woman speaking of her lord and someday king that way.* I tighten my lips. "He is a fine man. He seems to be loyal to his country."

She nods her head, the mischief leaving her eyes, and there is disappointment left there. *I will not join her in speaking of him that way.* She brushes her hand firmly across Blått's head. "Aye. That he is. Loyal to all those he knows, from the little I have seen of him. He is a good leader. Loyal and steadfast. We are grateful for him—Havard, Fitzclaste and the others here. We all are."

She brightens. "You know he took the emissaries out for a ride today? I would have liked to have gone. It is a beautiful day out there and I wanted to get a look at the lady's riding dress. Everything she has worn thus far has been intricate like nothing I have seen since I left home. The first one looked like it would have taken a full moon of days to embroider."

There are figures in the hall, moving into the meeting room, voices blending together in a chorus of words and laughter. She grins again, not waiting for a reply, and her pace picks up. There are people around us now, laughing, voices raised above each other, in the talk of evening. I slow before them, my eyes flickering down. Anna is gone, off into the crowd, her laughter joining the others in a breath. Blått glances at me, hesitating between her and I. He steps off into the crowd.

I turn my head, duck around a man and he nods at me, stepping to the side, a hobble in his step. *Tollak.* I nod back, step past him. *I have not checked his wound again, since my own slowed me. His will have been more than healed by now, with more than a full moon between it's coming and today.*

My eyes flicker over the crowd. Landlots are pressing in, their faces all mirroring their conversations, voices both loud and quiet ringing in the room, inaudible over each other. There is no sign of Ciaran, no sign of Havard or Fitzclaste, or even Tejan. There are no faces that I have not seen before. *How different would Menantians look, from those I see here everyday?*

I glance at the table spread with food ahead. There are baskets on it, glimpsed between the crowd of people, with thick rolls in them. *Anna was right.* I half-smile. The two large pots are on the table on either side of the rolls, bowls stacked, figures moving between me and them, laughing, talking.

I step up in the back of the line, and the man at the front moves away, speaking to the man beside him. *Severin and Jakob.* Two more people step away, and I am nearly there, the crowd thinning. Someone stops beside me, their head nodding. "Healer." The voice is curt.

I glance up. There is a man beside me, his eyes forward, posture straight, but not like that of the soldiers. His eyes are rimmed with lashes, thicker and darker than I have ever seen. *The storyteller.* I half-smile, incline my head toward him. "Goodeven, Ágë."

A smile tugs at his lips, wry, like every expression I have seen from him, outside the woods. "Goodeven."

My eyes flicker to his, and the women ahead of us step away, their voices murmuring together. *Unn and Norla, Jørn beside her.* I lift the ladle on the pot in front of me, slide a bowl toward it. "Your niece has grown much this last moon. She is precious, a chubby babe if I've seen one."

A smile brushes across his face, bright, real. There is pride in it. He inclines his head. "I believe she is. Amalie and Caj are proud. I am glad to see that they have brought another new life into this place." His voice is almost bitter, though there is still pride in it, blending strangely. He lifts the ladle, pouring the stew into his waiting bowl.

My eyes flicker upward. "Is it not a good thing, to be bringing children to this world?"

His eyes stay steady on his hands, setting his bowl down. "It is. These are dark times and the war will not be won without them." He grips a knife from the table, sliding it into a strange pale substance in a crock. It moves like lard as he cuts into it, only its tint is yellowed. *That must be the butter Anna spoke of. It has been many turnings since I last saw any.*

I lift the knife from next to the basket beside me. "That is a strange statement, sonyá. Children are a blessing, but it does not seem right to say the war will not be won without them. Surely, they are more a gift for any time than a means to ending or winning a war."

His brow shoots up, expression sharp. *That seems to be his only manner of expressing himself, across those sharp features.* "Are they not part of the means to ending the war, to truly turning the tide?" He turns, facing me, a roll in his hand. I glance back over my shoulder. There is no one behind us, everyone else moving around the room, laughing, talking, taking seats loudly. His eyes are fixed on mine. "Raising children to know what is good and to pursue it is one of the surest ways to fight a war and to see to it that the next days will not be as ours are. Who are we fighting for, if there is no next generation, being raised to know what is right? Wars are not won in a day, and there is much more to it than the man or woman who takes the seat of power. Surely of all the people here, you would know that. You have seen this war fought in words and minds."

My hand tightens on the bowl. "Would you use your children as a weapon of the mind?"

He lifts a brow. "I would use the children as people. We have nothing to fight for if what is coming after is only more people trained up to think like those that followed blindly before. Raising up children with a sure foundation, with wisdom and knowledge of good from evil, is one of the most potent things you can do in a society that is crumbling. Ours has half-broken. That is a call for more families to raise children up to know what they are about, what we are living and fighting for, and I would have more people answer it. We need more couples settling down and setting to work, faithfully, earnestly to raise families. And we need more stories about it."

My chest tightens. "You do not worry then, about the danger of raising them in a place where they may be hunted for speaking the truth? Children are known to speak out of turn. They do, often. That is what towns are being burned for, villages slaughtered." *Jørn is a prime example of children speaking out of turn. He and Lila both. If they were not here and knew what they do, they could bring down their homes with a breath out of turn, believed by the wrong man.*

His eyes settle on mine, steady, but there is something troubled behind them, pain in the creasing of his eyes. "There a risk. There will always be risk. But if we do not raise them to know truth from falsehood, right from wrong, someone else will be teaching them something else. In a generation, they will be back where we are, if not further into the darkness. This is a fight we should be fighting."

This is what Iris spoke of, in the sewing rooms, days ago. I incline my head. "So would you have all those who support freedom from her rule hide and raise children?"

He looks down at me again, stepping away from the food table. Someone moves up beside us, grabbing a bowl. "Gót. We need those preparing to work on the front lines. But we have a country following the whims and prophecies of two religions that claim to move this world. It is easy to control millions, where truth is not taught. I would push back against their words."

His eyes catch on something, over my head. He pauses, inclining his head. "Excuse me." He turns, stepping away quickly into the crowd. Tejan looks up as he approaches and inclines her head. *She is here now, then.*

A laugh rings out, high and loud, like a hen cackling. My eyes flicker that way. Iris's head is tossed back, her face scrunched with laughter, the sound still high through the voices. *I did not know she could laugh like that.* Ágë is standing not far from her, speaking with Tejan. Iris's gaze is half on him, as though she does not care that he is near. His back is mostly to her, as though he does not see her, does not know she is watching. *Have they spoken yet, of this, since Iris spoke of it in the sewing rooms? Of him?*

My eyes flicker over the crowd, over the figures. The three heads of the children are stooped over the table across the way, their parents beside them, laughing, talking. *Is it wise, to not take children far from this place? To not keep far from civilization? If death were to come here, their punishment at the hands of the queen's men would be the same as their parents. They would not be spared, for being young.*

A figure moves through the crowd on the other side of the room, clothes bright red like poppy blooms. It is a man, his eyes scanning the room, face caught up in a strange smile, his clothing matching it. His hair is combed back, slicked, the sleeves on his tunic thick and puffed, cuts across them accented, fabric showing gold beneath. He is short, not taller than the shoulder of the prince beside him. *An emissary. No one here would wear clothes that ostentatious to the hall.* His beard is long, slicked into a point down by the thick collar of his tunic.

I turn, and Ruidún lifts her hand before me in a wave, smiling. There is an empty place on the bench beside her. I drop into it, turn my head away from the prince and Menantian man. Ruidún is speaking, Tollah across from her, smiling, the story one of creeks and fields and home.

I set the bread down, my eyes flickering toward the children, across the room. Lila's head is bowed, a silly grin plastered across her face, her head close to the boys'. A tooth is missing from her wide smile. Jørn laughs, half-falling off the bench and Lila folds her arms against the table, proud. The other child laughs shortly and stops again, taking a bite too big for him. He grins through it, a piece of bread falling from his mouth. Norla nudges his arm, speaking softly, and Jørn laughs again, half-falling off the bench as though it were the silliest joke he had ever heard. *Perhaps it is wise to keep them here.* I smile, and it is heavy on my lips.

Tollah is speaking across from me. "How far do you think they will have gone with the Menantian party today?"

XLI

Emissaries from the West

Blåthjortt looks up sharply, his ears raising just barely. I tilt my head, the chatter of Jørn and Lila loud and high. I follow his gaze, press a strand of hair out of my eyes. A man steps down the last stair, Fitzclaste. His eyes flicker toward the children, a smile creasing at their corners. "What brings the children down to the healing rooms?"

I shake my head, straighten. My ribs ache, dull today. "Lila's fár is on watch and she was to play with Jørn." I incline my head toward the child. I drop my voice lower, beneath the noise of their chatter. "I was asked to keep Jørn down here, as company, since my work is quiet and his mother has gone to the gardens today. It looks to rain and she did not want him out there with her." I half-smile.

He nods, eyes flickering toward the children. "Speaking of quiet, I would speak to you, for a moment, quietly, if you have the time and there is nothing on to burn."

I shake my head, flick my eyes toward the children. "Blått." The hound lifts his head, eyes seeking mine. I whistle a short command, to stay, and he drops his head, the children near him still chattering.

Fitz does not move until I have turned, stepping through the arch into the room beyond. I glance back at him, swipe my hands against my apron, and he is turning toward me, actions calm. "You were supposed to be spoken to earlier, I apologize for that. It was lost in the busyness of the day yesterday." He inclines his head. "There have been some questions asked about you."

I raise my hands from my apron, lift a brow. "Questions asked by whom?"

"The emissaries."

I blink, lift my head. "The emissaries? I have yet to meet them, or to even see more of them than one."

He nods. "We are not yet certain what they know of you, nor how they came to know it. They have been asking about you more since last evening, when they have come back from the village, but they have been asking about you for a few days now. It is nothing concerning yet."

I shake my head. "I have not been down to the village. No one there should know of me at all, much less enough to offer questions, to have stirred up any." *Unless one of the men spoke of me, on the ride. One of the men from here who went with them to the village. Would they have done so?*

He inclines his head. "You have not, but the healing man who came to tend your arm is from that village. My guess is that his mouth has not been silent, though what he has said about you, we cannot determine. He was told to keep silent, but we knew there was little hope of that, so there was little that he was told or shown. There was not much he could have found out on his own. A watch was kept on him through every moment of his stay and he was not here long."

The paste man. My eyes burn. "I was not conscious during his stay. What could he know about me other than my wound? If I was ranting with fever, would Sradfaang or anyone else nearby not have removed him from the room? He should not have given credit to ramblings, if he is worth his metal as a healer." *He is not, not if he rambles about paste, and if all of his work had to be redone by a soldier with little knowledge of the healing arts scraped together.*

He shakes his head and my heart sinks into my chest. "He would have. We do not know yet, what he has said, or if it was him that spoke with them. But I am afraid it will not be long before they attempt to address questions to you directly, if they do not give up on it. We have kept them upstairs and busy until now, but there is only so much they can do here. There is not much to see, after they have been through it all, as they have these last days. And they have given no hint of leaving. We wanted you to be warned, before there is a greater risk, so that you will be prepared."

I lift my head. "What reason is there for not encouraging them on their way, if they have already come and have seen all there is to see? If they are pressing in where they should not, it will be a risk to many more here, if they ask questions."

Fitz's jaw tenses just barely beneath his beard. "We will be encouraging them to go, as we can. But with emissaries, there has to be caution involved, or we will find ourselves in a place we do not wish to be. We need Menantia on our side, or out of the war. That is our priority, beyond the safety of everyone here." I incline my head. He inclines his back. "You will be wondering why they are here in the first place. I know we have explained a little, but with all that is going on, I think it would be wise to let you know a little more."

I wait, and he continues. "A noble we know saw fit to share Ciaran's title with them. She is a woman we trust and have for many turnings. She has been of great aid to us in much of Ciaran's work around the country in the early days. They came, so that we could speak with them about making a treatise. With the way things have gone since they arrived, however, we are sending Sradfaang for a lord who knows more about them and their culture to see if he can figure out more about what they are looking for. Until then, we do not want you to be alone, just as a precaution. I can ask one of the boys to come down here and help you, each day, if you would prefer that, or I can ask a guard. It is your choice, what you would be most comfortable with, but they are less likely to speak with a child nearby."

I fold my arms around my ribs. They are aching, burning. *They said they are stretched thin, with guards now. If they have not proved to be a threat yet, I will not ask for one.* I incline my head. "Aye. One of the boys will be fine. When is Sradfaang expected back?"

"They could be back tomorrow evening, or it could be another half a fortnight. It will depend on weather, and how readily Lord Baldwin is able to leave his properties to come with them." He inclines his head, respect. "I need to return to the halls above. I have left my wife long enough with them. Ciaran is seeing to other matters. Keep to these rooms, healer, and they are not likely to trouble you. Send Jørn for me if anything changes."

He inclines his again, and turns, moving back through the other room. I follow after him. He stops by Jørn and Lila, stooping to speak with them. His hand rustles over Blått's ears. He glances back at me. "I do not think there is much for you to worry about, healer. But it would be wise for you to continue to do as you have done. Their lady is especially tenacious. She has been looking into every corner."

I incline my head. "I will be cautious. Thank you, Lord Fitz. If they come down here, I will set the hound on them."

He laughs. "Your hound? I have seen his attentive skills. You had better deter her or shout than try him."

My eyes flicker back to Blått. He is lying on the floor, his belly up, eyes shut, tongue lolling out against the stone. The children are around him, rubbing his stomach, their giggles high and soft in the room. *It would be better to shout. Blått will attack nothing that is not a squirrel or a rabbit. He will be of little use as a guard, little use as a warning or aid if there is trouble. Trouble that we do not wish to begin a war with. What would happen, if an emissary was wounded by a guard hound, here?*

Stars. There must be something better than a child or him as a guard. How will a child be sent, if any of them arrive down here? I cannot send them, not without alerting the emissaries that the child is going.

Fitz laughs, running his hand over Jørn's head, and the boy grins, his face imitating the hound's against the floor, tongue out, eyes closed, a grin pulling back his rounded cheeks. Lila is giggles, poking at his face. He squeals and Fitz tosses his head back in laughter.

XLII

The Lady

There is a step in the hall, unfamiliar, treading softly. I flick my gaze back toward the stairs, my hands slowed on my apron. A woman is standing beneath the archway of the first healing room, her head held high, eyes on the room around her. She is dressed as the emissary man was dressed, her sleeves large, puffed, the etching on them delicate and fine. Her skirts are slender, each panel of them its own work of art, a picture of fine handwork, and they hug close to her hips, only barely moving to let her step.

She smiles, a soft, surprised smile, and there is delight in it that is not trustworthy. "Ah. You must be the healer."

I set my apron down, over the chair. "Aye. I am a healer."

Her smile widens, eyes not leaving mine for a moment. *I should not have sent Miel up to dinner early.* She steps forward, a slow, deliberate step—closer to me. "I have been wondering when our paths would cross, but I hear you have been wounded. How are you healing, healer?"

I incline my head. "I have healed well. Would you care to join me on the walk up to the great hall? It is time to gather there for evening."

Her eyes widen and she shakes her head. "After your injuries, I scarcely think you are fit to handle those stairs. I heard they were no small wounds. Why ever did they ask you to stay here, in this hole, though? It took me days to find it. There is hardly any light down here." *She has been looking, then.*

I swallow and step toward the stairs, toward her. "I will be well, handling them. Will you join me?"

She shakes her head. "Do not worry with them now at least. I should like to see these rooms, to hear more about your work before we return above, and it is hardly beginning gathering time. They will not miss us and I have only just arrived here. I should love to see the rooms before I return above."

I half-smile, force my eyes to soften. "I am afraid you have seen all that there is to see here, kúráh, unless you would dig through herbs. My work is simple, all things you would not like to hear of, or things that you have already seen in your own healers work at your home."

She steps forward again, around the table. *She is nearly to me, too close.* "Oh, do not deter me. I love to hear about other tasks, like this. And I have heard about your work in these particular arts. I hear that you are quite skilled. Gifted, in that area." She smiles, eyes watching, studying me with the corner of her gaze. Her hand trails the tabletop. "This woodwork is fine. It would be more fitting in a dining hall."

I shake my head. "It has been damaged by time. And I am quite out of practice in healing work. The healer who was here before was far more able. You will have heard more of him, of his skill and time here before and not mine. I have not been here long enough for there to be tales about me." I step around the table, past her. "I am going up to the hall, whatever you would like to do. I am hungry, and they will not wait for us to come to them. You may look at the herbs, if you like."

Her eyes widen, pleading. "Oh, but we could at least have a chat first. I have not been down to these halls before. They are quite different from the ones above and I would love to hear more of their history."

I shake my head, move toward the stairs. "I am ready to head up to the hall, and I can tell you little of their history. Tejan will be who you are looking to speak with, if you would like to learn of them, or Fitz. I have not been here long. You will be missed in the hall soon.

They will already be wondering about where you have gone." *I will not be missed, not until she has asked far more questions than I can answer. But she should have been missed, should have someone looking for her.* I step around the table, and there are foot falls behind me, hard and loud against the stone. *She was walking nearly silently before, when she came down.* My heart sinks into my stomach.

She steps up beside me, her eyes casting down toward mine. *She is tall.* "You said there was another healer. You have not been here long?"

I turn away, toward the stairs ahead. *Keep your eyes forward.* "I have not. And there was." I plant my foot onto the bottom step, start up the stairs. *Deter her.* "How was your ride out to the village and back?"

She smiles on the edge of my vision. "It was delightful. So many wonderful folk down there, who were wonderfully full of conversation. We hear little about your queen in Menantia, only the last of the bits of information, unless you have a direct scout line to relay information. Really, we hear little about anything that goes on here, and they were more than willing to give us what information and news they could. It was delightful. Every bit of it was delightful. I could have stayed so much longer if we had had more daylight." She looks at me, her eyes never straying to watch her steps on the stairs.

I plant my foot on the top step, turn into the hallway. She is still beside me, her steps loud. I pick up my pace. "I am surprised they had anything to share with you. Small villages rarely know anything trustworthy. Especially not those in the mountains. News comes there late, and through too many tongues, to be reliable. This village must have a chain of information somewhere to have known so much."

Her eyes flicker to me, almost sharp for a moment, and then they are soft again, easy. "Much of the news they had to share was local news, as you will know, I trust. News from soldiers?"

My heart slows. I shake my head, move around a bench out of place in the hall. *The boys will have moved it while playing.* "I have not been to the village. As you have said, I have not been here long.

The time I have been here has been spent in Tejan and Fitz's home." *What soldiers, have been there but Einion?*

I pull the door open into the next hall and she steps through, eyes ahead and confident. She smiles. "You may not have been to the village, but that does not mean that you have not seen the villagers, or were you not conscious yet, when the healing man came?" My jaw tightens.

There are voices ahead, echoing up the hall, and she is standing ahead of me, the hall not wide enough for me to pass her here. Her steps are barely inching up it. She glances back at me, lifting a brow. "He seemed to have much to say about you all that I had never heard in the time I've been here. He seemed to know much of these halls."

I lift a brow back at her, force my eyes to stay calm, to remain gray, only gray. "Likely more than he should, given that he knows nearly nothing about any of us. He seems to have said a lot for a man who was only here for a matter of watches, all within one or perhaps two rooms."

Her smile twists into a grin, delight in her eyes again. "So, you were awake then? I thought you to have been unconscious, from what I had heard. The wounds seemed…troubling." She turns back up the hall, her steps moving no quicker. My heart sinks in my chest. *Surely someone must notice that she is missing.* She flicks her sleeves between her fingers, pulling the heavy fabric between them. "Your answers are sharp, for a healer. Have you been to the cities, to Blackwater or Gnor? Those are the nearest ones, are they not? The nearest ones worth mentioning to a woman like yourself, I think?"

Aye, to Blackwater. I shake my head. "Gót. I have spent most of my turnings in the middle of small lands that you would not care for, not a kúráh like yourself." There are steps in the hall, moving this way, the voices louder. My head lightens, heart thuds against my ribs. "Would you care to join the others now? They will have begun eating."

Her eyes flick back to me slowly, over the curve of her shoulder. "I do not know. There are so many questions I would still like to ask you. Is there a sitting room nearby that we could go to?" Her smile is sharp in her eyes, like a dagger.

I shake my head, step forward. "I doubt there will be time for that. I have my own tasks to keep to, and you are not here to see me. It would be a dishonor to the lords and lady here, for me to keep you during your stay, when you have come to see and learn of them." I bow.

She pouts, her lower lip jutting out. *The footfalls are not getting close to us quickly enough.* Her lip is still jutting, a pitiable expression. "But we will be here for so long, it would be a shame to not get to know all of you, especially someone who is so crucial for the survival of this place, for the survival of your prince as a healer. We will have plenty of time to learn of them and you."

I push back the burning of my eyes, lift my chin. "As you know who he is, you would know better than to speak of him in open places like that. We should return to the hall. I thank you for your compliments, but I would not deter you from those higher than me."

Her eyes are grinning, mouth still pouting, and my spine crawls. There is a step in the hall, just around the corner. She straightens, turning. "I will see you again then, now that I know where you are. Perhaps we can take tea together one afternoon, while we are here, just you and I, or perhaps one of the ladies? You must allow me to get to know you better. Our healers are not half so engaging, nor so fascinating."

I half-incline my head, and Iris is walking around the corner, her steps slow, head bent over some kind of cloth in her hands. The lady has not moved. I lift my head. "Iris." Her eyes snap up, widen slightly. She blinks, lowering the fabric, her gaze flickering between me and the woman. I keep my eyes on her. "Has everyone gathered for dinner?"

She blinks again, her eyes flickering to the woman for just a moment and back to me again. "Aye. It is that time of day." She straightens. "You all should be there, I would imagine. Ágë may tell another story tonight. I hear he has another one spun together, for our guests, of whom you, I believe, are a member, kúráh?" There is a ghost of pain on her lips, as she speaks Ágë's name.

The Menantian lady inclines her head, turning toward me. "A story from your storyteller. I would prefer a longer talk in person, but

I see you are taken with the idea of going to the dining hall. It has been an honor." She inclines her head to me, turning and moving up the hall. I step after her, Iris moving between us, and she is gone past me up the hall. The lady steps into the doorway, the men standing before it heavily in conversation—one of them laughs a kind of snort and the others join in, patting him on the back.

The lady glances back at me, waiting. I step up beside her, and she moves into the bustling of the room beyond. My heart presses in my chest. I move away into the crowd, put them between me and her, and Havard's eyes meet mine across the bodies, flicker toward the lady. Concern flits across them. He straightens, moves behind someone, and is gone into the crowd.

The lady laughs behind me, not far enough away though there are many people between us. One of the men she must have come with is beside her, his laugh matching hers, both loud, louder than the voices around them as if they have not a care in the world.

I lift my head, turn away. *That was too close. I will not let the boys go up early to dinner again, not be alone down there again. Blått could have at least been with me. I should have asked for a guard, a man to stay with me below. I did not think they would come so soon.*

I press my hand against the table beside me, glance back at the woman. *She is prodding close. I cannot tell where she is looking, what she is aiming toward, what she knows of me or if it is only a guess, a game. It cannot be wise to let her close again.*

Her laugh cuts across the room again. Fitz is approaching them, his gait steady, eyes focused on the party, the eight of them together. He nods to them and they smile in return, follow him across the room to the table and the pots of stew on the table not far from me. Her head is high, as though she were not pressing where she should not have been a moment ago, as if she were not playing games a breath ago.

XLIII

Dark Hall

Voices are loud, urgent, catching in the halls where there should be morning stillness. I press my hand against the wall, step up the passageway. *Has the party returned, then? Sradfaang and the lord he was sent to retrieve?*

There is a call, alarm echoing, and my eyes burn. "Get the healer." The voice is gruff, somewhere not far up the hall, and it carries strangely. I bolt forward, dart around a corner, and there is a crowd suddenly before me, a huddle of figures blocking off the hallway.

One of them turns, moving toward me—Eon, Nellie's husband. He stops sharply, relief and alarm mixing in his gaze. "Healer." His voice is high, sharp. "I was coming to get you." He sweeps his arm backward, and someone steps out of the way.

A figure is slumped against the wall, stretched on the floor, clutching his arm. His clothes are familiarly unfamiliar. *The garb of a Menantian man.* He flicks his eyes up toward me and they are raw with pain, hazy around the edges. His lips are a pale line, his shoulders hunched, blood coating his arm. I step forward, and my ears ring with warning.

I drop to the ground beside him. His hand is coated in blood, the cloth of his sleeve soaked, and his skin is pale. I push his hand back, shove the cloth to the side, and my stomach swirls. I press my hand sharply against the wound. There is a gash, across his skin, carving through the vessels that carry his blood to his hand. It is deep, clawing nearly to the bone.

I press my hand down further but it does not cover all there is of it, the cut jutting up his arm. I snap my other hand over it, press down against his leg. My head snaps up, to the men standing around us. The Menantian lady is among them, her eyes watchful, and there is something wrong in them.

I turn my head away, toward Eon. "Get cloth from the healing rooms, several rolls for bandages. Quickly!" The crowd presses against the wall and there are steps behind me, jerky, fading up the hall. I turn back toward the Menantian. My hands are still squarely over the wound. "What is your name?"

His face is pinched with pain, his eyes unfocused. *The unfocused look that all the wounded have when they are fading.* "Gulliame." The word is a shallow breath.

I nod, press down with my whole weight against the wound. "Gulliame. Focus on breathing. How did this happen, what happened to you?" The blood is oozing up between my hands in a gurgle, soaking between each finger. His eyes flick to mine and there is no sight in them. *He is losing blood quickly, too quickly. I only have a few countings left to stop the bleeding or he will be beyond saving.*

I lift my voice above the crowd. "How did he come to gain this? What happened to him?"

One of the other Menantian men turns his eyes from Gulliame to me. They are wide, face alarmed. "He was sharpening one of his blades and did it clumsily. I found him this way, he was half out into the hallway, to get help. Couldn't really stand, so I had to pull him over here." He chokes, turning away. "I dragged him here." He gestures vaguely up the hall.

There is pride in the eyes of the Menantian lady at the corner of my vision. I turn back to the bleeding man, his blood trickling down my wrist. A drop of it splatters against my skirts. *Creator, please stop this bleeding, save him. Please stop this and save him.*

If I sing, what will they do to us? Can I let him die, knowing that I could but lift my voice and save him?

Someone moves up behind my shoulder, too close behind me. "Is there nothing more you can do than sit there?" The man's voice is sharp, accented like the lady's—another of the Menantian men. "He is *dying*. We heard much of your skill, but this here is pure idleness and our friend is bleeding to death on your own knees. Will you do nothing? A child could do more."

Blood drips against my skirts. *Creator.* I lift my head, keep my eyes down, on Gulliame. "If I move my hands from this wound, he will bleed out before we can get anything to save him from the rooms below. I am doing all that I can until my help gets back." I lift my eyes to the Menantians. "But I beg that you would step back. Let me tend him. I will do all that may be done."

I look back at the wound and the man steps closer, his knee pressing against my shoulder. "But is there not something greater that you should do? He is bleeding out, you have said so yourself." There is panic in his voice. "You should save him, healer. Are you not a healing woman? Are you not the healer here? Is this all that can be done?"

A voice speaks up. "I trust the healer is doing all that she can." *Severin's voice, calm, even.*

The leg presses further against my back, form looming high over me, his leg jostling my hands. I shift them back into place. "All that she can? She is holding his arm, letting him die without even an attempt to be made. This is your miraculous healer? My friend is bleeding out, and she is sitting by and letting him, holding his hand while he wastes away into nothing, like an idle woman. Do you call that helping? Do you call this your healer?"

"I trust the healer to work. Step back." Severin's voice is hard.

The leg presses forward, voice turning to me. "You could save him, but you are letting him die. Do you call this the work of a healer, to let a man waste away while his very blood soaks through your hands, through each of your fingertips? You are coming away bloodstained if he dies, I swear it!"

A step sounds on the floor of the hall. "The healer is doing all that she can. Step. Back." *Sradfaang.* My eyes burn. Blood drips against my skirts and it is soaking through them, warm against my skin. The

leg is gone from my back, no longer pressing me forward. Sradfaang is still speaking. "Move. If he is wounded I will take him down to the healing ward. You standing here will accomplish nothing." Landlots behind me are moving out of the way quickly, the goblin beside me. "Healer. I can move him."
Another droplet of blood drops against my skirts. "Gót. He cannot be moved. If we move him before we bandage this, we will lose him." I swallow hard. "Goldenrod and horsetail." I flick my gaze upward. "I need someone to gather a crock of horsetail and goldenrod. Quickly. They are labeled on the middle shelf in the first room." I glance up again. Severin is already darting up the hall, gone, dark head gone between the bright colors of the standing figures. *The Menantians are the only ones left.*
Sradfaang shakes his head, a short, sharp movement. He is coated in dirt, his face grime covered. His eyes meet mine, grim. They shift to the man beside me. He turns toward those standing by. "You do not need to be here to watch this. Move. Back to your workplaces and tasks."
The Menantian lady shakes her head, her chin lowered, eyes wide, blinking. "You would have us leave our companion, here, injured? That wound is serious, she said it was serious, and we are not leaving him like that, alone, to die here, untended." Gulliame's eyes roll shut, and his head lulls forward, limp.
I nudge his leg with mine. "Gulliame, look up. Keep your eyes open. Gulliame. Keep your eyes open."
A foot stamps, voice raising. "Damn you, goblin. You are letting him bleed out, ordering us away, and she is doing nothing. If he dies—"
I click my tongue, whistle sharply, high. "Gulliame. Keep your head up. Lift your head, Gulliame." His eyes blink at me, consciousness slipping away again. *Where is Eon?* His eyes are unfocused, blinking up at me, his neck crooked. My heart thunders in my chest. *They are here for no good end, but I cannot let him die, not like this. I cannot let him bleed out.* Blood drips heavy against my skirts.

"You will leave, or you will do more harm than good. She will do all she can, but you are in the way. Move, kúráh." Sradfaang's words are sharp.

"In the way of her doing nothing?" The lady's voice is high. "She is not even pasting a bandage over it, or sewing it or anything closed. You call this your healer?"

"You will get out." Sradfaang's voice is low, hard, no argument in it, and there are steps in the hall, voices high and protesting. But they are moving, walking away.

"I will not leave him. He is my cousin, and I will not leave him." *The lady's voice.* A shudder crawls up my spine, creeping along my arms.

The air of the hall presses down on me, hard, thicker with every breath. "Standing and staring will help neither him nor you, if he is dying. Unless you like to watch death, kúráh. Do you like to watch death come?"

She straightens on the edge of my vision. *He is dying beneath my hands.* There are tears on her cheeks. Her lip trembles. "I do not like to watch death, goblin; I have never seen it. But I cannot do nothing, and you all are not helping him, not saving his life, and he is fading away at her feet. I cannot let my cousin die alone, like this." Her voice is a protest, watery, high. My heart clenches in my chest.

"The healer is staunching the wound, the first thing that must be done if your cousin is to heal. Go help Severin in the healing ward, if you would do something to help." The woman's lips open again, her eyes looking to protest, but Sradfaang does not move, staring, watching, his head high above hers.

She steps to the side, lifting her hand in a point toward him. "If he dies while I am gone, I will take it out on your head, not hers. And I *will* have your head, sonyá. There is nowhere that you can hide that I will not gain it, if he dies today." She steps up the hall and is running, her gait and steps awkward in her narrowed skirts.

Sradfaang drops to his knees beside me. "What is to be done here?"

I swallow hard, and Gulliame's head lulls forward onto his chest, limp, sight gone fully like a torch blowing out. Blood taps against my skirts. "He is bleeding out, as she said. The wound is deep, thick, and it has cut through the vessels."

His eyes flicker to mine. "If you do this. they will not cease to ask questions until they learn fully what you are. They are already pressing where they should know nothing." There is no one else in the hall, no one but him and I.

I bite my tongue. "Then I will do just enough for the bleeding to cease, to halt his death. I cannot let him pass on my hands. I cannot let him die like this."

His jaw is tight, eyes hard. "Then you will not do it here. I am moving him." I bite my lip, nod, and he slips his arms under the man, lifting. I keep my hands on the wound, and blood trickles down my arm, into my sleeve as he lifts the body. I stand, shift my grasp. Sradfaang moves. He turns through a door, kicking it open, and we are through, my shoulder bumping hard against the doorframe.

Sradfaang steps forward, dropping the man against the arm of a low bench, and he steps back. The man balanced for now against the bench, his head propped up. I drop to my knees, my hands on the arm, the wound, and his blood drips. His face is completely ashen now, eye lifeless in his motionless head. *I am nearly too late. Creator, please help me save him. Preserve him, please.*

I suck a breath in through my teeth. My eyes flicker back toward the goblin. "Will you keep watch outside?" My heart pounds in my chest, sinking. *What will they do, if they hear the song, learn what it does? What stone will they not over turn to learn what I carry?*

Sradfaang nods, stepping from the room, and the door taps shut behind him.

I lift my voice, raise the song, long and low, and blood drips against my skirts, dripping down onto the carpet of the floor.

XLIV

Gulliame

I drop my voice, curl off the last note, and I cannot tell if he is stable, or if his life's blood is still oozing new between my clutched fingers. There are voices in the hall, loud, urgent, moving nearer.

"What have you done with him?! He was not fit to be moved! She said he could not be moved. Dammit! That healer of yours—"

Sradfaang's voice cuts off the lady's. "Is doing everything she can to stabilize him and thought it best if he was not in the hall, where there are prying eyes and stepping feet. Would you have preferred we left him here to be tread upon?"

"You call yourselves barbarous enough to tread upon the dead?"

"The dead are often tread on, upon the battlefield."

The door creaks open, steps moving in. I glance up. Severin is moving toward me, Eon behind him. The lady's figure is in the doorway, her back to me, her sleeves filling its frame. She is still speaking toward Sradfaang in the hall beyond her.

Severin takes the bundle of cloth from Eon, moving to kneel beside me. "How can I be of aid to you?"

I shake my head. "Go for Ragnar. I can tend this wound, but it will be quicker and simpler with his help. We need swiftness, if this man is to be saved." I swallow hard. He nods, setting the items on the floor, and is gone, gone through the doorway again, the lady stepping out of the way.

She turns, moving through the doorway, her head high, eyes staring hard and focused on me. I look away, back toward the man propped against the bench, his arm limp across his waist. I speak. "Do you need something, kúráh?"

Her back straightens on the edge of my vision. "You can help me by healing him. I have heard of your great skill, and if he dies, it will be on your head and the goblin's both. This man is a lord in our homeland. He is a lord and should not die from a simple wound like this. This is no fitting way for him to fade. If you fail him—"

My jaw tightens. "I am doing all that I can, kúráh, but his wound was not my doing, and neither will his death be. The Goldtide Officer is doing his duty. I am sorry for your strife, but I can only do what may be done and I assure you, I am doing it."

"Brunhild." Ciaran's voice is sharp, from somewhere behind me. "You would be wise to come wait in the sitting rooms with Tejan, across the way. She has refreshments there. I think that you have done all that you can to help here, if you will give up those bandages. This will be well. Let the healers do their work."

My eyes move up, toward the woman's hands. There are cloths in them, tightly wound from the baskets downstairs. Her hands are clenched around them, but her hair is still perfectly placed, her eyes calculating. Ciaran is beside her, his eyes patient and unreadable.

Her jaw tightens, and she nods slowly, her eyes flickering back to me, sharply, too sharply. Her eyes flicker toward the wound, and they narrow, just barely. "Prince Ciaran," She turns toward him, but I can still feel her gaze on me. "I am glad to have your best healer on this. But you understand that I am worried for Gulliame. I will take tea only if doors can be left open so that I can hear what is going on here. I do not wish to be an inconvenience, but you will understand that I have not had the chance to get to know this healer, as you have, and she has shown me little to trust her with. I will not be absent when he dies. I will not go quietly if that cannot be done, and you will not move me."

Ciaran smiles, a slow, gentle smile. "That will not be necessary. Let Eness do her work. I will send for more help if you like, but I have full faith in her, and as you trust me, trust her. She will do everything that she can to help him, as she has said. Come wait. There is no help in worrying here. Tejan is fetching tisane for you."

The lady's lips tense, eyes studying his face. She nods slowly, gaze flickering to me. She turns, walking from the room, her sleeves buffeting around her.

Ciaran turns toward me, his gaze moving to my blood-soaked hands on the man's arm.

There are steps in the hallway. Ragnar steps into the room, a bag slung over his shoulder. He inclines his head toward the prince—respect and honor—and moves past him, not breaking his stride. He drops against the ground where Severin was only moments ago. "What do you need, healer?"

His eyes lift to mine, ready, sharp. I purse my lips, drop further back against my heels. "I need you to stitch the wound shut. My hands will take time to clean, and I cannot move them until it is time to stitch or he may bleed out." I tighten my jaw. "It is deep. Bone deep."

He nods, and the prince is stepping forward behind him. The door closes beneath Sradfaang's hand. "What has been done?" His voice is quiet, steady.

My throat clenches. "I sang." I swallow hard, shift my hands on the arm. "Briefly, to stabilize his life, but I do not know if it was long enough to stop the bleeding. We will sew it up and put the herbs on it, but that is all that I can do, unless we can keep them away for long enough for me to sing again. I will not risk your lives for his if they may be close enough to hear again."

Ragnar is pulling a pouch out of the bag on his shoulder. He draws out a curved needle, thread with it. *He keeps it ready.* Ciaran nods at me, slowly. I cast my eyes back toward Gulliame.

Ragnar has the needle threaded, his eyes waiting. I pull my hand back, grab a cloth from the ground. I swipe it through the blood on the man's arm. My skin clings to it, blood half-gelled between my fingers. I swallow. "She is asking too many questions, my lord. She knows something, and I do not know what. I think that after today it will be unwise for me to stay here, for your sake, or she will continue to ask and put you all at risk of being hunted down." My eyes burn. "I will not be the reason you are found out, lord."

The blood comes away from his skin, cleanly, all but a faint ring outside the deep ring of dried red. *The mark of the song, barely sung, and the clotting blood, one inside the other.* I swallow. The wound does not shift, does not gape or pull wide. *It is clotted, closed.* It is wide still, cutting across both blood vessels too cleanly.

Ragnar sucks in a breath. "What did they say did this?"

I swipe the cloth over my hands, blood moving between my fingers. "Sharpening a blade. An accident."

Sradfaang laughs, the sound harsh and hollow. "They might have picked a better excuse if they had said he did it with a wooden kitchen spoon. I have heard better excuses from fools."

Ciaran's face is dry, his eyes on the wound. They flick to me. "Do not speak with them again, healer. I will look into this and see what more can be done to remove them from here peaceably." His eyes shift to Sradfaang. "You will stay down in the healing rooms with her, whenever you can be spared. Baldwin and I will speak with them this afternoon. If he finds them lacking, we will send them on their way at once. I do not think we have misjudged them, and that worries me a great deal. I do not care for having that woman under this roof any longer than need has it." His eyes flicker to me again. "But healer, do not leave. That will benefit no one. We will uphold our promise to keep you safe. I will uphold my word to see you safe."

The goblin bows, short and deep—respect and acceptance, head tilted to the left, hands at his sides. "If she is my charge, I will stay with her even when I am needed. You all can manage without me until that woman is gone from these halls, or else I am not guarding her. I will not do a half-hearted job. If she is willing to risk her cousin, she will risk more."

Ciaran inclines his head. "You will stay down there."

Ragnar's needle slips through the man's skin, his stitches even, if not graceful. My eyes flicker toward him. He is in commoner's clothes, his face strange above the simple brown tunic, shoulders odd without the gold trim of his rank. I swallow hard. *He has not worn his gold trim since the Menantians arrived.* There has been none of it here, on any of the three soldiers.

Ciaran speaks again, his eyes on me. "I will look into this. In the meantime, I ask that you wait and trust us. We will speak to you, when we know what is to be done. Continue to heal and stay in the rooms below. They will have no more chance to trouble you today, nor to ask questions, with what Tejan has planned and meeting with Lord Baldwin this evening, when he has recovered from his travels. Sradfaang can handle them well enough if they come below, and you need not be cornered again. I heard what happened a night ago." He jaw clenches. "I thought we had put measures in place to prevent that. I am sorry that was not true. You should not have had to speak with her." He inclines his head to me and turns back toward the goblin, speaking calmly, too softly for me to hear.

I cast my gaze back to Ragnar. His hands are moving the needle through the skin, between the two circles around the wound. I lift the crock off the floor, pinch out the goldenrod powder. *And if they find me while the goblin is not around? She cared little that men were there when she questioned me in the hallway. They will go further yet, if they see their time here closing. If they were willing to play with the life of one of theirs, what else will they do?* I sprinkle the powder over the finished stitches.

What does a threatened animal do, when its prey turns on it? My eyes move to the prince. He is still speaking, his face calm, steady. *They will turn on him, if he tests them again. Then there will be far more in their hands than just the knowledge of my gift. If he is the man he claims to be, he is the life and hope of this country.*

And if not, he may be its downfall.

XLV

Lord Baldwin

Sradfaang's arms are folded, his back against the wall. He glances up the stairs. "I do not care for this."

I set the half-stripped stalk down, press a hand against my side. "Did you not imagine they would have much to speak about?"

He lifts a brow, expression dry. "I do not imagine it should take this long. There is not much for them to discuss, in the speaking, unless she is playing her hand." His ears flick just slightly toward the staircase. I turn my gaze toward the stairs, cast it back toward him. His eyes do not move from it. "Havard." He straightens. "Finally, then."

There is a step, faint and steady on the lowest step, and a figure moves out of the shadows of the stairs - Havard. His eyes move toward the goblin and then to me. "Lord Baldwin has asked that you come to the meeting hall." Sradfaang does not move, waiting, and Havard continues, still looking at me. "The woman has requested to speak with you, to ask how Gulliame is doing and to thank you for your work in saving him. Baldwin thinks it will be wise, to see how much she will reveal of where she gained her information. Ciaran and Fitzclaste have agreed with his reasoning. It will be better for her to try in front of many than a few." He inclines his head toward Sradfaang. "Even if you are the few, sonyá. Will you come, Eness? If you do not wish to speak with her again, you need not. But if she is willing to play her hand so openly, we may learn more of what she knows, and that would be beneficial before she leaves to learn what she may do with the information she holds."

I swallow. "And if she does not play her hand?"

Sradfaang's eyes move to mine. "I trust the word of all of the men that will be in that room. They are wise and will take council together. Ciaran and Baldwin do nothing on a whim. If they want to test her, go to them. They will not leave you out to dry too long. It will be worth seeing if she will, to gain what information we can, healer."

I incline my head toward him—respect and appreciation. I turn toward Havard. "I will go, then. Does the Gold Tide officer come?"

Havard glances at him. "Lord Fitz asked that you not come in the room. The Menantian party does not think well of you. But I think you will be able to hear everything from the other side of the door if there is trouble, which I would appreciate."

Sradfaang grins, his teeth starkly white. "Then I have done my job well. I am coming."

I slip the apron over my head, set it aside, and my eyes burn, twisting. *There can be little good out of speaking with them again, others present or not. What can we do, but assure her of her own assumptions? Confirm what she already seems to know? That will bring nothing but destruction down on this place in the days coming.*

I step onto the stairs, Havard in front of me and Sradfaang's steps nearly silent behind. Havard turns at the top, ducking through a doorway. I step after him, move into the room, and he is already walking out a door on the other side of it. *A shortcut. I have not seen this here before.* I move through after him and he pauses, glancing back at me. He pushes the door open before him, waiting for me.

The room is lit by the late light of afternoon, filtered through the blurred glass. There are figures in the room, six of them, the lady seated at the far side of the room. Ciaran stands, inclines his head toward Havard, and Havard bows, stepping back out through the door. Sradfaang is gone, no sign of him beyond the door as it closes.

I fold my hands before me, lift my eyes. There is a man across the room, his face unfamiliar. His skin is dark, shoulders broad, eyes honest, calculating. They are on the lady in the seat near him. His robes are fine, finer than those that Ciaran and Fitz have worn since I arrived. His head held steadily, shoulders broad and set. He turns his gaze toward me and bows, low and careful—honor with knowledge. "Eness Finch. It is good to put a face with your name. I believe the Lady Brunhild wishes to thank you for the deed you rendered to her cousin today in saving his life."

The lady stands, her height nearly matching his, and she sweeps an arm out, her great, large sleeves fluttering around her. Her head inclines gently—a mimic of our bows, honor, without respect. "I do wish to. I owe you an apology for doubting your skills in healing. The prince trusts you, and I should have taken his word, if I could not take yours. When you sat there and did nothing for all that time, it seemed as though everything I had heard of you was false. I apologize for that, for my fickleness."

I incline my head back to her, the gesture she made—respect without honor. "You have no call to apologize. A man was dying, your cousin. There was call to doubt me. I am only glad his wound did not prove to be more serious than it did. Elnial was gracious to him."

Her eyes widen, and she steps forward. "But did it not? I am still not sure how you staunched it. With all the blood upon your hands, I did not think it would stop bleeding until his body was drained of it. You have worked a miracle this day. I am glad Prince Ciaran will have such a capable healer on his side when he rises to the throne." There is a strange light in her eyes, shielded by the expression plastered across her face.

I lift my head. "Gót. There was no miracle in it but the grace of Elnial." My heart stings, eyes half-burn. *A lie. Creator, please forgive me. That gift is from You, and I have lied.* "Staunching it was easy enough once it was sewn closed, and I did not even do that task. It was done by one of the men."

Her eyes narrow, the smallest fraction, and they widen again. Innocence is in every line of her face, sweet and gentle as a child. A shiver creeps up my spine. "That may be so, but I am still convinced that a gifted healer like yourself does not belong in a place like this, out of the way. I have heard that you have a singing voice that cannot be matched, along with your considerable skill in the healing arts. Those both would suit you far better for the cities, for the forefront of this land. Would you not be better suited for the courts?"

My heart slows in my chest, eyes half-burn. I bite it back. *She should know nothing of my voice, unless one of the men I saved spoke to her. Surely they have not.* My head shakes, a smile twisting my lips. "I have little enough skill in healing and, as I have told you, it is out of practice. I am thankful to the Creator that your companion lived, but this place is rather too grand for me than not grand enough. All that I know I learned from a peasant healer, the daughter of peasant healers. This place is more than sufficient for my knowledge in the arts."

She shakes her head, laughing lightly. "I do not believe you for a moment. You will have to grant at least that you are skilled in song. What I have heard cannot be refuted there. The soldier who spoke to me in the village had never heard anything like it. Clear, mesmerizing, and strong, like something out of the tales of old." There is a glint in her eyes, and they are sharp again, watchful, like a lynx closing in on prey.

I shake my head, press back the swirling of my eyes. "He must have been mistaken. I know of no soldiers that have heard me sing, as it is a rare thing. Whoever this man was, he must have had me mixed up with another."

She laughs. "Another that looks like you? A healer with hair nearly white, pale like the full stråle sun? He said that he heard you singing in the forest, a fortnight or more before the healing man ever came here. Hair like yours would be hard to miss in the dark places of the woods, as he said. It would shine through the trees, pale, even on a night without stars. He heard it cleanly, clearly, the song, like healing. It must have been yours, high and clear like the Night Song of old."

I force a laugh, and it is faint. The men have not moved across the room, watchful, their eyes unwavering, waiting. I cannot push back the tightening of my chest. "Well then, he has greatly exaggerated my skill. The Night Song is far too high a compliment for any civ. I have not learned at the feet of a bard or master. It is all from singing about my worktables and in fields, alone." I incline my head, shallow and to the left, lifting my hands together—appreciation and nothing more.

Brunhild steps forward, her eyes still that strange soft-sharp, her gaze locked on mine, as though no one else in the room is here. "It is I that should be thanking you. How is Gulliame, my cousin? He looked a whole different man, when I saw him last, paler than smoke, than ash. I trust he is better this evening?"

I incline my head. "You will have to ask Lord Fitz. I believe he has seen him most recently, just before he arrived here, if I am not mistaken. I will see him again shortly, but I have not checked on him this last watch. That was the work of the other healer. Is that everything you would speak to me of, kúráh?"

She laughs, waving me away. "I only wished to thank you, so of course I will not keep you. I leave it to your men folk, whether they have words they wish to share with you, before you return to those rooms below. They are rather dark and separated from the rest." Something flashes through her gaze.

I flick my eyes to Lord Baldwin. He is watching me, his eyes startling, sharp. I look down, look away, my eyes burning, and I cannot stop it.

Ciaran steps forward, toward the woman. "It would be wise, I think, for you to rest now, Brunhild. You have had a long day, and will have a long day again tomorrow and in the days to come, while your cousin is healing. Rest would be wise while you can before you take to the roads again with your journey home."

She inclines her head, sweeping him a bow in the style of Menantia, her hands clasped within her sleeves, body bowing at the waist, twisted, and she brushes past me, toward the door. She pauses by it, glancing over the curve of her shoulder, and I look over mine, toward her. She half-smiles. "I would like to hear you sing, someday, before we return to our homes. A beautiful voice is hard to come by, and it would be an honor to us to hear yours. Our culture values singing highly. It would honor us greatly to hear your voice once, before we are gone."

I shake my head. "I appreciate the gift you bestow with your words, but I do not sing for entertainment. You will forgive me if I decline your request. I am sorry. I am not accustomed to singing for the public."

She laughs, shaking her head, and Fitz is pulling the door open before her. "I will forgive you, but I will continue to attempt to convince you otherwise, and my companions will join me. It would not have to be for the whole of Sikkerhet, but only us, if you choose. I hear there is healing in good song, and the soldier spoke of your voice highly. It would be an honor to us." There is the glint in her eye again, and I incline my head.

Fitz's voice is gentle, soft. He takes her arm. "I have not heard that saying. Is it from your homeland?" A shiver crawls up my spine.

Brunhild's voice is faint in response, and the door clicks shuts behind her. Someone moves through it as it closes. *Sradfaang.* He glances at Lord Baldwin, his eyes landing on Ciaran. "She cannot stay."

Ciaran nods, leaning forward on the table. "I know. I will speak of this with you all this evening. For now," His gaze flicks toward me. "Eness, you would do well to help in the kitchens, to aid there. It is too noisy for any conversation to be truly held this time of day there. Sradfaang, I would send you to the village, if you can be spared for a watch."

Sradfaang half-grins. "You would find the paste man?"

Ciaran inclines his head. "Aye. They spoke with him. If there is a soldier that knows of what Eness carries, I would know it. I think he knows more than he should. I would have you speak with him."

Sradfaang bows. "I will go, if Severin or Ragnar can be spared to stay with the healer."

Baldwin shakes his head. "I will stay with her. It will give me time to rest from my journey, and I would welcome the quiet. Brunhild was willing to speak at face with all of us present. She will not be stopped by noise or the presence of others in the kitchens. I do question how she gained this knowledge. How came she to speak with a soldier?"

Fitz folds his hands neatly in front of him on the table. "The village healer came to her, while she was riding through the village. They took to each other immediately, and there was little to be done about it, and little reason at the time to suspect that he had anything of import to share. The man was here for a matter of watches and should not have known all that he did. She rode off for a moment with him, when there was a scuffle around us. That fault is mine, for letting them speak unhindered while Sradfaang was not present to hear. I thought it a simple thing, and now I see that it was a foolish mistake. She will likely have spoken with any soldier that was there then." He runs a hand over his face, looking older. "I am ashamed not to have paid closer attention to them."

Lord Baldwin lifts a brow. "Something does not sit well with me on this. We have all underestimated how much the villagers know about you all, especially the healing man. And the presence of a soldier is off putting. How long ago did those soldiers come to be under your roof?"

Ciaran speaks. "A full moon ago. A fortnight before the village healer was here."

I shake my head, wrap my arms around my throbbing ribs. "I would not worry about the paste man. He does not seem to be a calculative man."

Fitz's eyes flicker to mine. "'Paste man?'" He half-smiles. "I suppose he earned that. He was not a skilled healer." His gaze moves to Baldwin. "I agree with the healer. But I do not like the extent of what he knows, nor how Brunhild will use it. We will speak more later. Sradfaang should go quickly and have a long word with the village healer. Ciaran's mind there is more than sound."

Baldwin nods his head, his face impassive. He turns toward me. "Did Brunhild learn anything when she spoke with you before tonight?"

I shake my head. "She did not. But I do not care to speak with her again. I would welcome your company downstairs, if you will bear with mine."

He inclines his head. "Thank you, Eness. We will see to it that you do not need to speak with her again, if it can be by any means avoided. I would not put you through that again. Thank you for speaking with her. It has made many things clearer, for me." He inclines his head again, respect. He turns to the prince, to the lord beside him. "I will speak with you both this evening when Srad has returned. Until then, I will be below." He bows, low and courteous, and gestures for me to go before him through the door.

XLVI

Before Dawn

Someone's voice is soft in the darkness, a breath. "Eness." I lift my head and sleep is heavy, my sight blurred in the darkness.

I swallow hard, drag myself from the covers. There is a figure, faint, the light from beyond the door. I suck in a breath. "Aye? Is someone ill? Or is it the Menantian?"

The figure shakes their head, curls shifting in the darkness. *Tollah.* "Gót. Ciaran and the Lord Baldwin wish to speak with you. They are waiting in the hall."

I blink, press back sleep. "Hall? Has something happened?"

She shakes her head again. "Gót. I do not know. Hurry. The hall across from us, two doors down on the left. They are waiting for you."

I throw the blankets off, press my hands against my eyes. My hand fumbles with my cloak on the chest at the foot of my bed. I sling it over my shoulders, and there is light in the room, bright, blinding. I jerk my hand up and stumble forward. The shadows are long across the floor, the door open now, torch light bright and fluttering in the hall.

I step through the doorway and Tollah is vanishing up the hall, off toward the kitchens, her steps quick. I blink again and tug at the edges of my cloak. *I cannot go speak with them, half-awake. They will have news from the village.* I draw a long, sharp breath and press it out. My ribs throb, faintly, the torchlight flickering again, fizzling, low. The air feels crisp, still heavy with night and the heat of the day long gone. *There cannot be many lots up, not with this silence pressing in. The night watches must still be here.*

I pull the door shut, step down the hall toward the meeting room. There are voices, faint, murmuring in the heaviness of the air. I slow by the door of the room, and the voices are louder, muffled by the wood between us.

I lift my fist, rap it lightly against the door. The voices do not stop, but there are less of them, steps moving closer. The door swings open, Havard behind it. His eyes are dark rimmed, but they are alert, not addled by sleep or the night watches. He inclines his head toward me. "Healer. You rose swiftly. Thank you." He steps to the side, his hand gesturing into the room. I step past him, into the smokey haze. There is a torch on the far side, burned low, sending the ring of choking smoke into the warmth of the small space. *My cloak is too heavy for this room. But I cannot take it off, with only my night shift on beneath it.* I purse my lips, turn my head toward the men.

Ciaran is standing, half-stooped over a table, speaking to Sradfaang in a low tone. The goblin is nodding, his arms folded, back against the wall, legs far out before him so that he is nearly at a height with the prince.

Lord Baldwin is watching me, his clothes still perfectly pressed, not a hair out of place, eyes calm. He inclines his head. "Eness Finch. It is good to see you again, though sooner than I had hoped. Will you have a seat while we speak? It is early yet."

I move over, lower myself onto the edge of the chair. Ciaran is speaking with Lord Baldwin, and the lord is nodding his head, eyes watchful, upward. He nods again, stepping backward. Ciaran turns to me. "We have told you that we had a plan in place, to protect those who would both be endangered and would endanger others in the event of trouble here. With the precarious nature of my standing in the country right now, it was necessary and has been in place since not long after I first arrived. It has been decided that it would be wisest for us to implement that plan, as soon as it can be arranged. There was some new information tonight that has made that action a matter to be dealt with swiftly."

My eyes half-burn. I flick them toward the goblin. "You spoke with the healing man?"

He nods. "Aye." He does not continue, offers nothing more.

The prince glances toward him, and at a movement of the goblin, continues, turning his eyes back to me. "There was a soldier. One from the night that you healed our men." My heart twists in my stomach. *Baldwin spoke of this possibility, this evening in the healing ward.* Ciaran continues, "From what Srad has gathered, he was in the trees above you, when the song was sung. He was only barely healed by your gift, but heard at least a fraction of your conversation with Srad and the others. He made his way to the village, wounded, and was cared for there until just after the healing man came to aid you. He left, when he heard you were wounded. We can assume from this, he will be spreading news of your gift." There is sorrow in his eyes, and mine are swirling, burning. I turn them away, turn them toward the floor. *Creator. Gót. Were the men that knew not enough, that I would be hunted now?* "Brunhild did not speak to him personally, but to the healing man of him."

I lift my head, and my throat is thick. "Will they not hunt you, if they know you have gone with me? The soldiers do not know yet who you are. I should go my own way. Would that not be the wisest plan, to keep them off your tail?"

Lord Baldwin steps forward, speaking. "I would see my prince traveling with the most skilled healer of our time, and even if the soldiers have not found out who he is, it will only be a matter of time. We will keep eyes on Brunhild's party when they leave, but there is little we can do to slow the spread of what she knows to the world."

Ciaran lifts his head. "I do not pretend that she is not selling what knowledge she has to both her government and ours. She will have it out, as soon as she is back in a location that she can bargain from. The higher-ups in Auvridal's military will know within a fortnight, if not sooner, that I am alive. It is you that will be running the risk by traveling with me. You will still be a myth, a hope in a legend. I am known and hunted. Would you travel with us?"

I fold my hands against the edges of my cloak. "Where can you go?"

He is watching me, eyes barely rimmed with red, but they are alert, guarded as they always are. "That I cannot say. It would be wisest for as few lots as possible to know where we are going until we are well outside of civilization, to minimize risk to all. Words travel. They can do nothing to Fitz and Tejan and those here if they cannot prove that you or I were ever here, but if it was known where we went, that would bring about consequences I would not like to think of. Where we go to is a place both remote and safe, if we can make it within its borders. That is why it is imperative that we leave swiftly, whether you come or not, to act before the soldiers reach here again."

I look down, grip my cloak between my fingers. My lungs ache, head swims with night. *There will be soldiers out, looking for the prince, others soon looking for me. I cannot go alone.* I look up at him, and my eyes are burning, churning. "Can you give me your word, that you will not cease to work to end the reach of your mother, while you are beyond it? I do not ask where we go, but I would have your word that it is not to run, but to continue somewhere without endangering others and yourself."

His eyes meet mine, and he bows. "You have my word." There is something faint behind his eyes—grief?

I shift my hands, nod my head. "When do you wish to depart? I will go, when you go."

Relief washes over Havard's face on the edge of my vision, matched by Lord Baldwin's, though it is calmer in his eyes. Ciaran inclines his head, acknowledgement in it. "So be it. We will leave within the next half-watch. Before the sun, if you are able to be ready by then. No one beyond this room will be aware, other than Tejan, who will help you ready yourself. She is already up. If there is anything you desire for the journey, you have only to ask."

I incline my head. "I will go then."

He inclines his head. "Iris has made you two travel gowns, to make the riding easier. I apologize again for the secrecy. Everything that can be told, I will tell you once we are on our way, safely far from these towns, but until then, I thank you for your trust."

I stand, tighten my shawl about me. "I gladly give it."

He inclines his head—respect and honor—and gestures towards the door. There is a softness in his gaze, that look almost like grief flashing through his eyes again, and it is gone.

Fitz steps forward. "Tejan is waiting for you in the sewing room. I trust you know your way there?"

I nod.

I turn and Lord Baldwin's eyes meet mine. He bows, his face solemn, but there is confidence in his gaze, pride, and my heart lightens. I incline my head toward him, and his hand reaches for the door, drawing it open before me. *We are going. Not to freedom, but to the wilds once more.*

I step into the silence of the halls.

Tejan's hand presses against my shoulder, gentle. "Supplies will be on the other horse." She steps forward. "Is there anything else you need? Oh! I nearly forgot." She stoops and turns back toward me, something large and leathered in her hands. *Boots.* They are simple, brown, and look soft to the touch. She smiles, offering them to me. "They will not be comfortable for the first few days. We ought to have had you start wearing them when Ciaran first decided you would be part of their party, if it ever came to this. It would have been wise, but it was not thought of, so we are here. And they are there, new and unworn and uncomfortable for you."

She places them in my hands. "The trail will be long. Wear these for a watch every day, to help your feet get used to them, before the days when they are needed. They will be painful at first, but you will regret it later if you do not. I do not know where he is taking you, but snow days may not be far off if it is north. Harvest is around the bend here, and I do not know whether he takes you North or South. Wherever you go, we will miss your presence here. Thank you for all that you have done for us."

I lift my head, "Thank you, Teja." I nod towards her, my eyes burning. "But you have done far more for me than I have for you. You and your husband both. I thank you for all that you have done. There will not be trouble for you, on account of our departure? Ciaran said the queen's men cannot touch you?"

She shakes her head. "We have weathered many a storm, and our family is of too high a standing to be taken down easily. There will be a stir, if anyone tries, and Georwyn's officers will not touch us without undeniable evidence. Do not trouble yourself. We are kept by the same God that keeps you. You must go now. I am late getting you to the men and they will be ready." She ushers me up the hall, slinging my bag over her shoulders. I adjust the boots in my hands, press my free hand against my side.

The skirts swish around my feet, heavy and full, fuller than any dress I have worn since I was a child, and they catch around my ankles. I tuck the boots under my arm. She pushes a door open into the hall beyond. I step through after her, and she is moving down the hall, her steps swift and certain, even. She pulls open the last door, and Sikkerhet is gone. *I am leaving, without saying farewell to anyone. They will not know that I have left. I will just be gone, when they look for me, at evening tide. Who will Tejan tell that I have gone, to pass ruse until the Menantians have left?* My eyes flicker up the hall, and there is no movement but Tejan's sure steps.

I step through the doorway, her hand leaving it to fall closed behind us.

The air is heavy on my skin, mist drifting faintly through the dark outlines of the trees, torch light orange against the wall of the stables. A horse snorts, stamping its foot, and the sound is echoed by another across the clearing. My eyes flicker to them. They are already saddled. Men are moving between them, figures faint, a torch held in one of their hands, illuminating his face. *Tollak.* He is giving orders, his voice a low rumble in the clearing. There are few other men here, men that I know.

Teja's eyes flicker toward me, and there is a man beside her, taking the bag from her with an inclination of his head, taking the boots from my hands. He turns away and is gone, his shape dark in the shadows of pre-dawn.

Teja half-smiles, reaching for my hand. She presses it, her grip firm and gentle. "May Elnial the Almighty bless you on your way and give you His joy. May He make your steps secure and your way straight and steadfast, that you may know the path which you should take, and may you return to the land of your fathers in joy, knowing peace in the work that only His hand can do. And may you have success in all your ways until you and I meet again, in this life, or the next." She bows, low—care and honor—and my eyes burn.

I lift my voice. "And may He add all and more to you, Tejan Jornamn. May Elnial go with you in all your ways, and keep you secure, and may He make and keep your home, until you and I meet again, in this life, or the next."

She smiles, faint in the darkness, and steps to the side, watching the men work around the horses. There is the signal of a hand, off to the left. *The sign to mount. The same used on the trail with the soldiers.* My throat is burning, air brushing with the warmth of a strálé night against my skin, and a firefly flickers, faint off in the trees.

A figure is moving toward us, his head up, gait fast, even. *Fitzclaste.* He smiles to his wife and she returns it, soft. He takes her hand, turning to me, his eyes only half-visible in the dancing torch shadows. "It is time to mount." He smiles, and it is only there in his eyes, the rest of his face soft shadow. "I am grateful to you, for the care you gave our people and home while you were here with us. May the Creator go with you as you take the roads, and may He give you rest at last with the healing of His hand." He inclines his head toward me—honor and respect—and turns, his hand extended toward me. "May I show you to your mount?"

His wife nods in my periphery, and I place my hand in his, his grip light. He turns, moving between the two horses on the end. One of them side steps, half a prance, and he clicks to it, not even shying away. I grimace, flick my eyes over my shoulder. *Where is Blåthjortt? I have not had time to go search for him in the stables, to ask of his coming. But they would surely not expect him to stay. Unless the way is unfit for a hound.*

I tilt my head back, Fitz's hand still steady around mine, leading me forward. There are shapes moving everywhere, growing in the flickering orange light, horse and man, and there is Tejan, giving soft instructions behind me. I whistle, low and sharp. There is a bark—something moves around the side of the fort, fast and blurred. It swings around a man's legs, tail wagging furiously, smacking at the legs of the horse beside him. *Blåthjortt.* My heart lightens. I whistle again, high, and he moves toward me, steps frantic, head held high. I smile, extend my hand.

Fitz's steps are slowing. "This is your mount, healer." His hand releases its grip on mine.

I turn toward him and incline my head, my hand brushing the top of the hound's head. Blatt's tongue swipes across my forearm, warm-damp trailing across my skin. I smile at Fitz, the pull of it faint on my lips. "Goodmorn, to you, Fitz."

He smiles, and the men are mounting, all on horses now. "And to you."

I plant my foot in the stirrup and swing my leg over, skirts moving easily, not catching like each time in the days coming here.

There is another hand signal before me, gold glinting off of a shoulder. My eyes snap forward, toward the figure. *Ciaran.* His head is lifted, hair bound back at the nape of his neck, gold around it, shining in the light of the torches. *He is wearing gold trim, this morn.*

A figure swings up beside him, tall, astride a dark horse that is larger than life. *Sradfaang. He will go with us, then.* My heart lightens. *Auvridal's hopes will be safer, with him with us.*

Ciaran shifts and he is moving forward, men filing in behind him, all dark figures I do not recognize. Blått's head bobs beside me, his steps easily matching the beginning paces of the horses into the darkness of pre-dawn.

XLVII

Light of the Road

The man beside me glances back, his face rose-colored in the light of the rising sun. He smiles, up toward the sky, something like wistfulness in his eyes for a moment and it is gone again. His curls brush backward in the wind, catching in the wisps of a beard along his jaw.

I glance out, over the side of the mountain. The ridges of the mountains are purple and pink, one rolling into another in line after line, ending only where the sky begins. *Sunrise.* The blue ridges of the mountains are quiet, only the sounds of morning in the trees. Saint John's wort dances sun gold beneath their branches, azaleas bobbing along above them, and there is a single chicory plant, the flower bright blue with morning.

The curly haired man glances back at me, the strands of his hair passing over his eyes for a moment in the gentle breeze. His eyes are still bright, still eager, his face barely scuffed with new growth. *The dazed soldier, from the healing ward.* He smiles at me. "Good morn to you. It's a fine day to start a travel, like this. A good omen, to crest the mountains at sunrise."

A smile tugs at my lips, and I let it. "I do not know that it is cresting a mountain, to walk here. There is still much mountain above us."

The edge of his lips quirk up, humor dancing in his eyes. "With a view like this, I'd say we can call it a crest. You can see seven mountain ranges from here at least. That's a view, if I've ever seen one. That's a crest, where I come from." He grins. "Though granted, we have few crests still above us, if you want to climb up shale."

I laugh, and Blått looks up at me, his head brushing against my foot. "A crest, then. What is your name, sonyá?"

He extends a hand toward me, shying his horse toward mine. I offer him my hand and he grips my forearm, a greeting of new friends. "I am Peren, of the fifth Mark."

I let go of his wrist, the horses plodding evenly beneath us. "Peren. I am Eness."

He inclines his head, acknowledgement. "And I am one of the soldiers who would not have been here, without your interference in the woodlands. It is an honor to ride with you, Eness of Sikkerhet."

A wry smile pulls at my lips and my heart dips. "It is an honor to ride with you, Peren of the fifth. But you need little speak of that." My eyes flicker over the other men. Ciaran is ahead, Ragnar not far in front of him, leading the party. *They both know of the song, if that is what he speaks of. Sradfaang will be behind, at the rear, as he has always done on the road in the days before we reached Sikkerhet and in the ride to find these men.*

There is a dark-haired slender man in front of Peren, with the bearing of a soldier. *He will be the third of their party, the third to be brought in. How did they decide they were trustworthy enough to let them take the road with us?*

Peren's eyes are on the mountains again and then there are trees, between us and them, and they are gone. I glance backward at them—wisps of pink clouds curl on the horizon.

Peren turns back toward me. "You have a fine horse." He nods to the mount beneath me.

I glance down at it, hold the reigns to the side. "If it is fine, I can take no credit for it. I did not choose it, nor could I have picked a good one if I had been given the option of any horse. I know little of them, or any animal."

He cocks his head at me, curls brushing across his eyes again, thick and pale brown. "Not any animal?" He makes a curious noise, under his breath. "I'd have thought a healer for a fortress would have known both animal and landlot. Did you not tend the livestock at Sikkerhet? If not you, then who?" He glances at Blått beside me, confusion in his features. "I did not think it big enough, to have two healers."

I shake my head. "I did not tend them. In truth, I could not tell you who did, but gòt. I only tended the landlots in my time there, which was brief."

He looks up at me, surprise flicking through his eyes. "You were not there long?"

I shake my head. "Gót. Only a little more than a moon longer than you." He looks forward, toward the figures ahead. *Toward Ragnar.* He turns back toward me, slowly. "Did you come then, for the same reasons as the others? To hide there from the Mark?" His eyes are earnest, intent.

What should be shared, with a man I barely know? With soldiers I will now be traveling with for unknown days? I incline my head, look ahead toward the men at the front. "For similar reasons, aye. Where were you serving, before you were taken in to Sikkerhet?"

He straightens, moving fluidly with his mount. *An experienced rider.* "We were merely a scouting party, newly transferred to the area. There had been some news of strange activity in these parts, so we were sent. More than that, I cannot say." He grins again, leaning to the side on his mount. *As though he does not fear falling.* "Though it was a fair sight that we were sent on that task. They thought it to be useless, but it got Ragnar and Nils to stop speaking about conspiracies in dark corners and start living in one, as you see now. Here we are, on the road."

I glance at him and he is straightening in his saddle once more, our horses turning along the cliffside with the road. "They spoke often of conspiracies, in the Mark?"

He shakes his head, face growing solemn. "Gót. Only when things were quiet and the other soldiers were far off, gambling and the like around camp. I was Ragnar's guard, so I was never far off. Nils is a lieutenant, so they spoke alone about many things to do with the Mark." He glances at me. "That is more than you need to know, I'd guess. My apologies, healer." He nods backward, his expression regretful. He looks forward. "Do you know the other men, traveling in this party?"

I glance over my shoulder. Sradfaang's eyes meet mine. He lifts an eyebrow, expression blank. I turn my eyes toward the other men. There are two of them, their heads turned toward the forests, one of them speaking in an animated tone, his hands waving all directions as he speaks. I can see little of the other man behind him, other than his nearly shaved head. *I have never seen a man's hair cut so close to his skull.* I turn forward. *They are not familiar, either of them. But I must have seen them before, unless they came with Lord Baldwin last eve.* I shake my head. "Gót. I have never spoken with them. Where were you kept in the halls, during your stay?"

He lifts a brow. "I thought you should know as well as I did. It was a room in the back, under the stairs that lead skyward. It was a room without window or light. A prison of sorts. Fitting for Ragnar. That man could sleep for a whole moon if left alone."

My eyes half-burn. I bite it back, turn my gaze toward the ground. *The space behind the stairs leading to the upper level of Sikkerhet. That was only a hallway away from the healing ward. They were kept so close?* There is a glimmer of blue, another chicory bloom on the edge of the path. *I did not know Sikkerhet so well as I should have, for being there through all those days.* "You are thankful to be out?"

He grins, shifting his reins to his other hand. "Aye. Quite thankful. I've missed the light of day. And the mounts. I had a beautiful one, a glossy mare, the night of the ambush. She should never have been a military mount that one, but out in the fields to roam and raise her own foals. A beautiful mare. A mane like fire."

The slender dark-haired man—Nils—tilts his head back in front of us, speaking over his own forehead. "You think every horse is too good for the ranks. If it was up to you, we'd all be walking and you'd have a farm somewhere as overrun with horses as the North Banks of the sea is with selkie."

Peren grins, shaking his head. "Your poor sod of a mount fits right in with the ranks, thank you. She is as much a soldier as you are. Even has the same face."

Nils grunts, looking forward again. "Looks more like you than me, with that posture. Watch her gait a moment and see who she looks more like."

Peren laughs, throwing his head back, and it is sudden and loud. "I'd say her nose favors yours more than mine, though I'd grant the trot. It's even set at the same angle. You could pass for siblings in a marketplace on a warm day."

One of the men behind us laughs, sharply, the sound rough and muffled. "He's got you there."

Peren grins, and Nils shakes his head, turning forward again. A faint smile pulls at my lips. *There will not be silence on the road, not today. But there may be, in the days to come, if there is trouble at our heels, as there is expected to be.* I glance forward, at the prince. *How quickly are they expecting trouble to find us?*

And how fast will our steps have to be, to keep ahead of it?

XLVIII

Campfire Talk

Vidar is moving on the far side of camp, his hair cut strangely short, and its color cannot be told by daylight. Tonight, it looks faintly red. He nods his head toward Ciaran, the thick scars along his jaw glinting in the firelight. Ciaran says something more and settles against a tree, listening to something the other man is saying. I turn away, toward the pot hanging over the flames. Steam curls up from it, blending with the wisps of smoke. Blått's head presses against my side. I run my hand along his head, grip a cloth from my pocket. I grab the pot, lift it from over the flames. "Would any of you care for a tisane, tonight? The water is warm now."

Nils looks up from beside a tree, Peren at his back. Firelight flickers across his face for a moment, turning it all angles in the shadows. He inclines his head, Peren mirroring the movement behind him. "Aye."

I glance behind me, at Sradfaang and Ragnar. Their eyes are on the forest, Sradfaang's hands working over a sword blade. *Not his. It is not the massive blade he wielded more than two moons ago, on the road.* I glance at the ground. His blade is leaning upon his saddle, at his feet, stretching out to the roots of the tree beside him.

Ragnar looks up at me. "Aye. I'd take some. If you are not one to put bitter roots in it."

I shake my head, smile. "Gót. That is saved for sickness. This one will be mild." I pour the water into the waiting mugs, and there is a figure beside me, movements fluid and carefree - Baard. His face is all edges, eyes soft, as they have been all day, unreadable and easy.

He crouches, drawing mugs from the bag beside me, setting them out on the earth. "How many do you need, healer?"

I draw back the pot, cut off the stream of water. "If Ciaran and Vidar will take some, then there will be seven. I do not imagine the goblin will take any."

He lifts a brow, setting out two more mugs beside him. "Does the Goldtide have something against tea?"

There is a snort across camp, from Sradfaang. He glances at Baard, hand still working a cloth over the sword blade. "The rest of the Goldtide does what they will. I do not care for mixtures of herbs that I cannot speak to."

Ragnar laughs, a short, high laugh. "If you died of not being able to tell the difference between the scent of chamomile and stronger herbs, you deserve to go."

Sradfaang lifts a brow at him, his lips curling into a smile in the firelight. He inclines his head. "If I died of that, you would be correct. However, I have made it my policy to not drink unknown blends of anything. I will not be breaking that tonight." He turns away, back toward the trees, eyes outward. *On watch.*

I crouch beside the steaming mugs, pull the bag of herbs from my pocket. Baard is watching, his hands relaxed and idle between his knees. I flip the bag open, dust out a pinch of herbs. Baard's eyes flick upward, watching something across camp. *Watching the prince.*

Ciaran is moving, his conversation with Vidar over. He lifts his head, glancing across the camp toward the goblin. "Srad. Is the area clear?"

Sradfaang lifts his head, lifting the sword by the blade. He turns toward Ciaran. "I neither hear nor smell anyone nearby. It is clear, but for us."

Ciaran nods, turning toward the circle of firelight. He leans back against the tree behind him once more, crossing his legs at his ankles. "You all will have questions, after being pulled from your beds during the dark watches. Today, the chances of altercations were small enough, this close to Sikkerhet, that it seemed best to wait until we could stop to answer your questions and speak of the roads ahead."

The soldiers have snapped to attention, the other two men relaxed in their posture beside them: Vidar with his arms folded, scarred like his face, and Baard beside me, still crouching, relaxed. Ciaran continues. "We will not speak of this again after tonight, so if you have questions, I would bid that you ask them. The risk of others on the road will grow as we continue."

There is silence for a moment. Blått drops to the ground beside me, curling up beside the flames.

Ciaran speaks again. "My mother or one of her generals will already have men on the roads after us. They will be alerting outposts to be on the watch for me. For that reason, we chose mostly soldiers, for the skills each of you possess, as well as for the tale we are spinning. They will not be looking for other soldiers on the road." He shifts his shoulders, and the gold trim along them glints in the light. "While traveling, if there is an altercation, we will attempt to solve it by words first. We do not need to alert the whole of the queen's army where we are. Taking up swords against any of them will do so. Sradfaang and I will speak first. I will be going by Captain Saar, but the rest of you will be able to use your own names. None of you are high enough rank to be easily recognized. If you see someone you know, any of you, you may break form and start speaking to the hound. That will alert the rest of us."

Ragnar looks up. "What reason do we have to believe that we will be hunted? I and my men will be guilty of desertion, but that will not be enough to make them send out forces, and unless the lady sent out a message while she was still within Sikkerhet, the Menantians cannot have gotten word out to send a party after us so fast. I understand the danger of being caught, but do not understand how we could be hunted so soon, lord."

Sradfaang inclines his head. "One of your soldiers escaped." Ragnar's face pales. Sradfaang continues. "The night that you were caught and taken in, there was a soldier in the woods, whom we can assume knows Ciaran's identity and will have sent others after us. You know the other secrets he will have heard while he was there."

Peren stands. "Which of them was it, sonyá?"

Ciaran shakes his head. "The bodies had been taken and damaged by animals by the time we found them. We did not attempt to have you identify them or confirm whether or not any were missing for that reason. Every hand was needed that night to get the wounded back to the fort."

Ragnar shakes his head. "How long ago did we learn of this?"

"Last night." Ciaran's voice is even. "Brunhild spoke of it in our meeting. Our steps will be taken with care. For now, while time is on our side, we will take the most direct route to our destination, keeping away from cities and towns when it is possible. We will act as any partial mark. In the event that we are met, the three of you who are not military will keep your heads down and act the part of those hired by the military. Eness has done it before, as well as Baard, and Sradfaang tells me that Vidar looks the part of a guide. That is the role he will play." He turns toward Vidar. "You will ride at the front with me, for the next few days at least." He glances at Baard. "Baard. You will be our scout. I have heard of your skill with the bow. That may be needed, in the time to come. You will ride ahead to alert us of bands and parties on the roadways."

Silence falls. The fire crackles, Ciaran's eyes every man for a moment. He inclines his head. "To the eyes of everyone on the road, we will be as any military band. Commoners will fear us, and anyone within the Mark will not question us with a Knoc'gnori in our company. We will travel fast and light, as we have begun, and will speak only to those that need requires. What questions do you have?"

There is silence again.

Ciaran inclines his head once more. "Thank you, then. The road will be long. We made good time today. Tomorrow, let us put more distance between us and those that would track us down." He inclines his head, moving to the side of the tree, and sits down against it. Blått stands and pads toward him, dropping to the ground at his feet.

I lift the mug from before me, light from the flames glittering on the dark surface. Baard lifts two other cups, inclining his head toward me, and he steps off, toward Ragnar. I glance toward the prince. *He is in the open, now. No longer hiding. And yet not running.*

Auvridal's hopes and dreams ride with him, to fear and cowardice or to a hope for tomorrow.
 Or to death. If he falls on the open road, the work they claim to have done will fall with him. Will men follow a cause, without a man to stand at its head?
 Will the men of Auvridal follow a man who works in shadows, who has worked in shadows since he was said to have betrayed his country, or fallen to the men who rise against it? He runs his hand over my hound's head, a small book in his other, hardly the size of his palm. Sradfaang drops down beside him, and asks a question, his voice low. He flashes a sign with his hand, two symbols, fast and sharp. Ciaran's eyes are forward, on the ground, as though he did not see, but his hand forms a sign over Blått's head -, three, small and close together, but clear and there.
 They speak in hand signs among their own men.
 What man, who trusts them, does that?
 What do they hide, that they would not even risk a whisper being overheard by those that travel with them?

•▶|◀▶|◀▶|◀▶|◀▶|◀▶|◀•

The horse jolts beneath me, stumbling. She whinnies, a soft, high sound, her head tossing. *Irritation.* I purse my lips and she starts forward again, her head low, close to the hound prancing beside her.
 Peren lifts a brow beside me. "Tricky one?" I glance at him, tilt my head. He laughs. "Tricky horse? She seems to stumble a lot."
 I half-smile. "I think that is more due to error of the rider than anything of the horse."
 He grins, shaking his head, and his curls shift brushing across his ears. "I was surprised not to have run into you ever back at the fort. I never got to thank you properly for saving our lives. I should have done it yesterday, on the road. But it is strange to be speaking to you, after I have faint memories of your work that night."

I half-smile, and the horse stumbles again. I grimace, shift my weight in the saddle. The men around us are quiet, eyes on the road, on the woods. I glance back at Peren, keep my gaze half on the trees. *Is there trouble, today, that they would watch so closely?* "I was not on my feet for a time, after Ragnar was released from custody. I assume you were not released before him, given all that happened."

He lifts a brow, the arch of it nearly vanishing beneath his hair. "All that happened? Your wound and the lady? I saw the way she watched you, the first time she saw you in the great hall. I do not know what she wanted of you, but I would not have liked to have had a long chat with her. I've met bush vipers that seemed more pleasant."

A smile twists my lips. "Aye. My wound and the lady." I look back at him. "Did you serve long in the queen's army, before you were taken?"

A wry smile tugs at his lips. "Gót. No more than six moons. Fresh blood, I'd guess. A green sapling barely up in the world. Now I'd wager I'll never make even private now." He smiles again, a dry smile. "Do you think they'll put up a reward for the return of a recruit deserter? I doubt they'd make it worthwhile for anyone to haul me in at least, if I am ever caught." He looks away, toward the woods.

The horse shifts under me, stumbling again—I grunt, my hand flailing for the reins. My side aches for a moment, and it is gone. "Did you look forward to being a private?"

He smiles softly, his eyes flickering back to mine. "Aye. I looked forward to proving to the skikes in my regime that I wasn't chopped curds. The recruits in my mark were a scraggly lot of horse burrs. I doubt most of them would make private if they were not desperate for recruits, as they are now."

I grip the saddle horn with my rein hand. The horse glances back at me with a single eye, plodding on. "Are recruits usually sent out for patrols? Do they not train for their first turnings, before they are sent out to any task?"

He looks at me and snorts. "Not hardly. Training ended moons ago. Do you not have family in the military?"

My eyes half-burn—I look away. His face is quiet, question light-hearted, guileless. *He does not know of my heritage yet. Nor of my song.* He thanked me only for saving him as a healer. I shake my head, force a smile to my lips. "Gót. I have no close relatives in this world. They have all passed on to Glory. Is the Mark so desperate that they would put unqualified men into the ranks?" Nils' gaze flickers to me behind Peren, barely a glance. *He is listening.* I turn my gaze ahead.

Peren straightens, an apology written in his eyes. He inclines his head sharply—regret. "I am sorry, healer. I did not realize or I would not have spoken."

I shake my head. "You meant nothing harmful by asking. It was many turnings ago now. You have little to apologize for." I turn my eyes toward the road, toward Peren again. "Do you have family, back home?"

He grins. "Aye. Two sisters and their families, and my fár. He is an aging man now, with scars from the Guard."

I smile. "Which guard?"

He turns his head away, out toward the trees. "The Guard." *The king's guard?*

Baard's voice cuts out from ahead, even and calm. "Traveling band ahead. Seven of them." Silence falls, and my horse stumbles again, snorting. I glance down at her. She is watching me with one eye, the other one on the road.

I turn toward Peren. "Your father served in the king's guard?"

He glances back at me, and away again, his smile gone. "I should not have spoken of it. I am sorry. I forget that outside the Mark, the guard is not often well thought of."

I incline my head. "I understand why there would be uncertainty about the guard, after what happened fifteen turnings ago, but I do not understand why the Mark would be any different. Do the Mark think differently about that night?"

Ragnar's voice cuts from behind me. "The Mark understands that you cannot always stop what happens to your charge. Even the best soldiers fail. Most folk outside the Mark do not understand that."

Peren inclines his head back toward Ragnar, respect. "Most of the Mark still honor and respect the queen's guard. It is an honor to have a father who served in it. My family has served for generations. My village was mostly those that served or had served in the queen's Mark. There was nothing that could have been done that night, to stop what happened. The Maa'eulé were prepared, with fire and instruments of war. They knew what they were about, and the Guard was unprepared. That is not the message that many believe, not anymore. Some even say the Guard was involved. I forget, when I am with soldiers, that you will not all be of a mind with me."

He glances at me. "I do not know where you come from, healer. But I imagine that will not have been the story you heard, if you were far enough away from the capital. My father fought with the Guard that night. Many men died, before they apprehended those fians. There was nothing they could have done that they did not do, but that was not the word that was spread. Not to the villages."

There are footfalls ahead—the sound of more horses on the road, approaching. A figure rounds the turn ahead, on horseback: a man. He is a short man, a half-hearted beard upon his face. He draws his horse toward the side of the road, bowing toward Ciaran and Vidar at the front. His head inclines, low, too low. A woman rounds the corner behind him, a child in her arms. She clicks to her mount, nudging it quickly to the side, and Ciaran keeps his eyes ahead, on the road. The woman's eyes are wide, fear in them, fear in the eyes of the man behind her, bowing toward each man in turn, toward me, twice. *Does he think I am a noble, that he would bow so often to me?* They pass by, silent, still bowing, and the pattering of their hooves fades out into the distance again.

The first roadside party, passed by.

I lift the spoon, tap it against the side of the pot. Something thuds to the ground beside me—my eyes snap over to it. Baard glances up at me, grinning. He half-bows. "Healer. I thought you might need bowls to go with that stew. It smells more pleasant than a thousand flowers."

Nils snorts behind him, his hands slowing on the surface of a saddle. "Flowers do not smell pleasant to a hungry man. You would think that grit smells good right now."

Baard laughs, kneeling beside the bag. "Quite so, but I have rarely smelled something so heart-gladdening as this stew. I take it that it will be ready soon."

I incline my head, turn back toward the pot. The fire licks around it, a carefully groomed flame, the work of Vidar. I glance at Baard. "It is ready now. If you will hand me a bowl, you may take it back to your seat, full."

Baard grins, standing, a stack of bowls held in only one hand. "Serve them all at once. I will take mine in a moment, when all are done."

I half-smile, incline my head. I set the spoon on the edge of the pot, draw the ladle from my pocket. My eyes flicker up, ladle slipping beneath the surface of the stew. It is watery for stew. *Not enough time to thicken, but evening is gone, night closing in, and they are tired. It was a long day, to wait longer now.*

Ragnar is on the far side of the fire, arms loaded with wood. He stoops, the wood clattering to the earth, branches tumbling over each other. He straightens, brushing the dust and bits of moss and branches from the front of his tunic. His eyes flicker up, land on the bowls in Baard's hand. They brighten. "It is ready then." There is relief in his tone.

I smile, lift the ladle, Baard's hand shifting the bowl closer to me. I take it, pour the stew in it, and steam swirls into the light of the fire, white above the flames. "It is."

I offer the bowl to Baard, and he shakes his head. "Pass it to the lieutenant commander. I will take mine when they are all served."

My eyes flicker over, following his gesture to Ragnar. *Is Ragnar's rank so high?* I lift the bowl to him, over the pot. He takes it, a smile across his features. "Thank you, Eness." He inclines his head toward the man beside me. "Baard." He turns away, moving for the trees.

I dip the ladle, lift it, pour another bowl. *He is an officer. I had not heard his title before, his rank. He carries himself like one, though not with the presence of the captain, or Sradfaang. He does not move like a man who is merely a soldier. I should have seen that before, back at the fort, in the healing rooms. There is confidence in his steps that is not matched in Nils or Peren or the soldiers before this.*

Peren is dragging himself up from the ground, Vidar already on his feet, moving toward the flames. I offer him a bowl and he takes it, inclining his head. I turn back to the fire, take another empty bowl from Baard. The wood of it is smooth beneath my skin, cool. I lift the ladle, turn, and Nils is beside me, waiting, his hands behind his back, posture sharp. *Like a soldier, and not an officer. Did they serve under the lieutenant commander, or were they part of a larger Mark?*

I offer him the bowl, and he inclines his head, shoulders barely relaxing as he takes it. He sniffs at it, straightening. He sniffs at it again. "Thyme." He smiles. "You have used thyme in it, and something else. Where did you gain some?"

I half-smile. "Aye. Garlic, thyme, and rosemary. I found a cluster of it in the woods when we stopped at midday. Are you fond of the herb?"

He inclines his head. "No stew is as good as it could be without it. I am grateful you found some. It was lacking in the halls of Sikkerhet." He inclines his head again, moving away. A wry smile twists at my lips. *I did not notice it lacking in Nellie's stews. Nor did I look for its presence.*

I shake my head, offer the bowl in my hand to Peren. He turns, moving back to the far side of the camp, his eyes on the woods. *He will be on watch, then. He and Sradfaang. Always Sradfaang.*

The prince steps up beside me, his eyes flickering down to mine. He inclines his head, the brush of a smile on his lips, his eyes on the food now, like any other man. I turn my head away, lift a bowl from Baard's hand. "Lord Ciaran." I lift the ladle, my face strangely warm. "Would you like stew?"

He inclines his head again. "I would, but you may take your own, Eness. I can serve mine. Thank you for making it tonight. You do not have to serve us like this on the road."

I shake my head, turn toward him, the bowl in my hand, and my eyes meet his. "It is no trouble. It will only take a breath longer to get mine and today's riding was long. You may take your rest."

His eyes meet mine, brow lifting, just barely. "And when will you take yours? You rode with us on that ride today, and have worked to tend this since then. I will serve mine, if you will allow me. Take your seat."

My face warms. I look away, toward the fire. "It was little enough trouble. It is good to tend something after being on the horse so long." I offer the bowl to Baard, take the last two still empty from his hand. He takes it without a word, turning away. I grip the ladle, pour the stew into the bowl on top. I turn toward the prince, offering the filled bowl. He does not take it, does not lift it from my hands.

"Take it, healer. I will tend mine."

I purse my lips, meet his gaze. *What noble chooses not to be served?* I look away. "The stew will have to come off the fire. I will sit when that is done. It is no trouble." He takes the bowl from the top, and I turn back, dunk the ladle back in and pour mine. The prince is not moving, has not turned away from beside me, standing still. I set the ladle on its hook upon the rack and reach my hand down, toward the cloth hanging from my skirt pocket.

Something reaches past me—Ciaran's arm. His hand grips the pot, lifting it from the fire, the glove between his skin and the hot metal. I grip the cloth useless in my hand, and he turns, setting the pot upon the stump beside me, steam curling gold into the darkness. He glances at me, bowing—respect and care. "It is finished, then. Will you take your seat?"

My face is warm, the bowl hot against my fingers. "Aye." I keep my eyes away from his, bow my head. "Thank you, lord." He inclines his head, stepping away toward the far side of the fire.

My eyes swirl, twisting with color, and I do not know what they will tell. I turn away, toward the fallen tree, only a step away. The goblin is still watching, his eyes on the forests, a bowl in his hand.

Nils is across from him, on the far side of the flames from him, his eyes outward, his legs crossed, head up. *Two men on watch at all times.* A shudder creeps up my spine. I glance at the prince. He is speaking with Ragnar, the tones of his voice low, the bowl in his hand.

A stick snaps in the forest. Sradfaang lifts his head calmly. "There are men about. Keep your weapons at hand."

I drop against the ground. Ciaran lifts his head, the bowl still held in his hand, but there is a sword beside him now, laying near his grasp. "How many?" His voice is low, even.

Sradfaang's eyes are on the woods. "Two. There were three a moment ago, but one has left." He shifts his leg, propping it up before him. "One has left. I doubt they will challenge us." He lifts his hand, his bracelet glinting in the light of the fire.

XLIX

The Horse Plains

Nils' eyes are on the fields, the heads of wheat shifting with the wind, still green. His gaze flickers across the field and back to where it ends in old oaks, head held high. Ragnar is before him, his back straight, eyes scanning. I flick my gaze out over the fields. The men are silent, silent as they have been since yesterday's dawn.

There is a figure ahead, riding toward us, his horse moving quickly. *Baard.* He reins his horse up short, before the prince. Srad-faang moves his horse forward, around the outskirts of the road, to the front. The prince inclines his head. "What is it?"

Baard swipes sweat from his neck. "Nothing urgent. But if there is another road to be taken, we might take it now." He shifts his horse to the side, its feet prancing, restless. "I spoke to a woman a minute ago, who asked me about myself when I slowed to let you catch up. She spoke of many things, before she left. The one that stuck with me the most was that she said its been busier here of late. There is an outpost being reestablished after orders from their duke. This road has become a common one for soldiers." He bows. "If we are looking to avoid conversing with them, this will not be the path."

Ciaran wheels his horse around, his eyes moving to the goblin. "Do you know anything of this, Srad?"

The goblin's eyes are tight. "I do not. But Novik is a friend to Georwyn, as you know. He would build a hundred forts if it would solidify his place in court." He shakes his head. "I would take the road up through Rhtith if we can. This corner of Tokhápenah will be no friend to us, if he has invited more soldiers. We are too far from the cities to not stand out to soldiers. They will begin speaking of us, if we meet many bands. I do not like the idea of that kind of trail."

Ciaran inclines his head. "Then we will make for the west." He turns his mount back, starting up the road again, his pace easy, Vidar falling in line beside him.

Ragnar's jaw is tight. He flicks his gaze toward Sradfaang, and their eyes meet. Something passes between them, and Sradfaang looks away, his expression grim.

My eyes burn. I turn away, toward the roads. A bird calls out overhead, joined by another, and there is a cloud of them rushing by— blackbirds in the oak trees.

•▶|◀▶|◀▶|◀▶|◀▶|◀▶|◀•

Fields stretch out before us, grasses rolling in a wave under the winds of the plains beneath the clear sky. The grasses sway and the air is sweet, sweet with strálé, flowers dotting between the stalks stretching out toward the blue sky. I shift on my horse, and it steps sideways, the pace slowed for a moment.

There is a whistle, clear, loud and sharp. My head whips back. Peren lifts his head, whistling again, the same high call, his hair catching in the breeze, throwing unruly curls back from his brow. He grins, his eyes on the plains.

Baard swears, his eyes bright. *Angered.* "You didn't need to go startling the world like that." His voice is sharp. Vidar's brows are drawn low over his eyes, and in the sunlight there is red stubble all along his face where his beard should be. Now there are only traces of it, like the hair on the top of his head, marred by scars and barely there. His eyes are scanning the fields sharply.

Peren shakes his head, and my heart is slowing in my chest. My horse steps to the side, nervous. Peren smiles at the plains again. "My hometown was near these plains. It is a good omen, to whistle out a call to the wild steeds of Eronil, before you enter the Horse Plains. A good omen and a good word that we mean no harm to those that live within them. If we mean to seem as travelers, this is the way of it, to call out a greeting before we enter."

Nils' horse is moving up, beside the curly-haired man, his face dry. "And if anyone has been following us these last days other than the Wandering Men, then they know exactly where we are now."

Peren shakes his head. "We have not covered our tracks. If anyone has been following us, they do not need my help to know where we are. They will already know."

Sradfaang clicks to his horse, his head high above the others on top of the great black steed. "They would already know where we are. Covering tracks would slow us down by days." He whistles, high and clear, a strange call that curls with the grasses, blending with the rolling of the winds over the hills to where it ends in the tree line. A smile brushes his lips, a half-smile, and his horse is starting forward again, through the others that step easily out of the way of the massive beast. *Is there no need for caution, then?*

I frown, press my horse forward, after Nils. Sradfaang's horse is beautiful among the grasses, its head high, long black coat draping its hooves and flanks, brushing against each blade of grass and each small flower.

A call sounds, out over the plains. A whistle, off in the distance. The horses snort, prancing sideways, their heads all up, alert.

Peren grins beside me, his eyes fierce, bright. "The Horse Call. They heard the goblin. They responded." His grin widens.

My eyes flicker out toward the plains, burn, my horse dancing sideways, her head thrown high. "Who heard him?"

He grins, eyes flickering toward me. "The horses of Eronil. Eusebus's offspring. The white horse of the Seven Stars. These are their fields." He clucks to his mount, moving forward, after the goblin. My eyes burn, a shiver crawling up my spine. My eyes flicker over the fields. They are quiet, winds rustling through the grasses, the plains still silver-green with the fullness of the season of growth.

My horse moves into them, the seed heads colliding with the side of my boot, thumping rhythmic with each step of the horse. I glance upward, toward the open blue sky. There is a dot sailing through them, its wings barely arched. *A buzzard.* The bird circles, a wide arch, high above our path through the open plains, its wings glinting silver and black in the light of the sun.

Vidar snorts, moving his horse ahead. "A vulture and a call to let all who live here know there are travelers. I thought the goblin wiser than that. A good omen, aye." He snorts again, shaking his head, and his horse trots past mine, back to the front lines.

L

Vidar

Leather creaks, metal taps, horse hooves clattering against the ground. Dust curls up, around the steps of the horse before me, each one knocking against stone beneath the dust and dirt. Vidar's head is down, dust curling around him.

Leather creaks, metal tapping, horse hooves clattering against the ground. I lift my head, press my hand against my ribs. I half-loosen my arm, flick my eyes toward the men ahead. All of them have their heads up, watching the road in all directions, except Ragnar, whose eyes are ahead, always ahead. The air is sweltering against my skin.

Leather creaks, metal tapping, horse hooves clattering against the ground. My throat is thick, dust heavy on my lips. *We have been silent for more than a watch.* The men's eyes are above, watchful but vacant, tired, though we are only a watch and a half into the day.

Leather creaks, metal tapping, horse hooves clattering against the earth. Someone hums out a note, a single sound.

The note sounds again, a little stronger. Baard glances up, his face focused, dust curling up, clinging to the sweat on his skin. He smiles, humming again, a song I've heard before. He glances at me and speaks, his voice quiet. "If we're being traveling soldiers, we might sing a little. They do." He hums again, the note high and even. *Off tune.*

Sradfaang snorts, behind him. "I've heard hunting calls with more of a tune than the noise you just made."

Baard half-laughs, glancing back at the goblin. "You want I should try to compete with them?"

Sradfaang shakes his head, his eyes going back to the trees.

Vidar speaks ahead, and Ragnar laughs, a snort of a laugh, but there, and they are speaking again, voices quiet but present in the dryness of the day, with the leaves rustling in the winds and the leather still creaking beneath the dust of the road.

•▶|◀▶|◀▶|◀▶|◀▶|◀•

I turn toward the pots, my eyes flickering over the camp. Nils' arms are already half-full of firewood, his head bowed beneath the branches of a tree, and he vanishes behind it. I turn, move toward a bucket.

"Healer." *Ciaran's voice.* I turn toward him. He is still moving, lifting a saddle from the horse beside him. "Take someone with you. It's a long walk to the stream. Vidar can be spared from the camp to go."

I incline my head, turn. Vidar is behind me, setting down the woven saddle of Sradfaang's massive horse. He glances up and moves away, snatching up all three buckets in one hand. He turns back, nodding at the prince, and starts down the slope, off into the trees. I start after him.

He ducks under a tree, glancing back at me. His face is half-lit in the faint blue of dusk, all ridges. His steps are long, fast, his movements a harsh thing, not like the grace of the goblin or the prince, nor the practiced steps of a soldier. He ducks under a branch, knocking it to the side with a bucket. I pause, and the branch swings back into place and past it, swaying. It brushes against my skin. I duck around it, needles of the pine catching in my braid.

"Healer." Vidar looks back at me, only halfway once more. "How did you come to be out here, with this lot, and why does the queen want your head? Fian blood?"

My eyes burn. I grab my skirts, pull them away from the branches of a thorn bush, and my eyes flick upward. The man is walking, his gaze on the trail, double-bucketed arm steady beside him, moving around branch, brush, and stone. I swallow. "Do you guess, or do you know what you guess at, sónya?"

He glances back at me, sharply. "I thought I might have heard the like. But I could never be sure. There were many stories told, under breaths, many different things said of you, in corners and by the women. One of my men back at the Safe Haven had a son who liked to speak of you." *Jørn. It will have been him.*

I incline my head, step around a branch. *He had men, who served under him?* "I would have thought they would have found better things to speak of quickly. I was not there long. Were you there many turnings?"

He starts around a bolder, his movements sharp again. "Three."

I glance up. *So long?* "What drove you to it? To go to that place?"

He shifts the buckets in his hands, a smile flashing across his face, sharp, almost feral. "I said the queen was unjust the way she taxed and murdered without trial. And the queen had my home and family burned. Or one of her officers did."

My eyes sting, shift. "And you escaped?" My voice is soft. The trees shift, throwing shadows across the earth, green in the underbrush.

He glances back at me, eyes still sharp, though the feralness is gone, not a trace of bitterness in them beneath the trees. There are faint lines I did not see there before, in a glimpse of light, white across his forehead. Praor marks. *Nelöhrra.*

His head shakes. "Gòt. I was stabbed and left for dead, on the outskirts of the city." He starts forward again. "I was found, brought into a home for a season, and then taken to Sikkerhet by one of Fitzclaste and Tejan's sons. He found me there, on his travels, though I am suspicious that they were told to go find me by their informants." He steps down the slope. "My family's blood is on my hands, for my words. But I will one day have the queen's for hers."

My stomach drops. I shove a branch away from my eyes, the edges of it swiping my skin. "You would kill your monarch, cut her down, for what she has done? Why then are you here and not with the men who would attain that end faster? If you seek her death, you might have joined the Maa'eulé. They fight to that end."

He glances back at me, a wry grin flashing across his features, faint. It is gone again, with the blue shadows of the growing night. "I ought not to have spoken rashly." He turns away, holding a branch back for me to pass under. I duck under, and he speaks. "I would not spill her blood, not when I know all who are fighting to put this kingdom to rights again. Not when I know who her son is. I trust him far too much for that, to take this in my own hands. What he says will be done, and I will not hinder it, not for all these lands. I should not have spoken as I did just now. It was rash. If he were not here, then aye. I might. I might do far worse."

My lips tighten. I shake my head. There is the sound of trickling water, through the trees, faint still. "You would put away bitterness, for loyalty to him?"

He looks back at me, and there is the stream, glinting behind him, the sound louder now. He slows. "I put away my bitterness because bitter men tear worlds down. No justice will be served by chasing it. Our country had best learn that before it finishes tearing itself apart. I spoke in bitterness now, but I will put it away for him. I would follow that man to the ends of the earth, if he asked me to." He glances at me. "Why do you carry bitterness against her? Was it at her hands that your family passed?"

I purse my lips. "I do not carry bitterness toward her for any wrong that was done against me or anyone that I know, but for wrongs done against her own people. My family did not die at her hands. I would hold her accountable for the actions she has done, in word and deed. Whether that be, in the end, to the sword or gallows, I do not know. I have not known the prince long enough to be sure of him, nor have I known long enough of the hope of a man who might could take the throne after her. My mind was only to make peace in pockets until her reign ended."

He lifts a brow. "You speak then as I do. But without the turnings of knowledge to learn what kind of man you hope in." His eyes quiet. "How did they die, Song Weaver?"

My throat tightens. I lift my skirts, step around a stone. "A wagon roll, hills that were too wet, and a får that was ambitious. The queen's doings were only wrapped up in the reason they were there and not in our own home, and that was a fight that was seasons old, even then."

His eyes are on mine, face solid, expression faint in the shadows, and there is quiet but for the flowing of the stream. He lifts a brow. "I thought you fought against her for your families' deaths. Do you not blame her then, for that and for your hiding, all those seasons, to keep your song hidden? I assume that was the largest reason you hid."

My jaw tightens. I force my eyes to stay calm, stay gray. *He is looking now, watching.* There is a pool of light on my skin, from the periwinkle sky above. "What do you know of songs, that would cause someone to hide their life away?" *Did not Ciaran and Fitz say it was to be kept secret, from those who did not need to know?*

He smiles, a sharp-edged smile. It softens, and he turns, dunking the buckets into the running water. He pulls one out again, grunting, his arm straining against the current of the stream for a moment. "I was there, that night. That was one of the reasons I was chosen. That and that I might be recognized. I was from not far from the fort. The soldiers near it might have known me, so I am here, guarding my prince, and no longer hiding. It was a fair trade."

He grins again, pulling the bucket from the stream. He glances at me, inclining his head. "The men were right about you. They all were. They said you were quiet steel. I did not believe them until now." He draws the last bucket out and turns. I grab the handle of the one nearest me, the water still faintly swirling, casting glints of light off into the shadows of the forest floor.

I glance at him. "And Ciaran? What have they said about him, the men who know him, know his heritage?"

He turns back up the slope, buckets in his hands. "You will have time to gather your own knowledge and words about the prince in the days to come, to add to the ones you will have heard back in Sikkerhet. I am glad to have you with us, if only so that you are not there, a temptation to any soldiers that catch wind of the rumors about the pale-haired healing woman, with life in her song." His shoulders sway, buckets balanced perfectly in his hands, his head dodging between the branches of the trees.

I swallow hard. "If they catch wind of it, will it be enough, to not find me there, to keep them from tearing it apart?"

He glances back at me, eyes gone beneath the shade of the evergreen. "It may be. But if you want the truth, it will depend on who their captain is. Soldiers are only as good as their leader." He steps up the slope, the snapping of fire the only sound from the growing circle of light above.

LI

Night Songs

Ragnar looks up, his movement different, almost sharp. My eyes flicker off into the forest. Birds are chirping, the breeze heavy and thick with strále warmth, and my dress clings to my skin. Something scurries across a branch, high on the edges of a tree. It vanishes out of sight.

I flick my gaze back to the lieutenant commander. His eyes are still on the forest, watchful, his hand on his knee. *Close to his sword hilt.* I lower the waybread in my hand, crumbs falling against my skirts—they drop softly against the leaves. The men are talking, their voices cheerful, sunlight bright around the ring of trees.

I glance at Sradfaang. His head is low, ears lifted, listening. I swallow hard. *If there was truly trouble nearby, he would speak, urge them to quiet, would he not?* I glance toward Vidar. He is laughing, his head thrown back.

Sradfaang's gaze flicks up, scanning the men. Ciaran stands on the far side of the circle, his steps careful, moving toward the goblin. He stops beside him, his eyes drifting toward the forest, and speaks, his voice low, and I can barely make it out. "Trouble?"

Sradfaang shifts his free hand, the bread in it crumbling across his knee. "Not now. It smelled mostly like a deer. Perhaps an elk that came too far toward the southlands."

Ciaran's eyes snap down to him. "And a moment ago?"

The goblin turns, looking up at him. "There was a band of soldiers that sounded near, a quarter of a watch ago. I thought they might have come back. They came within shouting distance of us this time."

The prince nods, raising his head. "What would you advise, Faang?"

The goblin glances out toward the woods over his shoulder, far from where his gaze was a moment ago. "Nothing needs to change, not now. We have taken the less traveled trail and kept away from nearly everyone. There is little more we can do than that." There is quiet, for a moment, the murmur of the other men's voices continuing. "The healer cannot go into the villages, when we get to them. You are obvious, but if they have word out about her, they will have her description with it."

Ciaran nods at the top of my sight, turning back. "She will not. You might refill that water skin before we start out again, Srad. It looks flat."

The goblin grins, taking a bite of his waybread. "Just as flat as your bedroll. It's a miracle you can yet ride after sleeping on that. It's like a single cloak, lordling. I'd have expected you to be stiff after the first dawn, walking like an aged man after the third. You might make a good cripple. You'd at least have enough tales to tell in trade for your upkeep."

The prince laughs, the sound even and clear. "Perhaps I was sore. Or perhaps I am not as soft as a lordling these days. I might become a cripple if you keep choosing the trails." He turns, jest in his eyes, in his movements. He turns back to the others, stretching his shoulders, his gloved hands dark in the shadows of the sunlit trees.

I turn away, a smile ghosting my lips. *He is young, around his men.*

I look up. *We are near villages. That will be the caution, today.* Ragnar's hand is still near the hilt of his sword, resting easily on his knee, waybread in his other hand. *How much further, on these roads, before we rest? Where do they know of a place, where soldiers are not near?*

•▶|◀▶|◀▶|◀▶|◀▶|◀▶|◀•

Firelight crackles, flickering across the faces of the goblin and men, catching on the grass that shifts with each breath of the breeze. The plains stretch out, gold under the night sky, the silver of stars brighter than I have seen in many turnings with no trees to block them, only the rolling fields. I draw my knees up, press my chin against my hands. Golden plains, fields stretching out forever beneath a darkened sky.

'Auvridal, the golden kingdom...'

Ragnar lifts his head on the edge of my vision, straightening his legs. He stretches his arms out, his movements exaggerated. Nils snorts. Ragnar glances at the other men. "We should have a song, around this fire. It would go well with these skies."

Vidar's eyes flicker to him, and mine follow, the other men mostly still but for Nils, his hands working at a strap of leather—saddle tack, or the like, broken from the day.

Vidar lifts a brow, his hand running over Blått's back. "You'd have a song in these plains? There are folk that live here. You think they'd like to have their nights disrupted by songs in the dark? Settling down for rest and then oh, there's a song of the Mark."

The soldier grins. "I'd have a song in these plains. There is a dare in the wind, life unlived, and I would have a song tonight. No one is near enough to hear it, and those that may, can enjoy it for what it is: a song of travelers. I would not choose a song of the Mark if I had a choice." He grimaces.

There is a snort from behind me, back in the grasses. *Sradfaang.* "It is no dare, to sing in these plains. We would see anyone coming for a half a league before they could reach us." He snorts again. "And I could smell them. Or I would, if you lot didn't smell so bleedin' awful."

"Would you then have a song tonight?" The prince's voice is careful. He does not move, his hands working a small carving between his fingers.

The goblin shifts forward, movements like the swaying grasses. "That would depend on who is doing the singing. I would rather keep company with these weeds than hear Ragnar attempt to carry a tune. Or any man here."

Ragnar grins. "Well then it is fortunate that I had not planned to, nor to ask them." His eyes flicker to me. "Healer, would you favor us with a song, if the ears of our Goldtide officer do not object?"

Sradfaang tilts his head, his smile sharp. *He is amused, though. His eyes are half-bright.* "Well thought, lieutenant commander. I would not object. What song would you choose?"

I flick my eyes toward Ragnar. His gaze meets mine and he inclines his head. "Healer. I had no knowledge that you could sing until a few dawns ago on the road. Sing for pleasure that is. Would you favor us with a song? You may choose the tune." *He should not speak like that, not in front of the men. They do not all know of my Song.*

I incline my head, eyes half-burn. I flick my gaze out toward the darkness. The sky is lit by only stars tonight, pale light a shimmer over the fields. *We are marching, running across our own lands from our own people. Auvridal.* I turn my eyes back toward the fire, incline my head toward Ciaran, toward the goblin. "I will sing, if you will have it. But I am no bard. It will be a simple song, simply sung, the way I know how." *Goblins are known to not care for songs and voices not their own.*

The prince inclines his head, a half-smile on his lips. "It will be an honor on a night such as this."

I turn my eyes away, glance at the faces of the men. I shift my legs. My joints ache, sore with the road and time. I lift a note. *It is strange, to sing like this, like a harper or a ballad master, before men. I have not done this since I was young, in my own home, before Aílé went on to the Bright Halls of Glory.* I clear my throat.

"Auvridal of the plains and hills, through tempest and storm you are met.
On the plains of Foriear your men in blood were bought.
Auvridal of the high hills, your cattle have spread abroad.
Your king was slain, your throne was claimed, your people clothed in blood.

I climbed to the mountain high; your king was pierced to a tree,
His son was born, a lad not crowned, a king beneath the green.
Auvridal, your queen a maid, a peasant, and a slave.
Her voice was lost, the battle gone, the people locked in clay.

Auvridal, the golden kingdom. Silver and gold
you have wrought.
Silver and gold are your people, metals forged of fire.
Auvridal, you have been bought, been purchased by His blood.
Elnial, He knew your pain, and your people all in name.

Your king a lad, a growing man, through sight he saw the dark.
A leading man, a golden man, to lead a growing land.
Halvdel, your father's son, your mother's not in fear.
A gifted lord, a faithful friend, a man his life out poured."

I drop the note, drop the last of the song. *I cannot remember the next verses. They are lost, to my mind.* Wind brushes, heads of the grasses knocking softly together once more.

Peren looks up, his expression caught in the flames. "How does the story end?"

I shake my head. "It is a common enough story, of Halvdel, the first of the golden kings of Auvridal. I do not know the rest of his song tonight."

There is a voice, lifted across the fire, slow, low, and steady, the tune of the song raised up to life again.

"Halvdel the boy king, raised in the wandering way,
A mother slaved, a father slain, a guard to guide the day.
A people brought from misery, the land anew again.
And Yarkenar a deadly man, a broken crown no friend.

Your land was bought with your own leg, a stump
where it once grew.
A humble man, a laughing man,
through futures you once knew.

You rode the fields, your crown regained, bathed in blood and fury.
And all your people raised their voice,
to aid the king usurping."

Ciaran's face is quiet, his voice trailing off the last note. His eyes lift, to Peren. "I would have thought that that tale was still taught, in the street corners and by the ways. Halvdel, the Seeing King, before Auvridal was named. It was his friend that named it, a man with no record of his life, nor of his death. Halvdel's mother's faithfulness is the reason our kingdom stands today, though she was a woman of no account. It is a cursed man who says that the task of mothers is of no report. A'reanhod proved that wrong, as has every mother who raised her children in the fear of Elnial."

I flick my eyes to his. "Was she a queen?"

The corner of his mouth tugs, the faintest of smiles. "She should have been."

There is silence and grass heads knocking together in the fields, soft and sudden like the coming of wind.

Ragnar shifts, his legs restless. He stretches them out, toward the grasses and plains. "We should have another song."

I glance at the goblin. *I have sung enough. The voices of others are known to be shrill to them, sharp on their hearing.* He lifts a brow, not looking at me. "I am not singing."

I smile, and Ragnar snorts. "I didn't ask you to sing. But I'd ask the healer to, if she will." Srad inclines his head, a grin still on his lips.

I turn my head back toward the men, toward the prince and the soldiers. "What song would you have?"

Baard looks up, his head turned from the ground for the first time since food was finished. "Aívac Éníew. The song of the plains." *Song of the plains?* I incline my head, draw my knees closer to my chest. I drop my voice, the first notes low, like the song of the winds through the rocks in the night, far out over the grasses, never quieting.

"I saw my brothers marching out, out over plains.

I saw my brothers marching out, grasses waving in their wake.
By star and sun they marched throughout
The turning of the world.
By star and sun they marched throughout
The coming of the night.

Through these plains you'll come back home,
Your home and victory won,
And to your farmer's daughters,
And your weavers you will come.

Oh soldiers you'll be marching home,
To sweet arms you will come.
And to the love of little ones, your battling all won.

And all these plains will see you home, these grasses waving wide,
The fields that saw you go, will see you safe arrive.
And when all the marching's done, with the ending of this day,
Back to hearth and haven home, for which you've hoped and prayed.

"Oh soldiers you'll be marching home,
To sweet arms you will come.
And to the love of little ones, your battling all won."

There is quiet, through the camp, the flames of the fire licking up toward the stars with a scattering of sparks. Peren is still, his eyes cast up toward them, hand slung over his knees, like mine. He hums, the first notes of the song, of home again. *How many of them have homes still to go to? To return to, after all the destruction of these seasons?*

Ciaran's eyes are caught in the glow of the light, cast back the way we came, towards the capital, toward home.

LII

Eye Diggers

There is stirring, somewhere in the dark. I lift my head. Fog is curling across the campsite, blending with the last of the smoke puffing up from the charred wood.

Voices murmur together, horses stamping, the sound of tack clattering against itself. I press my arms beneath me, draw my body up. Shadows flicker, fog rolling off, away from the movements of the horse. *Dawn is not yet here.*

I push back my cloak and sleep slips from my eyes. Blåthjortt lifts his head, steps away. He is watching, eyes eager, tail thumping the ground beside him. *Have they risen so early?*

Sradfaang is speaking, his voice low somewhere in the mist beyond me. *The cots are all empty already.* "…The far side is easy to navigate, if you go north from the village and keep to the outskirts of the forest. We will meet you there tomorrow, before dark, if all goes well." The fog shifts, rolling in the darkness, and there are figures, moving quickly, quietly through it. *They are all up.*

I sit up, pull the laces on the side of my dress tight. The air is warm, almost stagnant, heavy with the fog. I step forward and there is a figure, moving past me. *Vidar.* He glances down at me, the markings on his face strange in the half-light before dawn. "You might get ready quickly."

I tighten my arms about myself, reach for my cloak. "Are we setting out early?"

He shakes his head. "You are not, but you had best be ready just the same. I do not know what the Knoc'gnori will want to do."

My eyes snap back to his. I pull my legs under me. "I am not?" He is moving away, out into the wisps of fog and they are curling around him, no answer.

"You are not." I spin sharply, the voice behind me dry, low. *Sradfaang*. He glances down at me, his eyes green in the darkness and fog. "The men are going for supplies. We are keeping to the road."

I tighten my arms. "Would it not be wiser to stay together, if there is concern about soldiers near here?"

He turns, hefting a bag over his shoulder. "We need supplies to go on, and it would be unwise for you or the prince to enter a village. Or myself. The prince and I would both be too noticeable, and you would be too memorable." He starts forward. "Not because of your eyes. Your hair stands out. No one who saw it would forget it again, if asked. There are not many with that color, in this part of Auvridal." He steps away, lifting another pack from the ground beside the smoldering fire.

A strand of hair brushes across my cheek, pale and soft as the gray around us.

Another figure moves through the mist, off to my side, his movements sharp. *Ragnar*. He is lifting the iron pot rack, the water buckets slung by their handles over his shoulders. He nods to me, a stiff nod, his back ramrod straight. "Healer. You'd best get ready to head out."

I purse my lips, comb a hand down my braid. "Who is leaving?"

His mouth tightens beneath his beard, eyes unreadable in the shadows. "All the soldiers and Vidar. Baard with stay. The goblin thinks it wiser to send a small party through the marshes." *The marshes?*

I swipe my hand down my braid once more, smooth the freed strands. "You all will be heading into a near village then?" *Did they not come to guard the prince, to ensure his safety? If they did not come for that reason, then why did they come, why all of them?*

His eyes flicker toward mine, scanning my face. He nods. "Aye. We will be. I…" his voice trails off. He shakes his head. "You all will be well enough with the goblin and Baard. Keep an eye on the prince. If we lose him…" He shakes his head. "And tell the goblin

Baard is an apt bowman. I have packed an extra bow in the goblin's saddle bag. Baard has his own."

I incline my head. "I will. May the Creator watch over you all."

He inclines his head toward me—respect and deference. "See you tomorrow even." He steps away. "If all goes well." It is short, under his breath. He turns and is gone, off into the fog where the others are mounting, preparing to ride out into the gray of dawn.

•▶|◀▶|◀▶|◀▶|◀▶|◀▶|◀•

My horse stumbles, crying out, the sound high. I jerk back on the reins too late and there is a strange sound, sucking, water sloshing everywhere. The horse falls forward, my chest thudding hard against her neck. I clamp my knees, pull backward. *We stumbled into the marsh.*

The horse steps sideways, my ribs burn, and water soaks through my boots, thick and warm. I grimace, press my hands harder against the horse's neck. "Steady, civ… Steady—" She jerks her head to the side, and we are sinking, sinking forward. My chest smacks against her neck again. *Oh, stars.*

A hand cuts past the horse's head, jerking on the reins, and the horse stumbles, up, and I am falling backward, the horse's rump sinking behind me, her front feet free, moving onto the solid earth. Sradfaang speaks to the horse, his voice low, language one I do not know, and he pulls the reins.

She turns, her front feet higher, and I am sinking, its back closer to the mud with each heartbeat, water crawling up my legs, into my skirts, up the back of the horse. I press against her neck, grip hard at the saddle horn.

"Up…up...up…!" Srad's voice is sharp, his hand pulling on the reins, and the horse is stumbling, trying, striving. *Creator, please.*

There is a splash, and water crawls up my thighs, hands soaked. The horse scrambles, her back legs sinking further, and she is up, crawling onto the ground. She shakes her mane, stamping her feet, on them again.

The goblin steps away, beside me. His eyes scan over the horse. He glances at me, flicks his gaze over his shoulder, toward the prince. Ciaran is holding the leads of the other horses. "We should keep moving. They are uninjured."

Ciaran nods. He glances back, toward Baard. "Baard, put the hound on a lead. I do not want him dropping into the swamp. It is deeper than it looks here." His eyes move to mine.

I incline my head, press my hand gently against my mount's neck. My heart is pounding, still thundering in my throat. *It would not have meant death, to have fallen into the swamp. But there is no telling what swims in waters so thick.* I turn my head away.

Sradfaang moves sharply, turning back toward his mount. Baard is kneeling beside Blåthjortt, looping a rope around his neck. Blått is motionless, sitting still, his tongue lolling, eyes content.

I click to Nyerla, start forward, away from the edge of the trail, from the churning mud of the disturbed waters. An insect lands on my soaked leg, buzzing loud.

The goblin is moving forward again, between Ciaran and I now. He says something, his voice low, and it is lost in the thick humming of the marshlands. Something hums close beside me, the sound constant beneath the thudding of my heart, the spinning of a hundred mosquitoes, and more. I shift in the saddle and my skin is clammy, hot with the marsh.

The buzzing is growing, a hum.

I flick my eyes toward the waters beside me. There is a swarm of insects, not far from my shoulder, humming, swirling, churning above the marbled surface, stagnant waters. I purse my lips. The humming is louder, growing with each breath. *Not a swarm of insects.* Horse hooves clatter against stones for a breath, and the sound is gone again, lost to the sucking of the marsh.

Grass widens out, marsh receding back, and the goblin halts, my mount mirroring his. "Healer, Baard, dismount." I grip the reins, flicker my eyes toward the sky. The goblin is already swinging out of the saddle, his feet sinking just barely into the damp ground. The prince follows suit and his gaze flicks back to Baard as he turns. Sradfaang flicks his gaze to me again, his hand brushing against the nose of his mount.

I slip my damp skirts over the side of the saddle and they cling to it—my feet suck into the earth, sinking, skirts slapping against my legs.

The goblin's great horse is moving to its knees, its head lowering with its massive frame toward the grasses. The prince says something low to his mount, pressing gently on its shoulders, and it lowers, dropping against the damp earth beside the goblin's.

I click to my horse, pull gently against her reins. She jerks her head back up, feet stamping restlessly, mud spattering from her damp fur, the sucking sound sharp beneath her hooves. I click again. "Down. Come down." She jerks her head once more, snorting, and a hand moves past mine, gripping the reins.

Sradfaang snaps out a command, pulling once, gently, and she kneels, the sound of the humming growing, almost deafening. My eyes burn, flickering toward Sradfaang. His hand presses sharply against my back, pushing me toward the earth.

"What is it?" My voice is lost in the hum. *Where is Blåthjortt?*

He is still pressing, still pushing me down. I duck my head, and my knees suck into the earth, the sound growing, growing, and Sradfaang is still beside me, his voice in my ear, hand pressing hard against my back. "Cover her eyes with your arms and get your head down. Whatever you do, do not open your eyes." His voice is a hiss, hard, fast. It lifts. "Ciaran, Baard, keep your heads down, eyes closed, and make sure your mounts do the same or they will lose them."

I flick my gaze toward the prince, and something dark darts past my eyes. Pain sears through my cheek, and Ciaran ducks his head, his arms around his mount's, circling it. Something else darts past my eyes, the same dark shape—small, like a bird. Sradfaang's hand presses hard against my back, forcing me toward the earth.

I wrap my arms around Nyerla's head, my eyes flying toward the ground near Baard where Blått was a moment ago, but there is nothing there, nothing but darting black shapes swarming in the air. Something wraps around my back, forcing my head toward the horse's, and the humming sound is ringing, filling the air. Something large presses against the whole of my back, covering me.

My hair jerks, and the air is full of sudden screeching, of the sound of a hundred wing beats, small and fast and furious. The hum is deafening, and an arm twists over my head, pinning it down, against the horse.

I curl my head forward. The horse nickers, jerking against me, pulling at her head, and my teeth snap shut, against each other. The arms around me tightens, Sradfaang's voice cutting out, lost in the screeching hum. I breathe out, press my eyes shut.

Nyerla jerks her head, slamming it against my jaw. My mouth tastes of blood. I force my arms around her, push her down. "Thust, thust. Stay down..." I breathe out, and the horse pulls again, jerking upward. I lift my voice. "Hush hush. It's alright. Thust, thust." Her pulling slows and the humming is growing, piercing, pounding against my head. *What are these?*

Pain cuts across my hand, sharp, and I yank it lower, beneath the horse's jaw. Arms tighten around me, Sradfaang's voice still speaking beneath the rushing sounds of the air, speaking to his mount.

Nyerla jerks her head up again, and my jaw slams shut, pain bursting through my teeth, through my jaw. I grimace, and my mouth tastes of blood. "Thust thust..." My hair tugs, a screech beside my ear, and it is gone—my scalp throbs. The sound is rolling, murmur of wings swirling. I shush again and I cannot hear my voice over the hum of the beasts.

The horse goes still beneath my hand. Her breath is hot on my skin, brushing up against my face with each jet of it puffing from her lungs. A sound brushes my ears, high, a horse calling out, and it is lost. *Elnial, please let them pass. Let them be gone. Keep us whole.* Something tugs at my hair again. Another horse whinnies, the sound high, alarmed.

Sradfaang's arms loosen just barely, his chest still pressing hard against my back, body still sheltering mine, mine sheltering the horse's heads. *The hum is lessening, sounds further away.* My ears ring, high and foggy, eyes sting. *Are they leaving?*

The softness is growing, the screeching of the birds fading away, almost muffled. A strand of my hair tugs for a moment, and it too is gone, a cry beside my ear.

The horse's breaths are heaving, sides shifting with each one. Sradfaang's breaths are thin beside my ear. The air is ringing, ringing now with silence.

Sradfaang shifts and he is gone from behind me, his arms lifting away from my head. I sit back. Hair wisps around my eyes, catching on my lips, strands pulled loose, and my mouth still tastes of blood.

My eyes flicker toward Ciaran. He is sitting up, moving to his feet, his hand patting the head of his horse, speaking softly to it. There are dark patches coating his breeches from the bog-soaked earth, covering his knees and coating his calves.

There is silence, not even the hum of an insect in the air above the ringing. I flick my eyes up, toward Srafaang. There are a thousand tiny cuts across his face, across his arms, blood beading out from them and running along his skin in tiny rivulets.

My eyes swirl. "Sónya." I stand sharply, the world tilting for a moment. I shake it off, step closer to him. *Claw marks.* He pulls away. I shake my head, flick my eyes up to his. "You are wounded."

He turns his gaze toward Ciaran, over my head. "We need to move."

I purse my lips. There is blood, slipping from the cuts along his arm, catching in strands of hair, each lowered line, a crooked, growing stream on his skin. I purse my lips, turn for my saddle bags. "What were those?" My hand stings.

He looks down at me, expression dry, and a cut glints next to his eye, thick and bleeding. "Vykopavoci. Eye diggers."

A shudder crawls up my spine. I force my eyes down, back to his skin, my hand fumbling with the saddle bags. There are lines across all the green-gray surface, tiny lashings all along his arms and neck and hands. *They will all be wounded, for shielding their mounts.* My jaw tightens. *He shielded me.*

His jaw tightens. "We do not have time to tend anything now. We have less than a watch before dark." He clicks, and his mount moves to his feet, towering suddenly beside me.

I shake my head, flick my eyes toward Ciaran. He is too far, the cuts on his skin there, but I cannot tell how thickly they coat his hands and face. I look up. *Where is Blåthjortt?* I turn.

A tuft of blue-gray shifts, beside Ciaran, head hiding behind the horse. My heart lifts. The hound turns, moving to the side, pace even, steps steady. He lifts his nose to Ciaran, mouth shut, eyes bright. *But there.*

I breathe out, tug the salve from the side of the bag, my eyes snapping to Baard. He is speaking to his horse, adjusting a saddle bag half-fallen off.

I lift the crock, turn back to the goblin. "We can have time. You are bleeding. The other two will have ones to match." I pull the wax seal from the crock. A long, jagged line glints on my wrist, dripping a small stream of blood into my sleeve.

His mouth tightens further above my head. "Is it your place to dictate time, healer? We need to move. These will not harm, but if we do not leave these swamps before dark there will be trouble."

I frown, run my eyes along the upper cuts where the blood is flowing less. In the center of his arm, his skin is nearly hidden behind the tapestry of cuts and blood, a slash board of them, running over old scars. My throat tightens. *He did not spare himself, to shield me. They attacked him.*

He shakes his head, high above me. "There is not time to salve all of them now, healer. You may tend them this evening when they are dried and I have washed, if you choose. If you are going to tend them now, you might tend the prince's first and not mine. I have healed from worse."

I shake my head. I brush my hand across his skin, the blood smearing, and it pools again on many of the scratches, a bead of red spilling over. My lips tighten. *There is no point in attempting to tend them now, any of them. They will only smear and the salves will be of no use, until this can be washed.*

I step backward, and my hand fumbles with the seal in my pocket. He shakes his head, looking up into the fog, hazy, drifting around his head. I slip the canvas back onto the salve pot, press it into place. "I will tend them tonight, when we have water. All of them. And aye, I will start with the prince's then, but yours will be tended when I am done. You shielded me."

He ignores me. Baard nods at the edge of my vision and he is stepping backward, moving to mount his horse.

Mine is still lying down, her eyes watching warily, grass tucked in her mouth. She chews, her tail swishing against the grass, awkward. *As though she was not fighting, was not trying to get away and get up moments ago.*

I purse my lips and step forward, toward her. Something bites my arm. I slap at it—a small black dot flies away. *Blood sucking insects and eye digging birds.* My eyes flicker over, into the murky water's edge. *This is no place to travel by choice.*

The prince turns toward us. "We should be to a safe place to camp," His voice is steady, "inside of the next watch, Creator willing. There should be no more of them tonight, but the sun will set early in these mists. We should move." He is gripping his horse's reins again, starting off, the steps of his mount strange in the sucking, damp ground. Blått trots beside him, his head lifted, unharmed.

LIII

The Sword Tree

Ciaran's steps are fast, his gait even, horse trotting behind him. Sradfaang's voice is soft beside me, clucking to his horse for just a breath, and it is gone, the air silent again but for the hum of a thousand bugs too close to my skin.

I swat at my arm, and the slap is stale in the thickness of the air. There is a dark smear across my skin, reddish where the insect was only a moment ago. I look away.

Trees jut up from the water, sunlight glittering in shafts off of it, cutting at my eyes, flashing here and then gone. I grimace , pull my gaze away. The waterline is low, roots curling up from it like great fingers, out and down through the underbrush and waterside where the water flickers. Pale mud clings to the twisted roots where the water once was. I swat at my hand, boots sinking in the mud.

A stick snaps ahead. *It is too far ahead to be the prince.* I whip my head up—my eyes burn. The trees are crowding in around Ciaran, full and thick where the water ends, and I can see nothing beyond him, beyond his mount. I turn back toward Sradfaang, stumble. My horse is nearly blocking him from view, her head raised, a leaf in her mouth.

The goblin's eyes are on the trees, watchful, but they are not watching the prince, not even glancing in the direction of the stick's snap. *If I have heard it, he surely will have as well.* His eyes are still on the trees, watching the forests everywhere but the prince's direction.

I turn back toward the trail. The prince steps down slowly, and he is gone around a bush, branches swaying where his horse once was. I start forward, duck under the branch, Nyerla's snout pressing against my back.

The forest is filled with the sound of steps, branches breaking, leaves crackling beneath the horses' hooves, and there are more than can be made from ours. I flick my eyes forward, and I can see nothing beyond the brush and the massive cypress trees. I glance back at Sradfaang. He shakes his head, not moving his gaze down to me. "They are ours."

My heart slows. *Our soldiers, or our mounts? We could not make so much noise.* A horse steps around a massive tree, Ciaran on the other side, where he cannot see it. My eyes snap to the man, to the horse. *Ragnar.* Nyerla's nose brushes at my hair. She snorts. *It is our men.*

"Were you successful?" Ciaran's voice is sudden, even in the forest, another man stepping around the tree that is larger than his mount. I step to the side, around the tree where horse prints mar the earth, and I can no longer see the men.

"Aye. We have supplies for a trek and two more horses to carry them. You all survived the swamplands." Vidar's voice is frank, solid, and I hear no reply. *The prince must have inclined his head.*

"Lord, did you run into a tree?" There is a note of humor in Ragnar's voice. I round the corner and there is Ciaran's horse before me, its tail lashing at the air, swatting at the insects that swarm around it.

Ciaran shakes his head over the horse's shoulder. "Gót. Vykopavoci. A cloud of them, a little more than a day back. We were caught in the swamps."

Someone swears. "And the healer?" *Peren's voice.*

"She is well. I would talk with you on the road, once we have taken to it again. Dark is not far." Ciaran nods back toward me.

Sradfaang grunts right behind me. I flick my gaze up toward him. His expression is dry, a cut down his cheek beneath his eye, thin and dark. There is another, up above his brow, and a third half-hidden beneath his hair, dark along the neck of his tunic. The rest of them have mostly faded. I look away, grimace.

"And Baard?"

I move around the tree, and Ragnar's head is visible through the bushes and vines, Nils on a mount beside him.

Ciaran speaks. "He is well, as you all are, I see. We will discuss the events of our travels at rest tonight. For now, turn your mounts around and file into your places. Baard, you may take the lead."

Baard knows the way? Out of the swamp, or to where we will go beyond? There is a shuffling of leaves, branches breaking, and Ciaran moves forward, his mount following, sure-stepped behind him.

I glance back. Baard and Blått were there only moments ago, behind the massive form of Sradfaang's horse, but there is no sign of them now. I turn my head forward again.

Sradfaang's eyes are watchful, on the trees, something off in his stance. I purse my lips. Someone laughs ahead—Peren, high and uneven. A shaft of sunlight cuts through the trees, catching on the swarm of flies before me, turning them to a glimmering swirl. I grimace, duck around them, and one of them hums past my ear, gone into the sounds of the forest.

• ▶ | ◀ ▶ | ◀ ▶ | ◀ ▶ | ◀ ▶ | ◀ ▶ | ◀ •

Something smells heavy on the wind that is barely filtering through the trees, wrong. My stomach swirls, churning. I swallow, horse steps easy beneath me, and turn my head. It is stronger now, the horse's steps moving swiftly toward the hill before us, a smell that I know, though I cannot place it. It is almost sweet, swirling in my stomach. *Foul.*

Nils' face is gray beside me, shadows of branches in the midday sun playing across his skin, and there is no sound from any of the men, not a word or a shuffling step.

I turn my head forward again and there is a brush of air across my skin, warm, putrid. Bile flushes up my throat and I gag, press my hand over my nose. *Death. It reeks of death. The sweet rot of the dead.* Nils' face is paler than before, the men still silent around me. Peren half-gags.

The horses begin up the slope and the scent is gone, air clean, leaves filtering overhead, sending swirls of light across the head of my horse, and my stomach churns more. *It must be nearby, to have smelled that strong. And it must be large, no hare or bird.* Ragnar's horse is cresting the hill. He turns to the side, eyes meeting the prince's. "It's coming from over there." He inclines his head sharply forward, horse starting down the slope beneath him. Vidar's moves down after him, mine sticking close behind him. Flowers dot the hillside, but the trees are quiet, not the call of a bird or sound of leaves rustling in the valley. Silent but for the marching of the horses and rocks skittering on the slope. The air is still, too still.

Ragnar's horse steps up the slope on the far side of the holler, Vidar just behind him. Mine plods after them. Shale slides, clattering beneath her hooves, and she snorts, lowering her head, sticks skittering in the leaves. I grimace, slipping in the saddle. She stalls sharply, throwing back her head, mane lashing at my face. I fumble with the saddle horn, and Blått barks once, a strange call, and there is silence, the horse not moving.

The horses before me have stopped with mine, someone swearing somewhere above. There is a lazy brush of air, and it reeks again, scent strong.

The men are staring out, ahead, horses motionless, and I cannot see the men's faces, nor what is ahead. I press my hands against the saddle horn, slide off the side, and the ground shifts beneath me, shale sliding, skittering.

There is a hum of insects in the wind, like a thousand bees. I step forward, grip my skirts. Warm wind hits me in the face, and I stumble, bile flushing up my throat again. I swallow it back, press my hand harder against my face. *This is no deer, nor yet a bear, that it would smell so strong.* I force my eyes down and my heart stops in my chest.

Men.

There is a bowl in the valley below us, shallow trees circling it, and the ground is filled with half-rotted bodies, their skin bloated, shredded in the sunlight, eyes lost, faces masks of death. There are swords jutting out of chests and sides, handles and hilts, the air swarming with the gentle hum of insects.

Someone gags beside me, and the sound is muffled, the world quiet but for the gently brushing wind, throwing the scent across the world.

Death. Men, all of them. There is not a woman among them. *Dead.*

My eyes flicker to the swords, their handles of simple make, oddly fashioned and formed. *These are commoners. All of them. All villager men.*

I start down the slope and there is a voice, sharp behind me. "Healer! No."

My head snaps around. Ciaran's eyes are on me, his face quiet, eyes watchful. My chest heats, eyes burn, swirl with a thousand colors. I shake my head sharply. "I would see who they were. If this was an execution..."

His eyes are still calm, face still calm, emotionless. His horse prances sideways. "It was."

My heart sinks in my chest, the wind brushing again, and I swallow back the taste of bile in my mouth. "How could you know?" My voice is muffled, half-choked in the world. "You were not there."

His jaw tightens and he nods his head to the tree beside him. There is a sword in it, stained dark and crusted, another one just below it, with a sheet of brittle paper pinned to the tree. *A notice, with a seal on it, falling off.* It is visible, where I stand.

The queen's seal.

I swallow hard. *The queen's seal. An execution.* "We cannot leave them here." My voice is distant, somewhere else. I turn back to the bowl of the valley, and my stomach heaves. *Death.* Too many bodies, crowded together. There will be more than fifty of them here, piled together like unwanted fruit left in the midday sun. *We cannot leave them here to rot beneath the sky, like waste.*

A step falls on the slope. "There is no choice, Eness. We cannot bury them here."

I lift my head and my foot skids on the slope, throwing me downward. My hand jerks hard on a branch and I slow, feet falling on loose ground. My eyes snap down and my lungs cease. I gag.

There is a man next to me staring at the sky with eye sockets vacant, skin purpled in death, and I cannot breathe or tear my eyes away. *They died traitors' deaths, died criminal deaths. Left to the birds of the air to carry off.* "What could they have done to deserve this death?" My voice is thick, a scrap of fabric on the branch beside me, bloodied, soiled. "What did they do that they would have been left to never be buried in this valley?"

A throat clears. "They are accused of being disloyal to the queen. So says the notice, on the tree." Vidar's voice is far away, muffled, like everything in this valley.

I swallow, my vision blurred, swirling. *With tears.* "These were common men. Villagers. They cannot have all deserved this kind of death." *I have seen this before. In Guncalk, when the goblins came. But their families were left to bury them there, a mass death and then torn homes.* "What of their homes, their families?" *What will become of their wives, their children, when the dark months come? Their mothers? They have already been here two days, if not more.* "What if they see them?"

A hand grips my arm, gentle. "Their families will not live near the execution site, Eness." *Ciaran's voice.*

My eyes snap up, away from the bodies, from the piled corpses. "Have you been here on all your travels that you would know where the village lies?" My hand is shaking. "Have you seen them before? They have been here two dawns at the most, Prince. Two dawns, and I have seen soldiers do worse inside villages at a command, with their children watching on. How do you know they will not come here, will not see this carnage, see what became of their fathers, their brothers, their husbands?" My voice is sharp, and he does not flinch, face only one emotion, like the men behind me who can no longer change what their faces tell. "How can you know that they will not have seen them fall?"

He tilts his head toward me, his eyes soft, though his expression tells of nothing more. "Gót." His jaw tightens. "My mother's men do not dump the corpses near the village when they perform an execution of this scale. They will have taken them far out in the woods to keep the village from illness, if they have moved them at all. You will find wagon tracks on the far side of this bowl."

I shake my head, turn back toward the bodies. My hand slackens on the tree. "Do they think that will keep the villages from failing? What will the families do when winter comes, and their men all lie in a bone heap—" Wind brushes, my voice catches. Bile flushes up my throat. I press my head hard against my shoulder, the air filled with sweet, heavy rottenness. *In a bone heap, in the woods, bodies left to the birds of the air, to be picked at by passing animals, unmarked.*

"Eness. There is nothing that we can do for them."

I lift my eyes from my shoulder, back to the bodies below. "Can we not give them a fitting resting place? Are you not their lord, Ciaran?"

His hand tightens, and he swallows. "We cannot move their bodies, Eness." His voice is soft, gentle, kind, and my eyes burn, but not with shifting. "It is too late for that. We can give them the burial of the battlefield, but nothing more can be done now."

I shake my head, press it harder against my shoulder. The wind brushes and the smell is stronger, putrid, rotted flesh. "We could have helped them. We could have saved them."

His eyes meet mine, and his head shakes. "We could have done nothing for them."

I shake my head again. "And their families? Can we do nothing for them? What will they do when gråsving comes, and their men all lie in a heap at the bottom of a valley? They will not survive the dark months, not without aid." My cheek is damp. "This is the way she crumbles villages."

Ciaran's hand shifts to my other arm. "We can do nothing for them by helping but bring destruction. There is a price on my head, and one on the head of each of the men we bring with us. If we go to their village, if we enter it, we will put them at a greater risk than what they face in the cold months. We cannot stay, Eness."

My eyes snap up to his. "And where can we go to, where this will not be haunting us, following? Where the soldiers who have carried out the edicts of the queen will not be there, carrying out the next ones?" My throat is thick. "This is everywhere, my lord. It will not slow, though we run from it. Where would you go?"

His eyes sharpen. "Do you think I do not know of these troubles? Of this death that reeks across our country? These people are mine, that my family has sworn to protect since the days of our country's beginning, and I have not forgotten, will not forget. Nor do I forget the old words and who you are, Blood Sparrow."

His eyes flash, bright. "I do not forget, where we go, and if you think for a breath that I will not be thinking of them for every heartbeat, every breath that we are climbing over those mountains, every moment that we are there, then you do not yet know where my allegiances lie. I will spend my life's blood to make sure that they are safe, that my country is freed from her grasp. But I cannot do that from here; can do nothing here but put them at greater risk by burying souls that have already gone. Would you have me risk all the plans laid for turnings gone to bury these men?"

My eyes are swirling. "You will work to save the many but forsake the few? What would it cost us to spare a watch to bury them?"

His eyes soften, only a fraction. *Always a fraction with him, with any emotion from him, always the mask.* "I am striving to choose the benefit that will save the lives of those they have left behind, over that which will only bring them a moment of comfort, when they see they are buried. I will not forget these that we could not. If we stay, Eness, it will take far more than a watch to break the soil and lay their bodies to rest in the forest. We cannot run that risk, not when we are being followed." He glances up the hill, a sharp look.

The wind brushes, warm, hot scent over my face, and I turn away, eyes burning, swirling with tears. I clamp my hands across my face.

His hand shifts on my arm, gently. It pulls, guiding me up the slope. I draw my hands away from my face, eyes drifting back to the men. *Can we not give them a covering?* My heart tightens.

There are too many. We could not reach those at the center of the heap.

My eyes flicker to the man nearest me, his skin shredded, hands torn. *Death.*

"Eness."

I do not look up. "Where will we go, when we leave?"

His jaw tightens on the edge of my vision. "To Grior." My heart slows. *To the north country?* "If we do not leave—" The prince is speaking over my head, his voice steady but soft, "—then we can do nothing for the rest of this country and those like these men being led to the slaughter. We have prayed and we have sought council and studied. We cannot remove my mother from the throne without the help of the other countries. Auvridal alone cannot do it. This is war. This is the way we end it."

I look up and his eyes meet mine. "If we do not leave, there will be many more slaughters like this, your corpse lying in one of them." My eyes swirl. His face sets again. "It will not be long before the soldiers behind catch up, if we slow for even a day. They had already heard of us, in the village. And you will be among those slaughtered first, a trophy among the dead, strung up in a tree to rot, as an example. I do not think my mother would choose to utilize you for long. Not for all the healing you might bring. She does not often utilize things that might be used against her."

I turn away. "And you?"

A grim smile brushes his lips beneath his beard. "I will be taken up dead or brought back as a prisoner of war. A traitor prince, to wear out my days as the queen sees fit, as a member of the Maa'eulé."

We slow halfway between the valley of death and the mounts above, leaves and shale skittering beneath my feet. I swallow hard. His eyes are studying me, watching, and mine are unfocused.

"There is nothing we can do for them?" My voice breaks. *Death. Death. Bodies piled, their heads untouched this time, but they are lost beyond aid this side of Glory.* My lips tremble. *Would that I could sing the dead back to life. Would that they could rise again.*

Ragnar's voice is distant in the muffled air of the forest. "The best we can do is sprinkle them with dust, sonyá. We can bury their bodies when we return, if their wives and daughters have not already. They are too far gone. We cannot give them a funeral pyre in the forest. It will risk too much damage to the forests and villages nearby."

Ciaran's jaw is tight, his eyes on the bodies below, his gaze broken, eyes torn like theirs. I swallow hard. I turn my gaze toward the ground. "Sprinkle dust to the wind if it will ease your conscience, but we cannot stay long."

Horses shift above. *Elnial, please be with the families of these men. Heal the wounds that have been carved open. Save this people from this present darkness, O Lord. Save them from the hands that seek their lives.*

Is there truly nothing we can do, nothing that can be done for these men until the winds of time have done it?

Ciaran's hand pulls gently. My feet follow, steps heavy. I slow at the top of the slope, glance back down, Ciaran beneath me now. He turns, eyes on the corpses below. His shoulders cave. I turn, step up the last bit of the slope.

The mounts are all prancing, their heads high, feet anxious, stomping in the leaves. My eyes flicker around the men. Sradfaang is beside me, on his mount, his skin paled, eyes glittering. *Angered.* My eyes dart around them. *They are all angered.* There are tears in Nils' eyes, his jaw set, eyes matching the violence of Sradfaang's stare.

The prince moves up the slope, his steps steady, fast. I step into the stirrup, throw my leg over, and the horse prances, moving sideways. The horses turn, away, not a breath of a breeze in the valley. My throat aches, eyes swim.

How long will darkness endure? How many more valleys will be filled with the dead before the shadows end and hope is not a thing tucked away, hidden in crevices and rocks? Not a thing to be ushered away into hiding places where the darkness cannot see?

Something slips down my cheek, spattering against my hand. I swallow hard, nudge my horse forward, after the others. They have started across the hillside. *How many more turnings will there be that death endures?*

Creator. Please, come save.

LIV

The Fields of Andelor

The air is quiet, only the steps of the horses and the slow sound of Baard's voice marring it. It is a breath, soft in the treading steps of the forest. I turn around a tree, and his voice is clearer, a tune, held low and gentle.

"Shadows dance, deepen, long,
We lift homeward our fading song.
Shadows cannot dwell, nor do days of death last forever.
Upon the fields of Andelor we will have peace.

Fields once stained in blood, now stretch abroad in joy.
The plains that once knew darkness, now hear a blessed noise.
The homes now built in peace, before the mountain's end.
Upon the fields of Andelor, we will know hope again."

His voice quiets, and there is light through the trees ahead, stronger, brighter. Ragnar steps through, his form half-swallowed by the brightness of it.

I follow and squint. The sun is harsh, and golden with evening. Peren's horse steps out of the trees and I look up and the world is hazy for a moment. I blink, half-lift my hand to block the light. *The air smells sweet, like life.* I lower my hand.

My breath catches in my throat.

Flowers—faded blue blooms—large and waving in the wind of the fields, stretch out, out and out over the plains, climbing up the hill that curls high, higher than any I have ever seen—straight up toward the sky. I swallow. There is something gray and sharp rising up behind the last slope of the plains, where the fields should reach the sky.

Mountains.

There is white against the gray of their slopes, peaks rising high, sharp against the dusk of the sky. *Mountains.*

Ragnar breathes out two words. "The border."

Clouds are brushed with the first traces of pink, flowers still dancing in the winds, their petals large, curling up at their edges. *Anemones. The fields are filled with them.* The prince's head is thrown back. His face is silhouetted against the darkening sky above the falling sun, the light gold about his face and somewhere, a bird calls.

Epilogue

Captain Einion Flint leans forward in the soft velvet chair, his hands folded evenly between his knees. "I have completed my duties. My mission now lies elsewhere, wherever the Queen bids me go."

The duke across from him smiles. It is not the smile of a friend, but a bitter smile. He lifts the decanter of brandy, pouring a glass, leaning forward until their heads nearly touch. "I am not blind to your coming, Einion Flint. Not ignorant to why you have come. My daughter knows nothing of my work nor of my wife's. If I go down, there will be no one to save her from what is to come. My wife's pull with the courts will not be enough after how she has dug. I would charge you with this, before you leave my home. You got her here. Take her from it again." He leans backward, the brandy poured.

Captain Flint lifts a brow. "I cannot guarantee her safety where I go."

The duke's eyes lift to his, and there is desperation in them, wildness. He speaks, his voice barely a breath. "And if she stays, there will be no end to what they will put her through, Captain. Her chances as a commoner with a soldier, where she can do no more harm are far greater than anything I can offer her. I know your way of working alone. I have heard of the jobs you have done for the Queen and other nobles."

Flint turns away, the guards at the door still motionless. "If she leaves with me, the life she will find will be nothing like what you have given her. I cannot protect her forever."

The duke sets the stopper back into the crystal decanter, speaking softly still, low. "I have told you what will happen if she stays. There is no choice, and no one else to take her, Captain Flint. I will beg if you ask, but if the guards learn what we have spoken of, it will already be too late for her. The queen's men would stop at nothing to tear me down, and take all that I know and love with me. I have earned that. She has not. Save her, if you will heed a dead man's wish. Save my daughter."

End of book one.

Acknowledgements

There are so many, many people that I want to thank for this.

But the biggest thanks, and any glory that can be brought up (or scrounged) from this book goes to my Lord, the God Who Is, and Who has been. His grace has been abundant and I stand humbled and amazed by His goodness through all of this. Thanks be to Him, now and forever, through all the ages that life endures, amen.

To my sisters, Lydia and Phoebe, who read this book in its infancy and told me it wasn't terrible, thank you.

To Cathryn McIntyre, to whom this book was dedicated; thank you. That conversation in the car is one I will never forget, and I am grateful, so grateful for you.

To my parents here, Dad and Karissa, I am thankful that you guys only ever said, 'write good' and then let me try.

To Joshua and Abbie, the best older siblings a girl could ask for, who wrote far better than I did for so many years, and whose writings I miss. Thank you for your joy and encouragement, and for always making time to hear me out on ideas when I had them. Y'all are joys.

To Elijah, Samuel, Victoria and Whit, thank you. You guys are the best.

To Ioan and Thomas; bless you both for thinking that I was cool, even though you thought Annie was cooler.

To Madeleine, who said, 'you can do that better' and then helped me do so. Blessings upon you. You are a joy and invaluable, two tremendous things. I am thankful for you.

To my alpha readers; Phoebe, Beka, Annie P, Katie and Madeleine. Thank you. Thank you. Thank you. I cannot say that enough. Your notes and all that you did were more helpful than I can say. Thank you for cheering for this from chapter one.

To my betas, Hayley J, Millie N, Nani V, Ellie T and Annie V, thank you, each of you, for being my encouragement through Christ during a time when I was questioning this story. You all are joys.

To all my street team, Abbie P, Anne Marie T, Annie P, Brittany S, Cara P, Ann D, Beta S, Cindy W, Gabrielle S, Julie R, Emily H, Jenny S, Julianne G, Karissa B, Katelyn W, Kayla Ann, Helen L, Katelyn W, Laken V, Maili L, Mary L, Meg C, Tess M, Naomi N, Abigail L, Phoebe B, Sam T, Nataleigh J and Bethany M, thank you all of you for your work in spreading the word.

To my editors: Madeleine Bullen, Katelyn Walker, Jasmine Fischer and Esther McIntyre. Blessings be upon your heads for all that you did, and all of your patience. Words will not due to thank you.

There are many others I could and should thank, time permitting: Kelly Vernot, Tim Vernot, whose lovely wife is mentioned above, David, Stephanie and Isaac Alford, Jo Lort, Naomi Nash, Autumn and Sam Tremayne, Carolyn Simpson, Jess Brinson, Jo Stam, Jesh Stam, Hannah Stam, Jesse Stam, Anthony Lort, whose lovely wife is also mentioned above and many, many wonderful people on Instagram, as well as the writing group I was adopted into by no merit of my own, founded by Angela Teal (you guys know who you are) and my own writing crew, February 17th and the Poiema crew: thank you.

There are others, but time will not allow.

God is good and I am thankful for each and every one of you. It takes a village to publish a book too, in a smaller way, and I am grateful for and to you all. God is good.

Amen.

About the Author

  Danielle lives in the mountains of Southwest Virginia on her family's farm, striving to glorify God by enjoying Him forever.
  She is the author of high fantasy books about life in the darkness of a broken world and the Light therein.

She loves prose, good food, good songs and campfires on clear nights and loves getting out into the mountains, especially those near her.

She has two published books, Frost Light and Sparrow in the Sun and you can find her by following the QR code below and leave your impressions of her books there.

Printed by Libri Plureos GmbH in Hamburg, Germany